THE
DEVIL
INSIDE

What Reviewers Say About BOLD STROKES Authors

❧

KIM BALDWIN

"*A riveting novel of suspense* seems to be a very overworked phrase. However, it is extremely apt when discussing Kim Baldwin's [*Hunter's Pursuit*]. An exciting page turner [features] Katarzyna Demetrious, a bounty hunter…with a million dollar price on her head. Look for this excellent novel of suspense…" – **R. Lynne Watson**, *MegaScene*

❧

ROSE BEECHAM

"…her characters seem fully capable of walking away from the particulars of whodunit and engaging the reader in other aspects of their lives." – *Lambda Book Report*

❧

GUN BROOKE

"*Course of Action* is a romance…populated with a host of captivating and amiable characters. The glimpses into the lifestyles of the rich and beautiful people are rather like guilty pleasures.…[A] most satisfying and entertaining reading experience." – **Arlene Germain**, reviewer for the *Lambda Book Report* and the *Midwest Book Review*

❧

JANE FLETCHER

"*The Walls of Westernfort* is not only a highly engaging and fast-paced adventure novel, it provides the reader with an interesting framework for examining the same questions of loyalty, faith, family and love that [the characters] must face." – **M. J. Lowe**, *Midwest Book Review*

❧

RADCLYfFE

"…well-honed storytelling skills…solid prose and sure-handedness of the narrative…" – **Elizabeth Flynn**, *Lambda Book Report*

"…well-plotted…lovely romance…I couldn't turn the pages fast enough!" – **Ann Bannon**, author of *The Beebo Brinker Chronicles*

THE
DEVIL
INSIDE

by

ALI VALI

2006

THE DEVIL INSIDE
© 2006 BY ALI VALI. ALL RIGHTS RESERVED.

ISBN 1-933110-30-9

THIS TRADE PAPERBACK ORIGINAL IS PUBLISHED BY
BOLD STROKES BOOKS, INC.,
PHILADELPHIA, PA, USA

FIRST PRINTING: BOLD STROKES BOOKS 2006

CREDITS
EDITORS: SHELLEY THRASHER AND STACIA SEAMAN
PRODUCTION DESIGN: STACIA SEAMAN
COVER DESIGN BY SHERI (GRAPHICARTIST2020@HOTMAIL.COM)

Acknowledgments

Thank you to Radclyffe for believing in my writing and for her input into this story. I could have found no better home than Bold Strokes Books and no better family to help me grow as a writer.

After two years I've grown rather fond of the characters in this story, so I want to thank Shelley Thrasher for taking such good care of them. She has treated them and me with such respect, helping me to tell their tale with her expertise and infinite patience in editing. Thanks also to Stacia Seaman for her input in bringing the final product to print.

Thanks also to my partner for constantly asking the most important question of all, "What happens next?" I'm looking forward to a lifetime of answering.

Dedication

For C
My guide, my love

CHAPTER ONE

A steady rain fell over a sea of dark umbrellas clustered around a pale canopy. Two lone figures sat beneath it, next to Marie Casey's gleaming, flower-decked casket. A dark-haired woman and a boy.

Father Andrew Goodman had feared he would one day preside over the funeral of a Casey sister but had never imagined Marie would be the one. He glanced toward the woman he had expected to bury young.

Derby Cain Casey—Cain to those who knew her—sat with one hand on her son's shoulder and the other on her sister's coffin. She looked deceptively calm, but beyond the face she revealed to the world, Father Andrew glimpsed a cold, terrifying rage. Before this was over, she would exact her own unique form of revenge. Blood would be spilled for the injustice dealt to the Casey family.

"Let us all remember Marie, the kind spirit whom God has called home." Father Andrew observed the large congregation gathered around him in the Metairie Cemetery just on the cusp of New Orleans and Jefferson Parish. The mourners seemed lost in their own fond memories of the young woman.

"To her parents, Dalton and Therese, she was a blessing from heaven whom they cherished from the day she entered their lives. They said that often after her birth. To her brother, Billy, she was someone to protect and love, and he did so until his final day here with us."

He removed his glasses so he could wipe tears from his eyes. The Lord could have cooperated with better weather on the final resting day of the beautiful girl he had baptized twenty-six years before. It didn't matter to the more than two hundred people who had turned out, though. Many of them were more familiar with Marie's family than with the young woman they were there to honor. The Caseys' contributions to the community through charitable giving and deeds were as renowned as the way they allegedly earned their money.

"And to her sister, Cain, and nephew, Hayden, she was a harbor from the storm." Father Andy put his glasses back on and smiled at them, hoping to provide a little comfort. "Derby, I'm confident your parents and brother were all waiting with open arms to welcome her home. And with your family, I'm sure they had a party that'd do all the Caseys proud."

Cain disregarded the sniffles and laments of the family members standing nearby, but graced the priest with a nod for his generous words. They were only words, though, coming nowhere near to quelling the fury she felt inside for what had happened to her sister. Her life had often been marked by loss, but to lose Marie cut deep.

The man who had killed Marie obviously intended for Cain to dream for months about what he had done. He wanted the images of Marie's rape and torture to serve as a permanent reminder of how Cain had not only failed Marie, but her father as well, since she had inherited from him the responsibility of watching over Marie after his death. The killer had wanted her to remember that her sister had taken her last breaths alone and in pain.

If his intent was to brand her brain with his savagery, he had succeeded. Marie's barbaric murder had killed a part of Cain's soul as well. She would long remember every bite mark, bruise, and cigarette burn on Marie's body.

Soon, though, she would temper those cruel memories with the salve that came only through revenge. The man who stole Marie's dignity before pulling the trigger to end her misery would pay with blood and a world of pain. His price would be a thousand of Marie's lifetimes before Cain was through with him and God heard his pleas for the sweet peace of death.

No one in her life had loved her so unselfishly as Marie. As Father Andy continued his eulogy, Cain remembered the day Marie had turned ten.

"Derby, do you think I'm pretty?"

"No, Marie, I don't think you're pretty. I think you're beautiful. You get any more that way and Billy and me will get into more fights than we'll know how to win. You're going to grow up so gorgeous, we'll be beating them off at the door, there'll be so many boys after you."

The little black-haired girl held out the sides of her new pink dress and smiled into the mirror. "No, Derby, I want to grow up and take care of you."

"Why do you say that, birthday girl?" Cain locked eyes with her and smiled back. No one could bring a smile to her face more easily than her little sister.

"'Cause you look like someone who's going to need looking after."

Out of the mouths of babes, wasn't that the old expression? At thirty-six, a much-older-feeling Derby Cain Casey lost track of what Father Andy was saying and looked to the oak box that held her baby sister. *I'm so sorry, Marie. You did such a good job of taking care of Hayden and me, and I wasn't there when you needed me most.*

Her sister had been special all right. No one in her family cared that her mind hadn't matured normally, trapping her in a world of her own while freeing her to be the child she thought she was. Marie had been an innocent who had done an admirable job of helping Cain take care of her son, Hayden. Hayden and her sister had become so attached to each other, she worried about the effects her brutal death would have on him. He had already lost his mother; it didn't seem fair to add Marie to the list.

The sprinkling of holy water dragged her away from her memories. All that was left to do was to place the casket in the family crypt so Marie could lie alongside their parents and their brother. For one eternal moment, Cain felt almost like an orphan as she stared at the headstones that marked the final resting place of her family.

She felt like crying but heeded well her father's voice on this one unbending rule. As the head of the Casey family, she had been trained never to show weakness of any kind in public, so now was not the time to grieve. The priest came and momentarily took her hand before patting Hayden on the head. "The church is always here for you, Derby, if you've a need to talk. May God bless you and your son."

Behind them, the line of mourners moved toward their cars, looking like dead flowers cast on a lazy river. None of the attendees wanted to bother Cain and Hayden as they said their last good-byes. The ever-present wall of guards had closed ranks around them, ensuring their privacy. When she didn't answer, Father Andy joined the others and left them in peace.

Cain felt Hayden's grip tighten on her arm, drawing her attention from the coffin to him. "Shasta daisies were her favorite. Aunt Marie always said they made her happy." She stayed silent and listened. Hayden had been beside her when they went to identify her body at the morgue. Like his mother, Hayden had stoically and with a dry face shown the world the strength the Caseys possessed in abundance.

That her son was almost a carbon copy of her was a relief. A relief not to have to confront the image of his blond birth mother every single day. For Cain, to see any resemblance to the person she hated in the face of the one person she loved more than life would have been one penance too many.

She plucked a flower from the arrangement and handed it to him. "Keep one, son. We'll press it into one of the books she gave you."

"Mom?"

She cocked her head to the side to acknowledge his question.

"Would it be okay to cry now? Everyone's gone."

God, it sucks to be a Casey heir, she thought. The boy had tried to be strong, but in the end he was only a child. "Honey, of course it's okay to cry."

"It's okay for you too. No one'll see."

She put an arm around her son and a fist on the casket. How absurd that on such a rainy day the wood felt warm. She silently let a few tears fall. She held her son and cried for the injustices heaped in the road that marked her life.

When, eventually, Cain turned and signaled they were ready, the mantle of power was back in place. The time to grieve, along with all the other nightmares unleashed when her defenses were down, would have to come later. Now it was time to find those responsible for making this day possible. She knew who had put her sister here and vowed to make him suffer. It wouldn't be long before he got his own wooden box for his family to cry over.

From a distance the people Cain trusted with her family's lives tried to ignore the tears in their own eyes as they looked at the casket upon which their boss's hand rested. They all thought it was a good thing she had such broad shoulders, since the world expected so much of her. But they weren't the only ones watching. Parked farther up the drive, two vans with darkened windows were abuzz with shutter clicks. All of those in attendance as well as the family were photographed for later cataloguing.

The mantle Cain was born to and had inherited from her father was the reason for the huge amount of interest. Just as her friends had gone into their father's professions after college, she too had joined the family business. For her, however, it meant becoming the head of one of the most powerful crime families in New Orleans. The strong woman had a reputation for being vicious and hard, but she did have her Achilles's heel. He was walking by her side—Hayden Dalton Casey—her greatest gift and her only heir. She held the umbrella for both of them as she put her arm around her son and started back to the car.

"*Derby*?" said Merrick Runyon, Cain's personal bodyguard. "The padre has guts, I give him that. I haven't heard anyone except Marie call you that since your mother was alive." She opened the car door for them.

Before getting in the car, Cain glared at the vans parked not that far away and snarled in their direction. "You'd think they'd give it a rest, especially on a day like today. Fucking vulture bastards." She spoke loud enough so the mikes trained on her would pick up every word. With a deep breath she let go of the anger and turned to Merrick. "As to *Derby*, let's not get into that today. If my parents had met in Paris or somewhere else besides the Kentucky Derby, I wouldn't have had so much grief over my name."

"It's not that bad, Mom." Hayden bumped shoulders with her and smiled. His eyes were swollen from the crying he had done over his aunt, but he was obviously trying to cheer her up. "Want to watch a movie with me when we get home?"

"Sure, I could use a day off in front of the television."

"It won't be the same without Aunt Marie there, but we'll make it through. Maybe when all this stuff gets better you'll tell me what happened."

Cain put her arm around him and kissed his forehead. "Are you willing to give me some time, little man?"

"I trust you, so take all the time you need, but don't forget I loved her too. I want to know who hurt her and why. I know she didn't drive, so something else put those cuts and bruises all over her."

Cain looked at her son and ran her fingers through his dark hair. "How'd you get to be so smart?"

"It's the Casey genes floating to the top."

She realized that her father's old expression was coming back to haunt her, and despite the gloom outside the car window, she laughed. Hayden was right. She would eventually tell him what had happened to their beloved Marie.

Hayden was the rightful heir to the family business, just as she had been her father's. And like hers, his education concerning the family business had started early. Hopefully, though, they would have more time together than she and her father had shared before circumstances stole him from her life. Hayden was eleven, but having been raised around adults, he was precocious and highly intelligent. He needed to learn what happened to those who hurt vulnerable innocents, especially when their name was Casey.

CHAPTER TWO

Two months had passed since Marie's funeral, and summer had faded like the fallen magnolia blossoms into an early winter in the city along the Mississippi River. Life had slowly returned to normal. School helped Hayden with his grief, and work helped Cain do the same. Over dinner one night, when he brought the subject up again, she told him what had happened to Marie and to the man who had taken her from them.

At first she didn't know how to react to the grim face Hayden wore throughout her story, but all he wanted to know was if the guy was dead. She nodded, which he mirrored, and no other questions were necessary between them. It was the last time they had spoken of it, and she hoped the story had helped relieve his share of nightmares.

She thought of that night often, realizing Hayden had picked up on more than even she could imagine. Never evasive, she had wanted more time for him to enjoy being a child before the realities of life consumed his days.

Maybe it was all the time she spent with him, answering all his questions with infinite patience, that helped him think beyond his eleven years. Or maybe it was his insatiable need to know and his consumption of books in search of answers and things to share with her. Whatever the reason, she had ended up with a son who would be a brilliant man when his time came, and the thought never failed to put a smile of pride on her face.

Setting her coffee cup down, she put away her personal thoughts, got up from the table, and donned her jacket, signaling her shadows that she was ready to head to work. The car idled a few feet from the front door, ready for the trip to her office in a local warehouse.

She owned two nightclubs, but spent most of her time in the building along the river her father had bought years before. The faded, chipped paint on the outer walls gave no clue to the posh offices inside.

What she did have a clue about was where every FBI and other government agency wiretap and bugging device was located within the walls of her offices and complexes. She irritated the agents no end when she often smiled and waved to the cameras. By now they had to know that for every device they garnered to perform the constant surveillance, someone was always willing to sell better equipment to find the nasty little bugs.

Merrick, the woman next to her, was adjusting the shoulder holster under her jacket, making her chest thrust toward Cain. She was tall, slim, African American, and one of the most beautiful women Cain had ever come across.

In a hand-to-hand fight with her employer, Merrick would lose. Anyone *else* who suspected her of any type of weakness soon found she was three times as deadly as Cain, because her boss used more restraint before ending someone's life. Usually Merrick didn't want the hassle of talking when action was quicker and, in most cases, more efficient. She had worked her way up the ranks by taking orders and keeping the Caseys' secrets until she was the one at Cain's side.

"What's on the plate today?" Cain asked.

"Could be me if you play your cards right."

Cain let her eyes stray to the all-too-tempting cleavage and sighed. "It's hard to turn down such a great offer, so don't forget it later when we're done here. Did you meet with Mook this morning before he left with Hayden for school?"

"Of course. Don't worry, sugar. I'm not letting anything happen to your boy or to you." She reached over and patted the inside of Cain's knee. "To answer your first question, your uncle Alex is waiting to see you. He wanted to talk to you sooner, but I told him the last couple of weeks weren't the best time. He wouldn't be put off any longer, so I figured you'd want to get this over with."

Alex Baxter, her mother's redheaded older brother, was the one person on that side of the family who had tried to act as a surrogate when Cain's father had been killed in a turf war fifteen years before. The same battle had taken her brother Billy and her mother three years later, leaving her and Marie to pick up the pieces. Alex was the most socially acceptable of all the Baxter boys, but just barely.

"Did he say what he wanted?"

"No, just said it was important and it wasn't family business."

Merrick took Cain's black coat and hat as soon as they cleared the door and handed them to Cain's assistant. When she saw that Alex was alone, she took her usual seat outside Cain's door.

"Cain, how are you?" Alex stood as if waiting for his niece to embrace him and just as quickly sat down when she bypassed him and sat behind her desk.

"I'm fine. Thanks for coming by to ask. If that's all you want, we'll have to cut this short. I had to postpone a lot of things to take Hayden on a short trip, and the paperwork piled up. As much as I love these little chats with you, I'm busy."

"I told your trained pit bull outside I wanted to talk to you about something important, so surely you can spare me ten minutes."

"Careful not to call her that to her face, uncle. She's been known to bite for less. What's so important you walked into the viper's lair to talk to me about?" Cain relaxed into the leather chair and put a fist under her chin. She was grateful these little talks didn't happen often, but they were annoying nonetheless.

"So much like your father, Cain. What my sister ever saw in that man, I'll spend my life trying to figure out." He shook his balding head, remembering the senior Casey and his sister's adoring looks whenever he was within sight. Time and years of marriage hadn't changed the way she felt about him or what she was willing to overlook.

"Considering you and Edith lived off his money, and still do to an extent, I'd think you'd talk about him with an iota more respect. I'll tell you for the hundredth time to tread carefully when it comes to speaking ill of my father or of my mother's choices."

"No need to get mad." Alex threw his hand up, starting in on his reason for coming. "I want to talk to you about someone close to you who recently called and asked me to soften the blow before they come to see you. Promise me you'll listen before you end up smashing something."

Cain ran her hand through her thick jet-black hair, trying to defuse her impatience with the annoyance taking up space in her office. It was always the same between them. He would blame her father and his family for her mother's death, and she would get mad enough to throw the windbag out. The only other time he became this much of a nuisance was when his monthly check was late.

"Either you spit out what you've got to say or get the fuck out."

Before Alex could reprimand his niece for her language, the voice of one of Cain's other uncles, Jarvis Casey, interrupted him from the open door. "Perhaps the person Alex is speaking of went to the wrong family member for help. They should've sent only the favorite uncle, instead of one from the side of the family you find extremely annoying."

Jarvis's teasing yet biting remark coaxed the first smile out of Cain that day. Her uncle Jarvis was the closest thing she'd ever get to watching her father, Dalton, grow old. Jarvis had been born a few years after Dalton, but in some of their childhood photos the brothers could have passed for twins, both fitting the clichéd tall, dark, and handsome description.

Alex studied the two as they said hello. Unlike the Baxter family, which produced a brood of short redheads, the Caseys had produced giants with dark looks and even darker blue eyes. It had been Dalton's eyes, Therese had told him, that had captured her heart the first time she looked into them.

"Merrick," Cain said into the intercom, "please come in here and show Alex to the door. We're done."

Alex followed Merrick out, knowing Cain's dismissal was genuine. The Casey clan was an inner circle the Baxter side of the family would never crack.

Cain jumped up and hugged Jarvis as soon as her finger had released the intercom button.

"How you holding up, kid?" asked Jarvis.

"Trying to convince myself she's gone, even though all this time has passed. Marie was an innocent. She didn't deserve what happened to her."

"You took care of your own, Cain. Don't go doubting yourself now. It's only been a few months, so cut yourself some slack. Walk across the street and buy an old man a cup of coffee, and I'll tell you a tall tale, I will."

The two strolled out, followed closely by Merrick and three other people. Under their assorted coats the four were wearing enough firepower to take out the entire block, if necessary. As backup, a team of ten guards looked on from the roof of the Casey warehouses. Each of them had a legally registered high-powered rifle strapped to his shoulder.

"What's up?" Cain cocked her head up from under the brim of her hat to give the telephoto lenses, always aimed at the warehouse to catch her in a misstep, a clear shot.

"Why do you always look up when you know they're there?" Jarvis turned the brim of his own hat further down on his head.

"I figure the ladies in the jury pool will never convict me if I provide enough good-looking photos for them to study in the deliberation room."

The joke made her uncle laugh and slap her on the back. "Ah, it's nice to hear a little of that ego back. I missed it." They walked across the street to a café where Cain ate lunch almost every day. "Your father loved coming in here for the eggs."

"You left your house in this rain to tell me about my father and eggs?" Cain waved to the waitress, holding up two fingers before she pointed to the coffeepot.

"It could be I just wanted to see you."

The finger tapping on the table clued Cain to the fact that something was bothering Jarvis. Once the waitress put down two cups mixed with the right amount of cream and sugar, Cain laid her hand flat on the Formica surface, ready to hear whatever was on her uncle's mind. "What gives?"

"Emma called."

Had Jarvis stood up and slapped her, he wouldn't have gotten a more stunned response. Cain slid her hand away from the coffee cup and curled it into a fist at hearing the name. "What did she want?"

Jarvis lowered his head and played with the top of the wet hat resting on his lap. He'd consider himself lucky if the fist close to him on the table didn't lift and strike him before he was finished. He felt like the room had become nearly glacial from the color and look in her eyes.

"She's in town and wants to meet with you. I offered her my protection as long as she doesn't try to contact Hayden without your permission. I'm not telling you what to do, kid, but you need to finish with this business."

"There's no business to finish, it's done. She walked out, remember?"

"She went home…" said Jarvis.

"*This* was her home, and *our* life." Cain's voice rose an octave, and she slammed her fist on the table, making the salt shaker fall to the floor and break. "I know where she went, Uncle Jarvis. For Hayden's sake, I know all about her. What does she *want?*"

Jarvis was surprised at the outburst since Cain was usually all about control when she was in public. He noticed that everyone else in the diner went about their business as if the two of them were sitting in a soundproof box.

"Just a chat, Cain. Then you're done." Jarvis put his hands up in an effort to calm her down. He knew he was taking a chance, but he thought it was the best decision for all of them in the long run. He was willing to gamble anything for Cain to be happy.

Cain turned in her chair and addressed Merrick. "Call Mook now. Tell him no detours today, straight home, and he doesn't open the door unless it's one of us. Any fuckups on this one and it'll be his last."

Merrick didn't ask why. She just pulled her phone out and relayed the message to the big blond who was in charge of Hayden's personal security.

Cain glared at Jarvis. "Tell Emma to meet me at the Erin Go Braugh at one o'clock. She's got twenty minutes. And next time, uncle, never pick someone else's loyalties above your family's. If you learned anything from my father, besides what foods he liked to order, it should've been that."

CHAPTER THREE

The guards left Cain to her thoughts when they arrived at the Erin Go Braugh, a pub she owned. The crew who ran the place were restocking the bar and finishing their cleanup in preparation for the nightly crowd, and they too worked in silence. Cain closed her eyes and revisited the night that had changed her fate.

Fourteen Years Earlier at the Erin Go Braugh

"Emma, pickup for table five, and try not to spill it this time." The bartender slid the tray toward the new server, thinking he was going to have to start taking the lost liquor out of her paycheck. He felt sorry for the kid who'd begged for a job so she'd be able to stay in the city and in school. Too bad she wasn't as graceful as she was cute.

"Don't worry, Josh. I think I've got the hang of it now. This place is so crowded it takes a miracle to make it to the tables without spilling something."

Emma Verde had walked by the Irish pub numerous times when she was out with her friends. The live music and selection of beer and native Irish whiskey drew a large crowd nightly, prompting her to wander in one afternoon and ask for a job.

She'd moved to New Orleans to attend Tulane, over the strong objections of her mother. The last thing Carol Verde told her as the bus pulled away from Hayward, Wisconsin, was there'd be no help coming from them since Emma had chosen a place so far from their Christian values.

The tips Emma figured she'd make would allow her the luxury of her tiny apartment and the part of her tuition not covered by scholarship and student loans. Tulane had offered her not only the most lucrative scholarship, but also a chance to get a long way from Wisconsin. Her mother had been right about one thing. New Orleans, especially the French Quarter, was a world away from the farm she'd grown up on.

As she walked toward table five, she thought about the shock that would kill her mom if she discovered her working in a bar. Laughing at her own private joke, Emma never saw the tall woman who crossed into her path. The one thing she noticed, though, was the tray full of ale the woman was wearing when they parted.

"I am so sorry. I didn't see you." She used her hands to try to mop the mess she'd spilled from the thick, heavily starched linen shirt. When Josh appeared at her side, she figured he was there to fire her.

"Josh, where'd you find this one?"

The deep teasing voice made her look up and study more closely the face of the woman she'd run into.

"I'm sorry, Cain. Emma's training day hasn't been working out quite as planned."

"Emma, huh?"

She held out her hand, now sticky with ale, but Cain took hold of it anyway. "Emma Verde. It's a pleasure to meet you," she said, grimacing at how wet her hand felt.

"Cain Casey. The pleasure's all mine," answered Cain, not letting go of her hand. "Where are you from?"

"Hayward, Wisconsin."

A low rumbling laugh bubbled out of Cain's chest, which made Emma's ears get hot for some reason.

"Any bars in Hayward?"

"Just a diner, but they only serve beer at night."

Cain peered over Emma's head at her bar manager. "Don't mind me, Josh. I think this hayseed's a keeper."

It had been their first meeting. A night they laughed over often after they had gotten together and Emma had moved in with her.

For Emma, the daughter of a diary farmer, Cain had given up all the women who had shared her life and her bed. For eight years it had been blissful. They'd had Hayden, and the happiness Emma had brought into her life grew. But then Emma had turned her back on all of it.

The hayseed, as Cain often called her, left her seven-year-old son and her lover behind when she couldn't live with Cain's darker side any longer. Emma returned to the farm she had grown up on and apparently forgot her life with Cain. Not one phone call, postcard, or letter had come south after she had left, and now after four years she was back. But it was far too late for talking now. She should have talked to Cain four years earlier.

❖

Emma took a deep breath and stared up at the sign over the door. "The Erin Go Braugh." Her inflection of the name never came close to the way it rolled off Cain's tongue. She felt like a thousand years had gone by since the first time she had stood on the sidewalk trying to work up the nerve to walk in and ask for a job. How different would her life have turned out if she had just turned around and walked away? The question was one she often asked herself, but she never bothered to find an answer because she had walked in and forever tethered her life to Cain's. No amount of running away was ever going to change that. And now she was back to face the one person who scared her almost as much as she'd loved her.

Merrick opened the door for Emma and scrutinized her before pointing to a table that overlooked a small courtyard at the back of the pub, where Cain sat nursing a beer. Emma hadn't changed much, thought Merrick; even the smile she graced her with as she passed was the same. A simple blue dress had replaced the designer clothes Emma was partial to when Cain's money was paving the way, but she carried it off well. The sophistication and style Cain had taught her transcended the clothes.

"Cain?" Emma spoke softly and stood a few feet from the table. The years hadn't changed Cain much either, and Emma's heart sped up as soon as she saw her. "It's good to see you."

"Don't." Cain didn't turn around, but the tone of her voice was unmistakable. There would be no forgiveness coming from her today.

"I'm sorry. May I sit down?"

"It's your twenty minutes, Emma. You can do whatever the hell you want."

She stepped closer and sat down, shaking her head when Josh held up a beer glass in her direction. "Thank you for seeing me. I thought after all this time you'd be willing to let some of the anger go. Can you try for just a little while not to hate me?"

"I don't think about you enough to hate you, so get off your soapbox. It isn't going to gain you any sympathy. What do you want?" Cain watched a blue jay out on the patio fly away with a forgotten straw and pretended Emma being there wasn't affecting her. Next to her sat the woman who had managed to do what none of her enemies had accomplished. She had cut deep and left a wound that still festered.

"Still not big on small talk, huh?"

"You walk out on our family four years ago, we don't hear from you in all that time, and you expect me to talk to you about the weather when you do decide to show up? Even you can't be that naïve, Emma. I'll ask again. What do you want?" Cain finally turned and skewered the woman she had loved with the intensity reserved for her adversaries.

"I want to see my son."

"Your son? That's rich. What makes you believe he wants to see you? He's not the same little boy you left behind without another thought when you went to look for whatever you found in farm country."

"I'd like to talk to him." Emma studied the strong profile when Cain's head turned back in the direction of the courtyard. To have gotten this far without Cain calling the dogs on her was a minor victory. The pit bulls Cain surrounded herself with were always on a short leash and ready to attack.

"Let me ask him and I'll let you know. Hayden's old enough to make his own decisions." Cain heard the surprised breath Emma took and laughed. "Don't get me wrong or act so surprised that I'm giving in so soon. I'm not stupid. I knew you'd come back one day and I figured that, if he was old enough, I'd let Hayden decide on what kind of relationship he wants with you. That is, if he wants to have any relationship with you." Cain leaned forward to deliver the rest of the threat, not caring who was listening. "Just remember you don't get to walk away for free this time, Emma. You hurt *my* son, or make me spend one more night holding him when he wakes up crying because you left without so much as a 'kiss my ass,' and I'll bury you. I'll bury you so deep, God Almighty won't be able to find you, and you know I can do it."

Emma never got to respond, and she never glimpsed the blue eyes that still haunted her thoughts, because Cain just got up and walked out, trailed by the two constant deadly shadows.

"Yes, Cain, I know you can do lots of things," whispered Emma to the forgotten glass of beer on the table.

She hadn't really thought much about how their meeting would go, so she was a bit dumbfounded at her good fortune. Now if she could only control the itch in her hands from wanting to reach out and touch Cain. Her ex-lover even smelled of the same fresh citrusy cologne Emma remembered.

The short visit convinced Emma that no amount of time would ever erase Cain from her mind, or her body. She'd been branded by the tall, dangerous woman, and that was the way it would stay.

CHAPTER FOUR

Hayden was waiting for Cain in the den where they often watched television together. "Why now?" he asked, hoping to find the right answer in the blue eyes that always reminded him he belonged to her. They seemed guarded for once, and Cain had been a little on edge since she'd gotten home.

"I don't have an answer for that, kiddo. She's here, and she wants to see you. Emma's your mother, but it's up to you if you want to see her or not. I don't want you in therapy in your thirties blaming me for keeping the two of you apart," Cain joked as she sat down. She brushed his dark hair back from his forehead, then placed her palm on his cheek. The big room in the back corner of the house was full of comfortable chairs and had a great view of the yard. "This is your call, son, and I'll abide by whatever you say."

Though big for his age, he squeezed in next to her, needing to be close. Emma was someone he chose to think of seldom, and knowing that she was back in town was making him nauseous. It wasn't something he wanted to admit, but the anxiety he had gone through when she had so abruptly walked out of his life had devastated him.

Till that moment he had fought through the despair of losing Emma by pushing himself mentally and physically. He had rationalized that if he could come close to perfection, Cain would never abandon him. He had come to trust that Cain wasn't going anywhere, and with that assurance the need to excel beyond everyone's expectations had started to ease. Having Emma come back as suddenly as she'd left threatened to disrupt his world all over again.

"Hayden? Did you hear what I said?"

"I heard you, sorry. She gave birth to me, but you're my mother and father all rolled into one. Mook explained it to me once when I asked, and I think he's right. With you, I don't really need anyone else."

"Thanks, and no matter what, you know I won't ever leave you, right?"

"I know that, Mom, and I love you for it." Cain had taught him that when he felt uncertain, he should always fall back on something he would never question. Since he never questioned Cain's love and faith for him, she was his best ally in case he needed to lean on her strength. "Will you come with me if I go?"

Cain kissed the top of his head and smiled. "I love you too, son, and if you want me to go, I'll be there."

"You always tell me to confront my fears and leave them behind. I'm not afraid of her, but let's see what she wants and move on, okay?"

Hayden stood next to her when Cain phoned her uncle to set up a dinner meet that night on neutral ground. Hayden hadn't wanted Emma in their house, not ready to see her in such a familiar environment. The memories he had of Emma centered on their house, but this was also the place she had left. He even picked a restaurant he and Cain hadn't eaten at before so neither of them would have bad memories when Emma went home.

In a way he was curious why she had come back to see him. Maybe now he could ask why she had left, why she never cared enough to call him, and what he'd done wrong to make her stop loving him. Four years was a long time, though, and his curiosity only went so far.

❖

Emma wasn't prepared for the physical change in her son when he and Cain walked into the Creole restaurant together. If he'd ever had any of her traits, they were long gone. Like Cain he was tall and powerfully built, even though she suspected he hadn't begun to fill out, with the Casey dark-tanned skin and black hair. And when he got close enough for her to see them, his eyes would complete the picture that was all Cain.

"Hello." Hayden politely held out his hand, closing the door on any embrace Emma might have had in mind as a form of greeting. She was sure the aloofness was the beginning of her punishment for her sins.

"Hello, Hayden. It's so good to see you, son." When he let go of her hand Emma brought it up to cover her mouth in an attempt to stop the tears. This stranger before her represented everything she'd missed in his life. As his mother, she had failed him. "If you like, you can call me Mama."

"I don't mean to be rude, ma'am, but I don't feel comfortable calling you that. Mom said I could call you Emma instead of Ms. Verde."

"Of course that's all right. Cain, are you joining us?" Emma turned her attention to the silent woman behind the stranger who was her son and tried to blink away the tears. Now that she knew how he felt, she resolved to start the journey of reconciliation.

"Hayden invited me, so unless he asks me to leave, I'm staying." Cain pointed to the empty chairs and everyone took a seat.

Emma noticed that the silverware on the next table had been cleared away and the waiters seemed to know instinctively to leave the three of them alone. She felt exasperated as she stared at the protection Cain was never without. "Did they have to come along too?" The fact that they were now a part of her son's life made her both sad and angry because maybe she was too late. She had helped cast the fate of the next Casey leader, and this would be the only life her son would know.

"Mom, are you ready?" asked Hayden, standing up.

"Where are you going?" Emma jumped up in a panic.

"Lady, you don't have to like us. We didn't ask you to. Nobody even asked you to come here after all this time, so you can take your opinions and go back north with them. We've actually been fine without you all this time. What makes you think you can come back and insult my mother like it's acceptable behavior? You coming, Mom?" By the time Hayden had finished, his grip on the back of the chair was so tight his knuckles were white.

"It's your show, kid. Whatever you want." Cain stood up and buttoned her black jacket, obviously waiting for Hayden to walk out, if that was what he really wanted to do.

"I'm sorry. Please don't go yet. I just wanted to see you and get to know you again. Cain, please." Emma turned to her ex-lover, hating the despair that she knew painted her face and hoping Cain could put away some of her anger and help her.

"How about this, Hayden?" Cain suggested. "I go over and keep the help company for a while, and you and Emma have some iced tea or something. After that, if you're ready to go, we'll go."

"I thought you said it's my decision."

"You want to leave now, kid, no one's going to stop you, least of all me. But remember what we talked about. Listen to what the pitch is before you walk away."

"Yeah, I know. If not, you spend your life asking 'what if.' Can I talk to you a minute before I order a Coke?"

Emma stood motionless as Cain bent down and listened to whatever grievances Hayden was putting in her ear, wanting to kiss her for talking him out of leaving. Along with missing how Cain made her feel physically, she missed the feeling of safety she brought into her life. Cain had fixed almost all of their problems, no matter what she'd had to do.

Hayden squared his shoulders at her answer before turning back to her. Cain headed to the bar instead of the table of bodyguards, took a seat on one of the wrought-iron stools, and kissed the brunette who had called her over.

"You don't have the right to look so jealous," said Hayden.

"I'm not jealous, Hayden. I came to see you, not Cain."

"Then stop staring at her."

Emma sighed at his hostility, but she had prepared herself for it. She had no doubt Cain had used the four years she'd been absent to twist Hayden's mind against her.

"How's school this year? You just started back. Is it fun?" Emma unfurled her napkin and placed it on her lap.

"Fine and yes."

"Do you have a lot of friends?"

"Yes."

She could tell the one-word answers were not going to change, no matter how many questions she asked. In a moment of weakness, she slipped into silence, not wanting to fuel his frustration with her.

By the end of the evening, it turned out that their first exchange when Hayden threatened to leave was the easiest part of the night. Hayden had inherited the Casey temper as well as looks, and if Emma was hoping for an open-arm welcome, it wasn't going to happen over her plate of perfectly cooked fish. A few tables over, the talk wasn't as stilted, and Cain was having a pleasant time while she kept an eye on her son.

"Thank you for coming tonight, Hayden, and I hope we'll get to a place where you can let me in a little bit. Could you get Cain to join us again so we can talk before you go?"

Hayden walked to the table Cain shared with the woman she'd met at the bar. Not too worried about keeping Emma waiting, he joined them for bread pudding with whiskey cream sauce before finally dragging Cain back to Emma's table. He reasoned his birth mother had kept him waiting for four years, so it was only fair.

"Thanks for bringing him tonight. I don't need an answer now, but I'd like to know if you'd let him come meet my parents in Wisconsin. That's all I ask. After that I'll go away forever if you want me to." Cain couldn't see it, but Emma had twisted the linen napkin on her lap into a knot while she was asking.

"Hayden, would you join Constance for a moment, please?"

The boy got up without question, knowing Cain didn't want him to hear whatever she was about to tell Emma.

"You want coffee?" he asked Cain before he walked away.

"No, son, we'll be leaving in a minute, but thank you." Cain watched as he sat with the pretty brunette she had dined with, not glancing in her direction again. "You came to see me alone this afternoon, and you just bring this topic up now? Did all that fresh air and open spaces you left us for make you forget who you're dealing with?"

"Are you kidding? It took me a year to build up enough courage to come here, Cain. Forget who and what you are? Not even if I tried hypnosis. I just want my mother and father to meet their grandson."

"I've met your parents, Emma. Hell, I listened to you complain about them for years. What would make them want to meet the child you had with me?"

"Because he's half mine, which means he's a part of them as well. A week, Cain. Surely you could see to giving me that. I can look at him and see he's more than a certified card-carrying Casey, but don't forget he has other family as well, and it's time he met them."

Cain leaned into the table a little and lowered her voice. "What makes you think that you deserve anything from me?"

"Because I gave him to you. He's your mirror image. He acts like you, thinks like you, and probably *feels* like you, but I'm foolish enough to think there might be something of me still trapped in there somewhere. I might not have called in all this time, but don't fool yourself that I haven't thought about him. I've thought about him every day, until some days it's hard to get out of bed, I get so sick over it."

"Like I said today, it's his decision. But whatever he decides, don't be stupid enough to think Mook's not going with him." Cain pointed to the man in question and watched Emma's head fall forward in defeat. She nodded to signal she understood.

Almost as if he knew their talk had come to an end, Hayden turned around and excused himself when Cain waved him over. "I won't go alone, and I'm not going if you don't come with me," Hayden informed Cain when Emma asked him to visit.

"A couple of days with just us, Hayden. Then you can bring the whole Casey clan if you want." Emma tried to salvage something of what she wanted, mainly a relationship with Hayden, before it all slipped away and Cain's watchful eyes exposed all her secrets. But in the end, if everything turned out like she hoped, even Cain's presence had its purpose.

"I'll come for two days. Then Mom comes for the rest of the time, and Mook stays with me. Neither one of us is going to talk her out of that," said Hayden. He liked the big blond bodyguard, and it would be a blessing to have him along. "He's a reality, so that's the deal."

"Is there something you're afraid of, son?" asked Emma.

"My name is Hayden, and I'd prefer you call me that. And no, I like being with my family and that's Mom, only Mom. We always spend Thanksgiving together, no matter what her schedule's like, so it's not fair for her to sit at home alone because you decided to get in touch again. Maybe you feel great about yourself for suddenly remembering you have a family, but she never forgot. Remember, I'm a Casey. Very little scares us."

The declaration made Cain lean forward and ruffle his hair, getting the boy to laugh.

"I can respect that," Emma said.

"Where are you staying?" asked Cain.

"Why?"

"His break begins next week, so if he's going, I need to know where I'm sending him."

Emma knew Cain wouldn't just let her leave town with Hayden without every ounce of information on where he was going and how he was going to get there. She was so close now to having everything she wanted. If things worked out, Hayden would eventually forgive her, and they could make up for the years they had been separated.

CHAPTER FIVE

The flight up north and the drive into Hayward passed in silence. Emma realized Hayden probably didn't resent being there; he was just comfortable with silence. When they had first met, Cain wouldn't talk for long stretches, which had taken some getting used to.

The more hours that ticked off in Hayden's company, the more he reminded Emma of Cain. Because of that similarity, her plan, which had seemed so foolproof months ago, now seemed like a pipe dream.

"Your grandfather owns a dairy farm here. His major buyer is Kraft, but he actually still makes all the cheese we eat at the house, like his father taught him." She was fishing for things to say and laughing at herself that an eleven-year-old could be so intimidating.

Hayden was thinking of the dozens of trips he'd taken with Cain and how different they were from this forced visit. He remembered when Emma was in his life, the stories she'd read him at night and the way she would run her fingers through his hair when he was sick, but the good of that relationship was gone. The sound of her voice held no comfort for him now, and a small part of him mourned that fact.

The scenery out the window of the rented Tahoe held his eye, so he answered without looking at her. "I don't know what you're expecting from me, but these people are as much strangers to me as I am to them. I came because I thought Mom would be disappointed in me if I didn't at least try. Aside from that, nothing else could've dragged me out here with you."

"What she thinks is so important to you?"

"What is it about her that you find so offensive? You just didn't leave her, you left me too. So whatever it is, it must've been pretty bad. I read a lot, and the moms in books usually don't just drop their kids. Unless it's something terrible or they're just not cut out to be parents. If you're telling me how much you care about me now, I have to assume you're laying the blame at Mom's feet."

Emma snorted in amusement and peered out her own window in an effort to find something to focus on to calm her emotions. She'd been right in thinking Hayden was intimidating. He had her in the corner without lifting a fist, which was something else he had in common with Cain when it came to her enemies. "Do you honestly think she'd have let me take you with me when I left?" She turned back when she felt him move in his seat.

Hayden did look at her then, and like Cain, his cold eyes told her she had no chance. "Do you honestly think I'd have left with you even if she had allowed it?"

"Touché, Hayden. Can we try and spend this time getting to know each other better? You might find I'm not the monster Cain made me out to be." Emma put her hand on his leg and prayed he wouldn't knock it off.

"You want me to tell you a story?" He glanced at her hand and turned his attention back to the scenery they were driving by.

"If you want to, sure." She gave his knee a little squeeze, glad he had left it alone. Emma was willing to take her small victories where she could find them.

"Every night before I go to bed, Mom points to a picture of the three of us and tells me somewhere you're taking the time to think just about me and saying a prayer that I'll be safe and happy. When I was seven and I cried for you, it's the one thing that got me to stop crying and made the pain go away. Her telling me that you were thinking about me made me believe it. Does that sound like she's been bad-mouthing you all this time?" His voice sounded as cold as the weather they had flown into.

"You love Cain a lot, don't you?"

"Do you make a habit of asking unnecessary questions? You have to know the answer without me saying anything, right? Maybe it's all this open space out here. It makes you fish for something to talk about so you can forget you're in the middle of nowhere."

"You don't act like a child, and you sure don't sound like one."
You let too much time pass, Emma. He's lost to you forever. And to think Cain did it by talking you up. Emma was sure when Hayden had figured out she was the only topic his beloved Cain had ever lied to him about, she looked that much worse. She could just imagine how much discomfort and anger Cain had buried to say anything nice about her.

"Mom says the uneducated grow up to be prey. If you want to learn to be a hunter, then you have to be smarter, quicker, and stronger than everybody else."

"Is that what Cain is to you, a hunter?"

"Cain is a god to me."

"And what are Hayden's thoughts? All I've heard from you is what Cain thinks."

"Why reinvent the wheel if you don't have to. There's plenty we don't agree on, and we know what those things are. What I talk to my mother about is no one else's business. I'm not a puppet, if that's what you're worried about."

Emma squeezed his knee again and smiled. "I do worry about you, Hayden. I don't want Cain to drag you into something you might think you have no choice in."

"Ah, it was the family business that drove you out here to this boring town. Save your worry and your pity for the times you need to pacify yourself for abandoning us. You were so worried it took you four years to check on me? I'm overwhelmed, and I shudder to think if you hadn't cared for me. I'd have never seen you again."

Emma was shocked, not only by his command of the English language, which was astounding, but by his cool, detached delivery. Any trace of the sweet boy who had picked flowers for her was gone, and she was left only with the memory of him. She would be fortunate if he didn't hate her forever, because he would never forgive her.

"Hayden, relax and look at the lake." Mook spoke up from the front seat of the Tahoe he'd rented at the airport. He knew the kid could slice and dice a person without ever laying a hand on them. Looks weren't the only thing he'd inherited from the Casey clan. As his guardian, though, Mook took it upon himself to guide Hayden when he veered toward unacceptable or rude behavior.

Emma removed her hand and prayed the tension in Hayden would relax a bit before they got to the house. She didn't want to add to the list of wrongs her mother kept well tallied in her head. From the time she had come home, she had tried to fit into the role her mother expected as a way of atonement, but she was finding the righteous road wasn't so easy to walk. With the baggage she'd brought home, every time she stumbled, she dug deeper to find the woman her mother wanted.

Carol Verde wasn't the most forgiving of women, so Emma found herself stumbling a lot. She was supposed to have had the life Carol hadn't been able to achieve. Instead she had run off, found Cain, and brought Hayden into the world. That was not the life Carol had missed out on, and she found it abhorrent that her daughter had chosen such a path.

Carol hadn't been thrilled to open her home to the boy, no matter what it would accomplish, and Emma's father had just shaken his head at what she had arranged to do. Her parents had only met Cain once, but Ross respected Cain for never abandoning Hayden. Whatever happened or didn't happen in the coming week would occur without his help.

Emma rode the rest of the way in silence, looking out her side of the car and remembering happier times when she didn't know all she had learned about Cain. She recalled the terrified faces of those escorted to the office of the pub when she worked there. She didn't know who the men were or what their fear stemmed from, but after those meetings they disappeared. For so long her love had shielded her from realizing how Cain made a living, but the day came when it wasn't enough to make her stay.

Once she had left, though, when her longing for Cain almost overwhelmed her, she liked to relive those first years.

Fourteen Years Earlier at Emma's Apartment

"Thank you for dinner tonight." Emma stood in front of her apartment door and gazed up at Cain, hoping to get her to bend and kiss her before they parted.

"You're welcome. Maybe we can do it again tomorrow night?"

She watched as Cain put her hand on the wall and leaned in closer. "I've seen you with about ten different women in Erin Go Braugh since I started working there. What makes me so special?"

"I like talking to you, Emma. Trust me. If I just wanted sex, I would've turned on the charm by now and we'd be done." Cain moved her other hand to the other side of Emma's head, effectively trapping her in a human cage.

The deep voice was getting closer, and Emma battled herself not to lift her own hands and run them through the thick black hair. "That confident in yourself, huh?"

"Most of the time I go with what I know. That way I'm seldom disappointed, so yeah, I'm that confident. Let's say seven tomorrow night?"

"I'll be ready. And thanks for telling me you like spending time with me. That means a lot."

Cain leaned down and kissed her softly. "You're welcome again. Thanks for wanting to talk to me. That means a lot to me."

Emma remembered their courtship as a slow process that ended with her falling so in love with Cain that she thought the world would end if they ever parted. She'd never wanted for anything, especially Cain's time and affection, and she'd never worried about someone else replacing her in the mobster's heart.

Thinking back now, she acknowledged Cain had never shown her dark side around her, but she knew Cain was capable of violence against anyone who hurt her or the family. On long winter nights alone with just her memories, Emma sometimes had a hard time conjuring up a solid reason for leaving, but then the image of Cain's bloody hands would return, and so would the tears. As hard as being away from Cain was, Emma was certain in her justification for leaving.

"There it is." Emma pointed out the window of the Tahoe to a large two-story house with a barn standing near it.

The temperature was starting to drop along with the sun, and the cows standing near the fence huddled together for warmth. A man and woman stepped off the front porch when the car stopped, and like Emma, they were both fair and slight of build. The man stepped forward and held out his hand.

"Welcome. My name's Ross and this is my wife, Carol. We're your grandparents."

The boy, who was taller than all three of them, glanced at the hand before he took it. Ross was surprised by the strength of Hayden's grip, and by not finding anything about his looks that connected him to his daughter.

"Nice to meet you, sir. Thank you for having me." Hayden let go of Ross's hand and offered his to Carol. "Ma'am, I'm Hayden Casey." He smiled and cocked his head when Carol ignored his hand. His gestures reminded Emma so much of Cain, a sharp pain shot through her chest.

Ross stepped forward, obviously hoping to make up for his wife's rudeness. "Thank you for coming, Hayden. After watching you grow up in pictures, it's nice to finally have you with us. Would you like to take a look around the place?"

"Daddy, he might be tired," Emma reminded him gently.

"I'd love to, Mr. Verde. Lead the way."

Emma and her mother watched as Ross led Hayden and Mook toward the barn, pointing his finger in a hundred different directions as he talked. Ross had been a wonderful parent, but Emma could tell now it might have been a good thing for him to have had a son as well.

"He certainly looks like that woman." Carol glared as Ross walked the boy and his shadow closer to the barn. "If this works out, he'll only add to our shame when you go parading him around town. I warned you long ago that going to that godforsaken city was a mistake. You bedded down with evil, and look what it's gotten you." She pointed in Hayden's direction. "God won't look kindly on you for bringing that spawn into the world. It's a sin, I tell you."

"Hayden was never a mistake, Mother, and he's anything but evil. I don't give a damn how you feel about him. I'll never be ashamed of him, no matter what. And please try to be nicer to him. If he tells Cain we treated him like crap when she gets here, she won't let him come back if things don't work out. Not to mention Hayden's not going to want to come back."

"Don't curse at me, Emma. Wait, she agreed to come?"

"Hayden wouldn't come unless she was invited."

"I don't want her kind in my house. Though it might be nice to see that smug smile get wiped off permanently, and have her know who was responsible." Carol turned and went back into the house.

Emma talked to herself as she buttoned her coat and followed the guys to the barn. "Enjoy it, Emma, 'cause when Cain gets here and gets reacquainted with your mother, you'll either never see Hayden again or you'll attend a funeral when Cain orders Merrick to shoot the old windbag."

❖

Hayden and Mook smiled through dinner, and Hayden wasn't too concerned that no one spoke a word through dinner aside from the prayer when they had sat down. He thanked a still-unresponsive Carol for their meal before stepping outside with his cell phone to call Cain.

"Hey, kid, how are things in the sticks?" The static was so bad Hayden had to go inside and ask to use the phone, which sat in the empty living room.

"Cold and full of cows."

"You're in Wisconsin, Hayden. What'd you expect?"

"Where were we supposed to go this year on break?" Hayden looked out the front window as Ross closed the barn doors for the night. The older man seemed eager to please, and Hayden found himself liking him. Maybe the next two days wouldn't drag out too much.

"I think we'd narrowed it down to Vegas for some golf."

"You owe me, Mom."

"I do, huh? How do you figure I owe you?"

"The way I see it is, if anyone else had been my father, I'd be swinging a golf club instead of dodging cow patties. Get me, Dad?"

His laugh made Cain feel a little better. "I get you, son, but if anyone else had been your dad, all you'd know is cow-patty dodging. See how life works?" When Cain heard him sigh from the other end, she turned off the treadmill she'd been running on.

"You never have told me why she left."

"You're right. I haven't, even though you used to ask me all the time."

Hayden turned from the window and sat on a flowered print chair near the phone. "You don't think I can handle the truth? I didn't stop asking because I lost interest in the answer, you know."

"I know, Hayden. I just wanted you to form your own opinions about your mother. You may not want to hear it now, but you've got to have some kind of relationship with her. What that's going to be is up to you—not me and not her, just you. Accepting the things in life we can't change or can't take back will make you a man. Trust me on this one, buddy."

"Will you get mad if I ask her?" He picked at the tag on his hiking boots as he asked, and wondered for the millionth time what the answer to his question might be. This was his opportunity to ask Emma all the questions that had accumulated in his head since she'd left. But not at the risk of upsetting Cain.

"No, honey, that won't make me mad. I love you, and that means you'll never have to worry about disappointing me no matter what choices you make."

"Thanks, Dad," he joked.

"Anytime, son. Hang in there, and I'll be there soon to keep you company. Did they pitch a tent out with the cows for me?"

"You get the bunkhouse, but don't hold your breath on a warm welcome from Grandma Carol." He laughed at the thought of his grandmother, suspecting her hostility came from his large dose of Casey genes. "She's even quieter than you are, and I don't think it's because she's thinking deep thoughts, you know?"

"We've met, so don't worry. Go get some sleep. You want to be well rested for all the milking you'll have to do in the morning."

"You're so funny. Tell Merrick hi for me. Bye, I'll call you tomorrow. Love you."

"Love you too." Cain took the phone headset off and toweled her face. She battled the urge not to jump on the next plane to make Hayden feel better.

"You can't fight all his wars for him, baby." Merrick put the weights she'd been curling back on the stand and faced her employer. "We can be there by tomorrow night. Any sooner and it'll look like you're hovering."

"I'm his mother, I'm supposed to hover."

"Boss, you knew this day would come. The girl wasn't going to disappear forever unless you gave her a little push in that direction, if you know what I mean."

"Unless you have a death wish yourself, don't ever say that again. Emma's a bitch, I'll concede that point, but she's Hayden's mother, and I'd never do anything to harm her."

"I know that, baby. Emma just never gave you credit for your sense of honor. He asked again, didn't he?"

Cain let out a sigh of her own. Those things she'd told Hayden up to then had left her with her own demons, which would probably be with her forever. Emma had urged her to make choices with her heart, and she had capitulated, even though those choices went against her instinct.

Her father had harped on that subject more than anything when she was learning the business. He knew from his own experiences how easy it was to give in to the caring side of your nature, but therein laid the trap. Your heart kept your enemies around to fight another day, and when they did, most times they picked the easiest targets. The targets that inflicted the most pain to those left behind.

Up to now she hadn't lied to Hayden but had tried to shield him from the whole truth. She had done it to give Hayden the opportunity to have a relationship with Emma. It was a gamble, but once again she had turned away from her gut and gone with her heart. With Emma back in their lives, though, her decisions could return to haunt her. It would be Cain's main concern to keep Hayden whole if they did.

Remembering Merrick's question, she finally answered, "Yeah, he asked, and I don't have an answer for him. Not one I can live with, anyway. If Emma knows what's good for her, she'll clam up on the subject. If she wants any type of relationship with Hayden, honesty on her part won't be the mortar that'll pave that brick road for her."

"It's not your fault, Cain."

"The hell it isn't, Merrick. Marie would be alive if I'd thought with my head instead of my heart. You knew my father. He'd have never made that mistake. And for what? I turned a blind eye to what happened, and Emma left anyway."

Knowing better than to argue, Merrick held her hand out so Cain would come closer. "Come on, let's get you packed and ready to go. It's colder than hell up there, so we have to find your long johns."

CHAPTER SIX

The panic set in when Emma went to check on Hayden the next morning and found his and Mook's beds both empty. That he'd gotten disgusted with his visit and left crossed her mind, and it brought on a fresh batch of tears. Her eyes were still a little swollen already after eavesdropping on his telephone conversation with Cain the night before.

"What's the matter?" Hayden appeared in the doorway and appeared confused as to why Emma was in his room crying.

"Nothing. Just thinking about something. Would you like some breakfast?" The sweaty clothes and red cheeks could only mean Hayden was a morning runner, like Cain.

"Just cereal is fine, if you have it."

"It's no trouble, really. Let me make you something."

Hayden stripped off his sweaty shirt and folded it neatly before he put it in what looked like a laundry bag.

"Did you have a nice run?"

He nodded and grabbed another set of clothes to take into the bathroom with him.

"Let me grab a shower first. I'm not that picky, so don't knock yourself out."

Emma looked at his bag full of folded clothes and the order of the room. Both Hayden and Mook had made their beds before they'd gone out, and nothing was out of place. Hayden was neat, polite, intelligent, and thoughtful—all attributes she would not have put together with someone so young. The illusions she had spun with her upstanding

Christian mother's help were fiction. She could see now that leaving him with Cain hadn't been a mistake. Her son had become the person he was at Cain's knee, not at the end of her fist.

"God forgive me for what I've done." She got off the bed and left the room without another word. Her mother's disgusted look as she passed her in the hall didn't brighten her mood as Emma headed to the kitchen.

Carol had been standing in the hall like a sentinel on guard to make sure their guests didn't run off with her silver. "This isn't a café, Emma. The boy has got to learn we aren't here to cater to his every whim."

Carol had watched Hayden run off with Mook and felt her anger start to simmer. Seeing Hayden was like looking at a mirror image of the woman Emma had introduced to her and Ross on the day of her graduation from Tulane.

Thirteen Years Earlier at the Tulane Campus in New Orleans

"Hi, baby. Your mom and I are so proud of you." Ross hugged Emma and held her for a long moment before he let her go. He had already taken two rolls of pictures on the old Kodak camera he'd lugged with him from Wisconsin so he could remember the day his little girl walked across the stage in her cap and gown.

"Thank you both for coming, Daddy." Emma squeezed her father one more time before she turned to face her mother.

Carol studied her daughter for a long while before she said anything. Something was different about Emma, and she couldn't quite place what it was. "I don't know what you think you're going to need all this education for when you come home and settle down. All this was a big waste of time and money, if you ask me."

"I'm sorry, did anyone ask you?"

The question was asked with a touch of humor, but when Carol looked up, the blue eyes held no trace of teasing.

"Mom, Daddy, I want you to meet Cain Casey. Cain, my parents, Carol and Ross Verde." Emma stepped next to Cain and put her arm around her waist. "Try and behave, baby." They had been seeing each other for over a year, and Emma felt comfortable prodding the mobster when it was warranted. Emma laughed at the way Cain's brow arched at her comment.

"Miss Casey, it's nice to meet a friend of Emma's." Ross held out his hand, unable to turn away from the sight of his daughter leaning against the tall, strong-looking body. The image was making his brain freeze temporarily, since he'd never seen Emma act like this with anyone before.

"Thank you, sir. I know she's been looking forward to you two making it down for this auspicious occasion."

After Cain saw the way Emma's mother inspected the crowd, she was amazed Emma was as carefree as she was. The woman looked like someone was following her around holding a piece of crap under her nose.

"Are we ready to go out to dinner?" asked Cain.

Emma tried to act relaxed, but watching her mother size Cain up was making her nervous. "Cain made a reservation at one of the city's best restaurants, so I hope you guys are hungry."

Without one word Carol turned and walked away, leaving her husband no choice but to follow her. In all the years that followed, she never asked about Cain Casey. When she got the news of Hayden's birth, she had simply handed the phone to an overjoyed Ross.

Watching her grandson make his way down the stairs brought that day back to the forefront of Carol's memories. One look at Cain and she'd known she and Ross had lost Emma. When she saw the size of her daughter's smile and how comfortable she looked in that viper's arms, she knew exactly what was going on. Loving another woman went against everything she believed in, a lesson she thought she'd firmly instilled in Emma.

From that day she couldn't bring herself to forgive her daughter the mistake Cain had been. To see the proof of that mistake in her house was more than she should have to endure.

❖

Hayden detoured into the living room after he bounced off the last step, wanting to see who had driven up. Peering out the window, he could see he was mistaken; actually, someone was pulling away from the bunkhouse. It struck him as odd that anyone living in the area would be driving a dark sedan instead of a truck or SUV.

"Problem?" Emma asked, studying Hayden's back as he looked out the window. She was wiping flour off her hands, wondering what he found so fascinating in a place where almost nothing ever happened. As a child she'd never wasted time gazing out windows to the empty fields beyond. She spent her time reading and expanding her horizons through books like *Little Women* and *The Secret Garden*.

Her life in Hayward tempered the different lessons in those pages, and her mother had filled in the gaps of what was right and wrong, and good and evil. Though Cain had added to Emma's experiences, her moniker of *Hayseed* was never too far off.

"Are we expecting company?" Hayden didn't really need an answer as he watched the car drive to the gate and take a left onto the road. He was more interested in what Emma's response would be.

"Not that I'm aware of. Why, is someone out there?"

"Not anymore." He turned away from the window and went to sit at the kitchen table with Mook.

Behind him Emma glanced out the window to try to see what Hayden was talking about. The only thing moving in the yard was her father on his tractor, hauling a load of feed to the fence line.

She washed the breakfast dishes and put them away. A couple of hours later she stepped out on the porch to search for Hayden and found him reading a book, while Mook kept an eye on the road as if he were expecting someone.

"Would you like to go for a walk?" asked Emma.

Hayden put his book down and shrugged. "Sure, there's some stuff I'd like to ask you."

"That'd be great. What would you like to talk about?"

Mook put his sunglasses on and followed far enough behind to ensure their conversation would be private as long as they didn't start screaming at each other. The three followed the dirt road Hayden had jogged on that morning.

Emma put her hands in the pockets of her coat to keep them warm and waited to hear what Hayden had on his mind. The crunch of dead leaves under their feet sounded almost magnified as they walked up the path behind the house. It led to an open field where Ross grew hay for his animals in the summer. Now the ground was frozen and covered in leaves from the nearby woods.

"Why did you leave us?"

Emma hadn't expected the question, even though she'd listened in on his conversation with Cain the night before. She would have thought Cain had settled this issue long ago in her blunt, forthright manner. "I'm sure Cain told you the answer to that already, Hayden, so are you just testing me?"

Hayden sighed in frustration. Emma was going to give him the same runaround Cain always did on the subject. "Unlike you, I don't ask questions just to make conversation. I want to know. Did Mom hurt you or something? Is that it? Because she won't tell me."

"Really? And please don't ever think that about Cain. I don't like what she does, but she never hurt me." She waved her hands to emphasize the denial.

It surprised him, though, how quickly Emma had come to his mother's defense. "Cain thought it best for you to answer that question, not her."

"The Cain I knew would've answered something so simple easily enough, so it just surprises me she didn't."

"Maybe that's what your problem is—you don't know my mother at all. Maybe you never did."

Emma stuffed her hands into her coat again and looked back at the big blond trailing them. Mook was far enough away so he couldn't hear what she had to say and report it back to Cain. "I'm not stupid enough to think Cain has sheltered you from what the Casey family does for a living. I just hope you know it doesn't have to be your destiny."

"I didn't ask what you thought about my mother. I asked why you left us."

Emma sighed, knowing he wasn't going to let it go. As much as she didn't want to, she was going to have to answer him. Her memories of that day, every grotesque moment of it, were still a raw spot in her soul. She still grappled with the consequences when the events played in her mind.

Chapter Seven

Four Years Earlier at the Casey Residence

M rs. Casey?" Carmen the housekeeper stood in the doorway of the sunroom waiting to be acknowledged. She had seen Emma make her way into the house and away from the mob in the yard.

Emma's attention jumped from the cake table to the door. Carmen was, as always, quiet as a cat. "Please, Carmen, I've been here long enough for you to start calling me Emma. We certainly spend enough time together."

"And as enjoyable as it is, your name to me is Mrs. Casey," she said with a smile. "I need the key to the cellar, ma'am. We've gone through more liquor than we put out, and there's a couple of hours to go yet."

The basement, a rarity in New Orleans, was filled with cases of the best brands on the market, and in this case all of them legal. Cain was a gambler by nature when it came to business, but in her home everything was legitimate.

The key Carmen needed was in the top drawer of Cain's desk, which was why she'd gone in search of Emma. She enjoyed a high level of Cain's trust, but no way would she chance the mobster coming inside and finding her anywhere near her private office.

"Don't go jinxing us, Carmen. We've gone all afternoon with the whole of Cain's family having a good time, and there hasn't been one fistfight yet."

Emma's teasing made Carmen laugh as she accepted the key and headed off to replenish the bar.

Two of the guys who worked at the pub were waiting to do the heavy lifting, leaving Emma to her moment of peace once more. Outside, Cain was holding up a plate to the maid cutting the large lemon cake, their son waiting with a fork in his hand. She was about to sit in the sunroom and close her eyes a minute when she felt a hard body press against her back and a large hand clamp over her mouth. Even with all the people in attendance and the room's great view of the yard, not one person noticed when the man pulled her away and dragged her to a guest room near Cain's office.

When the door closed she heard his breathing and felt sick to her stomach when he pressed his crotch into her bottom.

"You believe in God, Emma?"

His speech sounded slurred, which she attributed to the liquor that had flowed so freely all afternoon.

"Do you know how God punishes the perverts of this world for being perverts?"

"Please don't do this."

He only pressed harder into her and laughed. "I asked you a question." He moved his hand from her throat and squeezed one of her breasts to the point of pain. "So answer me."

"My mother certainly thinks so, but God won't punish you near as much as Cain will if you do this."

"My cousin Cain plays at being a man, but she doesn't have what it takes." His hand moved lower to her abdomen, and Emma fought the urge to vomit. "She's led a charmed life, though, and I'm thinking I want a taste of the sweetest charm she has."

He pushed her so hard she landed in the middle of the bed, and before she could move he was on top of her, pressing her face into the mattress, yanking up her skirt. Her thoughts flew to Cain and how badly she needed her. Her tears began when she heard his zipper and his sickly laugh.

Outside, Cain looked around for the third time, not seeing Emma in the crowd, so she patted Hayden on the shoulder and pointed to Mook. Merrick and Lou broke away from the festivities when they saw her head into the house. The same laugh that was terrifying Emma zeroed Cain in on the closed door.

Once inside, Cain and her guards realized immediately what was happening when Danny turned and they saw the evidence of his intentions in his hand. In two strides Cain reached the bed and jerked him back into Lou, who dragged the idiot out of the room before Emma could straighten her skirt and sit up.

"It's all right, love." Cain's voice sounded soothing, but Emma could feel the tension building in the lanky frame. "I'm sorry for not getting here sooner, but it's all right now."

"He tried to…" She couldn't finish.

"I know, sweetling, but you're safe now." Cain pressed her palm to her lover's cheek and offered the only comfort she could at the moment. "And I promise you this won't ever happen again. No one comes into our home and touches what's mine. No one."

She pulled Emma closer and looked at Merrick over the blond head. "Clear the grounds and bring Hayden upstairs to our room. I want him to sit with his mother while I take care of this. And make sure Carmen sees to Marie."

Merrick left without a word, and Lou and his charge disappeared into the cellar. With no windows and cinder-block walls, the space made a wonderful wine cellar, but in this instance it would serve as a great place to swallow all of the screams that would issue from it.

"Cain, don't."

"Don't what?" They had started toward the stairs and Cain stopped, confused by the request.

"He just scared me, and I know you don't think so, but he doesn't deserve what you have in mind."

Cain took a deep breath in an effort to control her rage, not wanting to scare Emma any more, but she couldn't resist picking up an expensive vase and flinging it at the wall. "This can't go unanswered, love, you know that. What he did—"

"He did to me," said Emma. "So I'm asking you to let him live. I won't have his death on my conscience for a 'what if.' God is forgiving, but not that forgiving." A bit of her mother seeped into her speech, but she really didn't believe in taking someone's life. And from what she was seeing in Cain's eyes, that was exactly what was going to happen to Danny if she didn't do anything to stop it. "Promise me on what we have together you'll respect my wishes. I want your word."

"Why? After what he did today, why?"

She gazed up at Cain, trying to find the right words. "Because this time it happened to me, and I don't believe this behavior warrants such a rash act. That's the best way I can explain how I feel about it."

Emma's reasoning wasn't good enough, and the logical part of Cain's brain told her to send her upstairs with their son and be done with what had to happen. The guy had crossed an unforgivable line, and the price was his life. Cain knew that, but the trust in Emma's eyes made her turn away from logic and tell her what she wanted to hear. No matter the cost, Cain didn't want to destroy how Emma felt about her, so she answered with her heart. "I give you my word."

"Thank you."

Hours passed after the brief conversation, and when Hayden had fallen asleep, Emma went in search of her partner. The house was quiet and the sun had just set, so it was easy to hear the squeak of the cellar door as it opened.

"Get rid of him."

Cain's voice and her words made Emma grab the banister to keep her feet. When she turned the corner, she stopped. She felt sick when she saw the blood splattered across Cain's shirt and pants, and her crimson hands. "You promised me. I thought your word meant something to you."

In their time together she had never thought of Cain as a liar, but before her stood not only a liar, but also a vicious killer. A killer covered in the evidence of her crime, who had committed the act with her wife and son in the house.

"I promised you, and I kept my word." The blue eyes never wavered, and she delivered the words calmly.

All her mother's warnings crashed down on her. She sank into the nearest chair, disgusted with her own naiveté. She had wanted to believe so badly in Cain that she had refused to see what was right in front of her. How much more plainly could Cain show her the depth of her deceptions? This time she was covered in the truth of what she was and what she was capable of. Emma felt her heart turn cold at the fact that she was sharing her life, her bed, and her soul with a killer. To make it worse, she had given this devil a child to perpetuate what the Casey family stood for.

She loved Cain, but she couldn't ignore this evil woman who stood there and blatantly lied to her. Despite their love, she had time to salvage as much of her family as she could. She refused to become as guilty as Cain. She refused to teach Hayden that murder, revenge, and dishonesty were codes to center his life around.

"I said I kept my word," repeated Cain.

"Thank you." Those two empty words were all Emma could think to add.

"At a birthday party for your aunt Marie that Cain and I hosted, one of the guests got drunk and tried something he should've known better about, considering who I was and who I lived with. But I guess he thought Cain would tolerate it since the Irish whiskey was flowing as well as the ale, and everyone seemed to be having a good time. You were about to turn seven, and I remember looking out into the yard and seeing Cain help you get a piece of cake."

Emma took her gloved hands out of her pockets and brought them up to hug herself from the sudden chill the memories had brought on. She realized her voice sounded detached and devoid of emotion, which was a lie. With every detail she retold, she relived the anguish.

"I don't think anyone noticed when this guy dragged me into one of the bedrooms. Just when I thought something horrible was going to happen to me, somebody jerked the guy off me. One second I was in terror, and the next I was in the arms of someone I knew would keep me safe."

"Cain?" Hayden looked at her for the first time since they'd left the house.

"Yes, it was Cain. I don't know how she knew, but she saved me."

"So as her reward, you left her?"

His voice sounded so incredulous his mother almost laughed. Her son wasn't yet twelve, but he already thought like the heir to the Casey name. Every sacrifice she'd made to get Hayden back was in vain. Cain was too ingrained where it mattered most—his heart.

"I didn't leave because of that, Hayden. After she calmed me down and let someone take me upstairs with you, she cleared the grounds. I waited up because I was so worried about her, and because I wanted her to hold me and make the humiliation go away. After what seemed an eternity, I went downstairs to look for her. The man was gone, but Cain hadn't cleaned up yet.

"I saw her hands. Her hands and her clothes are etched into my brain, and I'm sorry, but I couldn't live like that anymore. There was so much blood. She was covered in it, so much so that it felt like it would taint all of us like a flood. The sight of it made me sick.

"I didn't want to be responsible for getting someone hurt, or worse, just because I shared a bed with the head of the Casey family. I'm sorry if that's hard for you to hear, but it's the truth."

She put her hand on Hayden's arm to get him to stop walking. When he paused, she thought she had gotten through to him and he'd understood her position.

"Mom protected you, and you left because of it?"

Hearing it put like that, her actions didn't make much sense to her either. "I'm not one of my father's cows, Hayden. I don't belong to Cain like some piece of furniture. As much as I respect her sense of family and honor, this isn't feudal Japan where I'm expected to walk four steps behind her. I was her wife, and I wanted to have some say in what happened in my life and the lives of my children.

"But she told me she didn't kill the guy like she wanted to because I asked for his life. I thought it was a job for the police—not Cain's hands or the muzzle of her gun. Do you understand all of Cain? What she's capable of, under the right circumstances?"

"I understand better than you. But you left one more person out there just waiting to hurt her or me. All because you were weak. Did you think of that when you were being so charitable? Sure, you did what you thought was right. But I can't respect you for it. You and your clear conscience. Too bad you didn't care as much about Mom and me. Why didn't you ever stop to think about me?" The anger that had been bottled up for four years came pouring out until Hayden was screaming at her.

Hayden's words hit her like physical blows, so she moved a little away from him, and her eyes filled with tears again. "Listen to you. No eleven-year-old should have to think that. This doesn't have to be your life, son. I more than care about you, I love you. It killed a big part of me to walk away. You, Cain, and Marie were my family. You're still a part of my family, and I want you to know you have options other than Cain." When Hayden didn't object, she moved back close enough to put her hand on the sleeve of his coat.

"What, I could come live here and learn to milk cows? Better yet, I could spend the rest of my life trying to get Grandmother Carol to not look at me like she hates everything about my family and me. No, thank you. You wanted me here so we could get to know each other. Well, you're no one I want to waste my time getting to know better, lady." He jerked his arm out of her grasp and walked farther away from her, wiping his eyes as he went.

Emma just watched him leave, not thinking of anything that would make him stop. The hope she had so fragilely pieced together when she left for New Orleans to see him again shattered with every step he took away from her. She was sure this defeat would hurt as much as giving up her life with Cain.

Hayden turned back toward the house, ignoring Mook as he passed. He wanted nothing more than to leave when Cain arrived. Coming here was a mistake, and Cain would have to respect his wishes about not caring to have a relationship with Emma. He had done his part. He had tried because of the precious memories he still clung to when he remembered his mother. This time around he would walk away, and she could spend the rest of her days reliving the pain of loss.

"Let him cool off, Emma. Don't worry. He'll be fine. You just hit a raw nerve without knowing," said Mook.

"What do you mean?"

"He still misses Marie. It upsets him sometimes when someone mentions her name, and he wasn't expecting it."

"Did Cain have to institutionalize her?" Emma remembered Cain's younger sister and the afternoons she'd spent listening to Cain read to her. She recalled Marie's blue eyes looking adoringly at Cain.

"She died almost three months ago."

"What? How?"

"You aren't getting the story out of me, and I'll have to insist you don't ask Hayden about it again." The bodyguard broke out into a run when his charge disappeared into the house, leaving Emma to fill in the blanks however she wanted.

The two houseguests spent the rest of the afternoon and early evening behind the closed door of their bedroom. Emma walked past it more than twenty times but took Mook's warning seriously.

CHAPTER EIGHT

The sun had set by the time Emma felt comfortable enough to knock and see if Hayden and Mook wanted to come down for dinner. Her hands flew to her chest when, before her knuckles made contact with the wood, the door opened. Hayden had his coat on and rushed past her toward the stairs, obviously heading outside.

She heard the front door open and close and ran down after him. *Is he leaving?* Her worst fears were confirmed when she saw the entourage of people standing in her father's yard.

Pulling back the curtain in the living room, she spotted a large SUV parked near the barn. From the light spilling out of the large building, she saw Hayden clinging to Cain. He stayed in Cain's arms for a long time, as if trying to make himself feel better after the horrible morning he'd spent with his birth mother. He'd obviously called, and she'd come early to take him away.

Cain and Hayden strode into the barn, leaving all the help, as Cain liked to call them, outside near the car. The head of the Casey family surely wasn't expecting a mob hit or trouble here, since she'd brought only Merrick and a couple of others with her. In New Orleans, depending on what was going on in the business, anywhere from four to eight guards trailed Cain every day. They had also been a presence in Emma's life, and of all the things she missed, the guards weren't one of them.

Emma looked on as Hayden told Cain something and kept pointing toward the house. Cain cocked her head to the side as she listened, looking in her direction every so often as if she knew Emma was standing at the window.

When the boy finished, Cain hugged him again before she put her hands on his shoulders and started to explain something to him. "Hayden, she didn't know about Marie, so try and let that one go, buddy."

Cain squeezed his shoulders, trying to get him to look up. The death of her sister was still a raw spot for both of them, but especially for Hayden, who had spent so much time with Marie. Cain would arrive home on many an afternoon to find him reading to her from one of his textbooks so she could learn whatever he was studying in school.

"If she called more often than every four years she'd've known."

"And as my grandmother used to say, if you were born with wheels you'd have been a bicycle," said Cain in a light voice.

"Mom, what in the world's that supposed to mean?"

She laughed as she watched her son's face go from an expression of gloom to one of confusion. "I'm not really sure myself, but it seemed like the right thing to say."

"Come on. I'll show you where we're staying for the night. We've got a lot to catch up on." Hayden moved away from Cain for a minute and went to welcome Merrick.

When he did, Cain looked back up at the house, saw her ex-lover standing in the window, and wondered what had brought their talk around to her late sister. Something had, because she knew Emma well enough to know she would use all the time she'd been given to win Hayden over, just like she had won her own heart so many years before.

Cain hadn't gotten this far in life without being smart enough to suspect this visit was Emma's first step in a plan to lure Hayden away from the evil Caseys. Cain would find out what had upset him soon enough, but now it was time to get out of this fucking cold. If Hayden wanted to leave, the morning would be soon enough.

"Cain?"

She turned toward the masculine voice and broke into a smile. "Ross, how are you?"

"Fine, thanks for asking. And thank you for letting young Hayden come visit. We've really enjoyed having him." Ross stood at the door of the barn wearing a heavy plaid wool jacket with matching hat.

The hat, with flaps that covered his ears, looked almost comical, but Cain found herself wishing she had one of her own. "Thanks for having him, Ross. Hayden's a great kid." She patted her son on the back.

"Yeah, and now he can go back to the city with the knowledge of how to milk a cow under his belt."

They all laughed at the statement, making the young man blush.

"Let me show you where you're bunking down for the night, Cain."

"I'll get it, Mr. Ross. Go on inside with Emma."

Ross quickly moved toward the house, acting as if he knew Hayden and his mother needed privacy.

"What's up?" The question came out of Cain's mouth the minute the door of the bunkhouse closed.

"I just want to leave here. Does something have to be wrong?"

Cain took a deep breath and let it out slowly. She had wanted her son to know Emma, but not at the expense of his happiness. Heading down the path of sleepless nights and nightmares again wasn't high on her agenda. They had gotten through the pain of Emma's desertion together the first time, and she would always help him. But if she could avoid a repeat of that cycle, she would do whatever was necessary for Hayden's peace of mind.

"Right this minute?"

"No, you're right. No sense spending the night in one of those uncomfortable chairs at the airport, but tomorrow I want to go. I came so you wouldn't think I was afraid to try, but I don't want to stay. It's just..." Hayden turned and faced the front door of the bunkhouse.

"Finish, son. You know you don't ever have to do anything just to make me happy. Someday I'll start asking you to do things for the good of the family, but that's far in the future. The best thing my old man did for me was let me live before he gave me too much responsibility. I love you, Hayden, and if it's in your best interest I'll move heaven and earth to give you what you want. If it's to leave here, you don't even have to tell me why."

Cain put her hands on her son's shoulders. As smart and mature as her kid was, he was still a kid.

"It's just that you're my family, Mom. You and Aunt Marie. I don't need anything or anyone else." He recognized the long intake of air and slow exhale he heard above his head as a technique Cain used to calm down.

"Did something happen, or did someone tell you something?"

"No, I'm just ready to go home." The big hands on his shoulders just patted him gently before pulling away. The loving gesture let him know she would give in and leave in the morning, if that was what he really wanted.

Mother and son sat with their guards in the small kitchen in the bunkhouse and ate. Merrick had brought supplies with her, knowing Carol wouldn't feed them. And considering they were in the middle of some frozen hell, they didn't have a slew of restaurants to pick from if she wasn't up to cooking.

A little after ten, Cain settled Hayden down in one of the bunks in the large open room at the center and waited for him to go to sleep. When he was out for the night, she and Merrick shared a look before Cain put on her coat and hat and headed outside. She hadn't made it halfway toward the front door of the farmhouse when Emma stepped onto the porch.

"He wants you to take him home?"

Cain looked at the empty fields, wondering how people didn't go completely insane living out here. "Tomorrow. Now you want to tell me what in the hell happened? I didn't think you two would be glued at the hip when I got here, but the phone call I got this morning surprised me. Hayden doesn't usually give up on anything so easily."

"He told me today all the stuff he talks to you about was none of my business, so why should it be any different for me?" Emma was hurting and tried to lash out at the person she blamed for her misery.

Cain just nodded again and turned around, headed back to the bunkhouse. "Please, don't go. I'm sorry. This isn't your fault."

"What do you want from me? I raised him to be strong, Emma. Not to be like me but to choose his own path and be whatever he wants. Hayden's his own person, and I happen to love the hell out of who he is. He's better than me and you put together. Whatever happened today, you're right. That's between the two of you, but don't expect me to get in the middle. Nor am I going to champion your side. So what is it you want? For me to shake him until he agrees to stay?" Cain took her hands out of her coat pockets and spread them out, obviously frustrated.

"I want to talk to you and not have you sound like you hate me. I want for our son to look at me like I'm a member of his family, like I'm his mother and not some woman he has to spend time with because that's what you expect. I want him to want to please me as much as he lives to please you." Her voice started to sound ragged even to her own ears by the time Emma was done.

The stream of air that left Cain's mouth smoked the air at least two feet in front of her. "You could've had all that and more, and you know it. You left for your own reasons, none of which were me asking you to go. In fact, if memory serves me correctly it was me who asked you to stay. You want him to look at you and treat you like you're his mother. You should've sent him a letter now and then. What I did four years ago was a mistake, but I'm not making any more where you're concerned. I'll give you the morning to convince him to stay, if you can. After that I'm taking him home, if that's what he wants."

"What do you mean you made a mistake?" Emma wondered if Cain really regretted killing the man for what he'd tried to do.

"I listened to you, and I let him live. It's a mistake that has cost me dearly."

Just as quickly Emma realized Cain was still a heartless liar. What she had put into motion didn't seem so horrible now.

CHAPTER NINE

Merrick was sitting on Cain's bunk when her boss stepped back into the room, and she watched as Cain stripped off her hat, gloves, and coat. She enjoyed looking at the long, denim-wrapped legs since she rarely saw Cain in anything other than a business suit. They shared a close relationship, but she had never been able to convince Cain to cross the line and add being lovers to their list of accomplishments. She knew what Cain needed was a woman like Emma, but one who thought like her when it came to business and family. Merrick loved and accepted all of Cain, whereas Emma obviously could only stomach the soft and gentle parts. Emma had never sat back and learned, like Merrick, that it was Cain's strength for all things that made her incredibly attractive.

"How's the ex?"

"A little miffed. It would seem her son doesn't love her as much as he loves us. It always amazes me the things people can do to convince themselves how the world around them should work and respond to their decisions."

"Baby, what have I told you about women?"

"I believe your advice was along the lines of staying away from them. Maybe only after Special Agent Barney Kyle finally snares me in the trap he's been laying for years and convinces a judge to send me to the men's prison do I see that happening."

When Cain mentioned the man who led the task force formed to bring down the Casey organization, Merrick stood up from the bed and prowled toward her. If any of the others were awake, they knew better than to watch them or comment. She pressed her body to Cain's and slid her hands up to the back of Cain's neck.

"I don't see that happening either." She smiled through the statement before she pressed her lips to Cain's and coaxed her boss into kissing her back. The kiss was long and convincing, and Merrick pulled away first. With Cain's head still hovering close, she moved around to kiss her neck and trace Cain's ear with her tongue. "The camera's set up in the overhead light fixture, and so far I've found four bugs dispersed throughout the room.

"Sorry, baby, but I think Emma's visit had more to do with getting Hayden comfortable with the idea of being here, so when the time came and he'd be here permanently, he'd be easier to handle. Little Miss Muffet's plan involved more than getting together with her long-lost son and feeding him curds and whey. Kyle's goons have been in here. I'm sure of it."

If Cain was angry, she never showed her feelings when she pulled back a little to look at Merrick's face. She kissed her again and smiled. "That sounds like a wonderful idea, but it'll have to wait until we have a bit more privacy. Maybe we'll stick around here for a couple of days to build up the suspense before we can take care of our problem. A little ache can sharpen the sense of relief when it comes. Don't you agree, sexy?"

Cain leaned closer and traced Merrick's ear with her index finger. "Remember what happened to the girl in that rhyme, sweetling. Along came a spider. Only this time Emma might just have found a black widow, and I do believe they kill and eat their mates when they're done playing with them."

She laughed and moved out of Cain's embrace, but not before slapping her in the stomach. Her boss had given no clue as to who would be hurting by the end of the trip, but if Emma and Kyle knew what was good for them, they would start praying to whatever entity they believed in now. Because "relief" as defined by Cain Casey could leave a person praying for death instead of salvation.

❖

Before the sun came up the next morning, Cain was sitting on the bed assigned to her, waiting for her son's eyes to open. Experience let her appreciate the quiet, knowing it wouldn't be long before Hayden would wake up and join her for a run. They enjoyed this time together every morning—first with her pushing him in a running stroller, then with him riding his bike to keep up, and now with him keeping pace on legs almost as long as hers.

If she was grateful for one thing, it was that her brother Billy had lived to meet Emma. When Billy saw the way his older sister looked at the small blonde, he'd gone to a local clinic a few times and left them a gift for the future. She could still remember the shock she'd felt when he'd told her about it, joking it was his way to keep the Casey legacy alive for the next generation.

Billy's gift had given them their son and his name, which Billy had picked out before he died, three months before the child's birth. Cain liked to think her brother was watching over them from heaven and that was why Hayden resembled their family so much and had turned out to be so terrific. If she had to have a guardian angel, Billy Dalton Casey wasn't a bad guy to have sitting on her shoulder and whispering in her ear.

"Get ready, kid. I want to go running in the boonies." Cain spoke in a hush so she wouldn't wake everyone else. There was no danger out here she couldn't handle herself, and she wanted the time alone with her son for a talk.

Hayden had opened his alert blue eyes while she indulged in thoughts of her brother, and his quickness to get out of bed showed he had missed their morning ritual. Cain might have lost Billy to stupidity, but the generous man had given her a little bit of himself before he died so she would never be alone.

Cain moved to Merrick's bunk and kissed her forehead while Hayden was in the bathroom. "Enjoy a rare morning off, sweetling, since I'm thinking no one's going to jump me from behind a tree way out here."

"But…" Merrick said, ready to complain.

"I'll take care of myself and the kid, don't worry. I even promise to be back in plenty of time to help you make breakfast."

"I can blend into the background."

Cain laughed softly, looking down at Merrick. "Honey, you're talented beyond words. I'm not going to argue that, but in my eyes you can never blend into the background. I never told you this, but your breasts are a major distraction when you come with us in the morning."

Merrick knew she was being teased. It would take a hard blow to the head to distract Cain from anything. "Then I guess me and my tits will be sleeping in today."

Mother and son stepped out into the frigid cold and completed the stretches they'd begun inside. Cain detested running in so many layers, but the Wisconsin temperatures wouldn't let her get by with less.

"Where to, Mom?"

"How about we end up somewhere nice and open that would take a lens from space to see my lips moving?"

Any hope of leaving today vanished from Hayden's mind as he started off at a slow jog. If they headed far away from the tree lines dispersed throughout the property, he was certain Cain would open up and tell him what she couldn't within the perimeter of the house and barn. It was hard to bug open spaces, and even harder to listen in on someone's conversation without being seen.

The two agents who followed them couldn't get any closer than half a mile when Cain and Hayden stopped to watch the sunrise. A small device Cain had turned on when they stopped running was giving the sensitive long-distance mike trained on them a steady stream of static.

"We aren't leaving today, are we?"

"I'll make it up to you, I promise, but no, we aren't. Emma invited you for the week, and I'd like for you to take her up on her offer."

"When we talked yesterday you said I could leave this morning, no questions asked."

"Hayden, I know being a month shy of twelve isn't exactly adulthood, but I want you to understand that sometimes opportunities come and you have to take them."

His full lips turned to a frown, and Cain could see he was about to get angry. Sometimes it was a plus to have a kid who acted just like her in almost every way, down to the mood triggers that his face gave off. "Since you got here, have you seen anything that didn't make sense to you?"

"What, a cow with five legs?"

"Kid, maybe you're spending too much time with me. You're turning into a smart-ass. Come on, I'm being serious here. Nothing made you scratch the side of your head and ask 'I wonder why?'"

Hayden shook his head and stared at the ground as if the dead grass would give him the answer. Then he snapped his fingers. "That first morning after I finished my run and was heading downstairs after my shower. I saw a black sedan leave the yard and turn back onto the highway. I asked Emma about it, but she didn't know what I was talking about."

Cain moved closer to him, not taking any chances of tipping her hand to anyone but her son. "Think, buddy. Who drives around in black sedans in the middle of farm country? Hell, we had to wait for them to find something other than a truck at the rental counter when we got here."

"Cops."

She put her hands on the sides of his face so only she could see his lips move when the reality of the situation obviously hit him between the eyes. "My father was right. Those Casey genes do float to the top. You're going to be something else with those looks and the brains to go with them." She moved one hand to the back of his neck and pulled him in for a hug. "Kyle's here, buddy, so watch what you say in the bunkhouse. You don't know a whole lot, but I don't want this to blow up in my face and they take me in and have you somewhere where I can't get to you."

"Why would Kyle be here? Who would have…" The rest of the question never made it out as the realization of what Emma had done hit him even harder. His birth mother had set them up, or at least Cain, to take a fall, leaving her as the concerned mother to pick up the pieces—the pieces being him. "That bitch."

"Hey now, don't blame her just yet, kiddo. Let's see how this plays out and what game's in motion before we rush out with guns blazing. I realize you think your mom just up and left you, but Emma's never done something like this unless the situation or someone drove her. Can you do something for me, Hayden?"

"Mom, you don't ever have to ask."

Cain still held him close and spoke into his ear. "When we get back, don't let your anger win out. I'm going to make an example out of Kyle and whoever helped him so he won't bother us anymore. Do you think you can do that? You don't have to play the forgiving lost son, but try and work on your relationship with Emma and see where it leads. That'll give me time to deal with Kyle and his goons."

From the trees, one of the agents had climbed up with the wand to see if he could get a better line and hear what Cain was talking to her son about. "Man, Kyle's going to shit a brick if we go back with nothing. I don't get it. There's nothing out here between them and us."

"Just go up a little higher and try a more downward angle. Maybe this thing's so used to hearing background noise it doesn't know what to do with only the occasional bird noise. Never mind. Pack it up. They're heading back."

After a few stretches the pair stopped talking and started back in the direction of the bunkhouse.

The two men watching them froze as both sets of blue eyes seemed to zero in on them when mother and son ran past, but they knew it was impossible.

CHAPTER TEN

R oss watched from the porch as the two dots on the horizon started to take shape and become more recognizable. Cain and Hayden had the same stride, and watching them run made him think back to his own high school track days. He had never been as comfortable when he ran as the two people he was watching. The door closing behind him didn't make Ross turn around and take his eyes off his grandson and his mother. He brought the coffee cup to his lips again and figured if Emma wanted to talk, she would eventually say something.

"Think they're leaving today?" Emma's voice cracked a little at the end of her question, so Ross figured she'd been crying again.

"I don't know, baby. Maybe you should ask them when they get back. Those two must have gotten up pretty early to beat me out of bed."

"Hayden's a lot like Cain, I guess. She'd get up, run, and be home in bed after a shower before I woke up." She felt the heat of her blush when she realized what she had just shared with her father. But she remembered how Cain had moved her run up an hour when she'd complained about waking up alone and hearing the shower. She had fixed it so she was there and holding Emma when she woke up every morning they'd shared together. "I'm sorry, Daddy. I don't know why I said that."

"Because you love her, and no matter how much time you spend here hiding from the fact that you do, you won't stop loving her. Though now, with all this, you may've killed any hope of getting her to feel that way about you again." Ross put his cup down and turned to face his only child in hope of getting through to her before the world started to crumble around her feet. He didn't want to have to stand by helplessly and watch.

"Honey, I don't know Cain as well as you, and you probably don't know her as well as Hayden does, but I'm guessing the one thing she's got going for her is smarts. She won't go down without a fight, and when she starts shooting back, do you really want to be standing on the other side hoping some other white knight comes charging in to save you?"

He took his hat off and scratched the top of his head before he glanced toward the barn. "I'm just a farmer and may not know a whole lot about a whole lot, but I'm thinking they don't send this many people to snare someone who goes around with their thumb up their butt."

"I know what I'm doing, Daddy."

"Don't worry, I've said my piece. You go on and listen to your mother and that fella who's come by to see you, and I'm sure he'll ante up on all those promises he made. When the dust settles I'll go back to tending my cows and working my land, and I can promise I won't say a word about the outcome. I'll go ahead and say it now. When it's done, you're going to be here with me alone because that big Irishwoman's going to strip you and Kyle of everything you hold dear. And, Emma, I mean everything and everyone. When it happens, I'll still love you and won't throw you out for the world to finish beating you down, but I'll spend my years trying to find it in my heart to feel sorry for you."

Emma evidently wanted to lash out at him, but it wouldn't change the way he felt. Ross Verde was a man of principle, and what his wife and daughter had conjured up didn't smell right to him.

"You're supposed to be on my side, Daddy."

He laughed and put on his hat, ready to get to work. "If you can't see I am, we don't have another thing to talk about on the subject. You just remember what your old man said this morning and think hard on your future. What you want it to be and who you want to share it with depend on what you do starting right now."

"Don't you remember, you win here too, Daddy, if this all works out. I think Cain will relax enough out here to let her guard down around those baboons she surrounds herself with, and if that happens, you and I both win."

Ross stopped his trek to the barn and turned around. "I didn't sign those papers, Emma, and there isn't a reason in the world you and your mother can come up with to make me do it, either. I've been in jams before and I'll get myself out of them just like always, and this time it won't be from taking favors from some idiot in a suit with a grudge."

The idiot Ross was referring to was standing behind the barely opened front door, listening in on their conversation. Special Agent Barney Kyle had started his career in the FBI on the fast track by cracking a couple of drug rings and giving his superiors the impression he would be a star in the Bureau. His success had landed him the Casey assignment.

The Bureau was tired of trying to get an indictment on Dalton, then his daughter, only to come away empty-handed. When Kyle took over, he expected the operation to last about a year before he had her in court. His plan ran into a roadblock by the name of Cain, so eight years later he found his star status had tarnished considerably, and he was about to be relocated somewhere not found on the average map. Because of that threat and Cain's constant smugness under the unrelenting surveillance, Kyle had come to despise her. All he had to show for his efforts so far were pictures of her impressive wardrobe and smile.

Ross was right in a way. The thing between him and Cain had become personal to such a degree that he wanted the satisfaction of taking her down. The main fantasy that played in his head about that day now involved doing it at the end of his gun barrel. He lived for the day he could squelch all of her condescending laughter and snide remarks about him. So this phase of the operation was his last chance, and he didn't care how many corners he had to cut to bring her down; he was going to do it.

"He isn't going to spoil this for us, is he, Emma?" Barney Kyle opened the front door farther and watched Ross walk toward the barn. Cain and Hayden were still too far away to spot him, and his earpiece was on to alert him to any movement in the bunkhouse.

In Emma he had found Cain's weakness, and even though it had taken only an hour to convince Carol, it had taken both of them months to get Emma on board with his plan. Cain was fighting a turf war over a major part of her business, so this trip came at a time when she couldn't put her affairs aside for a week to watch Emma play nice with their kid. The mob boss would never suspect the level of sophisticated equipment Kyle had installed in the bunkhouse, which would only make it that much sweeter when she started talking and conducting business as usual.

"You shouldn't be here, Agent Kyle."

"I was just in the kitchen having coffee with your mother. Don't worry. I watched Cain and Hayden leave this morning, and I'm positive no one saw me enter the house. I'm sure as hell no one will see me leave."

Hayden and Cain slowed their run down to cool off, giving Emma a few more minutes alone with Kyle. "I take it Cain hasn't started singing about her illegal activities yet?"

Knowing his subject, Kyle moved in for the kill. "No, all we have is her in a serious lip-lock with the pretty fluff piece parading as a bodyguard."

"When was this?"

"Last night after they put the kid to bed. Don't worry. It was just a little sexual innuendo, then off to separate beds. I don't know, though. One more kiss like that and Casey might not be able to hold out."

Kyle chuckled when Emma left the porch and headed to the bunkhouse, entering without knocking. Most of the guys were up and talking over coffee while Merrick and Mook moved around the kitchen fixing breakfast.

"Damn, I thought you two were in Canada by now, you've been gone so long," teased Merrick, assuming it was Cain and Hayden.

"They're on their way back, so I thought you might need a hand with breakfast." Emma's voice sounded slightly colder than the temperature outside.

All the men in the room watched as the minor turf war broke out, ready to jump in if it came to blows and Merrick tried to kill Emma.

"No, thank you, Ms. Verde. I'm more than familiar with what Cain and Hayden want and like."

"It's still Mrs. Casey. Try and remember that. And I'm sure you know a lot about what pleases Cain. But I'm not leaving, so get used to it," said Emma.

"Get used to what?"

The deep voice made the two women look at the door in time to see both Caseys strip off their jackets and shirts. Except for the breasts covered by a sports bra on one, the bodies were similar in build. Hayden had less muscle mass, but everyone could see that in the near future he would be as imposing as his mother.

"Get used to me coming over here in the morning for the next couple of days to help with breakfast." Emma tried to tear her eyes off

Cain but couldn't keep from staring. Every night she dreamed about her estranged lover.

"I see. Well, we're both starving, so I hope you're up to the task. Hayden, go grab a shower, and save me some hot water."

"Hayden, you can use the one in the house if you want," said Emma, trying not to sound desperate.

He just grabbed the things he'd need for the bathroom and walked away. Mook had been nice enough to pack their belongings and move them out of the main house.

Merrick and Mook walked out of the kitchen when Cain stepped closer to Emma and started talking. "Don't look so disappointed. He's staying the rest of the week like he promised. I hope you spend the time trying to get to know him for who he is, and not for what you want him to be.

"You can't change the past, Emma. Just try and get him to trust you a little bit and take it from there. Hayden's a happy kid, and I've done my best to keep him that way, but I've always suspected a big part of him misses you. There's only so much I can give him, but in the end he needs his mother in his life as an active participant.

"I'll help you as much as I can, for his sake, but don't try and get back in his good graces at my expense. You try and drive a wedge between us, and I'd like to think I know him well enough to guarantee he'll cut you off and never give you another thought, no matter how much that'll hurt him." It was the only warning she would give Emma about Kyle or anything else she might have planned. "Do you understand me?"

"Yes." Emma turned back to the bowl of eggs she had been whipping. Cain didn't sound threatening, but Emma couldn't look at her anymore in her current state of undress. "Thank you. I'm sure you helped him change his mind about leaving early."

While they ate breakfast in silence, Emma studied Hayden and Cain, trying to figure out a way to get her son to talk with her again. She wanted to kiss Cain when she asked him to take Emma for a walk after their meal. She and Hayden watched as Cain jumped a fence and started toward Ross, who was dumping feed into one of the bins he had placed throughout the pastures.

The coat Cain had on provided just enough buffer to the wind, and the snow that had fallen the night before had frozen, making a crunching noise as she walked through the grass. She had yet to see Carol, but

Ross had gone out of his way to make friendly talk since she'd arrived the night before. They had always shared a good relationship, and Cain had missed their telephone conversations when he would call to see how Emma was doing.

"Morning," Cain called out so as not to startle him.

"Morning, Cain. Enjoy your run?"

"Any more of this clean, fresh air and I might just keel over. I thought I'd come out here and help while Emma's spending some time with Hayden." She tipped her hat up and smiled at him. "Earn my keep, so to speak."

Ross smiled back and patted the seat next to him. They rode around on the tractor, filling the bins and pushing cows out of the way so they could get the job done. Four hours later he pulled up in front of the barn and went to put the bags they hadn't used back in storage. There weren't many bags left, so he didn't want them to spoil. After they were gone he'd have to use the hay he'd baled in the fall.

"You need to make a run to the feed store, Ross." The bag over Cain's shoulder joined the ones she'd already carried in and stacked neatly in the dry, dark room in the barn. Ross had been amazed when she hefted the eighty-pound sacks and hauled them into the barn without too much grunting.

"I don't think that'll be possible until spring."

He looked so uncomfortable with the subject that Cain changed her tactics and moved to something else. "Is there a restaurant in town?"

"Just a little place that does simple stuff. Not anything you're used to, I'm sure."

"Oh, I don't know. I'm kind of a joint girl, given the opportunity. Let's go get a bite."

They were sitting in Mabel's Diner fifteen minutes later, waiting for the waitress to take their order. Cain looked out at the guy on the corner, doing his best not to stick out on the small town street. The fact that he was freezing his ass off while keeping an eye on her brought its own perverse sense of satisfaction. Just watching him out there made her peruse the menu and plan to order every course she could squeeze out of the sparse number of selections.

"Cain, can I ask you a question?" Ross peeked at her over the top of his own menu but kept it near his face. Probably, Cain figured, to hide his face if she didn't like his question.

"Shoot."

"What is it you do?"

She looked at him and wondered if old Ross was a strand in Kyle's webbing. "Can I ask you a question before I answer yours?"

He followed her line of sight out to the guy on the corner.

"Have you ever heard the expression the walls have ears?"

Ross just stared at her silently, as if waiting for her to finish.

"In this day and age they have ears, eyes, and brains. And they always seem to be plotting my demise. The other thing is, they aren't confined to the walls, so I'm curious why you want to know what I do."

Ross couldn't take his eyes off the man on the corner leaning against one of the town's only parking meters. "I've been watching my daughter for the past four years, trying to find what spooked her. Granted, I didn't spend a lot of time getting to know you, but I saw how you felt about her. I could hear it in your voice when we used to talk." He finally turned from the window and scrutinized his daughter's ex-lover. "Why's she here and not with you?"

"She asked to go and I let her. I'm not a monster, Ross. I wasn't about to try and force her to stay somewhere she felt she didn't belong any longer. What I wouldn't allow, though—and if this makes me sound like a monster, then I'm sorry—was letting her leave with Hayden. He's my son, and his place is with me. If Emma wants to have a relationship with him I'm all for that, but it'll be limited to visitation rights. I'll pull out every bit of power and influence at my disposal to keep it that way. Don't ever doubt that."

"But that doesn't really answer my question."

Cain glanced at the man on the street again and thought of the best way to answer without upsetting Ross. "In my time and in my business dealings, some people have tried to test my resolve and my position every so often. Sometimes, they try to get to me through my family. At a party for my sister, one of my cousins tried to take certain liberties with Emma in our home. I caught him before it turned ugly, and after seeing she was upset but unhurt, I had a little talk with this guy. The blood on my hands after our talk scared her, and she left a week later. I figured she would come back here, and someday she'd return to see our son. As much as it hurt me, it was her decision, and I've tried my best to honor it."

Ross leaned back in the booth and stared at Cain's hands. Granted, her life did have slimy characters at the periphery, but Emma had left because Cain had done what anyone else not even in her position would have. *Baby girl, what were you thinking?* He reflected on Emma and how she'd spent her time at the farm since she came back in the middle of the night so fragile looking. She had been prime pickings, and her mother had finished the job of beating her down.

"Cain, there's something you should know." Ross stopped talking when she shook her head in a way only he would see.

"How about you explain why you aren't making a trip to the feed store until the spring?"

During the rest of lunch Ross told her about low dairy prices and rising debt. He didn't mind doing without, but the land he worked had been in his family for generations, and family tradition was a subject he was sure she understood.

"I can look at you, Ross, and see you're a proud man, but does that mean you're stupid?"

Her smile kept him from getting mad and made him laugh with her. "I'd like to think I've got a few brain cells left, thank you."

"Then how would you like a silent partner?"

CHAPTER ELEVEN

R oss laughed again and studied her face to see if she was serious. "Who? You?"

"Let's say me for now, but eventually Hayden. I know Emma's probably your heir, but Hayden's your grandson and the one chance you have to keep this place you love in your family. I give you my word you'll never have a problem with the authorities, and nothing will go on there that isn't going on now."

Ross thought of the number of FBI running around his property playing a cat-and-mouse game. He figured Kyle hadn't realized the woman sitting here with him was the cat. Very seldom did the mouse win when the cat was as conniving as Cain. "How about we say nothing will go on there but farming and milking cows if I take you up on your offer?"

Ross shook one of the big hands that came off the tabletop and extended toward him. "Deal, partner," said Cain, apparently not needing a written contract. She excused herself from the table and headed toward the pay phone at the back of the restaurant. Ross sat alone and had another cup of coffee, wishing he knew who was keeping Cain on the other end so long.

"Let's head over to the bank," was all she said when she was finished.

Ross didn't ask any questions and just followed her down the street. He noticed the employees of the bank looked a little wary when they saw him, probably not wanting to turn him down again for a loan.

"Ross, why don't you ask them to fire up the one computer in this place and tell them you're here to make a withdrawal."

He watched the manager step out of his office and behind the counter to the teller, apparently afraid there was going to be a problem. "Jodie, could you access my account, please?"

"How're you doing today, Ross?" The manager held his hand out and smiled. "How much will you be needing?"

Ross looked back to Cain and put his hands up in question.

"However much it'll take to bring your account up to date at the feed store and buy another load of feed to fill up the storeroom. And we'll want that in cash," said Cain, in answer to the silent question.

The number Ross told the teller obviously surprised the manager, who pushed the girl aside. "You know that isn't going to happen, Ross. How about we wait until the spring and you sell off some of the stock, and then we'll see what we can do?"

Cain moved Ross out of the way to get to the manager. "I believe Mr. Verde asked you for some money, so start tapping away on that antique sitting back there and let's get to it."

The manager smirked as he brought up the Verde account. He looked like he'd love to knock the cocky expression off her face. "Like I said, Ross, why don't we wait until spring?"

"Look at the screen, Fred," ordered Cain.

"My name is Herb."

"Look at the goddamn screen."

It took a couple of envelopes to hand over Ross's money, and ten minutes to make it out of the bank after the manager saw the new Verde account.

"Do I want to know how you got my account number?" Ross patted his coat pocket where his newfound wealth was stashed.

Cain leaned over and whispered in his ear. "Don't tell anybody, but I'm just a good old-fashioned gangster."

Ross laughed and felt a genuine affection for the tall rogue his daughter had shared so many years with. The sentiment had nothing to do with the fact that she was willing to help him, no strings attached, which differed vastly from the deal the government was offering. Still chuckling, he asked, "Does that mean I just cut a deal with the devil?"

"Ross, granted, you don't know that much about me, but I'll never harm you. Things didn't work out for Emma and me, but she's the mother of my son, so that makes you part of my family. I gave you the money freely on behalf of Hayden and myself, and I don't expect anything from you. Maybe you can send us some of the famous cheese Hayden was telling me about. In addition to the money, you have to accept that there's still a bit of the devil inside me. It's what makes life fun, though."

He patted her on the back, and they continued their walk in a companionable silence. Carol would probably leave him for taking the money, but at least he would be able to sleep at night knowing he wasn't ruining someone's life as a way to solve his problems.

The owner of the feed store seemed shocked when Ross handed over enough cash to not only bring his account up to date and get another load of feed, but to leave him with a large credit. Ross watched him lick his fingers and start counting, taking time to keep an eye on Cain.

"How's this afternoon for the delivery?"

"That's great, Roy. We'll have enough time to get back and help the boys unload." He shook hands with the old man and waved Cain through the door and back to his truck.

Cain watched the countryside go by on their return to the farm as if she was daydreaming, but when they were about ten miles away she asked Ross to pull over.

"Are you sick or something?"

"Or something, yes." She turned her attention to the side-view mirror and waited to see what the sedan that had slowed was going to do. The idiot couldn't very well pull over without causing more suspicion, so he passed them at the same snail's pace, like he was searching for a place to pull over down the road.

Cain put her hand on Ross's sleeve and just watched the car with a smile. There was no place to hide out here. "Let's just give him a head start."

"You know who they are, don't you?"

Cain looked at him and made a decision. She turned on the same small device she had used during her talk with Hayden that morning and expelled a sigh. "Ross, you asked me a question back at the diner, so I'll answer that one before we get to the buffoons driving around in the most conspicuous-looking cars they could find."

"You don't have to do that, but if you do, whatever you tell me won't go any further than this truck."

"I know that, Ross, but thanks for saying it anyway. I'm a saloon owner by trade, as far as the government is concerned, but I do dabble in a bit of a hobby."

"Hobby?"

"That's what I like to call it, but I didn't say it wasn't lucrative. See, Ross, when you go to the store and buy a bottle of liquor or a box of cigarettes, right there on the top is a tax stamp. The one on cigarettes is a real money generator for the state and federal government, but for the average storekeep, well, it really cuts into their profits."

"Unless they know you."

Cain laughed at his quick wit. "That's right, unless they know me. I move merchandise that doesn't go through all those pesky regulations. They make money and I make money, but Agent Kyle and his bosses— they just get mad."

"No drugs or prostitution?"

"Selling drugs in my organization or selling someone on the streets is a quick way to mount up some hospital bills or find yourself on a permanent vacation, if the infraction is serious enough. My family has just never been interested in drugs. Don't get me wrong. Those who do traffic in all that stuff are making a ton of cash, but it's no good for the kids who get sucked into that lifestyle. My business is slightly lower risk, but I have to deal with some who want to come in and undercut me. I'm thinking once I'm gone, they'll start charging more than if they bought from regular vendors."

Ross let out a low whistle and gripped the steering wheel a little tighter. "That's it?"

"What I just told you in less than five minutes is what Kyle's been trying to get me to say on tape for the last eight years or more, Ross. It doesn't sound like a big deal, but trust me, to the feds it is. I'm not trying to whitewash my business. Your daughter lived with a criminal for all those years, but I don't go around hurting innocent people, and I'm not a killer by nature."

Ross thought about what Cain would do if she uncovered Carol's and Emma's part in Kyle's trap. "Does that mean you can be driven to it?"

"That, my friend, is another conversation for another day. Why don't we stick to the basics today and let it go at that?"

"I'd really like to know the answer now, if it's all the same to you."

"How about if I answer it this way? Kyle's here. The car that just passed us proves that, but how he got here and who invited him isn't my concern. My concern is spending time with my son because he asked me to come here, and with helping you out. Aside from that, I'm leaving in a few days, and it won't be in handcuffs. And when I'm gone, you won't have occasion to use your one good suit to attend any funerals."

"How do you know I only own one good suit?"

"Call it a hunch."

Ross laughed before turning serious and facing Cain. "You remember what you said about the walls having eyes and ears?"

"Yeah, don't worry, Ross. I know what I'm doing. Can I ask you something?" He turned to look down the road to see if the sedan was coming back. "Why are you telling me all this? You have to know if Kyle finds out, he'll slam you with an obstruction charge so fast you won't have time to scratch your ass. I know your land is important to you, and you're in serious jeopardy of letting him take it away from you as leverage."

"Because that guy's a slime. I don't care if he's got a badge or not. You may be considered the criminal here, but you have more honor than he's ever thought of having. I just don't want you to walk away from here and take Hayden with you and never come back. We've missed out on so much of his life because of stupidity, and I don't want to keep making the same mistakes over and over again. I want to know my grandson and you."

"Thanks for saying that, and don't worry. Hayden and I'll be back. Who knows? He might not want to go into the family business and prefer to be a farmer."

"Sure, and the cows will be taking their afternoon flight around the barn when we get home. That boy idolizes you, and it doesn't hurt that he looks just like you."

"Of all the people in my life, I can say he's made me happier than I ever deserved to be."

Ross parked in front of the barn and turned the ignition off, trying to find the guts to ask the next question. The wanting to know overrode anything else he felt, so Ross just blurted it out. "Do you miss Emma at all?"

"Does it really matter? I mean, I'm not a woman who laments over anyone or anything I can't have. I'm too old to wish for the things I really want, so now I just try and make do with what I have. It's enough." Cain reached up and patted him on the shoulder. "Thanks for the great afternoon. I enjoyed it. Come get me when the feed arrives and I'll help you put it away."

Ross didn't push her any further and watched her head toward the bunkhouse. *You're good at avoiding answering direct questions when you want, I'll give you that, but your answer tells me you might just miss my daughter. As for you, Emma, honey, I hope you make the most of this time.* When he saw Carol waiting on the porch for him, he quit smiling. The frown she was sporting made him want to spend the rest of the afternoon with Cain.

"Let's hope my good fortune holds and I live out the afternoon." He spoke to the steering wheel, staying in the truck as long as he could.

CHAPTER TWELVE

W here's Hayden?" Merrick and two of the guys were playing poker when Cain stepped back into the room, and by the size of the pile of money in front of the only female in the game, Merrick was making out like a bandit.

"He left to take another walk with Emma after lunch. Don't worry, Mook went with him."

"He been gone long?"

Merrick distributed the money back to the others, putting away what she had started with. It was risky to actually gamble with the amount of federal surveillance in the room. "They're about fifteen minutes out if you want me to run and get him."

"I want you to run all right, but with me. Just let me get changed."

A short time later, Cain set their pace; the only sound that surrounded them was their running shoes hitting the blacktop highway in front of the farmhouse. They headed in the opposite direction of town, and Cain searched to find where Ross's property ended and the fence was replaced by another of different design. She broke her silence as they crossed the last fence post, allowing her to keep her word to Ross about not doing business on his land.

"Did you hear from Bryce?"

"Not since the airport in New Orleans." Merrick glanced around, hoping no one else was listening to the potentially dangerous conversation.

"Maybe I'll call him tonight and put this business with the Bracato family to bed. Giovanni's been strong-arming our suppliers for a better deal, and with his unfair advantage, he's starting to hurt us."

"Unfair advantage?" Merrick was lost.

"His guardian angel, sweetheart, try and keep up." Cain winked at Merrick as she took a right at the next intersection, following the new fence line. "When we get back to the bunkhouse, I'm going to call and tell Bryce to go ahead with the shipment and see what happens. I'm hoping tripling the amount will keep our guys from jumping ship."

Merrick just kept quiet, her mind working to try to decipher the conversation. By the way her body felt, they had gone at least four miles, and she wondered where Cain was finding the energy for two runs so close together.

When they passed a break in the fence, Cain glanced to her right where, unlike the Verde place, the house sat much closer to the road. Suddenly Cain slowed down, but her very visible breaths sped up. The color drained from her face, and she just stopped in the road, as if she had been coldcocked by an invisible fist.

"Are you okay?" Merrick moved closer and put a hand on Cain's chest.

"I'm fine, let's head back."

Merrick prided herself on the kind of shape she was in, but by the time they headed down the long dirt road in front of Ross's farm, she was about to drop from the stitch in her side. Cain was moving as if she were running away from something, something that had scared her.

Emma stopped in the middle of what she was telling Hayden to watch her ex-lover run until she fell against the side of the barn and promptly threw up. The move was so uncharacteristic that both Emma and Hayden ran toward Cain to see what was wrong.

"Mom? Mom, what's going on?" Hayden sounded upset, never having seen his mother this out of control.

"Just give me a minute." Cain leaned heavily on the side of the barn and looked down at her feet, trying to process the information running crazily through her head. The sight of Emma's face made her hands twitch and clench. Never before had she wanted to wrap her hands around someone's throat until they were dead.

"Honey, is there something I can do?" Emma forgot the years and circumstances that separated them, and put her hands on Cain's back in an effort to comfort her. She instantly felt the muscles tense and watched Cain's long fingers grow white from gripping the wood.

"I just need a minute." Slowly Cain shoved her emotions back into the recesses of her heart and took a deep breath. "Too much exercise for one day." With that short explanation, she smiled at Hayden, then left to clean up.

"Are you sure I can't do something for you?" repeated Emma. "Something I can get you?"

The questions and the concern in Emma's voice stopped Cain at the corner of the barn, which she leaned against again as if she were exhausted. "I think there's nothing you can do now, Emma. Nothing at all."

Not understanding what was going on, Hayden turned his fury on his birth mother. Cain had been fine when he had last seen her. "What did you do to her?" Hayden looked at Emma and frowned. No one had ever made Cain look that defeated, and the fact that she didn't move away from Emma's touch meant whatever was wrong was serious.

Hayden had been only seven when Emma left, but he was old enough to see how her absence had affected Cain. He spent a lot of time with her and knew how important he was to her, but it wasn't enough. Something had changed in her when Emma walked out, and it took Hayden time to realize that she was obviously lonely, and that he could do nothing to fill the gap his mother had left.

"Hayden, I was with you all afternoon. I'm sure Cain will be fine once she showers and lies down for a little while." Emma just stood there when Hayden left her to follow Cain, glancing back at her with suspicion.

She turned to Merrick and knew the woman wouldn't give her any information, but thought she'd take the chance and ask anyway. "What happened?" Emma had to admit Merrick seemed as confused as she did.

"She just overdid it. Nothing to worry about."

Emma fought a feeling of sheer panic that insisted something was terribly wrong. She knew the mobster would've rather been shot than show that kind of vulnerability in public. "I'll give her and Hayden a few minutes. Then I'll come over and help you with dinner."

"Look, Emma, how about you just skip tonight." Merrick saw the protest forming on Emma's lips, so she overstepped her position and tried to defuse it. "How about I try and talk Hayden into going up to the house to join you and your parents for dinner? That way I can take care of Cain." Merrick looked at the woman and tried one more thing to get her to agree. "If she's sick we'll have to leave early, and I know you don't want that to happen. I'm sure things will be better in the morning. Just let me take care of her."

I'm sure you'll take every opportunity to take care of Cain. The thought made a flash of jealous anger bolt through Emma's heart, but it quickly died away when her head reminded her that *she* had left, not the other way around. No, Cain had given her every chance to change her mind, only turning away when Emma refused to believe her and insisted on leaving. Whomever Cain chose to spend her time with, in or out of bed, wasn't Emma's concern anymore.

Four Years Earlier in the Casey Home, New Orleans

Cain dismissed the guards outside the door, wanting to spend a quiet afternoon with Emma. The memory of what Danny Baxter had tried to do to Emma had kept them up for a good portion of the previous nights. Cain was exhausted from holding her while she tried to comfort and soothe her, and Emma was worn out from bouts of crying.

Something had changed that morning, though, when Emma sent Cain off to work with a promise she would call if she needed anything. She had said that she was trying to put Danny out of her mind.

Danny was Cain's cousin from the Baxter side of family, who had talked her father into a job a year before Dalton was killed. Unfortunately, the young, short redhead was a little too aggressive for either Dalton or Cain to trust him with too much responsibility or information about their operations and business associates.

At first, Danny accepted his low-man-on-the-totem-pole position, since his family relations wouldn't get him a more important role in the business. But with each passing year he resented his status more, and he centered his hate on Cain.

He blamed her for locking him out of the main family business and was quick to complain to anyone willing to listen. The attempted rape was his way of trying to show those closest to Cain how weak she'd become, and he had gambled on her falling apart after she saw Emma broken and bloody.

He wasn't planning to take over the family. Even he wasn't so stupid as to think he could. He just wanted someone else at the helm who would give him a chance—the chance to prove he was man enough to expand their operation and up their profits, at the expense of the store owners who dealt with Cain. To him they were all pathetic sheep whom he could bend to the will of his gun.

"So close" became his mantra when Cain spared his life after he attacked Emma. With the woman's underwear feeling silky under his fingertips, he had come so close before the dark side of his cousin's nature turned its fury on him. It had taken months for the bones in his once-handsome face to mend, and weeks for the bruises on Cain's knuckles to fade, but she had let him live. His only punishment was banishment from her family and her business.

The reprieve that allowed him to keep breathing came from the most surprising of places. He owed his life to the woman he had tried to humiliate. The fact gave him no cause to be grateful. Instead, it reinforced his resentment of Cain and the fact that she had been given everything in life. Her decision to give in to Emma's request only strengthened Danny's resolve to crush his cousin through those she loved.

"Baby, where are you?" Cain called from the foyer as she flipped through the stack of mail on the small table by the door. When Emma didn't answer, Cain turned around and noticed the pile of luggage in the den.

The number of bags foretold a long absence, and Cain dropped all the envelopes when she spotted Emma sitting on one of the sofas in the room, wiping away tears with a tissue.

"Going somewhere?"

Emma flinched at the question.

Cain knew she hadn't spoken roughly and wondered if Emma was afraid she'd be angry with her answer.

"I'm going home."

She turned to the bags again before she concentrated on Emma. She unbuttoned her jacket and took it off before sitting down across from Emma, realizing she was going to be in for a long talk. "I thought this was home."

"I'm going home to my parents, Cain." Emma stopped and put her hands up to her face to wipe away the tears. "I'm not coming back, and

I'm begging you to not try and talk me out of it."

"I know you're scared, sweetling, but you can't just give up and walk away. Danny's never going to hurt you again, and I swear on my life, I'll keep you and Hayden safe."

"That's not enough anymore, Cain. I don't want to raise a child in all this turmoil. Can't you understand that?" Emma looked at her lap.

"Emma, you know I love you, right?"

"I know you do, honey. This isn't about me questioning your feelings or your commitment to me. It's this life I can't take anymore. I love you so much, but the violence and the people you surround yourself with are killing me. I can't stay."

Cain sat back in her chair and stared up at the ceiling for a minute, not saying anything. The woman she had trusted with her true self had blindsided her, and she was having a hard time figuring out where this irrational need to flee was coming from.

Once she'd become the head of the family, Cain didn't fear much because she controlled her life and how she lived it. What scared her was what she had to take on faith, and Emma and how she felt about her was a huge part of that fear. Emma's demeanor gave her the feeling that her blind faith was about to be tested.

"What brought this on? I know you're still upset, but I won't let anyone like Danny get close to you again. You have to trust me to take care of both you and Hayden."

Emma gazed out the window and watched Hayden trying to run around the much bigger man as he tucked the football under his arm like Cain had taught him. He had wanted to play and promised her he wouldn't get dirty, so she let him go outside. She was glad that in the safe sanctuary Cain created, his companion Mook could drop his guard and just enjoy a friendly game of tag football with the seven-year-old he had come to love. Emma thought of how oblivious her son was to this conversation and how it would change his life.

She took a deep breath and faced Cain. "You can't be everywhere, my love, and I can't take any chances by just praying you'll keep us safe. I know this is hard, and it seems like I'm not giving you a chance, but try and understand what I'm going through. I'd never dream of keeping Hayden from you. You can see him whenever you want. Though for the first couple of months it might be better if you came to us. Just until he adjusts."

Cain let out a loud laugh, thinking Emma was joking. She looked outside and saw how Hayden was dressed, and then scrutinized the bags. When she saw his sitting next to Emma's, she realized she wasn't kidding. "You want out, then get out. But don't be crazy enough to think you're taking Hayden. That'll never happen."

"Cain, he's my son." Emma put up her hands and scooted to the edge of her seat, ready to drop to her knees and beg if she had to.

"You made a commitment to me, Emma, one I'm willing to release you from, but Hayden stays here with me. Or have you forgotten who you're dealing with?"

Emma closed her eyes and saw again the blood all over Cain's hands. "No, I could never forget that."

She could only watch as Cain picked up the phone and called for the car. The driver loaded her bags and left Hayden's for the nanny to put back in his rooms.

"Is this your final decision? It's not too late for the staff to take your bags up with Hayden's."

Emma stood up and moved closer to Cain, stopping when one of her hands went up.

"I asked you a question."

"I can't stay."

Without another word, Cain headed for her study. The door closed, with a slam of finality.

When Emma moved to the patio doors leading out to the yard, one of Cain's guards stepped into her path and shook his head. She would have no tearful good-byes with her son. She turned next to the closed door of the study and let out a sob for what she was losing.

Because of the solid oak door to Cain's sanctuary, Emma would never see the luxury Cain afforded herself, crying out all of her pain alone. Nor would she see the extent of the hurt she left behind when the front door clicked closed, locking her out of Cain's and her son's lives for over four years. All by her own choosing.

When Emma left, she had never feared reprisal from Cain, but losing four years with her young son had been a steep price to pay. Now she found herself questioning whether she should have left at all. Cain had been very generous with her so far. But if she hadn't drawn the line when Cain killed Danny for something he had almost done, where would she have drawn it? The price of staying in the mobster's bed was just too high, and she had so much more to think about than just herself.

What had hurt the most, though, was the ease with which Cain had looked her in the eye and claimed she had let him live. That night and the words, "Just get rid of him," were etched in her memory. They represented much more than a lie between lovers; they were the essence of the person she cared for.

Cain's calm delivery of her order was the factor that had made Emma face the truth. Her partner was obviously familiar with that level of violence, and her impassiveness showed her comfort with it. Emma could only guess Cain had learned such callousness at Dalton's knee, since their relationship was so close.

She had never had the opportunity to meet Dalton Casey, but Cain idolized her father in much the same way Hayden worshipped Cain. Because every generation seemed to embrace it as a rite of passage, the family would never break its cycle of malicious tradition.

Emma's true nature gave her the strength to walk away, even though she still loved Cain. She wasn't a zealot like her mother, but some of Carol's lessons had taken root. She believed in the difference between right and wrong, but Cain believed the world revolved around her rules and if someone crossed her, she could eliminate him.

Danny Baxter had broken the ultimate rule and dared to put his hands on Cain's woman. At least, that was how Emma had felt when she was rescued, then shuttled upstairs like a child. Her opinion hadn't mattered because, while she'd been wronged, the insult to Cain superceded her feelings.

She couldn't stay with someone who treated her like a possession to be owned and killed over. She only hoped she wasn't too late for Hayden.

CHAPTER THIRTEEN

W hat the hell just happened to Casey?" Kyle had witnessed the whole scene through his high-powered binoculars from the trees near the road. In all the years he had watched Cain, he had never seen her so undone.

The two agents behind him were new to his team, so they had been stuck with the job of keeping pace with Cain and Merrick for their afternoon run. Hopefully the equipment they were carrying picked up more than just their own heavy breathing.

"We may have a problem, sir." The first agent to arrive was leaning over with his hands resting on his knees, trying to catch his breath.

"That's not a career-making statement, Simmons." Kyle dropped the binoculars into the bag at his feet with a dull thud. "I'm not going to ask you again. What happened?" he screamed.

"She ran by the Rath place, sir."

"And?" Kyle asked, waiting for the rest of the report.

"What Simmons is trying to say, sir," interjected the second agent, who sat on the cold ground nursing a charley horse, "is Maddie Rath had the kid outside. Casey just stopped when she saw them. Then she came back here. We're sorry, sir, but we weren't able to keep up on the way back. We did get a little on tape before she got there."

"Did Maddie see Casey or Merrick?" asked Kyle.

"Not that we noticed. She was still outside when we continued our pursuit."

Kyle pinched the bridge of his nose and took a couple of deep breaths. "Don't say a word about this to anyone else or you'll both be investigating moose droppings in Alaska. Get me?"

"But, sir, shouldn't we inform Ms. Verde?" Simmons was still breathing hard from his run, making his question sound hesitant.

"It's taken me close to four years to get Emma Casey to this level of cooperation, and I'm not going to jeopardize that with something this trivial. That means keep your mouths shut, gentlemen, and head back to the command post. I expect a transcript of what you picked up on the first leg of your run. You two worry about that, and I'll worry about Emma."

Kyle turned his back on the two men and watched Emma just standing in the yard, seemingly lost in thought. Yes, he had spent too many years on this case already, but his career wouldn't advance until he could justify the money and time he had invested in Cain Casey. He was just about ten years from mandatory retirement, and he wanted to spend that time heading up some other task force at FBI headquarters. The feds owed him that honor for his loyalty and diligence. History would gloss over how he brought Casey down, but his superiors would remember that he had. That's what counted.

❖

"Honey, where's Cain?" Ross asked as the feed truck turned up the road. He watched it approach, thinking that the unloading would be a good excuse to spend more time with Cain.

"She's cleaning up, Dad. She and Merrick went for a run and Cain got sick. Do you need anything?"

"No, she just promised to help me with something."

Emma barely heard the last part because her father was already moving toward the bunkhouse. He disappeared a moment later when Merrick opened the door for him and showed him inside.

"Just fabulous. I bring Hayden here so I can bond with him, and it's my father and Cain who end up forging a lasting relationship." Alone with her thoughts, Emma ignored the cold and sat on the porch wondering what was going to happen next. Two young deliverymen were the only ones who broke the silence as they flung bags of feed off the back of the truck into a pile by the front of the barn.

"Agent Kyle called while you were out." Carol spoke through a crack she had made in the front door. The windy, cold temperatures of a Wisconsin winter were becoming increasingly unbearable as she grew older.

"And what'd he have to say?"

"Our bird started singing this afternoon, so he wants you to try and keep her around for a few more days. I'm glad to see your father finally coming to his senses." Carol opened the door a little more and pointed toward the delivery boys. The only way Roy was letting that much feed go was if Ross had taken Kyle up on his offer of assistance. "Have you decided what you're going to do with the boy once this is over?"

"What do you mean, do with him?"

"Agent Kyle mentioned a good school in Virginia for him. Not that we can afford it, but I'm guessing they'll let the boy keep some of her ill-gotten money."

Emma watched her knuckles turn almost purple from gripping the armrests of the rocker. "I didn't do all of this to send him away, Mother, and his name is Hayden. It's not 'boy,' just like *her* name is Cain. What is it about my life you find so disgusting? Is it the fact that Cain's a woman or that my son thinks our family is a joke? God, can you blame him?"

"Don't get hysterical, Emma. If you want to know, yes, I think what you did with that woman is not only a sin, but also disgusting. Your boy's an abomination as far as I'm concerned, and if you want to make your home here, it's going to be without him. I didn't raise you to go off and whore yourself, sniffing around someone like her. I won't have it, and I won't be parading your little family at Sunday services when this is done. To tell you the truth, it took a lot of prayer to not send you away when you came back like you did, but I'm a Christian. The only reason I agreed to all this is because it'll mean it's over and I don't have to worry about you running off again to take up with that spawn."

The venom in Carol's voice was hard to miss, and Emma didn't understand where it was coming from. Her mother had never taken the time to know Cain, so her hatred was hard to comprehend. "What Cain and I shared was beautiful, and it gave me the opportunity to learn how to love. The only reason I even recognized the emotion at all was because of Daddy. You and your 'Christian' values were always too busy condemning the rest of us to teach me anything about the concept. I never did ask, Mother, but why did you ever marry Daddy and have me? Being here with the two of us has obviously brought you nothing but misery."

"Because it was either your father or Mark Liston, and even back then he was nothing but a drunk. If that's not a good enough answer, then make one up you like better. Women back then didn't run off and come back with bastards in tow. But you sure made the most of your choices."

A freshly showered, angry Cain stood ten feet from the porch looking like she was about to pounce on Carol. "You call my son a bastard again, old lady, and I'll teach you the meaning of the phrase 'raising the old Irish.' The fact that you hate me doesn't bother me, but Hayden's never done anything to earn your displeasure, so while I'm here, don't speak to him or his mother like that again."

The door slammed shut as hard as Carol could muster, considering how little it was opened, leaving Emma alone with a now-angry Cain. "Are you feeling better?"

"Yeah, it was just a fluke, I'm sure. Nothing to worry about, and since I offered your father my help putting all that feed away, I guess I don't have a choice but to feel better." Cain pointed to the large pile of bags.

"He likes you, I can tell. My father, I mean."

"It's nice to know someone in the Verde family does."

"That's not fair, Cain." Emma stepped closer so Cain could hear her over the truck.

"I'm an expert on knowing life isn't fair and on how people feel about me. You didn't just leave Hayden, Emma. You left me with some shallow reason as to why, and you never looked back."

"Hayden said the same thing to me, and like you, he isn't going to forgive me either, is he?"

"Why would you care if I forgive you? Worry about your relationship with your son and if you're going to have one at all. You killed whatever feelings I had for you with the closing of our front door just as effectively as if you'd used one of the guns you always hated being around. Forgive you? I don't mention your name or even think about you except for the benefit of my son."

"Cain, are you ready?" Ross called out across the yard.

"Cain, please, I want to finish," said Emma.

"We're not done. Don't worry. Just not now and not here."

❖

Cain and Hayden helped stack bags of feed until Ross's storeroom was filled. The sun was starting to set by the time they were done, and despite the cold, they had all worked up a thin coat of sweat before they brought in the last bag. Ross shook hands with Cain before walking back to the house to get cleaned up for dinner.

"Mom, are you sure you're all right from this afternoon?" Hayden leaned on one of the stall dividers and studied his mother's face closely for any residual illness.

"There's nothing wrong, kiddo. To tell you the truth, it was a temporary thing, kinda like getting kicked in the gut. You know what I mean?"

Hayden sat on a bale of hay across from Cain and stayed silent. He had spent the afternoon listening to Emma talk about growing up on the farm and what a shock it had been to leave Wisconsin. The biggest surprise was that she had ended up with Cain after growing up in such a sheltered place. From her stories, he didn't think she had it her to take such bold chances and go so against her upbringing.

When Emma spoke of going into the Erin Go Braugh and asking for a job, Hayden realized perhaps Cain wasn't the only chance taker in the family. As they strolled through Ross's pastures he found himself enjoying her stories, hearing about a side of Cain he knew nothing about. Emma spoke of her in a tone that had more than a trace of affection, which confused him. If Emma still loved Cain, why wasn't she with them?

"Let's go grab a shower and something to eat, then get you to bed, big guy," said Hayden. "You aren't as young as you used to be, so we have to watch out for you."

Cain laughed and threw a wad of hay at him. "Wiseass, huh?"

"I'm your wiseass, though, and I'd like to think I learned all my wise ways from you. Even when I'm being an ass."

With her chin on one of her fists, Cain looked at her son and sighed. So many things her father had said and taught her came back to mind when she had time to study her own child like this. "I wish you had gotten to meet my father, Hayden. He would've loved you, and my mother would have spoiled you until even I wouldn't have known what to do with you.

"They had three children and they loved us, but I always suspected we were just the down payment on what they really wanted—

grandchildren. Whenever I started seeing someone new, my mother used to remind me. 'I want grandkids someday, lass,' she'd say in that thick brogue. My dad would just laugh, but he told me one day he had practiced swing pushing until he wasn't going to get any better without a live subject."

Hayden moved and sat next to Cain. "As much as I'd have liked to meet them, I'd like to think I did get to know them through all the stories you've told me. You know what I figured out?"

"What's that?"

"I listen to you talk about Grandpa Dalton, and it's like hearing a story about you. I look at all those pictures, and I imagine what I'm going to look like when I'm older. And Merrick told me you two had the same hands." He put his smaller hand next to hers and smiled because the structure and shape were the same, no matter the size difference. "I want to grow up and have people look at me and say, 'that's Cain's kid and he's just like her.'"

Hayden could count on one hand all the times he'd seen his mother cry, but he knew his words had reached deep and when her eyes filled with tears.

"You *are* my kid, and I love you, but you're wrong. People are going to look at you and say we're alike, but you're better than I ever thought of being."

"Thanks, Mom. You ready?" He hugged her and enjoyed the slight citrus smell that always clung to her.

"Hayden, I want you to do me a favor."

"What?" The way she had asked made him think he wasn't going to like her request.

"I want you to go up to the house and have dinner with your mother."

"No. I spent all afternoon with her, and now I want to eat with you and the guys." He moved a little away from her and crossed his arms over his chest as a way to say his decision was final.

"Son, it's the last thing I'm going to ask of you while we're here. After tonight, if you want to spend the next couple of days in the bunkhouse and not see anyone, then I'll have to respect your decision."

Not needing any other prodding from Cain, Hayden got up to go get ready for dinner.

He never saw Emma crying behind the first stall in the barn, deeply ashamed she had eavesdropped on their conversation. Listening to the mother and son had proved to her that Hayden had been raised by the same loving person who had stolen her heart so many years before.

For all of Cain's faults, her one best quality hadn't changed. Even after Emma left, Cain was filled with love and devotion for her family. If Kyle succeeded now, Emma would never gain Hayden's love or his respect, and he would gladly be sent away anywhere, as long as it meant not having to lay eyes on her again. She was sure now that he would want nothing else to do with her once he found out the extent of her involvement.

The Verde dinner table was again silent as the four people sat eating their meal. In the bunkhouse Cain started an indoor football game that ended up with the ball hitting the overhead light fixture, tilting the camera it hid. The agents in the back room of the barn could only stare in horror at the monitor, now showing the ceiling tiles, and wonder how they were going to get back in again to reset the angle.

"You guys watch it. With my luck I'll have Carol down here suing me for damages."

They heard Cain's reprimand effectively stop the game.

"Why don't you head into town and eat at the little diner Ross and I tried today, and let me lie down and wait for Hayden. I'm still not feeling well from my bout of barfing today."

The agents cursed. If Cain wasn't leaving too, they would be listening to nothing until the others got back, unless Cain was going to be talking in her sleep.

"Don't forget to try the apple pie with homemade ice cream. It's to die for. As a matter of fact, bring me back a piece, minus the cold stuff. It might make me feel better."

Special Agent Rich, the senior agent working for Kyle, sat back in his chair eating an apple and pretending it was the pie Cain had talked about while he listened in case Casey decided to call someone after her henchmen left for dinner. The quiet filling the tape made him want to imitate the napping woman he was monitoring. Had he been paying attention, he would have seen the figure dressed in black crawl toward the nearest fence and head out to the dark pasture.

CHAPTER FOURTEEN

Cain slipped the night-vision glasses into place as soon as she cleared the fence and started out at a moderate pace. Since no one expected her arrival, she could take her time. Merrick had walked Hayden and Mook to the house for their dinner with the Verdes; they had instructions to stay there and not step into the bunkhouse until the rest of them got back from town. Cain was outside her destination less than an hour later and just sat watching for dogs or other security measures.

The woman she had seen earlier stood at the kitchen window. From her movements, Cain guessed she was rinsing dishes and loading them into the dishwasher. She crept closer and, almost in the woman's plain sight, she attached something to the window before she moved back. Sitting against the fence, she put the headphones on and turned up the volume.

"Jerry, will you pick up those toys all over the den? It's been too cold to take Hannah outside, and we really made a mess."

In addition to the woman, Cain could hear a child singing along with a video.

"Are you ready for your bath, Miss Hannah?"

"Yes, Aunt Maddie."

"You're such a good girl."

Through the binoculars, Cain watched Maddie carry the little girl upstairs to the bathroom, then to the bedroom to get her ready for bed. She devoured the sight of the child with shiny black hair and a very familiar face. Hannah's resemblance to Hayden made Cain ache. And it made her furious. Here, full of energy, was why Emma left. Only Cain viewed the little girl as what Emma had stolen from her.

"Aunt Maddie, where's Mama?" Hannah put her arms up for her nightgown.

"She'll be back for you in a couple of days. Do you miss your mama?"

"She said she's gonna bring me a prize."

Hannah held a teddy bear up to the side of her face and smiled, making Cain fall in love on the spot.

"I love prizes."

"A surprise, huh? Well, I'm sure it's going to be great. Get in here, baby." Maddie pulled back the blankets on the bed and tucked the little girl in. "You go to sleep, and I'm sure your mama's going to come and see you real soon."

"You promise, Aunt Maddie?"

"I promise, baby girl. Your mama's got something to do, and as soon as she's done she'll be coming by to pick you up. Until then you, me, and your uncle Jerry are going to have the best time playing and watching videos."

"Mama said she was going to see my brother Haygen, but I hadda wait to see him. He lives with my mama Cain far away. Why do you think she doesn't want me to live with her too like Haygen does?"

"You're going to have to ask your mama that one, sweetie. I never met Cain, but I'm guessing she loves you a whole world full, and one day maybe she'll get to show you. Does your mama tell you a lot about Hayden and Mama Cain?"

"Yes. She told me 'cause they're my family, and Mama said dat's important."

"It is, but getting some sleep is important too, so close your eyes and get ready to meet the sandman."

Cain listened with big tears running down her face when the little charmer said her prayers after the woman left. "God bless my mama, Grandpa Ross, my big brother Haygen, and my mama Cain. Amen."

Maddie stared out into the night from the kitchen window as she finished the dishes, obviously not seeing anything out of the ordinary. "Emma, I hope to hell you know what you're doing." The good friend was one of the only people in town who knew the whole story, and was the one who had helped Emma through the pregnancy and birth.

Cain gave her no answer as she ran back into the night. She had one more thing to do before retreating to her bed. After carefully climbing up to the roof of the barn, she attached some listening devices so she could monitor the hunters who were stalking her. She knew if anyone caught her up there, she would blow any chance to pull off her plan for Kyle, but she hadn't built her life on playing it safe. She crouched as she watched Merrick and the guys pull in from dinner, timed her jump from the roof with the closing of car doors, then slipped back in through the window she had left from.

Cain was lying down with her eyes closed, her breath slow and deep, when she heard the group walk in with Hayden. She listened to them get ready for bed, trying not to make too much noise. Then, when the last of the lights clicked off, she sat up and swung her legs off the small twin bed. Her every instinct told her to go up to the house and drag Emma to the next farm and force her to confess to Hannah's existence.

In bare feet and no coat, she stalked outside and reached the halfway point between the two structures before she stopped herself from taking another step. She was so angry she closed her eyes and took a few deep breaths to still her emotions. Her fury prevented her from feeling the cold or seeing the woman staring down at her.

From her window, the woman who was the center of Cain's storm felt a finger of fear drag slowly up her spine. Emma felt completely different than the first time she had looked out and spotted Cain outside her bedroom window.

Thirteen Years Earlier at Emma's Apartment

Emma leaned against her apartment door, listening to the receding footsteps on the other side. It had been an electric year, enjoying life on Cain's arm. She was about as far from her father's dairy farm as she could imagine herself. She had kept her job at the pub and her modest apartment because she didn't want to ever be thought of as a kept woman.

When she could no longer hear anything out in the hall, Emma moved to the window to watch Cain leave. Instead of getting into her car, she stood near the bottom of the window looking up, apparently knowing she wouldn't have to wait too long to see Emma again. The well-known Casey smile was in place when she appeared in the window. Tonight that smile undid her. Tonight, she realized, Cain was going to claim something that belonged to her from the moment Emma had laid eyes on her.

"Do you have to be anywhere else right this minute?" she asked, leaning out the window.

"I'll be wherever you want me to be."

As an answer, she dropped her shirt on Cain's head and moved away from the window. She laughed when she heard the footsteps out in the hall again, only this time she heard more of a run.

Cain opened the door and found Emma standing there holding an arm over her chest, looking like she wasn't so sure what to do next. In all their time together she had never teased Cain too much as she got more comfortable with taking their relationship to the next level. Some heavy-duty kissing and groping on her couch with Cain was about the extent of Emma's experience, and Cain didn't want to make a wrong move.

"I want you to stay."

"Come here a minute, baby." She opened her arms and waited for Emma to move. When her arms wrapped around naked skin she felt Emma relax. "Do you mind if we talk for a minute?"

"No." Emma sounded so nervous that Cain's libido cooled.

"Let's sit down." Wanting Emma to see how serious she was, she put her fingers under Emma's chin so she could see her eyes. "You're the woman I'm going to spend my life with, that's how I feel about you. If you want the same thing, no one will ever share my bed or my life until it's over."

"Thank you for saying that, honey."

"There's a reason, and it isn't what you think. Because I want to spend all my life with you, sweetling, I can be patient. When we make love, it's going to be the right decision for both of us."

"Don't you want to?"

She smiled and placed her palm on Emma's cheek. "More than anything, but I'm willing to wait. I love you, Emma, and because I do, it means I'll wait as long as it takes."

Emma closed her eyes and leaned farther into Cain's caress. "You do?"

"More than anyone or anything else."

"Could you say it again?" Emma asked as she looked into the eyes she adored.

"I love you, Emma, so very much."

"I love you too, and I want you to show me." Emma leaned back a little and moved to straddle Cain's lap. Then she picked up a big hand and placed it over one of her breasts.

The move lit a flame in Cain that truly never went out. She got out of the chair and felt Emma's legs tighten around her waist as they moved to the bedroom. To get Emma to feel even more at ease, she had her unbutton her own linen shirt and push it off her shoulders. They both moaned when skin met skin for the first time.

"Tell me if I do something that makes you uncomfortable, okay?" Cain's words were some of the last they spoke.

Emma lifted her hips and helped remove her skirt. She was hungry for Cain to put her hands on her body and sate the need growing between her legs. They had touched her before to help her out of chairs, or to hold one of hers when they sat in a dark theater, and sometimes through her clothes when they shared some quiet time in her apartment, but tonight Cain's hands felt hot.

Cain moved her hands constantly, never keeping them in any one place too long, which was driving Emma insane. As much as she wanted the hand to drift lower, any other need melted away when Cain lowered her head and sucked on her right nipple until it grew hard.

"Please don't stop." She clamped her hands around Cain's head and held her in place. Touching herself had never brought this kind of intensity.

"Relax for me, honey."

"Cain, relaxed is the last thing I'm feeling right now." She really wanted to whack the side of Cain's head when she heard the low chuckle, but doing so might pull the lips away from her body, and that just wouldn't do. "Could you take your clothes off for me, honey? I want to feel you when you're loving me."

Hovering a little over her, Cain pulled her mouth away, which made her open her eyes.

"I love you." After Cain made the declaration, which she had never made to anyone outside her family, she unbuckled her belt and shed the rest of her clothes. When Cain lay back down, Emma moaned as a trailing hand moved down to her most intimate place.

Cain took her time running her fingers through the silky wet heat, encouraging Emma to move with her to increase her pleasure. Just as slowly and gently, she moved her finger to the opening and her thumb to the hard clitoris, to help ease any discomfort Emma felt at first.

"Look at me, sweetling. This is the first night we give ourselves to each other, but the commitment that goes with this honor is one I'm going to take a lifetime living up to."

Emma gazed up at her and pulled Cain's head down so she could kiss her. This was how she'd always dreamed this night would go. Cain didn't disappoint, talking to her as she loved her. The talk of commitment and love made her glad she had waited. Giving herself to Cain was the best gift she could bestow. "Please, honey, make me yours."

Emma tightened her hands on Cain's shoulders as Cain broke through the barrier of her innocence, and again as the most unbelievable sensation of pleasure washed through her. Before the night was over she was hoarse from screaming Cain's name into the darkened apartment, and when they went to sleep, she felt very well loved.

Emma remembered how Cain had held her and whispered how much she loved her when the intensity of the moment had driven her to tears. One of the most beautiful nights of her life had started with Cain standing under her window.

The woman standing in the yard now had nothing to do with romance or gentleness. Emma had only one thought in her head, and the possibility of it being true made her feel like someone had poured a bucket of cold water over her soul.

She knows.

CHAPTER FIFTEEN

Emma stood as frozen as Cain was down in the yard, unsure of whether to go out and try to talk to her. Her breathing started to slow when Cain seemed to realize where she was and went back inside. She noticed something different about Cain's behavior, and she had two days to figure out what it was.

Cain, soon on the phone in the bunkhouse with her bar manager, ignored all the eyes looking at her as if she had lost her mind and forgotten they weren't the only ones listening. "Bryce, get in touch with our friend right now. Tell him I'll make it worth his while to meet me before I go home." She looked at the tag on the phone and gave Bryce the number he would need later.

"Cain?" Merrick put her hand on Cain's back, surprised at how cold it felt.

"Go back to bed, guys. I've got things to do." It was a clear dismissal and they all tried to comply, giving Cain some space. "Hayden."

He opened his eyes and sat up with no further prompting.

"Stay in sight of the guys and Merrick. I'll be back by morning."

"Do you want some company?" Hayden wished for the day Cain would say yes to the question, but her shaking head meant it wouldn't be today.

"I won't be long. Remember, nowhere tonight alone."

"I promise, Mom."

Cain pulled him close and hugged him longer than normal. She had planned this scenario before she left New Orleans, thinking she would drag it out a little just for the entertainment value, but now her anger was fueling the timetable. She didn't worry that it would make her sloppy. Kyle would never get that lucky. She wanted to flush the rats out of their holes and discover which of her enemies were helping Kyle set his trap.

"Should I go start the car?" Merrick tried again, hoping Cain would at least take her.

"I'll be fine, and I need you here looking out for Hayden." Cain finished pulling on her boots and reached for her coat. She kissed Merrick's forehead once she was dressed and walked out.

When the door slammed shut, Merrick put her finger to her lips so no one would say anything. The federal agents who had enhanced the room didn't need to know none of them knew what Cain was up to.

Outside, Cain pulled a satellite phone from a bag in the car and punched in a number. "You in?"

"When and where?" the male voice asked.

"Four hours, and you know where."

When Cain slammed the vehicle door like she had the door to the bunkhouse and started the engine, Emma ran back to the window at the sound.

In the back room of the barn's loft, Kyle pumped his fist and whispered, "Yes."

Cain's Suburban was on the road for less than two minutes before it had company. In no real hurry, she drove the speed limit and relaxed back into the leather seat. If Bryce did his job, losing the Ford behind her wasn't going to be a problem. A faint chirp from beside her drew her attention from the road for a second as she glanced to see who was calling.

"Mission accomplished, boss. I'm guessing your package will arrive in about three and a half hours, depending on the weather and tailwinds."

"Thanks, Bryce. I'll call back if I need you." Cain drove past the city limit sign and put her traffic signal on to pull into Ray's feed store lot, where one of the delivery boys who had brought Ross's order sat on the steps waiting for her.

Cain waved to him and pulled an envelope out of the glove compartment before hopping out. "Make sure Roy gets this, and here's something for your trouble." Cain handed him the envelope and a twenty-dollar bill.

"No problem. Do you think this will make much of a mess?" The young man looked like he dreaded the amount of sweeping in his future.

"If you let me out back it shouldn't be too bad." Cain followed him through the store to a large fenced area. A large quantity of farm equipment and parts was neatly stacked throughout the yard, but back by the delivery trucks was all the room she needed for her ride. She handed the kid another twenty to appease him about the dust and studied the north for what Bryce had ordered.

Special Agents Joe Simmons and Anthony Curtis both started cursing when they saw the approaching helicopter. Kyle hadn't planned for this type of contingency.

Curtis reached for the phone and pressed speed dial to the boss.

"Gentlemen, this better be good." Kyle's voice filled the inside of the car, and from the sound of it, he wasn't too appreciative of the wake-up call.

They knew their boss well enough to realize that after Cain had left, he had gone to bed to rest up for any media appearances he would be making in the morning, if the night panned out like he planned.

"Is Casey in town having a cup of coffee and you got bored, maybe?"

"The café closes at nine o'clock, sir, and Ms. Casey isn't looking for a midnight snack. She's catching a flight somewhere."

"She headed for the airport, and you just now felt we needed an update of her whereabouts?"

Joe was busy looking for a volume control, and Anthony rolled his eyes and secretly cheered Cain on. It surprised neither of the young officers that Cain had proved too much for Kyle over the years.

"Sir, we're half a block from the feed store, watching her get on a helicopter. We thought you should make the call to track where she's going, if it can be done." When Anthony finished, a dial tone replaced the bellowing from the other end.

❖

The pilot headed south, trying to keep his eyes on his instrument panel and not his quiet passenger. Their destination was a small airstrip right on the other side of the Illinois state line, which was all the information the man who had hired him said he needed.

When they landed, Cain sat with her eyes closed, obviously trying to ignore the cold weather that the cockpit didn't protect them from, and didn't open them until the whine of the arriving Lear engines came to a stop about forty feet from where the helicopter sat idle.

"I won't be long," Cain told the pilot before she stepped out and headed to the stairs that had been lowered when the Learjet's door opened.

He was mildly disappointed he wouldn't get to see who Cain was meeting.

Cain made the trip back to the chopper and scowled at the pilot. "I'll be highly upset if you decide to use any of the radio equipment or a phone before I get back."

The pilot nodded and held his shivering to a minimum until she left. His tremors had little to do with the dropping temperatures and everything to do with the icy blue eyes that had pinned him with their own silent threat.

Cain noticed a number of guards. She couldn't imagine her guest leaving the city without them, but they only waved in her direction and didn't attempt the normal pat-down. She knew their boss would have them beaten had they made a move toward her, except maybe to shake her hand.

Cain spoke to her host as if she were addressing a visiting dignitary.

"Vincent, you old dog, how are you feeling after your recent travails with the law?"

Vincent Carlotti laughed and stood from the plane's sofa to embrace his longtime friend. His thick gray hair set off his dark eyes well, and after he'd turned sixty he'd started to lose a bit of his waistline but was still an attractive man. He had watched Cain grow into the brilliant leader she had become after her father's death, and could only hope his own son would fare as well the day he departed. His only regret had been when he learned of Cain's sexual preference. On the day of her christening, Vincent had spun for himself a vivid daydream of a day the two families would merge at the marriage altar with Cain and his son Vinny.

"Cain, come over here and give me a kiss. I'm old but I'm not dead."

"The day you stop flirting will be the day I start worrying about your imminent demise."

After a friendly embrace the two sat down, and the others in the area moved to the front of the plane to give them some privacy.

"I imagine my trip north means you were right?"

"Vincent, the one lesson my father beat into my head by sheer repetition was to always be prepared. He said he learned it from your father. The reason I asked you up was to offer you Bracato's territory."

Vincent arched a brow and pressed his fingers to his mouth. If Cain was offering, it was almost a done deal, but why not take over herself, he wondered. "That sounds, I don't know, intriguing."

"I only have an hour at most here, Vincent."

"Why not do whatever you're planning and take over his part of the city and be done with it?"

The don stopped talking when one of the plane's crew stepped up and put a tray with coffee and cups on the table between them. He and Cain watched her pour and stir sugar into the espressos, then leave before they exchanged another word.

"I'm not interested in expansion. That was Billy's forte, not mine."

Vincent took a sip of the strong brew, leaned forward, and placed his hand over her knee. "You do realize, though, that whoever controls such a big section of real estate can become powerful enough to squash everyone else?"

Cain covered his hand with her own to acknowledge his concern for her. "Once this is over, everyone else will know who was gracious enough to give you this"—she paused as if trying to find the right word—"gift."

"And I'll owe you what in return?"

"Peace, that's all I'm asking. I've spent years and then some fighting the feds on one front and Bracato on the other. The turf war and the bullshit with Kyle isn't impossible, but it takes time away from my son, and I'm ready to be done with both nuisances."

"Cain, you know I would've helped if you'd just picked up the phone and asked. We aren't blood, but we're family nonetheless." He reached over and patted her hand.

"You've had your own problems, godfather, without having to worry about mine. What do you say?"

Vincent held out his hand to seal the deal. "Tell me what you want me to do."

The two spent another thirty minutes going over plans and the information necessary to pull off what Cain had in mind. Nothing was written down, and no one bothered them as their heads drew closer together. Some of the old guards smiled at how many times Cain made the old man laugh.

Dalton—Cain's father—and Vincent had grown up within two blocks of each other when New Orleans was a different and rougher town. Both their fathers had worked their way through their respective family ranks, and the underlings of both organizations knew it wouldn't take long before each ran his own show. They were smart, loyal, and ruthless when the situation warranted—all the ingredients that would land them at the top and keep them there. In all that time the one thing they could count on was the bond they had forged as boys when they threw rocks at old buildings and rode their bikes along the docks.

The two men served for each other in their weddings and were godparents to more than one of each other's children. Vincent had openly cried as he carried his friend's casket and then again when Cain laid her mother and brother to rest. It was his muscle who kept her business intact and allowed her the time to mourn without any worry that someone would try to usurp her position as the head of her family. He had been at the hospital the day Marie passed on and already had his underlings looking for the man responsible.

What Cain was doing now would give the old man tremendous power in the underworld. Enough so that, as he said, he could crush her if it came to a war. He would pass the gift to Vinny eventually, but Cain worried about neither of them. The friendship her father had shared with this man was the same bond she shared with his son. They had never thrown rocks together, but more than one can had died at the end of their pellet guns over the summers.

"Patrick," Vincent called to one of the guards.

"Yes, sir?"

"Cain, you remember Patrick, don't you?" Vincent pointed up to the wall of a man standing quietly for an order.

"He ate a truckload of food at my house last month, so he's hard to forget," Cain joked and held out her hands. "How's life treating you, Paddy?"

"Hey, Cain, I'm all right. How's my brother handling this shitty weather?"

"Mook's a good kid. A good kid with a big-ass coat, but he's hanging in."

"Yeah, he loves Hayden like the little brother he wished he'd had, so you got no worries. I've always told him the big-brother gig is a good one, if you can get it." Patrick put his game face back on and looked to Vincent. "What can I do for you, Mr. Carlotti?"

"You wanna go out and talk with Cain's pilot before we fire up to leave?"

The man left, knowing already what the talk needed to be about.

Vincent didn't like to intimidate any bystanders, but sometimes it was necessary, especially when the bystander was being watched from one of the plane's windows doing something colossally stupid.

Changing the subject, he asked, "What do you think of my new stewardess, or whatever the hell they call themselves these days?" He pointed to the young woman who had poured their coffee.

"Cute, but definitely not my type." Cain waggled her hand at Vincent.

He laughed again and made a mental promise to have dinner with Cain soon. He loved spending time talking with her. "Why not, too blond?"

"Vincent, you and I know one of my main weaknesses, as it were, is women of the blond persuasion."

"True, so what is it about her?"

"Graduate of Quantico, class of '98, I believe. There are so many of these young feebies running around it's hard to keep them all straight. Her being here, though, gives me a hint as to who's next on Kyle's to-do list, or at least his replacement's once he manages to apprehend me."

"Are you sure I can't marry you off to Vinny?"

"Not my type either."

"I know you wouldn't insult me by asking, but we swept before we boarded and the crew's checked methodically before boarding, so all she can report is where and who I met with. The problem for her is, no one else knows we left the city, and I'm the only one with a phone."

"Mind if I give it a shot before you treat her to a swim?"

Vincent put his coffee cup down and waved a hand in the woman's direction. "Be my guest." He reached into his shirt pocket and handed over a fistful of small chips. Listening devices courtesy of the blonde in the tight skirt, each one missing its battery.

Outside, Patrick stepped to the helicopter and tapped on the pilot's door. "Cold out tonight, huh?"

He watched the man at the controls try to hide the pad he had probably written the plane's name and identification numbers on. "It'll only get worse, believe me. I'm glad for the business tonight since winter's usually my dead season."

Funny you should mention dead, Patrick thought, and laughed softly. "How are Bonnie, Leo, and John?"

The question didn't sound threatening by any stretch of the imagination. It wasn't meant to be, but it grabbed the man's complete attention, and he came forward out of his seat as if in a panic. "Fine, but how do you know my wife and kids?"

"Your job is to fly, mine is to know stuff about you and your family. See, when you get back to the podunk town you're from, most likely there'll be these guys who'll want to know all about your grand adventure tonight. With me so far?"

The pilot resembled a bobbing child's toy, his head was moving so much. "Yes, sir."

"You tell them anything remotely interesting, like our talk right now for example, and I'll come back. Only it won't be just me, and it won't be to talk. After I've done my job you won't feel like such a hero for handing over the information, and you'll have only yourself to blame for what's going to happen to Bonnie and those two cute boys of yours. So now would be a good time to tell me how you spent your time out here all alone, stupid."

The pilot handed over the pad he had used, then pleaded tearfully with Patrick to leave his family alone.

Just once he wanted one of these guys to show some backbone, but the crying always replaced the smug machismo they so obviously felt as they sat outside meetings like this and planned how they would spend the reward money. The fantasies of seeing their overweight wives in a bikini on some beach in Hawaii seemed to override their brains concerning who they would be turning in.

"Take a deep breath, Mr. Jones, and try and calm down. To tell you the truth, I want to leave here tonight and never come back. This cold weather frankly sucks, so just remember what we talked about. That way I can stay home and work on my tan, and you can go back to doing whatever it is you do in the course of a day. Make me put this coat on again to hunt your ass down, and you're going to wish your parents never met."

"Don't worry, sir. I'm not going to say anything." The reassurance came out after a series of hiccups and a couple of swipes at his face.

Patrick pulled a bottle of water from his coat pocket and handed it over. The last thing he needed was for this guy to kill Cain from nerves on the way back. "Just a few more minutes and we'll be on our way. Try and remember the big plane over there has windows."

CHAPTER SIXTEEN

The atmosphere in the plane became a little more tense when Vincent called the young woman who stood near the cockpit over to them. Throughout their conversation she had tried to listen in without being too overtly obvious, but she wasn't concerned. Whatever she missed, the bugs she had planted would fill in the gaps. Being there to witness the meeting between two of the main figures who ran the city's underworld was enough for her, and would play well in court when the time came.

"What's your name again, darlin'?" Vincent asked when the blonde leaned over to await his order.

"Shelby, Mr. Carlotti. Shelby Phillips."

"Cain, meet Shelby. She's filling in for my usual girl until she gets back from having her second baby."

"I'm impressed, Vincent, giving maternity leave. What's next, a dental plan?" Cain joked as she looked at what could be a dead woman standing.

"We're looking into it, smart-ass. Shelby, this is my friend Cain." He pointed to Cain and saw the condescending expression the agent quickly tried to hide. "Cain was wondering if she could have a private conversation with you back in the office."

"If it's just a talk she's interested in, I'd be happy to." Shelby turned to Cain, plastered a fake smile in place, and asked, "Ms...?"

"Derby Cain Casey. That's C-A-S-E-Y. Do you also need my social and date of birth for the record?"

It happened so quickly Shelby didn't notice when she lost control of the situation, but she felt a tiny line of perspiration break out along her forehead. Remembering her training, she took a deep breath and tried to make her smile look more genuine. After all, the instructor who had lectured on undercover techniques had said most of the people they would be trying to bring in didn't have enough brain cells to string a correct sentence together.

"I'm sorry. I didn't want to be presumptuous and call you by your first name."

"Of course not. Do you mind if I call you Shelby, Ms. Phillips?"

"Please do." Cain led the way to the small room Vincent used as an office when he was on the plane and sat in the old man's chair.

"Shelby, have a seat." Cain pointed to one of the other two chairs available. "Can I get you anything?"

She laughed and pointed her index finger at Cain. "That's my line, Ms. Casey. That's my job here, remember?"

"Please, feel free to call me Cain. And I don't really know your purpose for being on this plane, but that's what we're here to find out."

The urge to wipe her brow was becoming overwhelming, but she didn't want to show fear. She felt like there was already blood in the water, and a display of weakness would only agitate the sharks swimming in her tank that much more. "I'm filling in, like Mr. Carlotti said."

"I see. So you graduated in the top 1 percent of your class at Stanford—political science, I believe, was your major—then from Quantico so you could serve drinks on Vincent Carlotti's plane. That's the story you're telling me?"

"I don't know—" She was scrambling.

"Please, Agent Daniels, don't insult me by finishing that sentence. One thing I'm always sure of is what I'm talking about. That was what the last part of your statement was going to be, wasn't it?"

Shelby felt like crawling out of her skin. She needed to get off this plane and now.

"I asked you a question, Agent, and I would appreciate the courtesy of an answer."

"Yes, that's what I was going to say. I think you must have me confused with someone else."

"Don't take this the wrong way, Agent Daniels, but yes, I do know Phillips is a cover name, so we aren't going around about that one too. But you're like a textbook study of clichés. That all you gleaned from

Barry's undercover class at the academy?"

"I'm not the person you think I am."

Cain stood up and started to re-button her coat. "Then we have nothing else to talk about, Agent Daniels."

The relief flooded so quickly through Shelby's body, she was afraid she might slide out of the chair if she weren't careful. Barry Trice had been right about the average bad guy's level of intelligence. "I'm sorry to worry you like that, and please call me Shelby."

"Okay, Shelby, but don't waste your air or your time on apologies. My parting advice would be prayer, or whatever it's going to take to make things in your heart right before you meet your maker." Her coat fully buttoned, Cain started for the door.

"What do you mean?" She laughed nervously.

"It means when Vincent is cruising at thirty thousand feet, you'll be doing some cruising of your own without benefit of a parachute. And I'm seriously doubting he's going to be giving you one of those nifty flotation devices for the dramatic water landing you'll be making."

"Do you know the penalty for killing a federal agent, since you're under the impression that I am one?"

"Capital offenses call for the death penalty, last time I looked up the section of law you're referring to."

Cain laughed at the shocked expression on Shelby's face.

"Never play a game you don't know all the rules to, Shelby, especially the penalty shots that come when you fuck up. The main thing you have to remember, though, is know who all the players are and what they might know about you. The government isn't the only one with good sources of information. Good luck to you."

Shelby was up and pulling on Cain's arm before she took her third step for the door.

"Don't go."

"Like you said, I have you confused with someone else."

"Is that what you're going to tell Mr. Carlotti?" Shelby's desperation was starting to bleed into her voice.

Cain stroked the hand on her arm and smiled. "As a matter of fact, yes, I am."

"Thank you."

"You're wasting time again, Agent. I'm going to tell him that, and since we all know it ain't so, you're going to enjoy the rest of your career as fish food. Vincent won't remember you by the time this thing hits the tarmac in New Orleans, and I'll just chalk it up as a waste."

Cain gave her credit for a viselike grip for such a petite woman. Fear was almost as strong a stimulant as adrenaline. "Because I guarantee you this baby's taking the long way back over the Atlantic." She waved her hand to the plane around her so Shelby would know what she was talking about.

"What are my choices here?"

"Very limited indeed."

Shelby tightened her grip on Cain's arm, trying to fight back the hysteria that was trying to force its way out and make her beg for her life. "I saw you with him tonight. He'll listen to you."

"Like a wise man said, Shelby, the truth will set you free, baby."

"I'm new to the area so I don't know a whole lot of information about the agency, if that's what you're after."

"I'm not after information, Shelby. Believe me, I just want to see you live out the night. You're a beautiful young lady who deserves a second chance."

"What will it cost me?" Her last two years of training and any hopes of an FBI career were quickly disappearing, but it wasn't worth her life to give in to her more noble side now.

"Very little, really, but that depends on how honorable you are. Because we can do it the hard way, or we can act civilly and live to fight another day."

"What's the hard way?"

"You promise me the moon until you feel you're safe. Then you run to whoever your supervisor is and start clearing your conscience about how close you came to making a pact with the devil. It will most probably land you a commendation or two and a big promotion."

"What makes you think I won't do just that?"

Cain started unbuttoning her coat and chose to sit next to Shelby this time. "You have guts, Shelby. That'll get you commendations enough. To answer your question, though, you could do that, which will get us to retaliate in some way, even if it's from a jail cell. Something like dropping by on Mr. Daniels and seeing how he and your mom are enjoying retirement. I mean, what's one more indictment in the realm of all things?"

"You're a monster."

"Maybe so, but like I said, little girl, know the game, its rules, but most importantly, the penalties that come from playing with the big dogs."

"What do you want?"

"Goodwill toward men."

Shelby looked at the serious face and tried not to laugh. Considering her situation, humor should have been the last thing she felt. The woman trying to make her feel better had, after all, just threatened her parents. But when Cain winked, the stress broke something inside her and she started laughing, though it quickly turned to tears.

"Shelby, I don't want to hurt you, and I'd like to leave your old man to build more of his model boats. This isn't why we're here. I want you, as a favor to me, to go home and forget about tonight. If you have to give a location, say it was Biloxi for a card game. Unless you're good and were able to send up smoke signals before you left town, no one with your team even knows you're gone."

"You don't have any respect for authority, do you?"

"Give yourself time, and with time comes skill. When you get to that level and you start to worry me, that I'll respect. As for the people you work with, none whatsoever."

"My career's over, so it doesn't matter, does it? I didn't do all this to become a mole or a puppet right out of the gate."

"Darlin', you need to work on those clichés, and why don't you listen to the rest of what I've got to say before you go hanging up your spurs."

Shelby laughed again and started to protest the blatant use of clichés.

Cain grinned. "I couldn't resist."

"I forget about tonight, and what else?"

"Somewhere down the line you'll get a phone call, and the caller will bring to light a different avenue to investigate. All I'm asking is that you do your job and look into what you'll be told."

"Trying to put some of your competition out of work?"

"It's not what you think, so no info on any less-than-reputable citizens, I promise."

Shelby was skeptical. The job and her scruples were important to her. "That's it?"

"That's it." Cain held out her hand. "Shake and you've got a binding contract and also a promise you'll get home safe to Coots tonight."

"You know my cat's name?" Shelby was thinking the government would do well to fire Barry and hire Cain to teach a few classes.

"It's the turtle's name I haven't been able to get yet."

"I don't have a pet turtle."

Cain snapped her fingers. "That would explain it, then."

"Why couldn't you be a nice accountant I could bring home and introduce to my mother?" She gripped Cain's arm again, only this time she felt like caressing it.

"You wouldn't find me this interesting if I crunched numbers for a living. Admit it."

"True, but as one of the senior agents in the New Orleans office is fond of saying, dating you wouldn't be a career-advancing move."

"But think of the fun you'd have if you took a walk with the devil in the moonlight. What do you say, Agent Daniels. Do we have a deal?"

"There's nothing like being painted into a corner." She laughed, then reached over and ran her fingers along Cain's jawline. "Sorry, I couldn't resist. I get to live out the night?"

"You have my word."

"Then yes, we've got a deal. I never really thought my fieldwork would end so quickly."

Cain looked confused as to why she would say that. "Do you think I'm going to post your picture on the gangster Web page?"

"The thought does seem reasonable, you have to agree."

"Shelby, I wouldn't recommend you take any other plane trips with Vincent to plant these babies." Cain dropped the minute listening devices into her palm and pressed her hand closed. "And I'll have a hard time forgetting such a pretty face, but the only way someone else will blow your cover is to do their homework like I did. It won't be because I sold you out. Despite my less-than-reputable ways, I understand you have a job to do. You've worked hard to get here, and I'm not about to mess that up for you."

"You're something else, Cain Casey." As their time together drew to a close, Shelby felt like she had run up a mountain carrying a boulder on her shoulders. "Thank you for not recommending he just toss me out."

"You're welcome, and you be careful from now on. The world's full of big bad wolves waiting for pretty sheep to come along."

"I'm a trained agent, Cain, hardly sheep material."

"Uh-huh. Does the term 'fish food' hold any meaning for you?"

Shelby laughed and thanked the heavens Cain had asked for so little in return. Gazing into the beautiful blue eyes any longer would have made it easy to forget which side she was on. "Point taken."

"Good, and good night." Cain reached for her coat and started to get ready to leave. The deal had taken longer than she thought, and she would be pushing it to get back before the good citizens of Hayward were awake and witness material. It was a safe bet to say helicopters dropping off outlaws at the feed store weren't normal occurrences in the small farming town.

"Cain, I hope I get to see you again under better circumstances, but I do want to thank you. I had no idea you two had made me."

"Rookie mistake, Shelby. You'll get better, I promise. I was impressed when I read your jacket, but don't believe Barry when he says all of us are idiots."

"How did you know?"

"I have a few tricks of my own." Cain smiled once more and moved to the door.

Shelby stopped her and pulled her down for a thank-you kiss. It was out of character for her, but at the moment she felt like celebrating life. "I won't forget what you did tonight."

Cain nodded, and they both made their way back to Vincent.

"Why don't you entertain Agent Daniels on the way home with stories about your last vacation, Vincent?"

"Are we set to all fly back to New Orleans?" Vincent asked.

His meaning wasn't lost on Shelby. The seriousness of her situation slammed into her brain so hard she had to sit down.

"Yes, sir, I gave my word you *all* were going to have a pleasant flight home."

When Cain stressed the word "all," Shelby wanted to kiss her again.

"Good. I'll wait to hear from you, Cain."

Cain waved them good-bye and headed back to the helicopter. She and her pilot waited for Vincent's craft to clear the runway before they took to the air themselves.

Shelby watched the ground getting farther away and shuddered at the possibilities of "what ifs."

"She's something else, don't you think?" Vincent's question dragged her attention back to her travel companions.

"Yes, sir, she is."

"Now you understand a little better, I think, why Agent Kyle's hair is a little grayer and a lot thinner." Vincent smiled at her and arched his brow. "You might want to fix that smudged lipstick before we land. We wouldn't want the federal government to think you were taken advantage of."

Shelby laughed and was grateful this was the last bit of small talk she would have to exchange with Carlotti for the rest of the trip. She spent the rest of the flight mentally writing her report of their night at one of Biloxi's casinos. She would have to ask Vincent which one he frequented most so there would be no other questions about her absence.

❖

Cain addressed the man who had just put down with a little too much force. "Thanks for the ride." If his shaking hands were any indication, he wasn't going to be having a long chat with Kyle's men.

"No problem, ma'am."

Cain drove back to the farm at the same unhurried pace, with the same company as before, only now the sun was just starting to rise. She used the time to consider her first problem before she could worry about Hannah. For now, she couldn't afford the luxury of thinking about the little girl or giving in to the anger she felt toward Emma. Now she needed to concentrate on all the pieces that would need to fall into place to make her plan work. Parking in the same spot, she took a deep breath before she stepped out into the cold.

"Morning, Cain, out for an early drive?" Ross stood on his porch drinking a cup of coffee.

"Something like that. I was having trouble sleeping, so I went to talk to a friend."

She heard the door to the bunkhouse open and surmised it was Hayden in the doorway. "How about breakfast in town, son?"

"Great." He moved to the passenger-side door in no time, bundled up for the cold.

"Ross, want to ask Emma if she'd like to join us?"

"She's out running an errand this morning, Cain. I'm sure she'll be sorry she missed out."

She could see his discomfort at telling the lie, but she wasn't about to push. Ross was too honest for the position he found himself in.

"I'm sure you're right."

CHAPTER SEVENTEEN

Emma ran around to the back door of Maddie's house, eager to spend time with her daughter. Being away from the sweet child was killing her, but she couldn't take the chance that Cain would see Hannah. It wouldn't take a DNA test to determine the roots of Hannah's family tree. The four-year-old was as much a Casey as Hayden.

A squeal greeted Emma when she opened the door and spotted the object of her secret covered in oatmeal. "Mama!" The blue eyes, identical to Cain's, lit up when Hannah saw her mother, and as they often did, they flooded Emma with memories.

Over Four Years Earlier in the Casey Home in New Orleans

"Good night, honey." Emma kissed Hayden's forehead and pulled the covers under his chin. She had just read their second book of the night, hoping Cain would make it home before she was finished and Hayden fell asleep.

"But Mom isn't here yet."

"I know, sweet boy. She must be running later than she thought, but I promise she'll be here when you wake up." Emma ran her fingers through his hair in an effort to relax him and help him go to sleep.

"Aunt Marie's party's coming up, Mama."

"I know. We'll have to sneak into our room and finish wrapping her presents. Now go to sleep." Emma kissed him again and watched the blue eyes flutter closed.

Outside the room Cain relaxed against the wall and waited for Emma to finish. A warm smile came easily as she listened to their conversation and thought about spending time with Emma. She wanted nothing more than to go in and kiss their son good night, but she knew it would take another forty minutes to calm him down again.

"Thanks for not coming in. He's been wired since seven, and sleep wasn't high on his list of priorities tonight," whispered Emma when she emerged. Together they peeked in on the sleeping child.

"Maybe he thinks he's missing out on something while he's doing all that sleeping."

"No, lover, that would be you who thinks that. He really missed you tonight. Come to think about it, so did I." Emma pressed closer and started unbuttoning Cain's blue shirt.

"I'm here, and I'm all yours for the rest of the night."

"Promise?"

"With all my heart." She kissed Emma, then scooped her off her feet and headed for the bedroom.

Problems at the Erin Go Braugh had kept Cain out late for the past week, and Emma had missed her touch.

Cain could feel her lover's longing. She opened Emma's robe and ran her hand down the lithe body.

"Sit down, baby," requested Emma.

The shy lover had morphed into a woman sure of what she wanted and how to get it. Cain sat at the foot of the bed and watched Emma take off her clothes. The robe pooled at Emma's feet, leaving her in a short silk nightgown that revealed her erect nipples. Before she lifted it over her head, Emma cupped her own breasts and pinched the nipples.

The move made Cain growl in a deep voice, "Take it off," and Emma complied, smiling.

Emma's body was, to Cain, perfection. Emma was what she liked to call curvaceous. Her breasts were full, with soft pink nipples, and her flat stomach gave way to shapely hips. True to her word, Cain had never desired another woman in her heart or in her bed after she found Emma.

Emma moved closer and finished removing Cain's shirt. She unbuckled the belt next, and after she unzipped the pants, she snaked her hand down the opening and pinched the hard clit. "I promise to take care of this, but I want you to make love to me first." Emma shoved the strong body down and pushed her own center over Cain's mouth.

Cain loved Emma's scent and taste. She took her time, pressing her tongue flat along the wet opening.

"Please, baby, I've been waiting for you all week," Emma begged.

She kept her tongue in the same position, waiting to see how badly Emma wanted it. The slow rocking hips were starting their dance, which made her wish Emma had finished removing her pants so she could have gotten her to touch her, when suddenly Emma dragged her wet sex back and forth over her mouth. She knew Emma was in the mood for it to last, which meant any relief for her would have to wait.

"I love the way your tongue feels," Emma moaned. "When we're somewhere we can't do this, I look at you and think about you licking me or sucking me, and it gets me so hot."

Cain pulled her mouth away and groaned. The added dialogue was about to kill her since Emma was still using the same slow movements.

"I crave for you to do this to me, baby. Then when I can't stand it anymore, you fill me up and make me scream." The thought of Cain doing that made Emma speed up for just a moment before she stopped and slid herself against Cain's mouth, filling it with the evidence of her desire.

Knowing she would have to wait a long time for satisfaction if Emma's pace stayed slow, Cain ran her hands up Emma's legs, along her body to the hard nipples. Maybe some more stimulation would accelerate Emma's tempo.

"Oh yeah, baby, pinch 'em just like that," Emma gasped, adding a roll to the movement of her hips. She was getting close, but she wouldn't be making the trip alone.

As Cain was about to take both breasts and squeeze, Emma swiveled around. The different angle made her suck on the now diamond-hard point. She was so focused, she barely registered her pants falling past her knees to her ankles, and the head between her legs made her moan loudly against Emma.

Slow was impossible now as they each tried to ride out the pleasure and not forget the other's need. Emma loved looking into Cain's eyes when she came, but this position was one of her favorites because she could feel the long body shuddering under her. It was the only time Cain gave up total control, and she was the only person who had gotten her to do it.

Emma kissed the inside of Cain's thigh and waited for the small tremors to stop before she finished taking off the forgotten shoes and pants. She stayed on her knees on the floor and enjoyed running her hands up and down Cain's legs. The toes digging into the carpet let her know they were just getting started.

"Honey?"

"What?" Cain took a deep breath and dragged herself into a sitting position.

"I love you."

Cain put her hand gently on Emma's cheek. "Come up here, sweetling." She helped Emma onto her lap and kissed her softly. "I love you too."

"Can I ask you something?"

"You can ask me anything. You can have anything you want that's within my power to give you."

"I want another baby."

Cain's hands came to rest on Emma's backside, and she pulled her closer. Children were something Cain wanted, the number limited to as many as Emma was willing to have. Because seven years had passed since Hayden's birth, she had given up hope for any more.

"Are you sure?"

"Honey, I know how you feel about Hayden. I just didn't think it was fair to cut into that, but he might be willing to share you with the rest of us now." Emma put her hands behind Cain's neck and pulled her into another slow kiss.

In a week, at Marie's birthday party, she was planning to give Cain her own special gift. In fact, she was about to move up her timetable and tell her now, but what Cain was doing with her hands made any other conversation impossible.

It was the love they shared that helped create the life growing inside her. Another baby was her gift to Cain and to herself.

That was the last time she had shared herself with Cain, and it was fortuitous she had waited to share the news of her pregnancy. When Cain had killed her cousin, Emma left with one of the good things she and Cain had created together. It was time to get the other one back.

Given time, Hayden would understand why she had decided to leave and what she was doing now. Cain would let the boy go and not come after Hannah only if she was somewhere she couldn't get to them. But Emma's craving for Cain, her desire to have her hands on Cain's skin, hadn't died away. Having her so close for the last couple of days was only making it worse.

"Girl, where'd you run off to?"

Maddie's laugh broke the spell and made her blush.

"Never mind. Maybe I'm too young to know, and this little one's definitely too young." Maddie put Hannah on the floor, and the little girl ran to her mother.

"Hey, sweetling. Have you been good for your aunt Maddie?" Emma scooped the child up and hugged her, loving the way Hannah's small arms felt when she hugged her back.

"I miss you, Mama."

"Oh, honey, Mama misses you too."

Hannah spent the morning showing Emma all the pictures she had drawn in the past couple of days. The little girl fought sleep when her naptime rolled around, and Emma knew she was afraid her mother would be gone when she woke up. She rocked her and sang to her until sleep won out and she was able to put her down. She spent some time just sitting on the bed watching her daughter.

Maddie interrupted her thoughts by softly asking, "Honey, what's going to happen if Cain finds out about Hannah?"

As Emma tucked the blankets around Hannah, she realized how her life with Cain had made her much more worldly wise than Maddie, who was a few years older. "That's not possible." She leaned down and kissed Hannah's cheek one more time before following Maddie downstairs.

"Emma, I'm not asking if it's going to happen. I'm asking what happens if she *does*. I'm worried about you, and I want to know what we might need to plan for."

Emma accepted the cup of coffee her friend offered and thought of a good answer. If Cain found out about their daughter, she might do something unpredictable. "I don't know how to honestly answer that question. Cain is like two different people. I fell in love with one, and the other one scared me enough to come running back here."

"Is there a chance you could lose Hannah?"

"If we were in Louisiana I wouldn't have a chance. That's why I'm here. Cain's reach is long, but even her power has its limits, or at least I hope it does."

Maddie put her hand over Emma's and squeezed it. "I want you to be careful, Emma. I just have a really bad feeling about this. You do what you have to do, and don't worry about Hannah. We'll take care of her as long as you need."

The loyalty made Emma smile. "I know you will, but don't worry so much. Kyle's got everything under control."

"How's Hayden?"

She felt like a ray of sun as she thought about her son, a smile breaking across her face. "Maddie, you wouldn't believe how big he's gotten. He's just like Cain—tall, you know—and smart. When he talks to me I have to keep reminding myself he's only eleven. We've had a rough start, but I think we're making headway. The biggest surprise in all this has been Cain. I don't think I'd have had much time with him if she hadn't prodded him to cooperate. She's been a good mother."

"You sound like a woman in love. Are you sure about all this? It isn't too late to change your mind." Maddie squeezed her hand and smiled.

"I can't go back now even if I wanted to. At one time, Cain would've forgiven me anything, but this..." She looked up the stairs. "This she won't forgive."

CHAPTER EIGHTEEN

R eady to head home in a couple of days, buddy?" Cain and
Hayden sat in the same booth she and Ross had occupied the
day before.

The café in Hayward was like a throwback in time. Oak floors,
scuffed by time and heavy foot traffic, needed a coat of finish, and
the countertop was a dated avocado green color, though clean. Their
waitress completed the atmosphere with a ruffled apron.

Cain ignored the nostalgia of the place and studied the anger
brewing just under the surface of her son's face.

"I'm ready to go now. I don't understand why we have to stay
longer."

"Hayden, what's wrong? And don't tell me it's nothing. I can see
something in there eating away at you." Cain tapped her finger against
the side of his head, making him smile a little.

"I've been taking all these long walks with Emma, you know?"

"Yeah, what's wrong with that? I know you're mad at her for
leaving and not getting in touch with you, but I've got to believe there's
just one little part of you that's been dying to see her again. It's all right
to admit that, son. Feeling that way isn't an insult to me. For better or
worse, Emma's your mother, and in her own way she loves you. She
gave you life, Hayden. Never discount that."

"It's just she never answers any questions directly. I'm trying to
get to know her like you said, but it's like she won't talk to me. She
doesn't treat me the same way you do. I know I'm a kid, but that doesn't
mean I don't have a brain."

"You want me to talk to her?"

Hayden slumped his shoulders a little more because he wanted nothing more than to answer no. If Cain was forever running around fixing his problems, she would never start to confide in him more about the business. "Can I give it one more shot?"

"You can give it shots for a month of Sundays, boy, if that's what you want. Good answer, by the way. You're growing up on me faster than I think is fair."

That got him to crack his lips in a genuine smile. Praise from his mother was something Hayden treasured more than anything else. "Thanks, Mom."

"You want to take a walk with me, or are you all walked out?"

"Are you going to talk about your feelings and how I should be playing with kids my own age more often?"

The sarcasm gave Cain some insight into how Emma had spent their time together. "That would be no. I want to walk down to Roy's and make sure your grandfather's all set for the winter. I don't want to see him have to sell off any of his…" Cain paused and tried to find the right word.

"What, land?"

"No, I was going to say 'flock,' but that's not right when it comes to cows. It's 'herd,' right?"

"You're looking at someone who's allergic to manual labor," joked Hayden. Actually, he had enjoyed his time with Ross the most during his visit. His grandfather talked about different things, not to just fill the silence, but probably because he thought Hayden should know a little about the other part of his family. Ross never seemed to expect anything from their time together, and Hayden had opened up in turn.

"Remind me to buy you an axe when we get home, then, son. Your new job will be to split logs for the fireplace." The two laughed as they got ready to leave.

The waitress ran over and asked if she could get Cain a cup of coffee to go. Hayward had never seen such a heavy tipper. She was used to the couple of quarters her regulars left on the counter, which wasn't an insult to the service, just a reality of tight budgets. With Cain coming in two days in a row, the new shoes she had been saving for were now a reality.

"Have a good day," Cain said as she put on her hat.

"Tomorrow the special is pork chops, if you're interested."

"How about you make plenty, and I'll bring my crew in for lunch?"

The waitress smiled and nodded enthusiastically as she pumped Cain's hand.

"If you eat in here and wink at her one more time, we may have to take her home with us," whispered Hayden.

The woman had run ahead and opened the door for them.

"If she can cook a pork chop as well as your grandmother could, she might be worth the airfare home."

Cain maneuvered Hayden between herself and the buildings they were passing, to protect him from any attack from the street. As they neared the corner, she spotted the same guy who had watched her have lunch with Ross the day before. The guy still looked cold and out of place. It was time to have some fun.

"Excuse me, could you tell me where the feed store is?"

The rapid eye movement was a giveaway that the last thing the man expected was for her to speak to him. He pointed in the direction they were headed and cleared his throat. "A few blocks down there."

"Thanks. Hey, does Bob carry any livestock?"

"Livestock?" The guy looked like he was about to jog down the street to get away from her.

"I believe she means live animals of any kind," Hayden added, trying not to laugh.

"I guess so, but I'm not really from around here. I'm just visiting friends."

She wanted to ask who he was visiting but didn't think the fun of needling the guy was worth the risk, not yet anyway. She wondered if he would bother to go down and find out the owner's name was Roy, not Bob. *Maybe in my retirement I'll offer to teach some classes on the art of what not to do when following outlaws, if the feds pay me well enough.*

Roy came around the counter and greeted her with a firm handshake, truly glad to see her. The fee she had paid him for the use of his property was more than generous, making the visit from Kyle inconsequential. They talked about Ross's account briefly, then spent the rest of their time shopping for a new tractor. The new piece of equipment was a gift from Hayden and Cain to thank Ross for his hospitality.

Another man unfamiliar to the storeowner browsed the sparse shelves during his transaction with Cain, declining his offer of help when mother and son left. Roy was about to call after Cain and warn her about the guy, but thought she looked like someone who could handle just about anything or anyone.

A few days after Cain's arrival, had the citizens of Hayward been responsible for her future fate, Kyle would have been hard-pressed to find anyone willing to convict her of a traffic ticket, much less anything else.

❖

When Emma pulled Ross's old truck into the Verde farm and stopped at the back of the barn, she noticed Cain's vehicle was gone. Taking a chance, she climbed up to the loft. Time was running out, and she wanted to know if Kyle had found anything useful.

"You shouldn't be here," Kyle told her in a more-than-irritated voice. He had spent the morning on the phone with his supervisor, trying to talk her out of pulling the plug on their whole operation.

"I have a right to know if you've made any progress, Agent. I want my son back, and you promised me results."

Kyle looked at her and found someone to vent his bad mood on. "I can't demand she start doing business as usual so your helping us bug her room won't go to waste, now can I? Get your butt back down there and let us do our jobs. You lived with the woman for years, so you know she's not stupid. Casey isn't going to suddenly start talking up a storm. She's too careful to say anything that'll lead us to a conviction. You and your mother knew going in this might not work."

"That's not exactly how you pitched it."

"This conversation is over, Emma. You are free to leave." Kyle bowed his head to his paperwork, fully expecting her to be gone when he decided to look back up.

When Cain spotted Emma coming down the loft ladder, something inside of her snapped and she curled her hands into fists. Here was her Judas, and she fought the urge to choke the life out of her. In her mind, helping Kyle was the ultimate betrayal, tantamount to throwing away everything they had shared. Furious, she decided to inflict on Emma the same kind of pain she was feeling now. The game had begun, and all she wanted now was to play it out.

"Hey, guys, I didn't realize you were back." Emma scrambled to think of an explanation for why she had been in the loft, in case Cain asked.

"We went in for breakfast at Mabel's," said Hayden.

"You must be full, then." Emma tried to make a joke as she watched Cain's face turn more glacial by the second. "Any way I can convince you to finish our talk from yesterday?" she asked Cain as she tried to find some of the affection the blue eyes always held for her.

"I'm thinking it'd be a waste of time since we have nothing more to talk about. Hayden, though, tells me he has more questions for you. Since we're leaving tomorrow, why don't you try answering a few?"

"Is something wrong, Cain?" Emma's worry was starting to grow, and she heard it add a quiver to her voice.

Cain ignored the question and turned to her son. "Why don't you try one more walk, and don't back down from the hard questions. You have a right to know who your mother is and why she's made the decisions she has, even if it changes the way you feel about me."

"That would never happen," Hayden said with confidence.

"Buddy, we all make choices in life that alter it in ways you can't begin to fathom. Hindsight doesn't make them better, and they change how you feel about yourself. So suffice it to say they change how other people see you. Even those who love you the most."

She put her hands on his shoulders and squeezed gently. "I know you hate when I say this, but bear with me this one time. It'll take you getting older to fully understand what I just said, but years and experience under your belt won't make it any less true."

"I love you, Mom."

"To hear you say that is my greatest accomplishment. I love you too, son, and at the end of your walk I'll be here to answer the questions Emma can't."

"Cain, I don't think this is a good idea." As much as Emma wanted Hayden with her, she didn't want to shatter completely his image of and feelings for Cain. To find out his parent was a cold-blooded killer would most likely make Hayden reject the one person he loved most.

"Like I said, Emma, I made a choice four years ago, and it cost me something precious. No amount of lamenting over it now is going to bring it back, so the boy has a right to know how we got here. He's young, that's true, but give him the benefit of an explanation for why his mother left."

"Are you sure?"

"Positive."

Cain patted Hayden's shoulder one more time and strode to the bunkhouse. Relaxing into the old chair next to the phone, she started making calls that in essence were the beginning of her downfall. Kyle's men recorded call after call, full of the information Kyle had been waiting for.

When she returned to New Orleans, her Canadian supplier would deliver a warehouse full of contraband liquor, and Kyle would be waiting. Merrick listened in horror as the agents in the barn exchanged hugs and congratulations.

"I have faith in you, but I don't understand why," Merrick whispered into her ear.

Cain leaned forward and kissed her lips. "I want you to trust me to know what's best for my family."

"I do trust you, Cain. It's the giving up I don't understand."

Cain smiled and kissed Merrick one more time. She cherished the woman's loyalty.

"My father once told me a story about when he was a young man just learning the business. His father took him to a cockfight one night. It wasn't something my grandfather did often, but some of his clients enjoyed that kind of thing. The sport of kings, I believe it's called."

Merrick, no matter what she did for a living, shivered at the thought of the barbaric sport.

Cain pulled the guard down to sit on the arm of her chair and kept hold of her hand when she got comfortable. "Pop said one of the last fights he saw that night was between a big bird with an impressive head of plumes and this small, insignificant-looking bird with a missing eye. As their owners threw them in the ring, the money started changing hands. This was back when twenty bucks meant a day's pay, but he said most of the people there saw that big cock and pulled their wallets out. They were slapping money down to cover the growing odds and the two hadn't exchanged a peck, but the spectators were sure the little one was going down."

Merrick relaxed a little more, leaning against Cain and starting to realize what the moral of the story might be, but asking anyway. "What happened?"

"My grandfather pulled five hundred bucks out of his pocket and bet on the small bird, amidst the laughs of those around him who warned he was throwing his money away. For twenty minutes that big, good-looking rooster chased the shrimp around the ring without laying a beak on him, Pop said. He chalked it up to the small one's fear of the inevitable, but when the big one showed the first weakness, he revealed his strategy."

"A bird can formulate strategy?"

"According to Dalton Casey, Jr., it could. He said that little bird, dismissed by everyone there including himself, and most importantly his rival in the ring, turned and sunk his talons into all those pretty feathers. It was over in nothing flat, and the big rooster was dead. He said that bird taught him a valuable lesson—never take for granted what seems like ultimate victory or defeat. The winning or losing in anything comes in the playing, even for small, one-eyed birds." Cain stopped and pointed to her eyes, hoping Merrick understood what she was saying. She wasn't running, and she wasn't half blind.

"When's the shipment getting to the city?"

"Two weeks at our dock offices. The boxes will be labeled 'sardines.'"

Merrick nodded and got up to start dinner.

Cain's only thought was "good girl." She had only two more things to do, and then they could all go home.

CHAPTER NINETEEN

R oss, it looks like you've got some shingles loose on the roof of the barn. Want me to climb up and check it out? It'll save you a service call." Cain looked up and pointed to the area she was talking about.

"You don't mind?"

"I can't wait." She scaled easily to the first section of roofing next to the loft, with a hammer in her belt and a box of nails in her coat pocket. It only took a few minutes to check the shingles and remove the tapes and equipment she had left the night before. She chuckled as she imagined the agents on the other side of the wall holding their breath and praying she wouldn't hear anything to alert her to their presence. She didn't care about them, though; she stared off into the distance, where she could see Hayden and Emma in one of the pastures.

She wondered if she was asking too much of her son, considering his age, and tried to bury her guilt. Not for the choices she'd made, but for her real reason for allowing the talk he and Emma were having. "I've had to live with the consequences of my life, Emma, but don't think you get to walk away unscathed because of what you believe were your noble choices." Her soft voice never reached the two people now in the middle of an empty pasture.

"I'm sorry, Hayden, for letting you find out about this in this way. As much as I love you, I've always been too afraid to tell you." Her apology was also a prayer the boy wouldn't walk away too scarred, but today Hayden would get the answer he had wanted for four years.

Two Weeks after Marie Casey's Death

No one on the street paid attention to the marked police car making a routine stop. In this section of town the men in blue routinely hassled the residents for the smallest infraction, as an excuse to search for something more illegal than failing to use their turn signal. As the patrolman made his way to his door, Danny Baxter studied his face in the rearview mirror to make sure he didn't have any traces of white powder around his nose.

"Is there a problem, officer?"

"Step out of the vehicle and come with me." The leather utility belt creaked when the cop placed his hand over the holster near his gun and waited. "Don't make me say it again," he added when Danny didn't move.

They walked to the unit together, and the patrolman held the back door open for him. Danny finally thought to look at the cop's face. "No fucking way."

"Come on, idiot. Someone's waiting to see you," said Merrick from the backseat. She pointed her gun at his head, and Cain's other trusted guard Lou pressed his to Danny's back.

Screaming or begging now would be futile, so he got in, deciding to save the dramatics for later when he could play on Cain's sympathies. He recognized where they'd stopped and laughed at Cain's sense of irony. Marie had spent her last tortured hours of life at this dilapidated shotgun house where most of the crackheads came to smoke their scores. Tonight it was quiet, but not for long.

The door lock clicked closed with such ease it belied the condition of the rotted-out building, and Merrick pushed him farther in to where Cain waited. Her boss stood at the rear of the house gazing out the kitchen window at the unkempt yard. In the center of the kitchen was the only piece of unbroken furniture in the place, a green Formica table with stained aluminum trim.

It had taken Cain some time, but she had pieced together where Marie had died. The table had to be the spot Danny had used, since she could still see traces of dried blood on one of the legs and at one corner.

"Anyone follow you?" she asked, without turning around.

"Lou was careful. Nobody but the rats know we're here." Merrick didn't lower the gun she had pointed at Danny's head, motioning for him to move farther into the room. "You ready, boss?"

"You should've brought a chair if you're tired, sweetheart. We're going to be a while."

"Who are you fucking kidding?" Danny decided to let his impatience show, hoping it would shorten the time he'd have to spend with his cousin. "Cut the bullshit and hit me some more if you want, but the tough act is crap."

"Do you know the proper way to kill a goat, Danny?"

Lou, Merrick, and Danny all hiked their brows at the question. Cain wasn't known for small talk in these situations.

"Lou, how about providing some incentive for him to answer the question."

Lou delivered a punch to Danny's left kidney that dropped him to his knees. The pained air escaping from her cousin's lungs caused Cain to turn around and give him her full attention.

"What's the answer?"

"How the fuck should I know?" he wheezed. "And why should I give a fuck?"

"That was always your problem, Danny." Cain put her hands flat on the table and just stared at him. "You grew up never wanting to learn anything. Your aunt Therese married well, and my father was supposed to provide you a gun and a wad of cash for being a wiseguy. That's what your daddy told you when he was sober enough, isn't it?"

"My father raised me to be a man. He didn't have to pretend like Dalton did." Danny let out another long stream of air when Lou kicked his other kidney. No matter what, he wasn't going to scream like he had the first time he found himself at the end of Cain's ire.

"You think having a pair between your legs makes you a man?" Cain took a pair of leather gloves from her back pocket and started to put them on. "Or because you're strong enough to make a woman do your bidding proves you're superior?"

"You'll never measure up to me, admit it. You need these assholes to hold me down to show how strong you are."

"Help the man up, Lou," she said.

Danny massaged his side when he got to his feet and glared at Cain. All of them could see he was getting angry.

"Just you and me, so show me. Show me what kind of man you are."

He lunged for her, obviously hoping to knock her down with his momentum, but she moved at the last second, sending Danny's head through the glass of the dirty window behind her. When he turned, blood was already running down his cheek. Her fist halted his next lunge when he got close enough. The blow to his nose made Danny double over and spit out a sudden spurt of blood.

When his head whipped back from the kick she delivered, she could hear the gurgle in his throat as he landed on his back. "Give up already?" She stood over him, careful to stay away from the spray coming from his mouth when Danny started coughing. "You should try a little harder, since we'll be here until you beg me to kill you."

"Fuck you."

The insult only made her laugh. "Given any more thought to my question?" Cain waved Lou over and pointed to her cousin.

During the sleepless nights after Marie's murder, she had spent the time thinking of how she was going to kill Danny. Many thought revenge didn't squelch the pain. Cain, though, was more concerned with responsibility than with revenge. Danny would pay with his life for what he had done.

As the head of her family, she was responsible for seeing that he did. She couldn't erase the pain of loss, but she could take some comfort in knowing Danny was burning in hell and she had stamped his one-way ticket. Yet she hoped she wasn't becoming the type of person Emma had accused her of being four years earlier.

"Playtime's over. For you anyway," she said.

Behind her, Merrick grabbed the length of rope that hung from the ceiling with a loop at one end.

While the guards had been out earlier picking Danny up, Cain had added one new fixture to the house. She had screwed a brass ring into one of the support beams over the doorway; it was so new it looked almost out of place. Pointing at it, she said, "My grandfather told me how his father had various methods for slaughtering different animals on their farm in Ireland."

"I thought Dalton always bragged about how you come from a long line of bootleggers?" After he asked the question, Danny winced as Lou locked his hands in the cuffs again.

"A man can't live on whiskey. You need a good stew to help you keep drinking."

"What in the hell does that have to do with me?" asked Danny.

After tying one end around Danny's ankles, Lou gave the rope a good tug. Danny pitched forward, slamming his chest and face into the floor. Lou kept pulling until Danny was hanging upside down from the ceiling. With his head even with Cain's waist, he could see perfectly what she was taking out of her pocket. The old switchblade had belonged to Dalton and had been one of the last gifts he'd given her before his death.

"What does that have to do with you?" she repeated his question. "Plenty." The tip of her blade rested at the opening of Danny's shirt. "You're nothing but an animal, cousin, so that's how I'm going to deal with you."

Beads of sweat broke out on his brow when the sound of tearing fabric filled the silence. "Think about what you're doing, Cain. I'm your family."

She stopped her hand just before she plunged the knife into Danny's heart for what he'd said. Instead, she moved to the hem of his pants, not caring that she cut into his hip when she got to the bottom.

"You stopped being my family after what you tried in my house, with my wife." The boxers he was wearing fell to the top of the pile on the floor.

"Shit, if you wanted some action you didn't have to go through all this to get me here. We're family, but if you want a piece of me, just ask."

If Danny wanted to jibe anymore, the attempt died when she sliced off his right nipple, instantly eradicating his promise to not scream.

"Somehow I don't think you would've accepted my invitation once you see what I have in mind." She sat back on the edge of the table and watched as rivulets of blood made their way from Danny's chest to his face.

"What'd you do that for?" Danny sobbed.

"Call it foreplay." She felt calm as she put the knife down and accepted a belt from Merrick. "We could waste each other's time with me asking why you lost your mind and killed Marie, and you denying it, so we're going to skip that."

"That's what this is about? Hell, you should be thanking me for getting rid of that anchor."

The slap of leather against his mouth opened a new cut on his lip, shutting Danny up once again. She hit him next over the open hole in his chest, wrenching another scream.

"You grew up around Marie. She was never an anchor to anyone who counted. That definition fits your family perfectly, so shut the fuck up." She swung again, hitting his chest and making sure the belt hit right on his wound again. "After all, we haven't finished our talk about the goat." She noticed his tears mixing in with blood when she picked up the knife again.

"If you're going to kill me, then go ahead."

"I'm going to kill you, Danny, but it'll be anything but fast. You know me better than that." She cocked her head to one side and continued to glare at him. "My grandfather told me when you kill a goat, to keep the meat from tasting gamey, you have to bleed it. You cut slowly." Belying her statement, she quickly sliced away his left nipple.

"You fucker," Danny screamed. He was crying and trying to pull himself up, almost as if to not provide her with such an easy target. Just as quickly he dropped back down when she slashed him again with the belt.

She hit him until he begged her to stop. She quit when her arm got tired. By that time Danny looked like someone had painted his body with red, cruel stripes, some of which were bleeding. The sun was starting to set, and the light in the room was fading as quickly as Danny.

"Please, Cain, no more." He could see the pool of blood on the floor under him, signaling he didn't have much longer to live. "I'm sorry for what I did."

"Granddad told me the last step was to slit the animal's throat and let it bleed out," she said, as if he hadn't spoken.

"Anything but that, please. I don't want to die."

"It's all right, Danny. I'm not going to do that to you." She watched as he laughed as if in relief through his tears. "No, I've got something else in mind." She picked up the knife and moved closer. "It's only fitting after what you did to Marie and the others before her. All those innocent girls your depraved little mind left scarred to satisfy your sick needs. Those women deserve justice just as much as my sister."

"Please, Cain. I'll do whatever you want. Just don't hurt me anymore."

She was surprised he had that much energy to scream when the blade came to rest on his scrotum. Without hesitation she cut all the way down, and Danny watched what had been a source of pride drop on the floor like a discarded turkey neck.

The fact that he was screaming made it easy for Merrick to slip it into his mouth right before Cain slit his throat.

Hayden studied his mother's face as if it were his first time to see it. "Are you going to answer my question truthfully, or do we just dance around the issue?"

"I don't want to do this, Hayden."

"Christ, just answer the question. Why did you leave? What's hard about that?"

"I don't want to change how you feel about Cain just because you're curious. It's hard because by telling you what she's capable of, that's what's going to happen."

"She's at least willing to take that chance. Why can't you?"

The question should have sent up a warning flare in Emma's brain, but her anger at Cain clouded her judgment. Hayden's reaction to the truth of her departure might be what she needed to win him over. "I don't see her out here answering any questions."

"She didn't abandon me. You did. Now I want to know why."

Emma glued her eyes to the ground and kept walking. Moving would make the tale easier to tell. "A little before I left, Cain and I hosted a party for your aunt Marie."

"I remember. We've been over this part already."

"The first time you asked me, I did tell you about the attempted rape Cain saved me from, but I changed the ending. I asked her not to hurt the guy too badly, but she went a lot further than that. She killed that guy for touching her property. He lost his life for something he almost did."

Hayden stopped and felt shocked. Cain was harsh when warranted, but she rarely lost control and made such stupid mistakes. "She told you she killed him?"

"She lied to me to cover for herself, but I found out later what she had done."

"Who was it?"

"What does it matter now, Hayden? It's done, but it doesn't change how she feels about you."

"Just answer me, and let me worry about how I feel about my mother."

"All right, but I found who it was the most disturbing since he was part of her family."

The cold weather intensified as he felt the blood drain from his face. "Who was it?" asked Hayden through clenched teeth.

"Cain's cousin, Danny Baxter."

He stumbled when Emma said the name, certain he had heard wrong. "Impossible." He felt her arms come around him, but he was too confused to care.

"It's hard to believe, I know, and maybe now you'll understand why I had to leave. My greatest regret, or should I say biggest mistake, was you, Hayden. I should've fought harder to keep you with me."

"You're lying, it couldn't have been Danny." He pushed Emma off him and looked like he was about to bolt.

"I'm telling you the truth, son."

"You're the one who begged her for Danny's life?"

The warning bells finally went off in Emma's head. Hayden couldn't possibly remember the man who had come so close to violating her, and Cain had admitted she hadn't answered Hayden's questions. His question was totally out of context to what they were talking about. "How do you know Danny?"

"I asked you a question first."

The anger, the straight body, the ice in his eyes and voice—it was all Cain she was looking at. What Emma didn't realize was that she was standing on a cliff of her own making, and by encouraging her to tell Hayden the truth, Cain was about to push her off.

"I asked her, yes, but she didn't listen to me."

"She listened to you, all right. It's your fault she's dead, and I never want to see you again. I hate you!" Hayden screamed the last part so loudly the people in the yard heard a faint echo despite the distance. He ran back as fast as he could manage through the tears, his lungs burning from the cold air.

Cain was waiting for him, and he lunged into her arms. As upset as he was, he felt better when he realized that Cain wore her usual suit and long black cashmere coat instead of jeans and boots. He wouldn't have to stay here any longer.

"Let it out, Hayden. It's all right. I've got you." Cain just held him until the tears subsided.

"Why, Mom?"

"It was a mistake." She shook her head when he began to blame Emma. "My mistake, and mine alone. I have to live with the lesson that sometimes you have to choose the hard road, because in the end it'll get you where you need to be that much quicker. I chose with my heart because it was easier, and it cost me, so it's my mistake, not hers."

"I want to leave."

"Go help the guys pack up. We're going home."

Cain sent him off knowing it wasn't the end of their talk, but they would have to wait for a less public area to rehash it. Kyle had access to her business here, but her personal life and her relationship with her son were off limits. She started walking to intercept Emma, now that she was prepared to finish their talk.

"Why didn't you tell him the truth?" Emma accused when she stopped in front of Cain, gasping for air.

"What truth is that?" She pointed her finger at Emma, almost poking her in the mouth. "The truth you spun for yourself to get you through the days?"

"You killed that bastard, and now all of a sudden I'm the bad guy here? I won't let you get away with this, Cain. He's my son and he deserves the truth."

"Emma, you left because you believed what you thought was a minor infraction on Danny's part sent me into a jealous rage and I killed him, right?"

Emma nodded.

"I beat the shit out of him—that part I'm not going to deny because to me it was no minor infraction—but Danny survived that night because you asked me and I gave in. I did, even though I knew he had done it before to other young women and no one was there to stop him. His punishment was the beating and banishment from my family. You know what that means, or at least you should."

"Why continue the charade now? I know the truth."

She kept going, not caring if Emma believed her or not. "He went to work for Giovanni Bracato's organization. I'm no saint, but I'm not an animal like Bracato. Danny waited and took his revenge on me by going after the most innocent of my family. He lured Marie away from her school and beat and raped her until she was barely alive. She was taking a fucking class she talked me into so she could keep up with Hayden better— God." She stopped and turned her face to the wind in the hope it would dry her tears before they fell.

"But Agent Kyle said…" Emma fell to her knees and couldn't finish as the shocking truth hit her.

"That answers my question as to who turned you. Be careful the company you keep, Emma, lest you drown in the shit they wallow in."

To cement the truth in Emma's mind, she threw her the picture the police had taken of Marie's swollen face just hours before she died. It was for their investigation, they had said, to help show the jury the damage when they caught the guy. She had let them take it just to get rid of them. She wouldn't need the police or a jury for Danny Baxter. Not caring to offer comfort, she left Emma there on the ground, staring at the picture.

"Cain, wait, please." Emma looked once more at the picture and remembered the sweet person Marie had been. No wonder Hayden had gotten so upset when she had brought up his aunt's name before. How could she have known what happened?

Cain was too far away to hear the plea to stay. It was one of the first times she had said all that out loud, in a way proving to herself Marie's death was her fault. Had she buried Danny like she had wanted to all those years before, Marie would be alive. She had failed her family by not killing him when she should have.

The group was ready to go when she got back to the farmhouse, waiting for her by the car.

"Ross, thank you so much for having us." She pulled out a business card and handed it over. On it was a list of numbers, should Ross need to get in touch with her.

He put it in his coat pocket and nodded.

"I really had a good time, and I'm positive Hayden enjoyed his time with you too."

"You sure you won't stay another day?"

"Hayden wants to head home, and I don't feel right about pushing the issue anymore. Stay in touch," she said, holding her hand out.

The farmer shook it without any hesitation.

"Hayden, come over here and say good-bye to your grandfather."

The boy stepped up and offered his hand as well, getting Ross to give him a warm smile. "Thank you, sir, for having me."

"I hope it won't be the last time you come up here to see us. Especially now that we're business partners," Ross joked and held Hayden's hand with both of his.

"Maybe next time you can come and see us in New Orleans," Hayden said.

Just as the large vehicle turned onto the road, Emma came running into the yard with the picture Cain had left. If everything Cain had said was true, she couldn't possibly undo the damage she had caused to all their lives by just walking away.

God, why hadn't she trusted Cain enough to just ask? She had just blindly sat and listened to Agent Kyle that day he had cornered her outside Hayden's school. The one time she had forced her hand about the constant protection Cain insisted on was the one day the agent had been able to get so close.

Four Years Earlier in New Orleans, A Week after the Attempted Rape

"Stay put. I'm just taking Hayden to school. That's hardly cause for a gang war." Emma grabbed her purse and car keys, wanting to get out of the house for a while.

"Ma'am, Cain said—" Mook tried to stop her, but Emma wasn't in the mood to listen.

"Cain's your boss, Mook, I respect that, but she isn't my keeper. The fact that I'm married to her should carry some weight."

"Yes, ma'am. I meant no disrespect."

Emma helped Hayden put on his sweater and smiled at her son's guard. "Don't worry, Mook. You can blame me if she gets mad. I just need some time for myself."

"Please be careful."

They made the short drive in relative silence, with just the radio tuned to a station Hayden had picked out. Emma kissed him good-bye at the front door of the school and waved to his teacher standing in the hall.

She didn't notice where the man came from, but suddenly when she got back into her car, he stood there tapping on her window. The badge he held up made her put her head on the steering wheel for a moment. Could she just drive away and expect him to leave her alone? His insistent tapping made her look up again and press the button to lower the window. Kyle handed over his ID.

"Ms. Verde, can I have a moment of your time?"

"It's Casey," she informed him as she ran a finger over the leather of the wallet that held his credentials. It was a rich calf leather and extremely expensive, if she had to guess. Interesting taste the agent had, and she wondered if it was government issue.

"Excuse me?"

"My last name, it's Casey. Would you like to see my driver's license?"

Kyle laughed and accepted his wallet back. "I see you've learned a few things from Casey about how to deal with the authorities."

"Agent Kyle, is it?"

He nodded at her question.

"If you want to talk to Cain, then I suggest you call her at the office. If you don't have the number, I'll be happy to give it to you."

"I don't want to talk to Casey. I want to talk to you. Would you like to have a cup of coffee? I promise it'll be worth your while."

"Do I have a choice?"

"You can drive away now, Ms. Casey, and I promise never to bother you again. But if you'd like to know the true nature of the monster you live with, I suggest you accept my offer."

She followed him to the location he suggested and hoped no one from the house would come searching for her if this took too long. In less than an hour Kyle painted a picture of Cain she had never considered. She couldn't conceive of the drugs Cain peddled and the number of prostitutes she owned. They went far beyond the image Cain had always painted of herself as a saintly bootlegger.

It was his last detailed account of Danny's murder that finally made the tears roll down her cheeks. If what Kyle said was true, Cain had looked her in the eye as she washed his blood off her hands and lied. The last lie in a long list of them.

"I don't believe you."

"Ms. Casey, what could I possibly have to gain by deceiving you? I'm not here to try and talk you into testifying against Casey. I just think you deserve to know so you and your son have a fighting chance at a normal life, if that's what you want."

He sounded so sincere as he described the makeup of Cain's business and the people she dealt with. However, when he asked what she would do when the ugliness Cain was involved in invaded their home again, but with more devastating results, she winced. What if next time the enemy went after Hayden? Could she live with that?

Kyle didn't miss her putting her hand on her abdomen for just that split second, and he realized that he obviously had more than one child to bargain with. He could see her swaying in the direction he had meticulously led her with his barrage of information, no matter that most of it was incorrect. He could never have guessed he would be so successful after just one meeting.

After trying everything else he could think of to snare Cain in some illegal activity and get rid of her, Kyle was gambling on trying to finish what Danny had started. If he could strip away all that Casey held dear, she would become sloppy in her grief. Danny Baxter had been stupid in trying what he had in Casey's home, but his idea and his reasoning were sound.

A few days later Emma had packed her bags and left. She sacrificed one child to save another, and when Hannah was born she had tried to make peace with her decision.

How strange it had been when they laid the baby in her arms and she had not seen Cain's blue eyes smiling down on her in pure joy. Her friend Maddie and her father had been the only ones at the hospital to make sure mother and child had made it okay, but they were outside in the waiting room, not standing by her side as Cain would have been.

Four Years Earlier at a Maternity Ward in Wisconsin

"One more big push, Emma, and we're done," the doctor coached as one of the nurses mopped her forehead.

It was a relief to finally be in labor after what seemed like more than nine months of misery. This time around she had no Cain to rub her tired back or to grimace in sympathy through the worst of the morning sickness. This time she saw only her mother's disgusted face, which grew worse in direct proportion to the expansion of Emma's waistline.

She screamed as a powerful contraction hit her, and she half sat up and pushed. She felt the baby slip out and heard the lusty cry a few moments later. Then she sobbed from the happiness of hearing the baby roar and the doctor say, "It's a girl."

Hannah Marie Casey was placed in her arms just long enough for Emma to know any chance of forgetting Cain was futile. Her first clue was a full head of black hair matted down from the mess that still covered the baby. Later, when she breast-fed for the first time, the innocent blue eyes that opened served to complete the picture. She had given birth to another Casey, and she had to keep it from the one person who would have rejoiced in the knowledge of her existence. Billy Casey might have provided the means for her conception, but Hannah was Cain all over again. Not only in looks but in spirit.

"It's just you and me, baby girl. Let me tell you about your family." Emma started talking to Hannah about her rich heritage, just like Cain had done for Hayden after his birth.

Rousing herself from her reverie about Hannah's birth, Emma murmured, "I'm sorry, Cain. I'm so sorry." She watched the dust settle after the departing vehicle roared away. Kyle had lied, and she couldn't begin to understand why.

CHAPTER TWENTY

Y ou want to talk about it?" Cain sat in the backseat with Hayden
in the Tahoe Mook had rented, and the others followed close
behind.

Hayden watched the scenery they drove past in silence, much
like he had done on the day they had arrived. Being strong now meant
keeping his mouth shut. He knew that was what Cain would have done,
so he shook his head. His questions could wait.

"It's all right, Hayden. Go on and ask if you want to."

"I can wait, Mom."

"Maybe this time I don't want to wait."

"Why?"

To most, the question would have been too broad-based, but Cain
understood it immediately. "Because Danny was a cruel son of a bitch,
and I made the mistake of underestimating him. That's the most succinct
answer I can think of."

"But why?"

Cain put her hands on her thighs and slid them down to her knees
and sighed. "You have to understand how much I loved your mother.
From the first day she came into my life, she set herself apart from
every other woman I'd known. Why? Because she asked me, that's
why. Letting Danny go wasn't going to impact the business or, more
importantly, my family, so I let him go."

Hayden was surprised Cain mentioned Emma and love in the same
sentence after all the woman had put them through, but she was always
full of surprises. "But it did."

"Boy, did it. Danny was such a pissant, I didn't keep tabs on him for too long. I just figured he'd end up on some street corner selling dime bags until the cops got ahold of him. I thought I'd hear from him again when Uncle Robert phoned, begging me to get his son out of trouble, because with Danny it was just a matter of time."

"Does he ever ask about Danny?"

"Who, our esteemed Uncle Robert?"

Hayden nodded. He had heard stories of how his grandfather Dalton and his family felt about the Baxters. They had only one redeeming grace and miracle, and Dalton had married her. All of Therese's brothers were varying degrees of losers, but losers nonetheless.

"I think Uncle Robert knows better."

Three Hours after Marie Casey's Death, at the Morgue

The room looked so sterile and plain. When Cain surveyed it, she grimly thought how strange and funny it was, in a nonhumorous kind of way. What did it matter now if it was sterile? The people here were dead. What did they have to fear from a mundane thing like infection? The living had to contend with that, and their guilt.

She could hear the low voices of her guards outside, one of them saying to keep it down. "The boss is in there alone paying her respects."

But she wasn't alone. Marie was with her. Cain had moved the sheet enough to see her face and hold her hand. As she caressed it, she noticed not how cold it was, but that her sister had more than one broken finger. Why hadn't she broken Danny before he smashed Marie like a china doll? She would have a hard time ever forgiving herself.

Most people would have considered a child like Marie a burden. Cain only thought now about how her days would forever be a little more empty without Marie's laughter in their house. Taking care of her had been a pleasure and honor, never a burden.

"Boss?" Merrick stood silently just inside the room, shadowing Cain, oozing compassion.

"Is he here?" she asked, turning her head a little toward the door.

"He's outside, but we can do this later if you want."

"Send him in, Merrick. Really, it's okay."

The small man was pushed into the room, stumbling a little from the alcohol in his system and the fear of not knowing why he was there. "Cain?"

"Uncle Robert, thank you for coming."

When a bunch of guys show up at your house and physically pick you up and throw you into the car, it's kinda hard to say no. Robert wasn't going to say the thought out loud, and he wasn't about to complain until he knew what was going on. He looked at his niece hunched over the sheet-draped gurney and wondered who the lifeless body belonged to.

"Why am I here?" Since Robert wasn't used to being subjected to the Casey muscle, he decided a direct approach might be best. This family respected guts and power, so he was desperate to hide his fear.

"Where's Danny?"

Behind Cain's back Robert pointed his index finger at her and tried to sound authoritarian. "Leave him alone, Cain. He made a mistake with you, I'll give you that, but he's doing good now. You tossed him out and gave him a good ass-whupping. He's not bothering you."

With a final pat on the top of Marie's mangled hand, Cain tucked it back to her sister's side and covered it. She must have tried to fight back the best way she knew how to get so many wounds. The cigarette burns so close to her nipples and scattered around her abdomen, though, had been hard to ignore. Cain realized Danny had probably used them to subdue Marie and get her to comply. *I should have killed him right after he touched Emma.*

"I didn't ask *how* he was, I asked *where* he was. Where is he?"

Robert raised his voice and tried to keep his courage up, but it was getting more difficult since he was so desperate for a drink that he was about to sell out anyone. "Come on, Cain. What's my boy ever done to you but try to have a little fun with a bitch who left you anyway?"

He started to shake and sweat when she took her jacket off and rolled up her sleeves.

The hospital workers who came running down the hall when they heard the scream emanating from the morgue just as quickly turned away when the five people by the door reached under their jackets and shook their heads.

Inside, Robert was reeling from the sudden pain to the side of his head where Cain had punched him, but he wasn't on his knees long before she grabbed a fistful of oily hair and yanked him to a standing position. With the same force she pulled him to the gurney.

"Look at her and tell me what you see."

The face was so battered Robert barely recognized his other niece lying there, and he fought a wave of nausea when he figured out why Cain wanted Danny. "Oh my God."

"No, God had nothing to do with this, so tell me where I can find your bastard son. Because, believe me, uncle, if I have to beat it out of you…" She stopped, not needing to finish the threat. "In the mood I'm in now, I may rid myself of the whole more troubling side of my family."

"Danny couldn't have done this."

"The idiot left a note pinned to what was left of her dress, so tell me where I can find him. I know he keeps you in booze and cigarettes, so you have to know."

The sniveling man tried to look up at Cain, causing her to tighten her hold on his hair. "What happens to me if you kill Danny?"

"You get to live, which is more than generous on my part. After all, much of what Danny turned out to be came from his upbringing. Be grateful he hasn't brought a plague on the rest of your house with this atrocity. Not yet anyway."

"I don't know where he is. Honest, Cain." A punch to the kidneys made him regret the lie, and this time she left him on the floor.

"I tried to do this the easy way. Remember that."

It looked like the worst of it was over and she was leaving. "What does that mean?"

"It means you stand with Danny on this one but, more importantly, against me. Go home and wait for your son and Giovanni Bracato to protect you. In your moments of lucidity, pray I'm kinder than this when I strike back and that I make it quick, but this is hard to ignore." She waved a hand toward the gurney.

"He's my son, for God's sake."

The slap to his face was so hard it knocked him into a table stacked with surgical supplies, and when he put his hand up to cover the sting, it came away with blood.

"You can live the rest of your life not reminding me of that fact."

"You stay away from my family, Cain."

"Just like yours stayed away from me and mine? Don't threaten me, you useless piece of crap. I guess the old saying 'the apple doesn't fall far from the tree' isn't just bullshit, now is it? Don't worry, though. I'm on my way home to fire up the chainsaw. Baxter trees from your orchard won't be a problem for much longer. Danny might have thrown the first punch, but you should know me by now. When I'm done there won't be a Baxter left standing. I don't give a fuck if you're my family or not."

"You can't do that." He tried to wipe off some of the drool and blood that oozed down his chin.

Cain grabbed him by the hair again and dragged him back to the gurney. With one flick of her wrist she pulled the sheet back and showed him all the damage Danny had done. "She didn't deserve this, or to be related to the human garbage you've inflicted on the world."

Robert gave her an address and dropped to his knees with his hands covering his face. Even if Cain left the rest of them alone, the memory of Marie's marred skin would sear his brain forever.

"I don't think Robert will ever invoke the name Danny Baxter in our presence again."

The boy nodded and gazed back out toward the farmland they were leaving behind at a fairly quick pace. "How can you forgive Emma?"

Cain picked a piece of lint off her coat as a way to delay her answer. The truth was love. Her love for Emma had blinded her to her responsibilities, a mistake she'd never make again. "I've lived with this memory from the moment I found Marie near our house and, trust me, blaming your mother was the last thing on my mind. I'm the head of the Casey family—me, not your mother. I blame myself every day for what happened. I don't need to forgive her."

Hayden turned in the seat until he was fully facing Cain. "Then maybe it's time you learn to forgive yourself and think about the good things you did while Aunt Marie was alive. Maybe you didn't give her enough credit, Mom."

"What do you mean by that? I loved her."

"I know you loved her, but you did so much more. All you had to do was give her a home and keep her safe, but you went way beyond that, didn't you? She told me you took her to a movie once, even though you didn't want to go. One of those old ones playing at the Prytania. She remembered how much fun she had going out to dinner and then that movie. She even told me how you took her over to the pub after the show and got her as many Shirley Temples as she wanted."

"Yeah, I remember that night. Marie always liked the pomp and circumstance that came from the idea of dating. She just didn't understand it was supposed to involve someone you loved or were interested in, not your sister."

Hayden laughed, remembering the stars in his aunt's eyes when she told him about the night. "But you did love her, and doing stuff like that for her only proved it. So what if she didn't know the rest. You were her hero, Mom. She said in the movie the character died at the end, but she told her husband that love meant never having to say you're sorry."

"*Love Story* is what she was talking about. That's the closest I've ever come to crying in a public place over something so, I don't know, trivial. We ended up going back the next night and seeing the damn thing again."

Reaching over, Hayden covered his mother's hands with his own. "Aunt Marie told me one day my mom would come back and we could be a family, but I had to remember Emma loved me, so she didn't have to say she was sorry for leaving. She didn't want me to be mad when she *did* come back."

"Your aunt was smarter than she let on. Hayden, I don't want to make this decision for you. Whatever relationship you want to have with your mother will be fine with me. Don't put my feelings first this time. It wouldn't be fair to you."

"I promise to do that, if you promise to stop blaming yourself for what happened to Marie. Danny did it, Mom—not you. Whatever his reasons were, they were all about him. You gave Aunt Marie a life she loved and enjoyed. It isn't your fault it was too short."

"You're growing up to be as wise as she was. Thanks, Hayden. Your saying all that means the world to me."

Cain stayed silent about Hannah, not wanting to add to the emotions of the day. She often had to put business first, and that necessary callousness probably added to Emma's decision to leave. But sometimes she couldn't ignore her responsibilities, no matter how much she wanted to.

She just hoped they weren't making her incapable of the type of love she had given to and received from Emma. Though that love had caused her to make one of the biggest mistakes of her life, it had also given her one of her life's greatest joys—Hayden.

❖

"Come on in the house, Emma. You're going to freeze out here if you stay any longer." Ross put his hand on her shoulder. "Why don't you go get cleaned up, and we'll run over and pick up the butterbean?"

"I'll get her in the morning, Daddy. Thanks anyway." Emma didn't move and wanted more than anything for some higher power to give her one wish. If she got it, Cain and Hayden would drive back up so she could make things right with them.

"Maybe she'll be just the thing you need to cheer you up."

A door slammed in the distance, and several cars pulled in. Kyle had changed and was ready to catch the plane waiting for him and his team at the small airport sixty miles away. He wanted to be in New Orleans before Cain so he could start planning. "Thank you all for your help. With what we got, we'll be able to nail Casey to the proverbial wall."

"Get off my land."

"Come on, Ross. You're making out all right here. I see you started using the line of credit we set up for you." Kyle pointed to the barn, talking about the feed he'd witnessed Cain and Hayden help stack up.

"I don't think you heard me. Get off my land now. And for the record, as you're so fond of saying, Agent, I didn't touch a fucking cent that belongs to the government."

"Hit the lotto, have you, Ross?"

Kyle sounded so condescending Emma wanted to slap him.

"Better. Cain and I became partners. The feed in there belongs to her, and she was nice enough to let me feed it to my cows. Now get out of here."

"As soon as we've packed the equipment." If Ross had become so chummy with Casey in the few days she was here, he would go down with her if he tipped her off to their presence. "Ross, I'm only going to ask you this once. Did you mention any of this operation to Casey?"

"No."

"Are you sure about that, old man?"

"No, I didn't mention any of you scum and what you were here for."

"Good. Keep it that way, or you'll find your own name on one of those indictments I'll be getting in the next few weeks."

What you should have asked, Agent Butthead, was if she mentioned your being here. Then I would've had to say yes, maybe. Ross laughed a little as he helped Emma to her feet and moved her into the house. He watched from the window as the agents carried monitor after monitor and other weird-looking equipment out of his barn. If only Kyle would take his head out of his ass and use it, he would have wondered about how easily the end had come after such a long road of trying, thought Ross. No way would he feel sorry for whatever happened to the man.

"Daddy, I don't know what to do now."

"Emma, I'm your father and I love you, but we've had this talk. I didn't agree with all this, and I was the only one in the house who thought about what could go screwy with this plan. I'm not going to sit here now and tell you what you did was wrong. The nights you sit up wishing you could take it all back will take care of that. You'd better start thinking about your next move, though. Hiding here listening to the wind and your mother isn't going to take you back to where you obviously want to be."

Carol wiped her hands on the dish towel as she stood right outside the door and couldn't believe her husband. "What are you trying to do, Ross?"

"I'm not blind, Carol. I could see the way Emma looked at the woman while she was here. You pulled her back here with all your holier-than-thou speeches, making her feel guilty about every one of the choices she's made in her life, and she's been miserable. Cain deserves to know about Hannah." He turned to Emma. "And if you leave now, it might not be too late."

"You run again, Emma, and don't come back here if she throws your worthless hide out this time. You can go back to that spawn if you want, but you aren't taking Hannah with you." Carol grabbed Emma by the arm. As a mother she had been cursed with Emma, but she saw another chance with Hannah.

"She's my daughter, Mother. Try and remember that. If I go back, do you think for one minute I'm leaving her here with you? You need intense psychiatric help if you think I'd give you the chance to make my little girl feel bad about who she is and where she comes from. That pleasure on your part will end with me. Hannah deserves to be happy, so if that means me letting her live with Cain and Hayden, that's what I'm going to do. You'll never get the opportunity to poison her mind with that garbage you call religion."

Carol turned around and raised her fist toward her husband. "You, this is your fault. Soft, you said when Emma was growing up. We shouldn't be so hard on her, you said. Well, this is what happens when you're soft with your children. They get taken by the first devil to come along. And did I hear you say you took money from that woman?"

"Shut up, Carol. This is Emma's life, not yours. You can't ruin someone else's life by stealing their chance to be happy. She's our daughter. She deserves better than your hate and constant judgment."

The fist opened, and Ross felt his head fly back from the force of the blow. "I want you to get out."

He put his hand over the heat on the right side of his face. "No, Carol. One of us is leaving, but it won't be me. You go home and see if your brother and his wife will take you in. This place belonged to my family, and now it'll go to my grandson."

"Daddy, wait." Emma tried to keep him from going inside the barn until the agents had cleared the yard. If Cain turned around and did try to come back now, all of them would be sorry.

"I'll give you the money to fly to New Orleans if you want to, and I'll check on Hannah every day over at Maddie's while you're gone. If you don't, then there'll be no more tears and asking 'what if.' It'll be done."

Emma tried hard not to cry in front of her father again. "I don't know where to even begin, Daddy."

"At the beginning, Emma. You need to give Cain the same chance you gave her at the beginning of your relationship. Because somewhere along the way you forgot what she meant to you and your children. Look where your blind judgment of Cain has landed you. She has a lot to atone for when it comes to you, but you aren't without blame. She stole Hayden from you, but what you've done with Hannah, that's not right either."

"I'll try, Daddy."

"That's all you can do."

CHAPTER TWENTY-ONE

The folks at the pub are going to get jealous." Merrick sat next to Cain as the driver took them to Emerald's, Cain's other nightclub, for the fifth night in a row. They were meeting with some of the players in the deal Cain had going and, much to her discomfort, they had left all their electronic playthings at home. Cain didn't seem to be too concerned as to who else was listening in on all these very public meetings.

"What are you, my agent?"

"No, darlin', just the eyes in the back of your head," she joked as the car rolled to a stop and the doorman bent to open the back door. Tonight was business, so she took her post behind Cain, scanning the crowd waiting outside for any familiar faces. Cain was more than capable of taking care of any threat that came from the front.

Cain stopped toward the head of the line and stared at a woman standing with two men, waiting to get in. She couldn't believe she had the guts to show up here, and with company, no less. Time to put her reputation to work and get a date for the evening.

"Morris, let the lady and her friends in." She pointed to the group. "They're with me."

"Thanks. I thought we'd have to stand there all night. Who's that?" the blonde asked the bouncer, referring to Cain.

"The name is Cain, and it's a popular club, miss," she whispered in the woman's ear as they made their way to the door. "People can't wait to take a walk with the devil, even if it's just for the night."

"I've heard it can be quite unforgettable if you let yourself go." Shelby tried to keep it clean since the small evening bag she was carrying had a powerful receiver.

"Can I interest you in a drink?"

"It's the least I can do since you were so kind to get me out of that line." Shelby wrapped her hand around Cain's bicep and trusted her two work companions to keep up.

In the van parked a half a block away, three other agents listened to the conversation, not surprised Shelby had been noticed right away. She looked hot in the dress she'd chosen for the night's assignment. Surprisingly, Casey had done the picking up.

"Just like a bitch in heat," Kyle commented as the technicians adjusted the device in Shelby's purse to drop out as much background noise as possible. They could easily hear the conversation over the loud dance music. "What an idiot. She didn't learn her lesson from the first blonde who burned her ass."

"What will you have?" Cain asked Shelby at the end of the bar, sending the staff into action. The bartender walked from the other end to reach Cain, ignoring the angry customers who were screaming that they were there first. "A mojito, perhaps?"

"Doesn't that mean 'little wet one'?"

"Well, I'd suggest something else, but I don't know of a drink that connotes staying dry." Cain's joke referred to what had almost happened a week before on Vincent's plane.

"How about just a club soda, since I'm not much of a drinker?"

"You heard the lady, Charlie. Club sodas all around." Cain could see her guest, Vinny Carlotti, had arrived and was being escorted to her private table. Vinny's entourage was shaking hands with her people. "Would you like to join me for a bit?"

Shelby was shocked Cain would even suggest it. She had tried unsuccessfully to get a transfer to another division since the night she'd met Cain. Her hostess had to know she was carrying some sort of listening device, but she didn't seem to care.

"I'm just here for the music."

Kyle almost blew the top off the van when Shelby gave that answer. To have Casey invite her into the inner sanctum of whatever was going on wasn't an opportunity that came along too often.

"Trust me. You can hear it from over there." Cain pointed to her table.

"If you're sure."

"What's your name, darlin'?"

"Shelby Phillips, and yours?"

"Like I said, why don't you just call me Cain? Come on. Charlie will bring those drinks over to us."

Shelby took the offered hand, and Merrick cut a path through the dancers for them as they made their way to the other side of the club.

The two other agents she had arrived with sat at the bar and kept an eye out in case Shelby needed them to intervene.

"Shelby, I want you to meet Vinny Carlotti. Vinny, this is my new friend Shelby."

"Shelby and I have met."

Cain arched a brow, wanting him to say from where.

"She works for my father, part time, I believe." Vinny got up and shook hands with her before she took a seat next to Cain.

The agent didn't knock Cain's hand off when it came to rest on her knee and hoped her notorious friend knew what she was doing.

"Have you made all the appropriate arrangements?" Cain asked Vinny, liking the feel of the skin under her fingers.

"We're all set to move for next week. My men will be there to help divide the shipment once you take control of it. Once it's ready we'll send it out from there. Dad added another truckload of cigarettes since some of the vendors we deal with on the Gulf Coast were interested. Overall we stand to make over five million apiece, if everything goes according to plan."

"Good. We'll be getting the warehouses ready to move the stuff out the same night we get it. I don't want to be sitting on this much merchandise for too long and get my ass popped for it." Cain shook hands with her old friend and made sure he and his party were taken care of for the rest of the night if they chose to stay.

"Want to join me in the office for a more intimate drink?" she offered Shelby.

"If she says no to this, I swear I'll have her ass transferred to the most disgusting place I can think of," Kyle said to the others in the van. He had already called the group assigned to Vincent Carlotti and informed them of the new alliance with Casey.

"Sure." Shelby followed a little behind Cain, enjoying the way the black slacks and black turtleneck Cain was wearing looked on her.

"I'm sorry, ma'am, but Cain doesn't allow anyone to carry anything in with them. If you'd like, you can leave your purse with me, and I promise I'll keep an eye on it." The big man standing at the front door of the office held his hand out and waited to see if the agent would comply. If he had to call Cain back out, it might look like he couldn't handle the situation.

"It's just a purse."

"And it's just her rules. Her club, her rules, that's the way it works. If you like I can go in and tell her you've changed your mind about joining her."

Shelby handed over the purse, knowing it was her last link to her backup. Not that she worried Cain was going to harm her, but Cain had made it clear it wouldn't be a good idea for her to keep up her surveillance. She noticed the two men move from the bar to get closer to the office, but they weren't able to get too close with the number of personnel Cain had between them and the door. To move in now would blow her cover not only with Cain, but also with Vincent. She hoped for the best and handed over the purse.

The office was a large space with only a bar, a desk, and a sofa that overlooked the crowd through what she assumed was a two-way mirror. Soft, low lighting made it feel warmer than it was, considering the sparse furnishings, but she could still see Cain clearly as she stood at the bar and poured two glasses of amber liquid.

"Irish whiskey," she informed Shelby when she handed over the glass before walking over and sitting on the sofa. "Come over here. I'm not going to bite. Unless…" Cain was obviously referring to any other wires Shelby might be sporting.

"Don't worry. Agent Kyle is most probably having puppies by now since my purse has left my person."

"I'm glad to see you again, but to tell you the truth, I'm surprised you're here." Cain drained the glass and sat it on the floor by her feet. Eventually she would have to finish furnishing the space to make it more functional, but it hadn't been a priority. She only came to the club when business demanded it or when she was in the mood for the rare evening out on the dance floor.

"I'd have put in another request for transfer this week, believe me, but any more of them and it would've started to look suspicious. I thought a few weeks of me coming up empty would do the trick, but you go and get all chatty on me. It's going to be hard to get rid of me now. Why did you do that? Was it a test or something?" Shelby took a seat and left a little room between them. Cain looked criminally good tonight, instead of just criminal.

"Maybe it was my way of helping you get that medal we talked about."

She slid closer and reached out for Cain's hand. "I appreciate what you did for me, Cain, but we agreed I have a job to do, and I'm not going to shirk my responsibilities even though you know who I am. You had to realize I was wired."

"I told you before, I'm not going to sell you out, and you've upheld your end of our deal, I would imagine."

She nodded. She had gone against everything she had been taught and believed when she omitted the truth of their flight. Cain had been right. No one from the Bureau had even known she was gone, so it was more of a lie of omission than anything more sinister. Either way, if Cain turned out to be less than honorable, Shelby's lie could come back to haunt her eventually. Pacts with the devil usually didn't come cheap.

"I gave you my word, Cain."

"Then that's good enough for me, and once this is all over, I'll see what I can do to help you get that transfer."

She tugged Cain's hand into her lap and ran her fingertip along the back of it, trying to find a way to say what was on her mind. "Not that I don't appreciate your help. After all, you saved my life, but please don't make any calls on my behalf."

The low, mirth-filled laugh made her relax, assuring her she hadn't insulted Cain. "I'm thinking more along the lines of your superiors being so impressed with your job performance they'll move you further along, than of me picking up the phone. As surprised as I was to see you tonight, I'm glad you're still around. Think you can lose your shadows tomorrow night and meet me for dinner?"

"I'd love to, but only if it's dinner. You fascinate me, that's true, but commitment is important to me, and even if you'd be willing to offer me that, I can't."

"My loss, then, but this is business. I trust you, Shelby, and I trust you to do the right thing with the information I'm going to give you." Cain turned her hand in Shelby's lap palm up so she would take it. It was sad in a way that they could never be more than friends. She liked the agent, and while Cain would never allow another woman into her heart, she would always welcome women like Shelby into her bed. "Are you ready? I don't need the feds organizing a raid because they think I'm in here having my way with you."

Shelby had played out the kiss they'd shared on the plane in her dreams more than once in the past week, and having the real thing so close proved to be too tempting. She moved so that she was almost in Cain's lap and pulled the dark head down so she could reach the full lips that had felt so good before.

Cain opened her mouth and invited Shelby in as she put her hands on the agent's hips and willed them not to wander. The door opening behind them broke them apart.

"Yes, Merrick?" She rubbed the side of Shelby's mouth with the pad of her thumb. She didn't need to turn around to confirm who it was. Merrick was the only one with the authority to open the door without knocking.

"The young woman's companions were wondering how long she'd be."

"Have Charlie pour them a drink on the house and tell them we'll be out in a minute, thank you."

The soft click left them in their quiet cocoon once again. Shelby figured the walls were extremely padded because of how quickly the music died away when Merrick closed the door.

"The last time I understood your actions, but tonight I'm at a bit of a loss," said Cain.

"Last time it was because I was grateful. Tonight it's just about wanting to. My life's so ordered that it's fun to put that aside for just one kiss and be happy in the moment."

Cain slowly kissed her again, coaxing Shelby's tongue to meet hers.

Shelby moaned at the contact, finding Cain's erotic pull impossible to resist. Perhaps it was the dangerous way she lived her life, or the way her hands felt as they ran along the fabric of her dress until one came to rest at the underside of her breast. Whatever the reason, Cain wove a spell that was hard to just walk away from, but that was what she had to force herself to do.

"There's a private bath behind the second door if you want to freshen up before we rejoin the party," Cain offered.

Shelby pressed her lips to Cain's cheek before she got up with a long sigh.

The man posted at the door handed her purse back with a wicked smile when she stepped out on Cain's arm. Per his boss's request, he had spent his time waiting for them to finish their meeting by singing along with whatever song the DJ was playing. Shelby would owe Kyle some aspirin when the night was done.

"How about a dance since you won't sleep with me?"

Shelby's face felt hot as she imagined the teasing she'd get later over the question. But she was also grateful to Cain for asking. A reputation for sleeping with the enemy was not something she wanted to add to her resume.

"Just one, then I'll have to call it a night." She waved to Special Agent Joe Simmons on her way to the dance floor with Cain, then stopped to hand her purse to Special Agent Anthony Curtis. Vinny was standing at the bar near them talking to Merrick, so it was the best place for it at the moment.

One dance turned into three before Cain signaled the DJ to slow things down, if just for one song. With Shelby this close, she took the opportunity to talk to her one more time. "You do realize why Kyle assigned you lead agent tonight, don't you?"

"The guys wouldn't have gotten this close?"

"There's that, and they aren't blond."

Shelby laughed and thought about what the outcome might have been had Cain not had such excellent information on who her watchers were. Would the untouchable Casey's Achilles's heel be a pair of pretty eyes and soft breasts? She hoped not, since it would be rather petty.

"Time for us to retreat back to our corners, Agent." Cain kissed the top of her head and walked her to the bar.

Merrick was waiting with Cain's coat and had already called for the car. In only two days all hell would break loose, and Cain wanted to go home and spend time with Hayden. If she went to bed soon, getting up for an early run wouldn't be so bad.

Kyle watched the car pull away, with a tail not too far behind. All he needed now was a definite time for what was going down. They had already worked out the logistics of mounting a raid. Until he had that information, he wasn't letting Casey out of their sight. He could almost taste the big payoff he'd get by bringing her down.

The two agents in the van didn't mind stepping out while their boss made a call. Being stuck in the cramped space with him for such a long period of time almost qualified them for hazard pay. Next time they would try a different approach on Joe and Anthony to get them to take the post with the boss.

"This is Kyle, put him on." He could hear a television blaring in the background before someone muted it and the person he'd called for came on the line.

"When?"

"I imagine sometime this week. Casey's been to every pay phone in the city, thinking it would make a difference. Then she had a meeting with Carlotti's kid tonight. With any luck I can catch two big fish with one cast."

"You do that, and I'll make it worth your while." With that, the line went dead.

CHAPTER TWENTY-TWO

The flight attendant gave final instructions for landing, and the grumbling, sleepy passengers complied, bringing their seats forward and refastening their seat belts. Emma scanned the familiar marsh surrounding New Orleans and prayed for the best. She planned to confront Cain with the truth and hoped her ex wouldn't add her to the marsh's treasures as a food source.

Her father, stern but supportive when he delivered his pep talk on the way to the airport, had been confident Cain would accept the news of Hannah with nothing short of happiness. No one who treated one child with such caring could reject an innocent who was part of her.

"For the rest, Em, you'll have to be patient. She loves you. Her heart knows that, but it'll just take some convincing to get her head to agree."

"If only it were that simple, Daddy."

"There's nothing simple about this, and you'll need to deal with your son as well as Cain. Hayden isn't going to let you into his good graces when he finds out. You have to commit yourself to not giving up."

"Having you think I can do it makes me feel better."

"You're a parent, Em, like me. No matter what, you love your children and have to fight for their happiness. Hayden is missing what you can bring into his life, and our Hannah's being cheated out of what Cain can add to hers. The most important thing missing here, though, is the completeness only you and Cain can bring each other."

"How'd you get to be such a fount of wisdom living out there on that farm?" Emma reached over and squeezed her father's arm with a smile, to let him know she was teasing.

"I watch *Oprah* when you aren't looking."

After her luggage finally appeared on the conveyer belt, she arranged for a cab to take her to her first destination. If her luck held, this course of action would be as successful as the first time she tried it. Of the very few avenues available to get to Cain, her uncle Jarvis was the only one she was sure wouldn't just toss her out at first glance.

The kindly older gentleman had always gone out of his way to make her feel like a member of the Casey clan. One of his niece's most trusted advisors, he was one of the only people in the city not afraid to rail against Cain's famous temper. She usually accepted his gentle rebukes because she knew Jarvis thought only of her best interests and those of the family.

Jarvis stepped to the front room of his house and hugged the woman whom he had come to love, regardless of how Cain felt. "Clara, please put Emma's bag in one of the guest rooms upstairs. What brings you back so soon, child?"

"I come asking forgiveness again, Uncle Jarvis."

"Of Hayden? Surely your visit didn't go that poorly?"

"No, of Cain this time. I'm not forgetting Hayden, but I've done something that hurt Cain more than anyone."

Jarvis sighed and waved to one of the chairs. If what she said was true, he could do only so much for her. "Emma, I never asked Cain what made you leave so suddenly, and I'm not asking you now, but you've got to realize what's happened since you've been gone. Cain isn't the same person you knew four years ago, and Hayden, he's completely different. Cain is, and always has been, strong and proud. What you did, or your reaction to something she did, ripped holes in the very essence of who she is."

"Don't you think I sit up nights thinking about that? That I miss her more than I can stand before I'm a teary mess again?"

He put up a big hand to silence her. "I didn't say all that because I think you insincere, Emma. You and I will come to an understanding today, or else I'll drive you to the airport myself and wash my hands of you."

"Just ask and I'll do it."

"It isn't that simple, lass. My brother and I had the good fortune to find and marry women who loved us with a fierce devotion." The more passionate he got, the more his brogue slipped into his conversation.

"They loved us and were able to turn a blind eye when the situation warranted it, because they knew what loving us meant. What acceptance they had to bring to their commitment of marrying a Casey."

"You think I'm not capable of that?"

"I've lived this long and enjoyed the fruits of my work too many years by not reading too much into any given situation. To survive, I accept only what's there. And I've seen you running away from your spouse and your son. Add to that not one phone call to check if they're doing well or if they need you. So no, I don't think you're capable of that kind of commitment."

His honesty stung, but she couldn't come into his house and argue with him over the truth as it had played out so far. "You have my word, Uncle Jarvis. Get me one more chance, and I'll never give you reason to doubt the depth of my commitment. Four years is a long time to learn a lesson, but I belong with Cain, and I'll die by her side."

"I took a chance on you already, Emma, and it cost me a little of Cain's respect. If I do what you're asking and you renege on your word, I'll lose my place with my niece. If that happens, Cain will be the least of your worries."

She knelt in front of his chair, put her hands over his, and gazed steadily into his eyes. "I give you my word as a Casey."

❖

"I'm sure it *is* important, Uncle Jarvis. I just can't tonight." As Cain put her shoes on, she paused to listen to him ask again. "No, it's not a hot date. I'll call you tomorrow, I promise, but tonight I'm meeting someone to go over something important. If I could reschedule it I would, but I'll have to ask your cooperation and flexibility on this one."

"I have your word you'll make time for me tomorrow?"

"You got it, and thank you for understanding. The way we left things the last time we talked has been bothering me, so I'll look forward to tomorrow." She hung up and hoped Shelby had been able to get the night off.

Jarvis tapped the receiver against his chin and closed his eyes. *Oh boy, she feels bad for screaming at me. Somehow I'm thinking she's going to forget her remorse really fast when I show up bearing gifts of small blondes again.* He heard Emma behind him, waiting to hear the verdict. "Tomorrow will have to be soon enough. She had dinner plans that she couldn't change."

"I'm not too late, am I?"

"Like I said earlier, Emma, four years is a long time. But if it makes you feel better, Cain hasn't had any encounters I've been able to confirm. With her reputation that's hard to imagine, but I don't think anyone's standing in your way. No one, that is, but yourself."

The thought of someone else pressing her naked skin to Cain's sent a swift pain through Emma's heart that just as quickly turned to anger. It was irrational to expect Cain to abstain until she came to her senses, but that was what she had done. As for Emma, no one else had remotely come close to engaging her in a long conversation, much less making her share herself in such an intimate way.

❖

The object of Emma's jealousy walked into an office supply store, sure that no one had followed her. What luck for the award-winning Emeril's Restaurant to share a wall with such a mundane business. The aisle with the pens and office paper was just where Cain said it would be, and at the end was a door. Shelby knocked and stepped back a little when Merrick opened it outward.

"Welcome, Agent Daniels."

She frowned when the woman called her by name. Cain had promised not to share it with anyone.

"I'm the only one here, and I'm the only one aside from Vincent's men who knows your name, ma'am, so don't look so worried. If you're ready, Cain's waiting."

Cain was seated in a beautiful private room waiting for her. As always she looked incredible in the custom suit she was wearing, and Shelby was glad she had put a lot of thought into choosing her own outfit.

Cain stood up and nodded to Merrick, who went to wait in the office of the business next door.

"Welcome, Shelby. I hope you're hungry and curious."

"You're just full of surprises, aren't you? If you ever decide to leave your life of crime, you can write a book on interesting tidbits in New Orleans."

"I would, but I hear a life on the straight-and-narrow path really doesn't pay," Cain joked back as she moved forward to kiss the agent hello.

"Isn't it a life of crime doesn't pay?"

"Bite your tongue, Agent Daniels."

"I'd rather you do that." She blushed. "I can't believe I said that. I really do need to stay away from you before you convince me bank robbery might be a good hobby."

Cain laughed and lowered her head. Since Shelby hadn't hesitated about her method of greeting, Cain lingered a moment longer and enjoyed it. "Why don't you try a curried shrimp, and I'll pour you a glass of wine?" Cain pulled Shelby's chair out for her and tried to squelch her libido.

"This is very nice. Thanks for asking me."

"My pleasure. Maybe after your big promotion you'll be the one to treat me to dinner."

"And why am I going to be getting a big promotion?" Shelby tapped her glass against the one Cain held over the center of the table and smiled at her before taking a sip.

In lieu of an answer Cain passed her a large file and sat back to enjoy her appetizer.

Twenty minutes later a waiter appeared with the next course, noticeably upset when he found Shelby's plate untouched and papers spread out around her chair.

"Leave it, Julian. I'll cut it up and feed it to her in small pieces so she won't choke while she's reading."

"Another twenty minutes or so before the soup, Ms. Casey?"

"That sounds about right. Why don't you bring that with a straw?" Cain teased.

Shelby finally looked up, an expression of total shock marring her features. "I'm sorry for zoning out like that, but there's no way this is true."

"Why wouldn't it be? Just because I gathered the information, it's bogus because it suits my interests?"

"No, Cain, because of what it implies. This is a serious allegation against someone who up to now has been beyond reproach."

Cain lifted a shrimp off Shelby's plate and held it up for her to take a bite. "I'm a Casey, Shelby, which makes me a bad guy in the eyes of the law. What you just finished reading doesn't make him any different from me because of who he works for. I asked you for a favor—for you to do your job. You have the rest of tonight and most of tomorrow to do it. Verify the information and then make your decision. That's all I ask. Forget now that you owe me your life. Your being here tonight has paid your debt. As your friend I'm asking you to do this. If you refuse, I still have options, but I wanted to give you first shot."

"Can I get some help from some of the other agents?"

"If you trust someone else, then knock yourself out."

"Cain, would you be terribly offended if I skipped the rest of dinner?"

"Eat one more shrimp to make Julian happy. Then get out of here."

Shelby ate the shrimp, gathered all the paperwork, and jumped up. She kissed Cain good-bye and was almost to the door before her benefactor stopped her.

"Is there room in your sensibilities for me to ask one more favor?"

"I'll owe you more than one favor if this checks out. What else do you want?"

"Tomorrow night is the one night your boss has been waiting for."

"Cain, it's not too late to call off whatever you've got planned."

"I don't want to call it off. I want this to finally come to a head, and I want you to be there. I'd like to live out the night, and with you there, I'll feel better that'll happen."

Shelby put her hand on Cain's cheek and nodded. "I'll be there. I promise no one will harm you."

"Thanks. Just one more thing. Do you want the video and audio tapes that go along with that file?"

"You have film to go along with all these pictures?"

Cain pointed to the box near the door.

"If you were a man, I'd have your baby, gangster or no."

Shelby kissed her and jumped a little when the door opened again and an acne-faced teenager from the office supply place waited to carry her box out for her. Cain had even thought to put it in a box from the place to make it look like a purchase.

"I'll keep that baby thing in mind, but it'll have to wait. You have work to do."

Merrick walked in, pulled the plate of salad in front of her, and accepted a glass of wine from Cain. "All done?"

"That should keep her and her friends busy for the next twenty-two hours or so. Anything more and it's just overkill, since we did most of the work."

"Are you sure about all this, Cain? I have the worst feeling."

"Merrick, nothing in life is a guarantee, but I promise you I've worked out all the angles. I'm through with playing by someone else's rules. I'm ready to take control of the game again." Cain lifted her glass and pressed her lips to the rim. The next question wouldn't come easy. "There's something I want to ask you. Actually it's something I want you to promise me."

"You know you don't ever have to ask me. Just tell me and I'll see it gets done."

She shook her head and reached across the table for Merrick's hand. "No, sweetheart, I want to hear you say it."

"What do you want?"

"If something should happen to me, I want you to take Hayden to Emma, and I want you to walk away. He'll have more than enough money, and I don't think anyone will go after him in Wisconsin."

"Honey, he's never going to agree to that. Maybe with your uncle Jarvis?"

"No, Merrick. Promise me you'll take him to Emma. I love Jarvis, but Emma's his mother. No one will fight harder to keep him whole than she will. He's young and maybe doesn't understand completely what's best for him, but if I'm no longer around, she's what's best for him. I'm counting on you to tell him that if I can't."

For one of the only times she could remember, Merrick's eyes filled with tears, which fell silently down her face.

"Please don't talk like that. I've never known you to plan something that didn't include survival ahead of everything else."

"I don't want to repeat the mistakes of my father and go without planning for all the possibilities. I loved Dalton with everything I was, and I've thought of all the 'what ifs' because he was taken from me so soon. I want better than that for Hayden. He needs a sense of himself other than what he is with me, and I think his mother is the best person to give him that. Trust me, sweetling. I don't ask this without biting back a whole bunch of feelings, but I have to do what's right for my son."

"I may have to tie him to the wing of the plane to get him there, but if that's what you want, that's what I'll do. Will you promise me something now, boss?"

"Anything."

"Promise me this is just one more cog in the wheel you're putting together and not a real possibility. Because if you're thinking like this, I'll tie you to a chair all day tomorrow and be damned with the consequences."

"There's no one you'll meet who adores life more than I do, Merrick. I put tomorrow together because I want to enjoy the years to come as much as possible. When this is all over, there's a girl I want you to meet."

Merrick lifted her brows in surprise. Having Cain mention anyone was cause for celebration. "The one who left just now?"

"No, I don't want to chance prison time every time I exchange pillow talk. This girl, she's special, and when you lay eyes on her you'll understand why."

Merrick lifted her glass and waited for Cain to do the same before she made her toast. "To life."

"And its infinite possibilities," Cain added, before she tapped her glass to Merrick's and took a sip.

CHAPTER TWENTY-THREE

The old chair creaked as Cain stared out the windows behind her desk at home. The branches of the bare trees in the yard swayed gently in the cold breeze. The sun hadn't shone all day, and the visibility on the docks that night would be extremely low. While she usually welcomed such a gift from Mother Nature, tonight it made her think of all the things that could go wrong because of all the people who would be watching.

"Cain?"

"Come in, Merrick." Her hand appeared from behind the chair and waved the trusted guard in.

"In a minute, boss. Your uncle's on line one for you."

She hesitated before she picked up the phone. She had honestly forgotten about Jarvis. Their last meeting had left her with enough bad feelings to make her ignore him, but he was family, which brought its own obligations, so she had to put her feelings aside. "Uncle Jarvis, I'm sorry about last night. I couldn't help it, though."

"I know you're busy, Cain. Think nothing of it. Could I talk you into stepping out for a cup of coffee with me?"

Something about the request made the hair on the back of her neck stand up. Jarvis usually just dropped by and dragged her away. When he asked, even so informally, he was usually up to something.

"How about the place close to the house? I'll meet you there in twenty minutes."

"Twenty minutes it is." Jarvis put the receiver down and faced the windows in his study. Emma had wrung her hands during the short conversation. He wondered if she realized how precarious a situation she had put him in. Cain was a special part of his life, one he would miss if this situation brought about his exile.

"Did she say yes?"

"Twenty minutes at the coffee shop near the house. Let me talk to her first. Then I'll send for you."

He knew she was about to protest. He heard the hitch of her breath as she told him she had come to see Cain, which was the only thing important to her.

"Cain has never struck a woman or me in anger. I don't want that streak to end today. Call it a selfish whim on both our parts."

"I trust you to do what's best, Uncle Jarvis. My fate is in your hands."

"As is mine in yours, little one."

❖

"Where do you suppose the mighty Cain Casey's going alone?" Kyle focused the binoculars in his hands and studied the way Cain's coat draped perfectly over her shoulders. He saw no guards, no Casey troops keeping watch as the crime boss strolled leisurely down the street looking like any other homeowner on her block. All she was missing was a big happy dog.

"Use another pay phone, perhaps?" The agent sitting with Kyle watched as well so that he could radio the next post to take up surveillance once she was too far away from them.

"Let's wait and see. Move it, Jones. We can circle the block and pick her up on St. Charles."

Cain heard the cable van start behind her, making her laugh when no cable guy emerged from her neighbor's house. *Maybe they just throw those nice new digital boxes on your front lawn now and let you fend for yourself.* She pulled the brim of her hat lower and glanced quickly down the street for their backup. She stopped at the sewer truck, thinking it was the most logical choice. It suited the way the government conducted its business concerning her family.

"Daniels, do the three of you see her?" Kyle's voice boomed though all their headsets.

Shelby, Joe, and Anthony popped their heads up from the vast amount of paperwork spread out in front of them and barely restrained themselves from answering, "Who, sir?"

"She just turned right on the avenue, sir. We've got her." Shelby scrutinized the tall woman like Kyle had, but with much different results. She wondered what it would feel like to have Cain wrap her up in that greatcoat. "She just stepped into the coffee shop. Her uncle's waiting at a table. Maybe it's just a social visit?"

"Jarvis Casey doesn't have a social bone in his body, Daniels. None of these Neanderthals do. Try to remember that. No, I'm guessing a last-minute advice session before our little escapades tonight." When Lionel Jones stopped short, Kyle lost his balance and almost smashed his head into the back door of the van. "Watch it, idiot."

"Sorry, sir." Lionel was praying the time would go faster so he could meet Shelby and the others before that night. After spending the day working with Kyle, he was ready to take a job as a security guard at an old folks' home if it meant never having to sit and listen to the pompous ass spout off about all the subjects he thought were interesting. The real action was happening in the other van, and he was missing it, though he was truly grateful to be one of the agents Shelby had confided in for the job none of their supervisors knew about.

❖

"Cain, thanks for coming."

"What brings you out on such a nasty day?"

Jarvis watched as Cain walked toward him, removing only her hat. He stood and hugged her. "Gloomy days are made to talk about love, don't you think?"

The server came over with the two espressos he had ordered, and Cain spooned some sugar into hers as she smiled and thought of the best comeback she could. "I've always thought gloomy days were made for making love."

"I remember," said a feminine voice.

The people in the coffee shop and outside it had two radically different reactions to Emma's comment.

"What in the holy fuck is she doing here?" Kyle screamed so loud they all yanked their headsets off. Even a woman riding her bike near the van stopped to see who had screamed the obscenity. "Get a mike trained in there now. God help her if that little farming bitch messes this up for me," he said. He had honestly thought when they pulled out of Ross's yard he had seen the last of the Verde family until they addressed the question of who got Hayden.

"I tell you, uncle, once is a moment of weakness for a pretty face from the past. Twice, though, is an act of stupidity, and that's not like you."

Jarvis's fingers, pinching the bridge of his nose, almost drew blood. Had the woman given him even five minutes, he could have ensured a much more successful outcome. "I told her to wait until we had a chance to talk." He raised his voice just enough to show his displeasure at having Emma go against his wishes.

"And you thought that would've made a difference?" Cain arched a brow at her uncle and watched the man actually blush. "What is it now, Emma? Come to make amends, have we?"

"Please, Cain, just listen to me. Once I'm done, if you tell me to go, I will, and I won't come back. There isn't enough forgiveness in the world for me, I know that, but I have to try and make this right."

"Shut up, Emma. I don't want to hear it. A pretty face and a pretty ass aren't going to work for you this time. Granted, the last time I fell for that was eleven years ago. My libido isn't what it used to be, so give it up. I gave you what you wanted, a chance with Hayden, and you blew it. He doesn't want to see you again, and I'm sure as hell not going to force him to do something he'd rather eat broken glass than do."

"I already knew that."

"Then why waste the airfare?" She turned a little in her chair to look at the woman who had not moved closer.

"To give you back what I stole from you."

Jarvis stood up so fast he knocked his chair over. "I didn't know she stole from you, Cain."

"Go home, Jarvis," she ordered the old man, not wanting to have more of a scene than they had already, given the other customers. She didn't need to complicate the operation that night.

"Come on, Emma."

"No, Emma's staying for a while," she said.

Her tone told her uncle to just walk out and not argue. Jarvis left without another word, hoping Emma would be all right.

"I just wanted—" said Emma, only to stop when a big hand went up.

She dropped back into her chair and exhaled so loudly the women two tables over could have heard her. "Come back for round two, have you?"

"Cain, please. I just want you to listen to me. That's all I want. I know I screwed up, but if I ever meant anything to you, I'm begging you to listen to me now." Emma stood with her hands out to her sides, her palms up.

"Don't you know you meant everything to me, and you threw it all away? That I opened myself up to you, and you ripped me to shreds without ever looking back? God, now you come back here and expect me to just forget all that?"

For the first time ever, Emma saw the weariness that seemed to cling to her partner. Cain looked almost defeated with her forehead resting on her palm, and Emma felt like someone was twisting a knife in her gut because she had made Cain feel that way.

"I love you, Cain. No time and no amount of distance between us is ever going to change that." She took a step closer, thinking that Cain's defenses were down enough so she wouldn't turn her away.

"What a joke that is. Love doesn't exist for me anymore, except when it comes to my son. The time and the distance, they changed everything between us, and nothing will ever make me want to go back to that place. So just run home to your parents and leave me alone. Take whatever story you have to tell and save it. I don't want to hear it."

Cain sounded like someone who had lived long with a broken heart, and as Shelby watched from the van she straightened up a little and ran her hand through her hair. Being a watcher for so long, she knew Cain was trying to center her feelings since they had obviously strayed too far from her normal cool self.

So this is the infamous Emma Casey who just walked away from Cain and her son. The thought took up so much of her attention, she blocked out the two other people in the van who were busy setting up the powerful microphone to capture the conversation. During all the hours she had spent observing people like Cain in cramped little places, this was the first time she had heard one of them sound so vulnerable.

Kyle's voice filtered up from the floor where her headset still lay. "They all turn out the same in the end. A big pussy who will fall, not because of a false move, but because of the weakness of some blond bimbo. They should study up on their history. Same thing happened to

Al Capone."

This assignment couldn't be over soon enough for her. "Excuse me, sir, did you say something?"

"Women, Daniels. They fuck up in the end because they let their emotions override their brains."

Are you forgetting I'm a woman, numb nuts, or perhaps the Bureau's policy against making such statements? She wanted to say her thoughts aloud, but Anthony shook his head and signaled her to focus on what they were doing. Getting into a fight with Kyle now was not in their best interests. "Interesting concept, sir. I'm sure that'll help us out tonight."

Lionel never turned from the scope sitting on the tripod he was peering through, but he had had enough of Agent Kyle and his low opinion of the people around him, including those who worked for him. "Sir, the Internal Revenue Service was the organization that brought down Al Capone. As for big pussies, I guess you could've called him that because he was afraid of needles. He died of complications of syphilis because he was afraid of getting a shot, but in the end it was the IRS that got him. Death and taxes, sir, not emotional whims or romantic fancies. Not to mention he wasn't Irish."

In the other van, three beaming smiles were testament that Lionel wouldn't have to buy a round the next time they went out.

"Shut up, you little geek. Who asked you anyway?"

"It wasn't an answer to a question, sir. More like a history lesson, in case you were interested."

Silence reigned after that as the five watchers concentrated on the coffeehouse.

Emma and Cain still faced each other. "First off, Cain, I'm sorry I didn't believe you about Danny. I brought Marie, a total innocent, excruciating pain, all because I chose to believe someone other than you. You had your faults, but you'd never lied to me about anything. I'm so sorry for Marie. If I could trade places with her, I would do it in a heartbeat."

"Don't apologize for things you had no control over, Emma. Marie was my responsibility, and I'm the one who failed her, not you. And don't try to be noble. If that's all you have to say, consider yourself unburdened and free to go about your life. I have things to do." She stood up and brushed past Emma without saying good-bye.

If Emma didn't know better she could have sworn she'd seen tears in Cain's eyes.

"You can leave, Cain, but you aren't getting away from me so easily."

Emma walked to the counter and ordered a cup of coffee. She wasn't anxious to go back to Jarvis and the lecture she was positive was waiting for her. The door opened behind her, letting in a cold blast of damp air and making her wish the guy behind the counter would hurry with her coffee so she could at least wrap her hands around the cup to get warm.

"She wants it to go," said a rough voice.

The young man holding the large ceramic cup nodded and went to pour the coffee into another container.

Kyle pressed up against her back and whispered in her ear. "You say one word, and I swear on any higher power you may believe in, I'll arrest you right here, right now."

"I don't have anything else to say to you, Agent Kyle, so I suggest you get lost."

"Why don't you take the bitch's advice and just shut the hell up, Ms. Casey, or I might make good on my promise, just to brighten my day. Think of what'll happen to poor little Hannah if Mommy's in jail."

The little condescending laugh made a surge of anger shoot through her, and she pushed back from the counter as hard as she could so she could turn around. "You leave my family out of this or I swear, asshole, I'll tell Cain everything you have planned."

"Isn't that why you're here? You're going to get back in Casey's bed by selling me and my people out?"

"I'm here for the rest of my family, so unless you want to give yourself away by being seen with me, I suggest you walk out of here and forget we know each other." The fact that the rest of her family included Cain was none of his business.

"You tell her anything about what we have planned, Emma, and I'll personally see you lose everything and everyone you hold dear."

She couldn't believe he would even say that, after his lies had cost her so much. Her anger surged stronger and surprised her more than it did Kyle. "You pompous bastard. You can't stand there and threaten me with something you've already done. You left my father's place before

I could talk to you and ask you why."

"Why what?"

"Why did you lie to me all those years ago? What did my leaving Cain have to do with anything you had planned? You left me alone for four years before you thought of something I could offer you, but it was never about me and keeping me safe, was it? This was all about you and whatever vendetta you have against Cain. The sad thing is I gave you everything I love without a question or a fight. You convinced me Cain was evil, and I ran just like you wanted me to. What in the world did you get out of that?"

When the young man handed Emma her coffee, Kyle pulled her next to a large display to try to keep their talk private. After Casey left, he had jumped from the van to go after Emma, giving the rest of the team orders to keep an eye on their target and leave the blonde to him.

"I thought your leaving would make Casey sloppy, but I guess you didn't have the influence over her I thought you did. You may not want to admit it, but getting away from here was good for you. Your mother told me—" Kyle stopped when he saw the green eyes narrow.

"What does my mother have to do with anything?"

The poke to his chest following the question was so hard it made him flinch.

"Tell me, or I swear on everything you believe in, you'll have to arrest me to keep me from going to Cain."

"Carol called me and asked me to help get you out of here long before Danny Baxter came along. Your mother's smart. She figured Casey had someone watching her, ready to pounce when the opportunity presented itself. Selling out Cain was her way of helping save your soul from the fires of hell. You should thank her for caring so much. When I found out what happened the night of Marie's birthday party, I thought I'd kill two birds, as they say. Your mother seemed nice enough, and I wanted Casey off balance. A little white lie saved your life, so don't bother to thank me either, since my job description doesn't include saving souls."

Hot coffee splashed on Kyle's legs when Emma dropped her cup in shock. Not once in all the time she had been home had her mother mentioned that she knew Kyle before he showed up at the farm. "Thank you? I damn you to hell along with my mother. How dare you play with our lives like that and keep us apart?"

Emma's voice was getting so loud Kyle was afraid he was going to have to take drastic measures and gag her with a small bag of coffee, if that was what it took.

Just as quickly it died away, and Emma narrowed her eyes, this time in suspicion. "Wait a minute. How did you find out about what happened that night with Danny? Cain made damn sure to keep that in the family." Emma saw Kyle's jaw tighten slightly and realized he was uncomfortable with the fact that he had said too much.

Shelby watched from the van with Lionel. She had hopped out and switched vehicles, knowing this was the more interesting conversation. "Yeah, Kyle, tell us how you knew about that little incident and in such vivid detail? Danny Baxter was your chance to snare Cain, but you have yet to find the body. And I'm willing to bet five years of my salary the little shit's dead." She asked the question as both she and Emma waited for Kyle to answer.

"I work for the FBI, lady. We know things." With a shrug and a laugh, Kyle was ready to move on to the next subject.

"The only way you got into the house was by turning someone else, because we all know what a good job you did on me. God, how could I have been such a fool? Leave me alone, Agent Kyle. Don't worry. I'm not here to ruin your plan. I'm here to try and get back something I too willingly gave away."

"Just remember, you tell Casey anything, and I will make you suffer." Kyle squeezed her arm so hard that she gasped.

"Are you all right, miss?" The young man had a bit of an acne problem and was wearing the green apron that was a standard part of the wait staff's uniform, but he seemed willing to stand up to Kyle if Emma was in trouble.

"I'm fine, thank you. I was just leaving." Emma smiled at her savior and felt Kyle's grip lessen. "You're too late, Barney. I'm already suffering." With a big push back, Emma broke his grip and turned to leave. If she could help it, she would never see or talk to the man again.

CHAPTER TWENTY-FOUR

A nthony and Joe watched as Cain strode away from her house. They didn't see her usual relaxed posture as she made her way down one of New Orleans's most famous streets. The two agents had become as familiar with Cain's gait as they had with her choice of clothes and her cool head. Emma had obviously thrown her for a loop with one short conversation.

For the first time they followed more closely than was prudent, in case Cain needed them. She was still locked in a heated territory dispute with Giovanni Bracato, and a walk alone to clear her head made her an easy target. Neither man was willing to let one of Bracato's goons get in a lucky shot just because Cain wasn't thinking.

Anthony reached for his ringing cell phone and handed it to his partner, who sat in the passenger seat chewing on a hangnail.

"What's up, Shelby?"

"Could you hop out of the van and hand the phone to Cain, please?"

"Are you going to support the wife and kids I hope to have one day when I get my ass fired for doing that?"

Shelby laughed more than she had when she had dialed Cain's cell and had to tell Merrick it was a wrong number. The juvenile stunt made her think of her teenage years when she and her friends used to crank call all the guys they were in love with that week. "Joe, you're going to have to trust me on this one."

Joe thought about what they had already trusted her on and made a quick decision. "Pull over, man. I gotta hop out a minute."

Anthony parked at a street corner, wondering what Joe needed out of the back that was more important than keeping up with Cain, who sure wasn't talking to herself as she walked down the street. "What in the hell are you doing?" he called after Joe when he opened the door and took off on foot after Cain with his phone.

"Making the book I'm planning to write that much more interesting."

Cain was close to the park entrance when she heard someone call her name. Seeing who it was only made her day more bizarre. "What can I do for you, Agent Simmons?"

"You know who I am?" Having her call him by name made him totally forget why he was talking to her.

"It's only fair. After all, you know who I am. Or did you think I'd mistake you for the Wisconsin farmhand who likes to hang out downtown in freezing cold temperatures just to see if anything exciting is happening in Hayward's local diner? Did you feel a sudden urge to confess your true identity? Because why else would you run out and flag me down? Even you have to admit that's a little unorthodox and probably isn't in the secret-agent handbook. Didn't you get a copy, with the ever-handy decoder ring? Am I supposed to start confessing now so you won't feel alone in your sudden honesty?"

"No, ma'am. Agent Daniels wants to talk to you." He held the phone out to her. "You were kidding about the decoder ring, right?" Joe tried to joke back. All of a sudden he felt like he was getting to hang out with the coolest kid in school.

"Please call me Cain, and no, just ask Daniels to show you hers." She took the phone and stepped away from him. "What a pleasant surprise. How's your day going, Shelby?"

"Please don't give him any more ideas about me showing him anything. Just listen to me and do what I say. Accept a ride from the two agents with you and go home right now."

"Darlin', don't you mean the two agents trailing me? Furthermore, I'm not in the habit of getting into cars with federal agents, no matter the circumstance."

"Cain, please don't argue with me. I need these guys to go somewhere with me, and I don't want to leave you out there alone."

She laughed as she leaned against one of the stone pillars that marked the entrance to the park. "Shelby, you do realize the only reason we know each other is because your boss thinks I'm a vicious killer?"

"Sure, and I don't really have time to discuss it in detail, so what's your point?"

"Dismiss Mr. Obvious here and his friend, and I'll be just fine on my own."

"I can't do that. Please don't be stubborn, and don't ask me why I'm being so obstinate. It's really necessary, believe me, so tell me you'll go."

"Okay, you win, but I expect an explanation eventually."

"You got it, hellion. Now put Joe back on the phone."

"Joe, is it?"

The young agent nodded and decided he liked the woman he had been watching for so long. She probably instilled such loyalty in people because of her humor and smile, which in his opinion lit up her face.

"Agent Daniels would like to talk to you."

A short talk later Joe pointed to the van and cocked his head to see if she really would accept a ride.

Cain stopped them a block from her house and promised she would be fine the rest of the way. "Thanks for the escort, gentlemen. I feel better about paying my taxes this year after such accommodating treatment from the feds."

"Anytime, Ms. Casey. We're always available if you'd like to chat," offered Anthony.

"I'll just bet. Run off to wherever Daniels needs you. I won't be going out for any more interesting meetings until around ten tonight."

As soon as she closed the side door, the van sped off down the street, headed in the direction of the river. Whatever Shelby had going was important enough for her fellow officers to abandon their post, so Cain would do her part and stay put. The afternoon would give her time to think about Emma's sudden appearance. Having her there might be for the best, if anything went wrong.

Merrick met her at the door to tell her Jarvis was sitting in her study.

Not ready for a fight, Cain took her time stripping off her coat and gloves. "Don't tell me. Bracato's out in the car and wants to talk to me?"

The sarcasm wasn't lost on the old man, and he held his hands up in surrender. "Cain, it hurts me that you would even ask me that."

"Why not? It's a fair question after your actions lately. What are you hoping to gain, uncle?" She took a seat next to him and put her hand over the one he had resting on the soft leather of the chair arm.

"I want you to be happy, Derby. You've lost so much in your young life, and the one person who's balanced all that and made you want to live again was Emma."

She didn't let go of his hand as she contemplated what he had just said. "But did you forget it was Emma who left and took so much with her when she did? Or is your matchmaking selective memory?" A picture of the beautiful little girl Cain had seen in Wisconsin popped into her head. *Yeah, Uncle Jarvis. Emma took so much with her when she left.*

"Do you remember the first day your father gave you a job to do for the family?"

"I'm not ten anymore, Uncle Jarvis. These little life's lessons won't work on me."

"Humor an old man, and just play along for a moment."

"It's hard to forget. I screwed up so bad I figured he'd pass me over and hand the job to Billy permanently."

"But he didn't. Dalton forgave you and gave you more than one chance to get it right. I grew up at our father's knee just like your father did, and when the time came he made more mistakes than you did when Papa started to trust him with more responsibility. At night we would sit out on the porch and smoke a cigarette when Mama wasn't looking, and he would tell me how tomorrow we'd have to try harder so the old man wouldn't just give up on us.

"The day he had you, he held you up in the hospital and showed you off to the rest of the family. 'This is my legacy, Jarvis,' he told me with those big blue eyes full of tears. I thought your mama was going to faint when he put that big finger soaked in Irish whiskey in your mouth."

Cain laughed and remembered her father telling her that story. In fact, she could remember his exact words. "The Catholics, they got ahold of you soon enough, me pride, but the whiskey—that was a Casey baptism. That spirited drink's in your blood, Cain. No oil and water a priest pours or rubs on you is going to wash that away. The whiskey's not only our business, it's our heritage, our history, and soon it'll be your turn to keep that tradition alive. Your mother didn't understand that first taste was a welcome home to a Casey. A bit of a reminder of who you are and what you come from. You're a Casey, and you're mine, but only for a time. When I set you out in the world, the one thing that's for certain is you'll be a hell of lot better than your old man."

"He said a lot more that made Mama's hair curl," she said, smiling. Suddenly she felt melancholy. "You know, Uncle Jarvis, he told me that story for the last time about a week before he died. When Hayden was born, I don't think Emma understood any better than Mama. 'A taste to welcome you home. You're a Casey and you're mine, but only for a time.'"

She had repeated the line when her son was first placed into her arms. The whiskey she had wet her finger from had been the same bottle her father had used on the day of her birth.

"You're so much like him in so many ways, lass. Your brother Billy had the brawn to muscle his way in life, but the brains and the tactician your father was, that's all you, Derby. For as much as you're like him, though, you're both very different people. You don't do business the same way, but that's how he wanted it. He was so hard on you at first because he wanted you to find your own way and lead your own way. Dalton learned from our father that experience makes the seeds of success grow."

Cain shook her head and walked over to the windows. "This is different, Uncle Jarvis. Pop forgave his family, but he never once had cause to question us."

"What's Emma to you, if not family?"

"My father was my family, as is my son, my mother, Billy, and Marie. But even they would have turned their back on me had I helped the snakes crawl so close to our nest."

"What's that supposed to mean?"

"That our sweet little Emma has changed much in her time away from us Caseys. I'm willing to bet Pop never had a day when Mama went against him or thought of walking out that door because of something he had done. I can't say the same thing about Emma."

"Don't be so sure about that, Cain. Your mother was a great many things, but she was never your father's lapdog. Your father never wanted her to be. She went against him plenty of times, but he never let it get in the way of how he felt about her. You had to let Emma go, if only so she could find her way back to you. Can I ask you one more question? I promise to leave you to your business once we're done."

Cain nodded but didn't turn around.

"Do you still feel anything for Emma? Look into your heart before you answer."

She closed her eyes and searched her soul for the most truthful answer she could give him. "A part of my heart will always love her. The sad thing is, it's the part that shrinks every day we're apart. But it'll take an eternity for it to fully die."

When she turned around to see if Jarvis was satisfied with her answer, she found his chair empty and the door slightly open. So much like her father, she thought. Dalton would ask questions that begged for truthful answers. In the end the answers mattered only to you, since you would be ultimately deciding how to change your life.

Could she forgive the woman who had shared such a large part of her life? Who had made her forget her responsibility to her family? Had her answer affected only her, she could decide more easily, but she wasn't alone. How would Hayden accept that his mother cared more for his unborn sister than for him? And what of Hannah? How would the little girl adjust to her after knowing only Emma and her parents? Carol had no doubt used the long four years to work on the little girl's thought processes.

When she had time she would find some answers, but now she needed to put Emma aside and think of the upcoming night and any possible complications.

❖

"Park out of sight and meet us on the roof of the American Coffee Company," said Shelby.

"Where in the hell is that?" Anthony asked as they drove through one of the roughest neighborhoods in the city.

"Look to your right. It's the abandoned building at the foot of the block."

"What are you, a walking historian of old city architecture?" He had never heard of the business, much less what building it had occupied.

"Yeah, I'm a genius who can read the company name and logo on the side of the building, even though it's faded. Hurry up and bring the audio booster with you, and be careful on the stairs. They were a little shaky when Lionel and I went up."

"A little shaky? I'd hate to see what you would consider dangerous." Lionel looked through his binoculars and laughed, thinking of the four times they had almost fallen through the wooden steps on the five flights up.

"Shut up and tell me everything's working perfectly, and we're taping all of this."

"Chill, Shelby, we're getting it all, and man oh man."

Lionel Jones was a mousy-looking little man who was never mistaken, at any time or by anyone, for a law enforcement officer of any kind. Fine brown hair and a milky white complexion, no matter the time of year, made him the focus of more than one bully on the playground that had been his life. He had passed the FBI's grueling requirements, not with speed on the obstacle course or high scores at the shooting range, but with his brain and computer capability. Kyle had been lucky to get him assigned to the New Orleans office to help with the wiretaps and other surveillance they had set up for Cain's case.

He turned back to Shelby, and from the creases around his eyes caused by his big open smile, she could tell he was happy. She noticed, not for the first time, that he had the lushest, longest eyelashes she had ever seen on anyone, male or female.

"What's got you so rocked today, Li?"

"You ever feel like a big bucket of shit and those two guys down there are a fan?"

"Don't worry about it, Li. We're high up enough here to come out of this smelling like veritable roses, once the manure settles down. Glad you guys could join the party. Took you long enough, don't you think?" She could hear the heavy breathing behind them, but she couldn't take her eyes off the meeting on the wharf.

"This had better be damned good, Shelby. I think we almost met a very messy end at least twice on those damned stairs." Anthony put down the equipment she had asked for and waited for someone to explain what he was doing there. Lionel handed him the pair of binoculars he had been using so he could add the new piece of equipment to what he had already set up.

"What's so interesting down on the water?"

"Jesus, Tony, could you just stand up here and wave a red flag so they'll see us?"

"Please don't call me that. *Anthony*. Is it so hard to remember?" he asked, as he reached the level of the short retaining wall that ran the perimeter of the roofline. "Oh my God, is that…?"

"Yes, I would say this confirms everything in that box Cain gave us."

Joe nodded as he adjusted his own set of lenses. "I just thought it was a big case of sour grapes on Cain's part when you first showed me all that stuff, but who would've guessed she'd turn out to be the class act."

"Am I the only one having a huge problem with the fact that you all seem to be on a chummy first-name basis with the head of one of the city's crime bosses?" Anthony asked as he reached into his pocket for a roll of antacids.

Shelby leaned back against the small half wall and looked at her team members. "He's right, guys. This is your last chance if you want out. I promised a friend I'd do my job, and that's what I'm doing. If you think differently, it won't hurt me if you want to just climb down and forget about all this. Because I can't promise there won't be any fallout once this goes down." Just because she owed Cain didn't mean they did.

"I didn't mean it like that, Shelby. You're right. This is our job just as much as bringing down Cain is. It just stings that she was the one who uncovered this. I feel like I've had my head up my ass to have missed something so big." Anthony reached over and patted her on the knee.

"She's really not all that bad, if you forget all the stuff she does for a living." She laughed and blushed a little, remembering the way Cain felt when she had pressed against her.

"Shelby, she's not worth losing your career over," said Anthony.

"The way I see it, Anthony, she's the one who'll launch our careers when all this is over. Can you live with that?"

Both Anthony and Joe looked back to the wharf and nodded, but Anthony answered for both of them. "I can live with that, if she isn't expecting anything in return."

"Maybe a nice dinner."

"We'll be happy to take her out for donuts."

All of them laughed at Anthony before they continued to monitor the talk still taking place below them.

❖

"My men tell me Cain's bitch is back in town sniffing around. Any truth to that?" Giovanni Bracato chewed on the end of the unlit cigar in his mouth and never took his eyes off the muddy, swirling waters of the Mississippi River. He had waited a long time for this day, and he didn't want anything messing it up.

Giovanni Bracato was what most people called swarthy when they were trying to avoid using the words "greasy" or "slimy," lest they be thought of as politically incorrect. Too much of the city's good food and liquor had put on the pounds over the years, and Big Gino, as he was known to his men, with his tight shiny suits and his trademark custom-made alligator shoes, looked like a movie depiction of a bad gangster.

Through the years the Bracato family had fought, along with all the other up-and-comers, for their piece of the city and their share of the action. The third-generation Italian Americans had chosen heroin and cocaine as the means to fill their coffers, setting them apart. They killed without hesitation or remorse, so people on the street had learned to fear the name. Forty years had passed since the first Bracato had immigrated to the States. The family still controlled the biggest part of the drug trade in New Orleans, but Big Gino was ambitious. He wanted control of what the other three families in New Orleans owned.

Vincent Carlotti and his son had their unions, women, and rackets. The Bastillo family, with women, gambling, and protection services, was the newest addition to the city landscape. The Cuban-born Ramon Bastillo and his twins got along with Vincent and Cain and had formed an easy alliance with the two less radical families. With what Giovanni considered a wise but costly investment, all that was ending. After the night was done, the other three bosses would regret ever laughing at Giovanni Bracato.

"Don't you think you'd be the first person I'd call if the bitch was a problem?"

Giovanni glanced at the man standing next to him, bit off the soggy part of his cigar, and spat it in the water. "I don't really know you at all, so why don't you tell me this isn't a problem."

"It isn't a problem. Don't worry about anything. I've got this all under control. Try and remember that we both benefit from Cain's demise tonight. I'll hold up my end. Try not to forget yours."

"Don't worry, Fife. You'll get yours when I get mine." With a laugh, Giovanni walked back to his office and the small listening devices in the walls. He had been so good for so long that even the feds just monitored him from the main office.

When both men went on their way, the young guns watching on the roof scrambled for the stairs. They had a lot to do before the witching hour of Cain's operation, and they had their own list of people to meet with.

❖

By seven, all the players were getting ready for the showdown. Those with a role in Cain's upcoming tableau felt like the city was doing her part to up the drama by dropping the temperature to almost freezing and enveloping the sky in a heavy blanket of gray, menacing clouds.

Jarvis didn't give out any more advice as he watched Emma come downstairs in a formfitting blue dress. It was the last gift Cain had bought her, and the color was Emma's favorite because it perfectly matched Cain's eyes.

A few blocks away the two Caseys headed to the door, dressed completely in black for their dinner reservation.

Merrick, Mook, and six others followed close behind, wearing long black coats that wouldn't come off that night unless they needed the firepower the fine wool fabric hid.

"Mom, is something going on?" asked Hayden.

"Saturday night and the natives are restless, I guess, son."

"Nothing else?"

"Tomorrow I'll have a hell of a story to tell, but for now think of this as a night to remember. Because for so many people it'll be a night hard to forget."

CHAPTER TWENTY-FIVE

The restaurant Irene's was dimly lit and full of soft conversations. Cain wanted to spend a few hours with Hayden before the business of the night started. "Hey, kiddo, thanks for having dinner with me. I want to talk to you." She sat back with a glass of iced tea, looked across the table at her son, and mentally clicked through her montage of memories. She relived the past years, which had given Hayden the fine-chiseled features that branded him a Casey.

"I'm kinda glad to get some time alone with you too. Maybe now you'll tell me what's going on. Please, Mom, I want to know, and it's not like Mook to be so quiet about stuff."

"Hayden, don't be in such a hurry to grow up, buddy. Life throws the years at your feet soon enough, so learn to enjoy each stage as it happens. When I was your age my main concern was a redheaded girl named Caroline who lived down the block."

"Grandpa didn't have you doing stuff? 'Cause Uncle Jarvis told me he was always teaching you things." The paper on the sugar packet in Hayden's fingers was getting thin from his constant flicking.

"He was always teaching me things, that's true, but not always about what you think. When I was eleven it was how to get Caroline to realize I was alive. Why? Do you feel like I'm neglecting your education?"

"No...well, sort of." Hayden's shoulders caved in a little. "I want to be ready, you know?"

"For what?" A quick dip of her head to try to catch his eye didn't work, so she tapped her finger on the table.

"I want to be ready when it's my time. You make running the business look so easy, and I don't want to mess up."

"Kiddo, all this isn't carved in stone. Is running the business, the family, something you want to do? You have other career choices, you know."

"No, I want that more than anything, unless you think I'm not cut out for it."

"Lesson one, sit up straight and square your shoulders."

The defeated posture melted away as Hayden smiled and took her advice.

"You control your life, son, not the other way around."

"What else?"

"Just remember you're a Casey and you belong to me, but only for a little while. The day will come when it's your turn to pass down the traditions we've held dear for generations, and I promise you on everything I hold dear, you'll be ready."

"What'd you want to talk to me about?"

Cain drummed her fingers on the table as a delaying tactic. Hayden wasn't going to like the rest of what she had to say, and in truth she could have just skipped the talk all together. Had they shared any other kind of relationship that was what she might have done. But the trust she had built with Hayden came from never lying to him, if she could help it, and preparing him for the worst.

"This is something my father told your uncle Billy and me when we were coming up. For Billy it made sense, but it forecast how my life would turn out."

"I thought he liked the way you turned out?"

The open look from Hayden toward her fingers made her stop the nervous habit.

"Yeah, he was proud of me and he loved me. Pop just didn't treat me any differently from Billy. He lived by certain rules, and because we were his kids he expected us not to stray too far from them."

Hayden sat up a little straighter and smiled as he sensed another Casey family treasure about to come out of the chest of his mother's memory. "Sometimes my one wish is that I'd known him."

"Oh, I think you, Hayden Dalton Casey, would have been one of his favorite subjects, so it's only appropriate for you to know his philosophy of life. To be a man, you've got to hold certain things sacred above everything else. To respect yourself so you can live with the decisions you'll have to make. To respect your wife because she's your mate and hopefully the mother of your children. To find someone whom you can trust with both your heart and your secrets. Being able to do that will give you a safe haven. The most important thing, though, is to respect your mother and your family. A man who doesn't respect them has no honor."

Hayden reacted as if he were a balloon and she had pricked him with a pin. Her father had shared this philosophy at Hayden's age because it had something to do with the pretty little Caroline. For her the lesson was easy, but her mother Therese had always been supportive and loving, so much of a fixture in their lives they never thought about the day she wouldn't be. This lesson for Hayden, though, presented more of a moral dilemma.

During the past four years, Cain had raised a smart, caring boy who thought before he opened his mouth, unlike his uncle. That trait of Billy's was why she had taken Dalton's place when her father died. *Hold your counsel, Cain, and only let those closest to you know your thoughts. To speak without thinking will lead you to an early grave, or to a very small cinder-block cell.* She could remember her father telling her that over and over.

"Where does that leave us?" Hayden was like Cain's mother, with her sharp mind and matching wit.

Cain laughed and waited for the server to put their soup bowls down. "In a bit of a quandary, don't you think?"

He laughed along with her, straightened his shoulders, and sat up again.

"Buddy, I'm giving you a sense of where you come from. Once you know that, it's easier to get where you're going."

"She didn't respect us, so it's not so easy to respect her. Maybe with time?"

"Your mother's in town." She watched him jump up and storm out to the front of the restaurant, with Mook and Merrick in pursuit. "Well, that went well."

"Are you leaving, Cain?" The waiter came to remove the dishes and cancel their order, if that was what she wanted.

"No, just hold these and reheat them when I reel him back in. Tell George to hold off on the main courses. We won't be long." She buttoned her coat and almost laughed when the rest of the armed entourage followed her out. "I'm going to move to a farm in Wisconsin," she muttered. The guards were necessary, but they were tough in private moments.

"Stop walking, Hayden." Her voice carried down the sidewalk, and he took another five steps before he stopped. *Rebellion is a good thing in small doses, but it only goes downhill from here the older he gets.* The thought reminded her of her youth and the more than many times she had pushed her parents' patience.

"Why is she here?"

Cain walked half the distance between them. If Hayden wanted to have this conversation, it would not be a screaming match in the street.

The boy took the hint and closed the gap.

"If you want the answer, then I suggest you go back in there and sit down. If that's not agreeable, then we'll go home, but don't you walk out and give Bracato a free shot. You do that again, and Emma Casey won't be at the top of your list of concerns. We understand each other?"

Her voice left no room for discussion. Cain had never lifted a hand against him, and nothing he could ever do would push her over that line, but he never wanted to face the consequences of truly upsetting her. "Yes, ma'am."

Two fresh bowls of soup arrived, and both Caseys concentrated on eating. Cain consumed more than half her bowl before she started talking again. "To answer your question, she's here to make amends."

"It isn't that easy."

The napkin returned to her lap after she wiped her mouth. "Another important lesson in life, son, is the disappointment you'll feel when you find out everything isn't always about you."

"What's that supposed to mean?" His smile could only mean his good spirits had returned.

"That before you came along and became the center of our world, there was an us. In other words, we were capable of enjoying life before you were born. She's here to make amends to me."

"What are you asking me here? You want her back, and you need my permission?"

She laughed, glad that her own good humor had returned. "My, aren't we full of spunk tonight." She reached across the table and took his hand to keep him in his seat. "Go back and think of a time when you didn't hate her."

"Why?"

"Because tonight I need you to do that. Life's a gamble if you choose this way of living it, Hayden. If you learn anything at all from me, let it be that, and take it to heart before you accept the reins that'll look all too enticing. Responsibility is more than just getting to give orders. It's sometimes sacrificing everything and everyone you love in order to protect them."

"Why tonight?"

"Dammit, son, because I want what was once my safe haven to be yours, if it comes to that." She stopped talking and ran her fingers through her hair to calm down. Tonight was not the time to say something she would regret or want him to look back at later and feel the same way. The last meeting with her father was burned into her memory, down to the color of the sky when she turned to wave good-bye.

She wasn't planning for her life to end in the middle of her warehouse tonight, but if it did, her son would look back on this night as one where his mother sent him on his way with as much knowledge as she could cram into their short time together. "Whatever else I feel for your mother, I know she'll protect you."

"I don't need—"

"Yes, you do. You're eleven, so yes, you do."

Hayden looked as close to panicked as Cain had ever seen him. "Then don't go. Wherever you're going, don't."

She moved around and knelt next to his chair. "Son, no one's taking anything away from you. Not me, and certainly not Emma. Remember, you belong to me, but only for a while. What do you think that means?"

The tears were shutting his brain down, and he couldn't think. "I don't know."

"That I can teach you everything I know. Tell you everything I've learned from every experience I've ever had, but the time will come when Hayden has to pick what Hayden wants. It's your life, and I want you to live it how you want. I didn't raise a coward, and neither did my father. I raised a boy who'll grow to be a strong leader and an accomplished man because he's sure of his life. If that means you become a cheese maker and farmer, a long line of Irish ancestors will haunt you as you churn, but so be it. But I want you to promise me you'll be whole and stay safe so the day *will* come for you to walk that road."

"Only if you promise to walk it with me."

She bent a little from the weight of his hug, but she returned it with the same intensity. "I promise, buddy. You never even have to turn around to check. I'll always be there for you."

They finished their meal with the same laughs they usually shared. When the dishes were cleared and she indulged him in a latte, Hayden had one more question. "Did Caroline ever talk to you?"

"You bet she did."

He leaned forward and put his hands up. "Well?"

"What's her name?"

"Who?"

"The girl who's got you so full of questions all of a sudden."

He blushed and dropped his eyes a minute. "Melinda."

"I see, and she hasn't noticed you? Hard to believe."

"Mom, please, what did Grandpa say?"

"It's easy. You walk up to her and just say hi. Introducing yourself is good too, and then ask her out for ice cream." She tried hard not to smile at Hayden's growing frustration.

"And it's that easy?"

"Make sure you're not wearing sunglasses at the time, and comb your hair."

The blue eyes squinted in his confusion. "What?"

"Hayden, your heritage is more than whiskey and business. Look in the mirror sometime. Not to sound like an egomaniac, but the Casey clan isn't a bad-looking lot. Big blue eyes and coal black hair will get you past whatever reservation she has and get you that first ice cream date. After that, it's up to you, but lucky for you we're known for a little charm as well. It's not just about the looks, it's the whole package, and you've got it. Trust me on this one. Women will never be your problem. You turn into a butthead about it, though, and you'll have one big problem."

"What, angry dads?"

"Worse. The fact is, I'm female too, and I'll be watching you."

Hayden blushed and laughed a little as he thought about some of the stories his uncle Jarvis had regaled him with. His time was just beginning, that was true, but it was hard not to compare himself to Cain. She was more than capable with the ladies, and if he fell a little short on that score, it would be hard to live down.

CHAPTER TWENTY-SIX

Are you sure about this?" George Talbot, the U.S. Attorney for the Fifth District in Louisiana, held the report the four FBI agents sitting before him had put together.

George had worked for the federal government, putting criminals away longer than these guys and gal were alive, he was willing to wager. Every crop of new up-and-comers had its conspiracy theorists, but this group had pictures and video to back up their outlandish claims.

"We're sure, sir. We've got a lot more in our files if you'd like to take a look." Shelby had been elected their spokesperson.

"No. As the saying goes, young lady, a picture's worth a thousand words." He held up the stills from that afternoon's surveillance atop the abandoned buildings.

"Sir, I know this isn't the usual chain of command, but we needed secrecy and discretion. We're the low men on the totem pole, so if things go badly our careers could be in jeopardy."

"Then why do it at all, Agent Daniels?" He cocked his head and waited. These young people had a fire he hadn't seen in years, the same drive and passion he had managed to retain.

"Because the law is the law, sir. No one gets to use it for personal gain, especially someone like Giovanni Bracato. Even if you take away our badges, we feel we've done the right thing."

"Okay, tell me this. Where did all this come from?" He pointed at the thick folder thrown down on his desk and looked up at four pained faces.

Anthony jumped in before Shelby could answer. "Mr. Talbot, that's confidential, sir. Agent Daniels garnered the information, and she trusted the rest of us with the operation because of the short timeline.

To betray the trust of our informant would jeopardize future operations where this person could be vital."

Shelby smiled at Anthony. He obviously wasn't happy accepting help from Cain, so to have him defend her made her feel better about the upcoming operation.

"I see. Well, I tell you what we're going to do." George almost laughed when four eager faces leaned farther into his desk as if he had started whispering.

They talked over their plan, and the four agents agreed to have some of the investigators who worked directly for George brought in for the final operation. The men who sat in on the final meeting had spent their careers with the craggy old attorney and were, in his opinion, above reproach. As far as Shelby, Joe, Anthony, and Lionel were concerned, they had to be for the whole thing to work. They had irrevocably set things in motion to coincide with whatever Cain had in mind for them that night.

"Why do you all think Cain's going through with this when she's got to realize the trap is set? I've known her from the time we were trying to chase her daddy down for running numbers and booze in the city, and she's an even more worthy adversary in the slippery department, but she's no dummy. She's like an old and wise warrior who's always three steps ahead of not only what you're doing, but also what you're thinking."

George watched Shelby's face as he talked. A few more years and a little more experience would help her temper her emotions, but she hadn't perfected the technique quite yet. He had his answer as to where the file had come from, and in a way it made him feel better. Cain was thorough in everything she did, so the information was as good as if it had come from the FBI.

"I don't know her well enough to answer that, sir. All I can tell you is we've been watching her for over a year, and all we've learned is how she takes her coffee and that she's got a keen eye for the cameras." Shelby laughed as the file of pictures of Cain's smile they had back at the office came to mind.

"Let me tell you something, Shelby. May I call you that, Agent Daniels?"

"Please do, sir, and if I may, this is Anthony, Joe, and Lionel." She pointed to each man in turn.

"Then you all call me George, not that I mind such a nice-looking group of young people calling me sir. As I was saying, I ran into Cain on the golf course about a year ago. She was playing a round with that big good-looking kid of hers, and she allowed my group and me to play through. She shook my hand and congratulated me for twenty-two years of tireless service to the community. After that, Hayden Casey asked how my daughter was doing and also said to congratulate her on my new grandson. I was out playing that day to celebrate the birth of my fourth grandbaby."

"Amazing," said Anthony.

"No, son, that's not amazing. It's damned good. Dalton, her father, was good, but he sired something when he and his wife were gifted with Cain. If I did anything else for a living, I'd say she was damned fun to watch, and that kid of hers. Well, let's just say I don't envy you your jobs when it's his time in the saddle.

"When I went to the hospital that afternoon to see my daughter, I discovered a flower arrangement there from Hayden, along with a note saying he had donated his month's allowance in the baby's name to a local children's center where my daughter does volunteer work. If she's ever sitting in a jury box fifteen years from now, do you think she'll be seriously considering whatever we're accusing him of, or will she be remembering that nice note he enclosed? And she knows better."

"It sounds like you admire her," said Joe.

"Cunning should be admired in any form, Joe. I'm not saying we should emulate her, considering what our jobs are, but know your enemy, because sure as I'm sitting here, she knows all about us."

Anthony was thinking back to the morning on the farm when he and Joe had followed her and Hayden on their run. "I would have to agree with you on that score, George. We're forever running around hiding behind bushes and trees, thinking how smart we are, and she'll just stop and look right into our eyes and smile. I'm waiting for the day she just waves and puts us out of our misery." If Cain had a special ability, the old man was right—her son had inherited it along with the looks and blue eyes.

"It doesn't hurt either that most people in this town feel like she's a hero to the little guy. For you folks, that makes life difficult. For me, it makes it impossible. No one wants to convict someone who's seen as a friend by most. Hell, I think Mrs. Talbot would run off with the outlaw if the opportunity presented itself."

The occupants in the room laughed and were happy to relax, if only for a few minutes. The investigators who worked with George were back, dressed in black SWAT uniforms with very few markings. They were getting ready to deploy to the warehouse and set up before any other company arrived. Almost simultaneously the beepers the four visitors were all wearing went off. The boss was calling.

"Daniels, where are you?" Kyle was riding shotgun, with his senior agent Samuel Rich behind the wheel. They had taken over as the lead car tailing Cain and her party.

"My group and I are going over last-minute details and waiting for a call from Agent Rich to get going, sir."

"She and that kid just left the restaurant, and I have a feeling she's going to be moving after that, so stand by and be ready to move. I don't want any fuckups tonight."

"Yes, sir, we'll be ready."

"Rocky, are we ready?" George asked his senior investigator.

"Yes, sir, we're leaving now. Agent Daniels, please be advised we'll be on the scene, so the four of you be sure and not take any shots at us," he joked.

"We'll keep that in mind, officer." Shelby answered her ringing phone and was glad they had brought along their own gear so they could leave from the federal building to wherever Kyle needed them. "Daniels."

"She's headed to the club, so let's see if she remembers you from the crowd, Daniels." In his usual manner, Kyle abruptly disconnected from his end.

Shelby unzipped the bag and pulled out a black minidress as her fellow officers just smiled. George finally had the guts to ask, "Where, Shelby, do you hide a gun while wearing that?"

"Trade secrets, George. If I told you I'd have to kill you."

❖

"You know who we're looking for, right?" Cain stopped at the front door of Emerald's and talked to the guy in charge of letting people in.

"Yeah, boss. Merrick gave me the heads-up earlier today. Don't worry if they show up. I'll make sure they don't wait in line."

Cain turned to Merrick and leaned in a little. "Where are they?"

"The trucks are en route still and about three hours away. That gives us enough time to meet with Vinny and finalize the distribution once they arrive. His father's monitoring the caravan and says we have plenty of company."

"Good to know I'm still so popular."

They entered the building and went directly to Cain's private table.

"Are you sure you don't want to let me in on what you're doing?"

"Sweetheart, you worry about my son and keeping him safe. Let me and Vincent worry about everything else."

Merrick tried to hide her hurt feelings at being cut out of Cain's inner circle.

"Don't pout, Merrick. I haven't lost faith in you. Believe me, that's not it. Vincent and I are the only ones on the front lines on this deal. I need you to be ready to move with Hayden, if it comes to that. Once my son is safe, you worry about me, understand?"

Merrick put her hands on Cain's cheeks and gazed into her eyes for a long moment before kissing her. "I may understand, but that doesn't mean I've got to like it. My place is with you."

"For now, sweetheart, your place is where I send you. Granted, Lou isn't as beautiful, but he's got my back tonight."

The big man of few words turned to the two women at the private table before he turned his attention back to observing the crowd.

"At least there'll be no tits to distract you," said Merrick.

"Yes, that's one advantage to taking Lou along tonight."

In answer, or perhaps a curse, to what Merrick had said, two women entered the club, neither of them noticing the other, but both looking for the same person. When they spotted the object of their search in such an intimate embrace with Merrick, they had identical frowns. Anthony walked up and put one hand on Shelby's elbow and pointed two fingers at her eyes to get her to focus on why they were there. The other woman's eyes never left the couple as she stalked toward the table, appearing ready to mark her territory.

"Heads up, boss," said Lou.

"Well, well, who do we have here?" asked Merrick.

"That, my dear, is what my mama would've called a devil in a blue dress."

"Can I talk to you?" Emma seemed ready to drag Cain away by the hair, if that was what it took to get her to cooperate.

"Sure, I'm feeling generous tonight. Merrick, take off and call me when you get home." Cain stood and kissed Merrick one more time before she left.

When she scanned the crowd, she noticed Emma wasn't the only surprise guest in the building. Shelby and her shadows were making their way to the bar and keeping an eye on both her and Emma. "Lou, call me in the office when our buddy gets here, okay?"

"You got it, boss."

For the first time in four years Cain wrapped her hand around Emma's and pulled her toward the office. It was their first prolonged physical contact since Emma had walked out the front door of their home. She tried to ignore the pull of her heart, but as she had admitted to herself earlier, Emma would always hold a special place in that sealed vault.

From her bar stool, Shelby locked her eyes on the mirror next to the bar. If Cain didn't know better, she would have sworn the agent could see into the quiet office where they had shared such an intense meeting not that long before. "Emma, you look like your old self tonight. What can I do for you?"

"I want you to listen to me and not interrupt until I'm done. Do you think you can do that?"

"I think I'm disciplined enough to pull it off."

Emma looked suspicious. She wasn't expecting Cain to be this accommodating. "Okay, I give. Why are you being so nice?"

"Because it's the only way I can figure to get rid of you, and like I said before—I've got things to do."

"Whatever you've got planned tonight, Kyle knows all about it and is waiting for you."

The admission took Cain by surprise. Emma had set her up to get Hayden back, and now she was willing to throw it all away by spoiling Kyle's surprise. "How?"

"He showed up at the farm and bugged the hell out of the bunkhouse. He knew you wouldn't let Hayden come alone, so he set a trap for you."

A dark brow arched at the news, and Emma wanted to run from the look in Cain's eyes.

"And you know this how?"

"Because he had to ask our permission before he was able to do that. I guess he could have gotten a court order or something, but he talked to me, and I listened again. You've got to understand that I thought this was the only way to get Hayden back. But then I learned the truth about Barney Kyle and what kind of help he had gotten from my mother. I can't take back the past, Cain, but I can try and make up for it, starting now."

Cain exhaled and leaned forward to rest her elbows on her knees. "Are you blaming your mother and Kyle?"

"That would be the easy way out, wouldn't it?" Emma sat on the opposite end of the couch and hoped Cain would listen to the rest without trying to kill her. "No, what I did, I did for my own reasons. I let someone else convince me of how evil you were, and even though I couldn't reconcile that person with the one who held me at night and loved me so well, I trusted a stranger blindly."

"You can never imagine just how deep you've cut me, Emma. I took Hayden out to dinner tonight so I could tell him how you were my safe haven, and I believed that at one time. What you've done, though, makes it impossible to go back and salvage any type of relationship. So if that's why you're here, then get out. I can handle Kyle, and I'll be fine without your last-minute confessions."

"There's one more thing, and you promised you'd let me finish."

"What? Let me guess. You're wired for sound too?"

"Don't you think I know what kind of chance I'm taking coming here tonight and telling you all of this? I have to live with what I did, and I have to live with the shame of what happened to Marie. I'm trying now to stop anything else from happening to my family. Kyle listened to everything you said while you were up visiting us, so whatever you planned, Cain, I'm begging you to think about backing away. I know you won't believe me, and you're nothing if not a fighter, but think of Hayden."

"I *am* thinking of Hayden. Everything I do is because I'm thinking of Hayden."

Emma moved closer and put a hand on the cold leather of the seat cushion between them. "There's one more person to consider here as well."

"Who would that be?" Cain wanted Emma to admit to the baby. She just wanted to hear it from the woman who should have shared it with her four years ago.

"Your daughter." Emma's voice was so soft she barely heard it. She had dropped her head and didn't look her in the eye.

"Hannah."

"How?" When she whipped her head up, a few of the blond locks fell from the knot Emma had pulled them into.

"Hayward, Wisconsin, has a lot of cows and expanses of empty, beautiful land. But do you know what there isn't a whole lot of?"

Emma looked at her and shook her head.

"Houses with dark-headed, blue-eyed children who live with two people so blond they'd sunburn in moonlight."

"I was going to tell you."

"Emma, don't insult both of us by saying something so colossally stupid."

"I just didn't know *how* to tell you. Once I left and went through all that alone, I didn't know how. Every night, though, I tell her about you and Hayden and how we'll be together one day. She knows you, Cain. Your little girl knows you even if you haven't met. When you do, her mom is someone she won't shy away from, because she belongs to you just like Hayden. Just like I do, but it isn't for just a little while. I belong to you forever, even if you don't want me."

"Promise me something. You owe me that much, at least."

"Anything." Emma gathered what courage she had and put her hand over Cain's. She would have traded her soul for Cain to take her in her arms.

"If something happens to me, you will keep my children safe, and you will stay away from me."

Cain got up and walked out of the office. This was not the time to become an emotional wreck, but she was close to losing her grip. To have Emma betray her trust and believe Kyle without even asking her was one thing, but to rob her of knowing her daughter was a bigger crime than she could even fathom.

Three feet from the office door was as far as she got before Shelby stopped her in the secluded entryway leading to the private space.

When Emma opened the door to go after Cain, she found them in each other's arms. Whoever the woman was, she was able to give her ex-lover something she no longer wanted from Emma. Shelby whispered something into Cain's ear and finally pulled the dark head down and kissed her. The two agents at the bar and Emma all looked away, not wanting to witness something that seemed almost special.

The urge to run again was getting stronger, and Emma wanted nothing more than to bolt and go home to her daughter. She could call it a wash—she would get Hannah, and Cain would get their son. Not the best solution and fair to no one, but she didn't want to end up alone, no matter how selfish that sounded. However, her father's words of not giving up bolstered her courage and made her look at the woman Cain was now holding and talking to.

"I won't go so easily, Cain, and I know you still care for me. If it takes a lifetime to knock down those walls you've built around your heart, then I'm willing to take the time."

All of the players in the upcoming game eyed their opponents and readied themselves for the final showdown. Time was growing short, and all of them were resolved to win.

Chapter Twenty-seven

Vinny Carlotti had arrived and made himself comfortable at Cain's private table.

His entry had prompted Kyle to send Lionel in to join the party and tell the other three to keep their eyes open, since the people they had taped all day had mentioned nothing but the weather.

"Boss, Merrick called a few minutes ago and said everything's ready." Lou stepped up and waited to see what Cain would decide. Interrupting her meeting with the pretty woman was the last thing he wanted to do, but he had no choice.

"I'm about ready to roll, Lou. Just give me a minute."

"It's not too late to pull out." Shelby locked her arms around Cain's neck and held her in place. The knowledge that Emma was looking on was, in a way, urging on her behavior, but the hurt look in the blue eyes she had come to dream about was hard to ignore.

"And do what instead, take you home so we can play cops and robbers?"

"Don't trivialize what I'm trying to do here, Cain. I care about you, and I don't want to come visit you where I'm forced to look at you through thick glass."

Cain rubbed her back and kissed her nose. "I'm planning on that dinner you guys are going to owe me when this is all over. Don't worry about a thing. You just keep your eyes peeled, and I promise I'll be fine."

"You'd better be."

"Honey, trust me. I've got some people to see once this is all over."

❖

Two semis were already parked on the dock when Cain's car pulled up. Ten more were just getting off the interstate exit ramp, and Kyle held his team back until they arrived. He was feeling almost giddy. His day had finally come, and he would live to see Cain Casey brought down.

Cain opened the back door of the car herself and stepped out to talk to one of the drivers. The warehouse workers had been dismissed, and she motioned for Lou to go open the cargo doors so the guy could pull in to start unloading. The drivers had followed her orders to the letter, and the first truck that pulled into her place was full of cases of Jameson Irish Whiskey. It had been her father's favorite and was hers as well, and she thought unloading it first would bring her luck.

Kyle spoke into the mike just in front of his mouth. "Sardines. Did she really think we would fall for that?" The headset kept him in contact with all his team as he looked through the night glasses. "If that's little fish, she must have cornered the market."

In a momentary lull between trucks pulling in, everyone heard the slamming of a car door, and all the federal agents stared as Emma walked directly over to Cain, who was standing alone, and grabbed her arm. None of them felt as stricken or as mortified as Kyle. He was so close to the biggest bust of his life, and some little blond bitch was about to mess it up.

"Kill the lights and move in," Kyle ordered, as the floodlights illuminating the docks suddenly went dark for almost a mile stretch. The cloud cover Cain had worried about was now a huge factor in who would hold the advantage.

"What are you doing here?" demanded Cain, as she pulled Emma inside.

"I couldn't let you do this alone. It's my fault they're out there now, and I'm not about to abandon you."

"Jesus, Emma, did you think for one minute I didn't plan for every factor, including Kyle? Just get out of here and wait for me to call you." They had made it through the large cargo doors and were just inside, next to the first semi that had been parked for unloading.

"FBI! Drop your weapons and come out with your hands on your head." The order came through a bullhorn, and for once Cain didn't recognize the voice.

"Lou, drop your gun now and step outside where they can see you."

Shelby heard Cain's order as she moved to the warehouse entrance. The dress had hindered her speed, but she had her weapon drawn and was ready for anything. As much as she wanted to believe Cain wouldn't hurt her, she couldn't predict how a cornered Cain would lash out. Anthony and Joe were right behind her, and Kyle was already at the entrance.

It was hard to pinpoint everything going on around them in the almost-dark, noisy warehouse. Cain forgot her hate for her ex and pulled Emma close. Whoever had ordered them to drop their weapons was nearby when she heard the order again, only this time without the bullhorn. Suddenly she recognized the voice and the danger they were in.

"I said drop your weapon, scumbag," Kyle ordered as he looked at Cain and Emma standing together. His gun came up, and almost instantly the bullet left the chamber.

With a quick move, Cain turned around and pulled Emma with her to protect her from the gunfire. Her swing was so quick it propelled them to the floor, where she landed on top of Emma, her arms still wrapped around her in a protective embrace.

"I knew you still cared about me," Emma whispered up to the ear so near her lips. She could hear only running feet before someone ordered a cease-fire. "Come on, I think the worst is over now. You can let me up." She said it as a joke, but Cain didn't respond. Only then did she feel it. The hot wet stain that was growing larger by the second on the front of the blue dress Cain had bought for her.

"Drop your weapon!" Shelby screamed from her defensive stance, gun aimed at Kyle.

"Daniels, what the hell do you think you're doing?" The gun he had just fired was hanging loosely at his side, but he refused to let go of it.

"Sir, I'm asking you to drop your weapon and step forward. If you refuse we'll have no other option than to take you down by force, and I think no one here really wants to do that."

Anthony moved behind their boss and aimed his gun at Kyle's back, in case he made any sudden move against Shelby.

"I'm beginning to think the stress has gotten to all of you, or is it the blueness of the bitch's eyes that turned you, Daniels? I'm ordering you to drop your weapon. It seems clear to me that you're working for Casey."

George stepped up and stared at his old friend. "There's corruption in the ranks in New Orleans all right, Barney, but it isn't from these fine young agents. Do as the lady says, and put down your gun." He was older than Kyle, but he'd used the agent in countless trials, always respecting his professionalism and expert opinions.

The lights came back on, and everyone quickly ripped off the night-vision equipment and blinked furiously, trying to adjust to the sudden brightness. It was then that they noticed the two women on the ground near the parked truck.

Emma was trying to roll Cain off her, whispering and shaking her furiously to get her to respond. She would have screamed sooner, but she didn't want to attract any more fire their way. "Cain, honey? Please wake up."

For a moment Cain did open her eyes and focused on her face. "Take care of Hayden. Tell him I'm…" The voice died away before she finished, and Cain slumped lifelessly against her.

"No!" The frantic call made everyone locked in the battle of wills focus in their direction. Joe, who was backing Shelby up, called for an ambulance and more agents. Lying on the ground was Cain with a gunshot to the back. Emma had two fistfuls of her hair and was screaming at her to wake up.

"She had a gun, I saw it," Kyle objected, before anyone accused him of any other wrongdoing.

"Agents Curtis and Simmons, take care of Agent Kyle and take possession of his weapon. If he resists, shoot him," ordered George. He had seen the shock that took hold of Shelby's features as she gazed past Kyle when Emma screamed.

Kyle stared at George and laughed at the absurdity of the situation. "You've finally lost it, George. We're surrounded by a shitload of illegal liquor, and I'm the one in trouble? I don't think so. This is my operation, old man, so you and your goons are free to leave. Jones, start inventorying the cargo in those semis."

George motioned to his lead man. He had tried the easy way; now it was time to wrap up. A second later Kyle was on the ground and cuffed, with Rocky practically sitting on him to keep him down. Another one of George's men read him his rights, ignoring the cursing and spitting coming from the big blond on the ground.

The government's head attorney in the city squatted next to Kyle as the paramedics rushed in and spoke softly enough for only the agent to hear. "Barney, you'd better start praying now that she lives, because if she doesn't, I'm going to bury you so deep you'll be wishing for death."

"Please, this is all a misunderstanding. I didn't do anything wrong."

"You shot an unarmed woman in the back in her place of business. I'd say that was plenty wrong. Take him in, and I'll be along shortly."

Cain was already loaded on the gurney when George got up. The fact that the three paramedics were still hooking up IVs and working furiously gave him some comfort. He hadn't lied to the young people who had come to him earlier that day. Cain Casey was a friend to a lot of people, most of whom owed her more than they could pay back in a lifetime.

Twelve Years Earlier at Cain's Warehouse

"Cain, you aren't going to believe who's on line one," Mrs. Michaels, Cain's assistant at the warehouse, said over the intercom. The woman had worked for Dalton for years and just kept coming to work when his daughter took over. Cain never questioned her presence, and the elderly woman kept her schedule and took her calls with meticulous care.

"Is it the police wanting me to turn myself in?"

"Close enough. It's George Talbot."

Cain picked up and accepted his invitation to play golf that afternoon. She didn't question why, or whether George wanted something. A little ruse on her part ensured that her conversation with George would be just between the two of them. Her constant shadows at the warehouse were still in the building across the street, thinking she was in-house. Not one of them noticed the bug exterminator truck that pulled out, or the fact that a different worker drove it.

On the fourth hole, as they drove out to take their second shots, George started talking. "Cain, do you have children?" He knew the answer, but it was easier to get the conversation started this way.

"I just recently started living with someone, sir, but I'm hoping she's agreeable to a family someday. Family is something that's very important to me. Do you and your wife have children?" She too knew the answer to the question, but it was an icebreaker to keep George talking.

"We have a daughter. Her name's Monica, and she's in the middle of her junior year at Mount Carmel Academy."

Cain stopped their cart well short of the balls and pointed to a bench under a large oak tree. "That's a beautiful name. Is she enjoying her year, getting ready for college and all that comes with growing up?"

"She was, and she seemed so happy until she met this guy. All I know is his name's Eddie, and he dropped out of school last year before he graduated. The headmaster of his school told me he had been in some trouble before that, and they were going to expel him soon anyway." George leaned forward and sighed like a man with a heavy burden. "When you become a parent, Cain, you discover the fine line between being too soft and having your child end up with someone like Eddie, or going too far in the other direction and having her hate you. Do you know what I mean?"

"Yes, sir. Times have changed. I don't envy you having to deal with a teenager."

"She's missing, Cain. She left for school two days ago and never came back. Her mother and I've looked everywhere. We called all her friends, but no one knows where she is." He dropped his head and grabbed two fistfuls of hair in frustration.

"Mr. Talbot, I feel like an idiot for asking, but shouldn't you be talking to the authorities?"

"I would, but I'm afraid of what they'll find. My career isn't important here, so don't think that, but we found some stuff in her room." George stopped and stared up at her, hoping she would understand his dilemma and what he wanted for his daughter. "I want her to have a future without something always out there threatening to drag her down."

"What sort of things did you find? I need to know what I'm up against."

He described the bent spoon and needles, along with the rubber tubing that meant Monica was in big trouble, the kind you were led into and never escaped just by sheer will.

"Sir, I want you to do me two favors."

"Anything."

"I need a current picture."

He pulled one from his shirt pocket.

"And I want you to go home and spend the afternoon with your wife. Do you think you could do that for me?"

George nodded and wanted to cry from relief.

"You go home and tell Mrs. Talbot not to worry. Monica's going to be just fine. I promise you that on my honor. It's going to take some time, but I'll return your Monica to you." Cain stressed "your Monica," meaning she would return the girl her parents remembered before Eddie had sunk his claws into her.

Three months later an elderly Carmelite nun pulled up to the Talbot home with a very contrite and apologetic Monica Talbot. Sister Mary Jude explained to the tearful parents that their daughter had kept up with her schoolwork and was fine after her bout of the flu. Monica's school was informed of her illness, and her teachers were anticipating her return the following Monday.

George never asked what had happened to Eddie, and his daughter never mentioned her time away. The thing—which didn't surprise him—was that Cain never called to ask for any payment. The rehab center Sister Mary Jude was in charge of was effective but expensive, but no bill ever came to their house, nor was their insurance notified. When George called to take care of the bill, he was informed that no record existed for anyone named Monica Talbot.

The only reminder was the small bouquet of forget-me-nots that Monica received on her birthday, with no card attached. Her senior year, George watched his daughter when he handed them over, thinking they were from a friend. She just stared for a long moment before dropping into the nearest chair. The flowers arrived religiously on every birthday, and after a few years, the scared expression turned from fear to almost comfort as she ran her fingers over the petals.

George surmised the flowers were from Cain, and like their name, she never forgot to send them. They symbolized something she didn't want Monica to forget. The troubled girl took the lesson seriously and went on to graduate in the top 1 percent of her class, both in high school, then in college. In law school she was first in her class, and then started on a successful career in the district attorney's office with no criminal record to hold back her career.

The young mother of four little boys, married to a cardiologist, bore no sign of being the teen who had run away from home. George remembered that afternoon when he had sat under the massive live oak with Cain, and how she had taken charge of getting his little girl back. This had been his opportunity to repay her kindness, and he felt like a failure. With the gravity of her wound, it was possible that no car would pull up to the Casey home and bring Cain back to Hayden.

"Gentlemen, Kyle was right about one thing. We need to inventory all this stuff before this group of drivers decides to go for a spin." He pointed to the trucks lined up along the docks.

The first truck was already open and a few of the crates unloaded. Lionel found the word "Sardines" stenciled on the sides, just like Cain had said in the bunkhouse when she made the deal. When they demanded the next few trucks open their cargo doors, they found the same stash of crates, stenciled the same way. It was over. Kyle had made his case, but none of them felt much like celebrating.

❖

"Call ahead, Murphy. Tell them to have an OR ready to go, and call the folks in the blood bank." The woman nicknamed Tex was barking out orders as she ran alongside the gurney holding a compress to the hole in the front of Cain's chest. Kyle's shot had gone completely through, leaving a much larger exit wound and one hell of a mess. The legs of the gurney folded under when they pushed Cain inside the ambulance, freeing Murphy to run for the driver's side.

Tex let her other partner climb in next and was almost knocked down by the two women trying to follow him. "Hold up there. Where in the hell do you think you two are going?" The paramedic held her hands up and stood in the opening to keep anyone else from entering.

"That's my partner in there. I'm coming with you," said Emma. She looked dazed but deceptively calm, despite the fact that she was standing there covered in Cain's blood.

"Ma'am, that's our patient, and you need to give us some room to make sure she's all right. I'd love to stand here and talk at length to you about it, but I don't have the time. I'm sure one of the officers will be glad to give you a ride. You sure don't need to be doing any driving."

"Come on, Ms. Casey, I'll take you." Shelby put her hand on Emma's shoulder and pulled her back so the ambulance doors could be closed.

The ride seemed to take an eternity as the two women followed the flashing lights of the large vehicle in front of them. Every so often Emma would look from the ambulance to the woman sitting beside her. The image of her comforting Cain was hard to erase as she took in the tight jaw muscles and worry lines across Shelby's forehead.

"Can I ask your name?"

"I'm sorry. I'm Shelby Daniels."

"Are you and Cain good friends?" It seemed ridiculous to have this conversation now, but she needed some reassurance of where she stood and what her role would be once they reached the hospital.

"We met just recently." Shelby took a hand off the wheel and put it on Emma's knee. "I work for the FBI, ma'am. That puts Cain and me in an awkward position for any romantic relationship, but it doesn't make it impossible for us to be friends." *Friends who share some pretty nice kisses, but that's all it'll ever be.*

Emma swiped at her veil of blond hair as she leaned forward a little. "I'm sorry. You probably think I'm just an idiot, but when I saw the two of you earlier I thought—"

"I know what you thought, ma'am, and like I said, Cain and I are merely friends. We got to know each other because Cain saved my life. If it weren't for that, I'd probably only know her as the voice on the tapes we have."

Needing some comfort, Emma put her hand over Shelby's and looked up at the ambulance. "Do you think she'll be all right?"

"I have faith Cain loves life more than anything. Giving up isn't in her vocabulary, so maybe we should have the same belief in her. I think she'll be just fine."

Shelby and Emma left the car in the emergency room lot and ran in after the gurney. Tex was now on it, almost straddling her patient as she held an ambu bag over Cain's face, pumping to keep her breathing. The sheet Cain was lying on was saturated, signaling them that the bleeding hadn't stopped.

So much had already happened, but in reality the night was just beginning.

CHAPTER TWENTY-EIGHT

The doors of the exam room swung closed, and Shelby and Emma neither saw nor heard of Cain for hours. Coffee cups still full of bitter-tasting liquid sat before them untouched. An intern had taken Emma into another of their exam rooms and checked her for injury and shock. She had only a scratch on her side where the bullet had exited Cain and grazed her. Once she rejoined Shelby, each, as if by silent agreement, took hold of the other's hand and didn't let go.

"I should call the house and ask Merrick to speak to Hayden." Emma was dreading having to tell her son what had happened but felt he would want to be there supporting his mother.

"It'll be okay, Ms. Casey. This wasn't your fault."

"Please call me Emma, and you don't understand our son. He idolizes Cain, with good reason, I guess. She never abandoned him, not like I did."

Shelby tightened her hold on Emma's fingers and smiled. "You're his mother and he needs you now, even though he's bigger than both of us and might not think so."

The cell phone Shelby was holding up looked almost frightening, but Emma rubbed her hands along her legs and accepted it.

"Casey residence." Merrick's voice sounded tight and cold from the waiting.

"Merrick, this is Emma."

"Ms. Casey, Cain's not home."

"Could you put aside your feelings for a minute and listen? I know Cain's not home, that's why I'm calling. She was shot, Merrick, and she's still in surgery. I need you to come and bring Hayden with you, but please bring extra protection. I promised Cain I'd look out for our son, and I need your help." Her grip on the phone was making her hand cramp as she anticipated Hayden's response.

"What hospital?"

She told her the name and where she and Shelby were seated.

"We'll be there in ten minutes."

The second hand of the large clock on the wall of the waiting room swept around with a low grinding noise thirteen times after she ended the call before Merrick, Hayden, and Mook filled up the small room by sheer presence. She stood up and prepared herself for whatever reaction Hayden was going to have. His poker-serious expression softened just a little when he saw the blood covering her blue dress.

"It's not mine, Hayden. Don't be afraid. I just don't want to leave until I know Cain's all right."

"She said you were here to make things right between the two of you. Did you?"

She was surprised by the question, thinking that he would have asked about Cain before anything else. "To be totally honest, it's going to take more than just one night to do that, but I'm hoping we'll eventually get there. You may find it hard to accept, but Cain and I were the best of friends at one time, over and above the love we shared."

"She told me that too. The nurse informed us on the way in that it'll be another couple of hours, but Mom's hanging in." The information was the only comfort he gave her.

Ah, of course he would have stopped to ask. He's Cain's kid, after all. The woman could have done commercials for the Boy Scouts— always be prepared. Emma knew Cain's idea of being prepared meant getting all the information about any given situation. Hayden was no different. "Thank you, and thank you, Merrick, for getting him here so quickly."

The room was small, granted, but Merrick had noticed how close the two were sitting. "Did you and Agent Daniels have lots to talk about before we got here?" She had already come up with two scenarios as to why Shelby was there—to either help finish Cain off or something more intimate.

"Agent Daniels was nice enough to give me a ride to the hospital from the warehouse."

Hayden walked nearer to his mother and the other woman sitting right behind her. "You were there?"

"We both were, Hayden."

"What happened?"

Riffling through her hair and taking out the pins that held only strands now, Emma took a deep breath. "It happened so fast that all I remember is standing next to Cain and then someone yelling at her to throw down her gun, which didn't make any sense. You and I both know Cain doesn't ever carry a gun."

Behind Hayden, Merrick nodded in agreement. Cain didn't need to carry a firearm. She was surrounded with them all the time.

"Before I could react she grabbed me and swung around, and something knocked us both to the ground. When the lights came back on I realized it was the force of the bullet that knocked her off her feet. She saved my life."

"It seems that every time she protects you from something, she loses big in the end, doesn't it?" said Hayden.

The tears came when Emma faced such anger in her son. Any chance of reconciliation with Hayden was as slim as with Cain. "I'm sorry. I can't say anything other than that. This may sound like an old cliché, but if I could trade places with her I would." The sobs that were threatening came spilling out then, and she ran out to escape any other sarcastic comment he had.

"Wouldn't it have been more effective to just slap her and get it over with?" Shelby asked him, never getting up from her seat.

"What do you know, lady? You're just here to try and drag my mother down."

"Check that attitude with me, Mr. Casey. I'm not Emma, and I'm not going to put up with it. Granted, your other mom is in there fighting for her life, but I'm almost positive that if she were out here, she'd have slapped you down by now herself."

It was remarkable to look into his eyes and find so much of Cain there. They held the intensity in their blue depths, and the same fire.

"Don't come in here and spout off about things you know nothing about. My mother lets you see only what she wants you to see, and nothing more. Even you can't be so stupid not to have figured that one out."

"I'm not stupid, Hayden. I just heard what she told you in the restaurant tonight. You're smart enough to know we're always listening. 'To be a man you have to respect your mother and your family.' Isn't that what she told you? One little setback and you have to lash out at the easiest target? One you know isn't going to fight back. Maybe Cain's right, and following her father's rules does show what caliber of man you will become. But you act as immaturely as you just did, and people like me will finally break you."

She kept her voice calm and waited to see if Hayden would make any other smart comments. When he turned away from her and leaned into Merrick, Shelby got up and went to find Emma.

"Do you think she's right?" Hayden asked Merrick, once they were alone in the room with only Mook.

"Boy, you got a lot of learning to do yet, so I wouldn't worry about it too much. Cain didn't get everything right the first time, and you don't have an edge on doing it any better."

"What do you mean by that?"

"It means that you are your mother's son, and nothing anyone can say will ever change that." Merrick pushed back the hair that had fallen on his forehead and smiled at him. "She has one fiery temper when she sets her mind to it, and it makes her say things she normally wouldn't. Lucky for us she doesn't give in to that part of herself often."

"I can't help but get mad sometimes."

"I know, buddy. Thing is, I'm paid to sit, watch, and listen, and to provide counsel when asked. I was there when Emma left and eventually realized why. I also knew that one day she was going to come back." She smiled kindly at him. "You were a heavy factor as to why she made the trip, but not the most important. I know that sounds cruel, but sometimes love is."

Merrick's words shamed him, and he couldn't hold back the tears, but he dropped his head so Merrick wouldn't see. "I know she doesn't give a rat's ass about me. You don't have to rub it in."

"Listen to me, Hayden. You're Emma's son, and half the blood running around in here belongs to her." Merrick tapped him on the chest over his heart. "But as important as the bond is between mother and child, it's as strong for the person who owns your heart. The woman didn't move to some out-of-the-way farm because she had a burning desire to stare at cows all day long and find someone else to fill Cain's place. She left her heart here with your mother, and dying is the only way she's going to get it back."

"I wish I could remember more about what that time was like. It seems like I should, but I don't have many memories of her. I like that

Mom sometimes talks about her so that I have some mental picture to go along with the ones in my room, but I just can't forgive her for leaving me behind. And if what you're saying is true, for leaving Mom behind too."

"My sweet boy, you're learning after all, so don't let the fed get to you. Your mother is proud of you. I promised I'd never admit this, but when you aren't around she just goes on and on about you."

One light pull on his sleeve was all it took to get him to collapse into her arms and have the cry he really wanted to have.

"She's going to be fine, Hayden, if only to kick some serious ass for this happening in the first place."

"Are you all here with Cain Casey?" A middle-aged man in green scrubs stood in the doorway of the waiting room, looking like he had sweated a bucket of perspiration on his outfit.

"Is something wrong?" Hayden stood up so fast he knocked Merrick back into her chair.

"No, I'm Don Elton, her surgeon, and I just wanted to tell you she's out of surgery and holding her own. Are you her son?"

"I'm Hayden Casey, and yes, I am."

"All I can tell you now, Hayden, is she'll probably be in intensive care for a couple of days, and after that's over I'll be able to share with you more about what comes next."

"She's going to be all right?"

The doctor ran his hand over his head, pulling off the surgical cap with his action. "I don't know yet, son. Your mom had a lot of damage, and she lost a lot of blood. I wish I could sugarcoat it, but I don't believe that's fair to you if something goes wrong later. The thing I know for sure is that it's been a while since I've had someone on my table who's in such great shape. That'll mean a lot later on down the road, and now that I've met you I know she has something to fight for. Could you pass the information on to the other family members who were out here earlier? I'm going to see about getting her set up for the night. Call me if you have any questions, or if you need to talk about anything. The nurse will have all the information you'll need to get in touch with me."

"Thank you, doctor. We'll take care of it." Merrick put her hand on Hayden's back in an effort to provide some comfort from the less-than-stellar report on Cain's health.

"Can I see her?" Hayden asked.

"Not tonight. Why don't you go home and get some sleep, and tomorrow morning we'll see?" The doors swished silently as he stepped back through them, leaving the family alone.

❖

"Are you comfortable, Barney?" George sat in the rigid chair across from the agent and took a sip of the coffee he'd brought with him.

Kyle leaned back in his chair and crossed his arms over his chest to try to intimidate the attorney into letting him go. Nothing else had worked, and he had been alone in the interrogation room for over three hours. He felt confident that whatever the problem was, he was only minutes from securing his freedom. All his years in law enforcement had made him an expert on the tactics they were using on him. It would take torture to break him, of that he was sure.

"You want to just get to it, George? I've got a crime scene to get back to, and all this bullshit is really cutting into my night."

"I'm afraid there's a little problem in just letting you walk out of here, Barney. Surely you can understand we have to follow the procedures, especially when someone such as you is involved. We can clear this up really quickly, though, if you just want to answer some questions and explain a few things."

The smirk George was more than familiar with was plastered on Kyle's face, and he returned it in kind. It would be a good feeling, he thought, to be the one who knocked it off.

"Sure, shoot. Give it your best, George."

"When did you become Giovanni Bracato's whipping boy, Barney?"

Anthony, Lionel, and Joe almost choked on their coffee on the other side of the mirror. They would have given their boss some more talk before just getting to it, the old proverbial rope that would eventually hang him. Maybe they could learn something from this old warrior. Kyle's pale face was testament to that.

Two minutes ticked by before Kyle felt ready to talk. He used the time to gather his thoughts and retrace where he might have gone wrong.

The silence only confirmed his guilt to George. Innocent people never shut up when they put them in these rooms. They were always eager to prove they didn't do it.

"I have no idea—" said Kyle.

"What I'm talking about," George finished for him. "Do you want an attorney present? I'm sure you've read that list of rights enough to know yours."

"I don't need an attorney. I didn't do anything wrong."

"This is the part where I usually tell the cocky bastard in the chair that if he cooperates things will go better for him. That is, when I took the time to come down to the bowels of the building and help out with the questioning. So, Barney, if you cooperate maybe we can work something out for you. I'm picturing something along the line of minimum security, if you play this right and help us out."

Kyle laughed and leaned forward, putting his hands flat on the table. "Go fuck yourself, George, and like I said, I don't know what you're talking about."

"I would imagine you took more than your share of psychology classes before getting that more-than-nifty badge you have, am I right?"

Kyle nodded and didn't say anything, wondering where George was going with this.

The other agents watching also wondered what everyone referred to as mind-bending classes had to do with what Kyle had done.

"Placing your hands flat on the table like that is a sign that you're lying. Rapid eye blinking is another dead giveaway." George almost laughed when Kyle jerked his hands back to his lap and tried to pry his eyes open and keep their movement down to a minimum.

"George, we've known each other a long time. You can't be serious in thinking I would help an animal like Bracato. My career means everything to me."

"It meant everything to that fellow in Virginia, I'm sure, but he sold out his country for the cash. What you did, though, is help someone bring more poison into our city and become a paid enforcer to get rid of Bracato's enemies. His main one just got out of surgery, and, like I told you at the warehouse, you'd better start praying she makes it through this. Because, old friend, if she doesn't, I'm going to add murder to the list of indictments. You shot an unarmed suspect on direct orders from a known crime boss. Are you sure you don't want an attorney present for this?"

"There's no way you can prove any of this, because it didn't happen." Almost as if without his permission, Kyle's hands were back on the table and he had started blinking.

It was getting late and George had tired of the game. He got up and tapped on the glass to get the others to join them. Three chairs had sat empty throughout their talk, and Kyle hadn't even bothered to notice. The veins in his forehead, though, were noticeable when his underlings filed in and took a seat.

"You all will be investigating ice-flow patterns in Antarctica when I'm done with you."

His glare didn't work, and Anthony placed the folder they had showed George in the middle of the table. The young agent started placing pictures on the metal surface and kept at it until the whole table was covered.

Kyle looked down and saw himself accepting thick envelopes from a smiling Giovanni Bracato. Whoever had been behind the camera had even gotten a shot of him counting the payoff.

When Anthony pulled out all the relevant photos, he put a small tape recorder in front of Kyle and pressed the play button. The volume was set so that the two people on the tape filled the room.

"You think she's set to go tonight?"

At the end of the question, everyone heard a spitting sound. In front of his boss, Simmons placed a picture of Giovanni spitting out the end of the cigar he was chewing into the river.

"The talk we're picking up is making me think so. We lucked out with the team I've been able to put together. Casey can't take a piss without our knowing about it."

The inside breast pocket of Kyle's coat was barely big enough for the envelope full of hundred-dollar bills Bracato had given him.

"Yeah, I'll admit, buying you, Fife, was the smartest investment I got going. Not everyone in my business has someone watch the watchers as well for them. I owe you for keeping my own team of federal pit bulls running around in circles trying to pin anything on me. As for tonight, how would you like to earn a big bonus?"

"What do you have in mind?"

"One million for that little retirement fund of yours for Cain's head on a plate."

Kyle made no verbal response, but Simmons showed a picture of the two men shaking hands. In court, that binder to the agreement, along with Cain being shot, would be good enough. Murder for hire would get both Kyle and Bracato the needle, if they were convicted.

"We have it all on tape too, sir. If you'd like, we can have equipment brought in so you can view the meeting. We also have hours of tape from the other meetings you had with Mr. Bracato, if you want to see those."

"I want an attorney. I have nothing else to say," said Kyle.

All the other men in the room pulled back from him because Kyle looked like he was about to be sick.

"Wise choice, Agent Kyle. I hope you can afford a good one," George told him as he stood up.

"Please, sir, don't insult the rest of us by addressing him as Agent. To some of us, the fancy ID you spoke of stands for something." Lionel stood with George and spoke in his usual quiet tone.

"Then, Agent Jones, why don't I give you the honor of arresting Mr. Kyle and locking him up for the evening."

"Stand up," ordered Anthony.

"You're under arrest," said Lionel as he produced a set of cuffs.

They were all anxious to finish with the traitor so they could go back to Cain's warehouse and wrap up.

CHAPTER TWENTY-NINE

S he's out of surgery and in recovery." Hayden spoke to Emma's back and didn't care that Shelby was also standing close by. "Thank you for letting me know."

"The doctor, he said we should go home and come back in the morning. They'll call if we need to return before then."

Emma wrapped her arms around her chest and held herself in despair. She was alone. No allies to ease the raging emotions of having Cain almost die in her arms. "I'll go with you, then. That is, if you don't mind?"

Had she turned around, she would have seen Hayden act his age for once. He stubbed the toe of his shoe into the ground, obviously fishing for the right thing to say. "If you want, you can stay with us tonight. If you want, that is."

Her tears started to fall again. For one brief moment, she almost heard the little boy who would beg her to hold him when something was wrong. "I'm sure Cain wouldn't like you offering that, Hayden."

"I think it'd be all right with her. That way we can come together in the morning and see how's she's doing."

The ringing of Shelby's phone disturbed the emotional scene, and she smiled sheepishly for the intrusion. "Excuse me."

The call was from Anthony to tell her they had finished with Kyle and were headed back to the warehouse. They would wait for her, since now she would be the head agent for the investigation. She would delay any questions about their talk with their boss until they were face-to-face.

"Ms. Casey, will you be all right? I really have to get going, but if you want a ride somewhere, I'll be happy to give you one," she offered.

"She'll be fine, Agent Daniels. She's coming home with me." Hayden stepped closer to Emma, as if he dared Shelby to say otherwise.

"I'm sure she will be fine with you, Mr. Casey. Have a good evening." Shelby gave him an approving smile before she headed back out to the parking lot. The sun would be coming up in a few hours, and she still had plenty of work to do.

"Are you ready to go?" Hayden asked Emma, who hadn't answered him about where she would be spending what was left of the night.

"Yes, son, I am."

A few minutes later Emma walked through the front door of her old house and had a strange sense of déjà vu when she found her bags sitting in the foyer. Only this time they would be carried upstairs instead of to a waiting car. From what she could see, everything was as she remembered.

The woman who ran the household was waiting for them in the den when they got home. "Carmen, would you please put my mother's bags in one of the guest rooms? I'm sure we're all ready to go to bed."

"I'll be happy to take care of that in a minute, Hayden, but first tell me, how's Cain?"

"You know Mom. She's hanging in and doing okay for now."

Carmen hugged the boy and patted him on the back. The look of sheer terror he'd worn when he first left for the hospital was gone, and having him come home with Emma was more than a little strange. "We're all praying for her."

"Thanks." He hugged the older woman back before turning to Emma. "Let's go." He walked her to a room at the opposite end of the hall from the one she had shared with Cain, but next door to his own. "Call if you need anything."

"Thanks again for doing this, Hayden. I know we have a long way to go before we ever become friends, but I'm grateful for you trying."

"You can thank Mom when she wakes up. She's the one who told me I should give you a chance."

"Is that the only reason you're doing this?"

He shook his head as if to emphasize his answer. "Yes and no is the best answer, I guess. I want to talk to you some more and find out why you did some of the stuff you did, but Mom made me want to do it."

"That's the best thing I could have hoped for. Could I ask for one huge favor before you go to bed?"

"What?"

"Could you hug me?"

The last time they had shared any physical contact Emma had been the taller of the two, but now he had become the comforter just by his size. He held her close as memories flooded his brain of all the times they had done this before. The longing of a child for his mother replaced the anger, and he felt warm inside for the brief moment he allowed himself to enjoy holding her close. It was nice to have someone other than Cain make him feel that way.

"Thank you."

"Yeah, sure. Have a great night." He turned abruptly and walked to his room without looking back. What Cain had tried to explain to him about safe havens made sense to him now, and he felt guilty for enjoying this newfound warmth, though the rational part of his brain told him Cain wouldn't mind if he ventured in that direction when he needed to.

The house gradually grew quiet, and Emma lay between the soft cotton sheets staring at the shadows the outside lights cast on the ceiling. Sleeping alone in this house now felt strange. Even on the nights Cain had worked late or was away on business, she had never felt alone.

The last four years she'd spent on her father's farm had been unbearable when the sun went down. Most nights she would sit up and read to Hannah, even after the little girl went to sleep, so she wouldn't have to face the empty portion of the bed, which taunted her for her stupid mistakes.

Twelve Years Earlier in the Casey Bedroom

Branches barren of any leaves cast almost scary images on the bedroom window. Emma was close to putting the covers over her face so she wouldn't have to look at them anymore. She couldn't explain her tears, but suddenly she was sobbing uncontrollably.

The bed dipped a little when someone sat down, and she was embarrassed to turn around and face who she was sure was Carmen.

"What's the matter, sweetling?"

In an instant she turned around and buried her face in Cain's chest.

"I was missing you."

With the hiccups and the tears, Cain almost didn't understand her.

"What are you doing home? I thought you were in Chicago until tomorrow."

"I wrapped up early because I missed you too." Cain ran her fingers through her wife's pale blond locks, and slowly Emma stopped crying. The repetitive motion calmed Cain as well as Emma. It still amazed her how quickly her lover had gotten by all her defenses and tattooed herself on her heart. "Why all the tears? Are you homesick?"

"No. I miss my father, but I was just feeling alone." A few of the buttons on Cain's shirt popped open, due to Emma's wandering fingers.

"And this lonely feeling, it makes you want to take people's clothes off?"

"I wouldn't exactly classify it as people, honey. I just like the feel of you. It reminds me there's somewhere in the world I belong."

The touches Cain returned weren't about passion, but enjoying what her partner referred to. Emma didn't possess her physical strength, but from the time they had met she had provided the kind of strength she did need. Emma gave her a place to come when the world overwhelmed her, and someone to share her victories with.

"I love you, Emma, and I hope you always feel that way. Your place is with me because I belong to you."

Emma thought of that night often—lying with Cain, just holding her until the bad feelings went away. She had never feared shadows or lonely nights after then because Cain had instilled such a permanent sense of belonging in her.

That she had so readily thrown away her sense of belonging for reasons even she couldn't explain anymore haunted her now. In the warehouse, being in Cain's arms had reminded her of what she had given up, but that was over. She needed to convince her heart she had no chance of standing at Cain's side again. She didn't think Cain would keep her from trying to develop a relationship with their son, but that was where their connection would end.

To admit her loss was hard enough; to accept it would be impossible, she feared. She rolled over, closed her eyes, and tried to clear her mind so sleep would come. That was when she heard it, the whimper from next door that could only be defined as fear.

As she entered Hayden's room, the thought of not being welcomed never crossed her mind. He was curled up into a ball like he was in pain, and he was crying. She held him tighter when he didn't push her away, and the little glimmer of hope Ross had lit in her heart before he put her on the plane flared just a bit.

"It's okay, Hayden. I'm here."

"I'm so scared."

"It's okay to feel that way." Running her hand over Hayden's thick hair brought back memories of the few times she had gotten to hold Cain this way.

"She promised she'd come back, and she didn't. I don't want to be alone."

As she tried to pull him closer, Hayden put up the first sign of resistance by rolling away from her. "You aren't alone, Hayden. You have me, and there's someone else." She had wanted to wait and tell him about Hannah with Cain, but she figured it would take his mind off Cain's condition.

"There isn't anyone else, and you already left me. Because Mom's hurt, I'm not just supposed to go with you. You didn't want us, remember?" Hayden sat up and pulled away from Emma. Without meaning to, she had distracted him from his worry about Cain by replacing it with his anger toward her.

"You have a sister, Hayden, who loves you very much."

The words had barely left her mouth when Hayden jumped up and twirled around to face her with clenched fists. "No!" he roared, loud enough to wake most of the house, and she heard the running footsteps headed for his room. "You'll say anything, won't you? I don't have any sister."

She spoke fast. "I'm not lying. Her name is Hannah, and she's going to be four in a couple of weeks. When I left I had just found out I was pregnant. I planned to keep that baby safe."

"How, by sacrificing me?"

"No, by coming back for you."

"I wish Mom had just ordered me to stay away from you. You not only left me, you love some other kid better? When Mom finds out—"

The door opened, and Merrick and Mook slammed in without an invitation.

"Go back to bed, this is between me and her." Hayden pointed to Emma, expecting to be obeyed.

"What's all the yelling about?" asked Merrick.

"I said this is private. Leave." Hayden never took his eyes off her as he shoved his hands deep into the pockets of his jeans. When they had gotten back from the hospital he had just collapsed on the bed, not feeling like undressing. "When Mom finds out, you won't be able to find a pit deep enough to hide in," he said, once the door clicked closed.

"Cain already knows about Hannah. I told her tonight, but she already knew."

"Liar. She would've told me. She tells me everything."

Emma stood and moved closer to him. She wanted to comfort him, but if she had to let him verbally attack her, so be it. "I don't know why she didn't tell you, Hayden. Maybe she was waiting for all this to be over."

When Hayden added betrayal to the list of things he felt, something in him snapped. "Get out. Go back to your room. You and Mom deserve each other."

"Let's finish this, son."

"I'm not your son, I'm not anyone's son. You've replaced me. Now, get out."

❖

"Mrs. Casey." Carmen shook her shoulder lightly, waking her to a very bright room.

Emma blinked in confusion until the previous night rushed back like some bad B-movie. If her original plan had been to alienate Hayden from Cain, she had succeeded. Only now, he totally despised her as an added bonus.

"Is something wrong? Did something happen to Cain?"

"No, ma'am, the hospital called and said Ms. Casey's doing better. I just thought you'd like to join young Hayden for some breakfast before you both head back to the hospital."

Merrick banged on the door. "Carmen, where's Hayden?" Merrick felt truly panicked as she asked the question. His dismissal of them the night before had caught both her and Mook off guard, but they had tried to give him some room. So much space that now they couldn't find him.

"I thought he was in his room."

Emma threw back the blankets, walked up to Merrick, and grabbed her. "What do you mean, where's Hayden?"

"I can't find him anywhere in the house, but he knows better than to be out alone. He didn't tell you anything?"

Emma tightened her grip on Merrick's arms. Hayden was probably just out blowing off steam like any normal eleven-year-old who had gotten into an argument with his mother. However, most young boys weren't the son of Cain and Emma Casey. They weren't walking, enticing targets for those who would use them as payment for the sins of their family. If he had let his anger override his good sense, then he could be in big trouble, now compounded by the fact that Cain wasn't there to fix any problems.

Mook ran in and had to take a second to catch his breath before he could talk. "We found his bike about a block from here, but no sign of him."

It was Merrick's turn to hold on to Emma, as she almost collapsed at the news. "Come on, Emma. Now isn't the time for you to fall apart. As much as I don't like it, we're in this together, and we have to get him back before Cain wakes up. She trusted all of us to take care of him, and let me tell you, folks, we aren't exactly doing a bang-up job here."

"Maybe he just went for a walk." Mook tried to think positively, but even he couldn't even imagine having to tell Cain they'd lost her kid.

"Mook, I love you, God knows, but if he left here on his bike he didn't go for a walk. We need to find out who exactly has him."

"I think I'm going to be sick." Emma took a deep breath and only for an instant leaned against Merrick for support. "Shouldn't we ask the feds outside if they saw anything?"

"They're not here anymore. The big fish they were trolling for is laid up in the hospital, so they don't have any real reason to watch us peons anymore. Unless your girlfriend did you a favor and called off the dogs."

"Back off, Merrick, and she isn't a friend of mine. I met the woman last night, and she helped me through a rough spot. That doesn't make us lovers. And as for Cain—" She was about to get on a roll when Mook interrupted them.

"Ladies, I don't mean to be rude, but we have bigger problems than who gets to walk home from school with the boss."

"He's right. We need to put our personal feelings aside and concentrate on how to get Hayden back. I think Merrick's correct about him not being out for a walk. Someone's taken my son, and I'm going to do something about it."

Merrick started laughing so hard she almost fell over. "You're going to take charge? That's rich. You're the reason he's not here now. Leave this to me and the guys. Then you can go back to milking cows."

"Mook, go downstairs with Carmen and assemble the men. We're going to the hospital first. Then I have a job for you. With Cain being hurt and Hayden disappearing, there's only one Casey left in this house and it ain't Merrick, so move."

The guard and housekeeper turned and left the room to do Emma's bidding.

She wrapped the ends of her robe tie in her hands and cinched it closed. "Not you, Merrick."

The guard had begun to follow the others, but the new commanding tone stopped her.

"I intend to resolve this situation before Cain gets too worried. She doesn't need any extra stress during her recovery, and I *do* plan to stay to see that she does recover. You can either suck it up and help me, or you can leave. Those are your only choices, so don't take long to decide."

"I don't take orders from you."

"Fine, get out. Leave now or I'll have you removed, and when Cain does wake up I'll explain your reluctance to help."

Merrick laughed again, only this time it sounded sarcastic. "My, the lady has claws, or is it the pit viper has fangs?"

"You're wasting my time, so leave."

"Come on, Emma. You don't think Cain's going to side with you on this, do you?"

Emma had a hard time maintaining her calm demeanor when all she wanted to do was run to the hospital and beat on Cain until she woke up and fixed things. She knew, though, that she didn't have the luxury of wasting time fantasizing. At the moment she knew two things with utmost certainty. The man who had taken her son wouldn't harm him without negotiating first, and if she didn't break Merrick now, she never would.

"I spent years being where you can only dream about, Merrick— in Cain's bed. You know what I learned in all that time, aside from the meaning of true passion?"

The guard's green eyes narrowed to slits, but she didn't respond.

"No clue? Let me tell you, then. I learned how Cain thinks and how she plans. Last night you weren't at the warehouse. The one night everyone's been planning on forever, and you're nowhere in sight. Why was that?"

"You think you're so fucking smart."

"I don't think, I know just how smart I am, thank you, but getting back to my question. You weren't there because your job was to watch our son. Cain counted on you, and now he's gone. I'm not blaming you, but I'll lay it on thick when it comes to telling her about the getting-him-back part. Because let's not kid ourselves, shall we? We know who has him and why." Emma strode toward the bathroom. The talk was over, and she had baited the hook. She needed Merrick, but only if the woman was willing to work with her.

"How did you know I haven't slept with her? You've been gone a long time."

"A wife knows, Merrick. Don't forget that. I'll see you downstairs in a minute."

The humor returned to Merrick's laugh. Cain's partner had won a decisive victory without throwing a punch, garnering a bit of admiration from her, the loser. Merrick had no doubt why her boss was still lamenting the loss of this woman. Any other woman would have fired her out of pride, but by allowing her to go wait with the rest of Cain's men, Emma was giving her a second chance.

Carmen and some of her girls were passing around coffee cups when Merrick entered the large den where they had all convened. The only men missing were the ones watching over Cain in the hospital. Mook tried not to smile at Merrick's appearance, knowing what it meant. He had no reason to dig into her wounded pride.

"What's the plan, Merrick?" one of the men asked, looking around Carmen, who was filling his cup.

"I'm sure when the boss gets down here she'll tell us what we need to do."

"Who, Cain? I thought she was still in the hospital?"

"Not exactly, fellas. For now we'll be taking orders from Emma Casey, and before you start grumbling, let's hear her out. This woman may surprise you. She sure did me just a few minutes ago when I had a run-in with her."

Mook and Merrick listened to the group's grievances, letting them vent before Emma came down. One man named Hank who had been with Cain for a little over a year sounded adamantly opposed to taking any direction from Emma.

"I don't know about the rest of you, but I ain't going along with no snatch ordering me around." Hank crossed his arms and leaned back into the thick cushion of the sofa.

"And your name is what?" Emma strode in and took a seat in the chair Merrick was standing behind. The fact that the guard didn't move sent a clear message to the rest of the people in the room.

"Hank."

"Hank, you are free to leave." Emma pointed in the general direction of the doorway behind her. "Don't let the knob hit you in the ass on the way out. Merrick, please settle up with him if Cain owes him anything for services rendered."

Merrick tried hard not to laugh at the shock on the man's face. Emma had effectively pinned him to his seat since he looked so paralyzed.

"We have plenty to cover, Hank, so get moving."

"You heard the lady," said Mook. He stood and walked over next to Merrick. It wasn't totally clear why Merrick was going along with this, but his job was Hayden's welfare, so to get the boy back, Mook would deal with the devil.

The guard walked out without any other response except to slam the door.

"Here's what we're going to do," said Emma. When she was done with her explanation, everybody in the room knew the woman had spent years at Cain's side. She was more polite, but what she was asking bore Cain's distinct cunning and resolve.

"You heard Mrs. Casey. Break into four groups and meet me back in the office at the club tonight. Don't even think about screwing this up." Merrick paused and looked at Emma before finishing. "It's a good plan."

"Thank you." Emma smiled and turned her attention back to the rest of the group. "Good luck and remember, Merrick's right. There's no room for error on this one. My son's life is on the line, and if one of you gambles with that I'll kill you myself. " She stood and paused to see if she would hear any other dissent. "Merrick, Mook, let's head over to the hospital and check on the boss."

CHAPTER THIRTY

A nother padlock slipped into place on one of the trucks the federal agents were using to cart away the mounting evidence against Cain. It wasn't yet ten in the morning, and the combination of too little sleep and the sick feeling over what they were doing was giving Shelby a massive headache. Why Cain had just given up and let them catch her so easily had been the question on her mind.

Lionel took a seat next to her. "We're going to have to call Agent Hicks to see where she wants us to store all this stuff. Eventually I'm sure it will all be destroyed. Since I like a drink every so often, I think that's a shame." He stared out at the warehouse, which was far more luxurious than he would have guessed from the outside. Cain obviously didn't use it too often the way the space was intended because of all the exercise equipment and the collection of cars.

Shelby had meant to call Agent Annabel Hicks all morning, but she had put it off until the inventory was done. Hicks supervised the New Orleans office and was no friend to their supervisor, Barney Kyle, so she had spent her morning at the federal lockup dealing with the ramifications of having a dirty agent in her employ. As Shelby went to call her, a forklift unloading boxes dropped one of the crates. It sounded as if every bottle had broken, and the stains on the wood confirmed that the majority of them had bitten the dust.

All of a sudden, a car door slammed near the entrance to Cain's property. A tall, dark-haired woman emerged from the driver's side, accompanied by a group of young, well-dressed men and women. One of them pulled out a leather-bound notepad and wrote down the number on the crate that had just been destroyed. Anthony stopped them from entering the premises and just as quickly pointed toward the table where Lionel and Shelby were sitting.

"Agent Daniels?" The woman in the lead held her hand out in greeting, not bothering to introduce the people she was with.

Shelby just stared at her, not lifting her hand. She knew clothes, and the outfit the woman had on cost more than the federal government paid her in two months, six if you threw in the expensive jewelry that adorned the hand at the end of her visual tour. "And you are?"

"Muriel Casey, and I believe you are trespassing on private property." Tired of waiting for the woman to break out of her stupor and shake her hand, Muriel dropped her hand and lifted an eyebrow instead.

"If anyone is in the way, it would be you and your little entourage of eager beavers."

"As Derby Cain Casey's attorney, I would like an explanation as to why you're destroying her property."

"Ms. Casey, we are investigating the illegal importation and sale of liquor and cigarettes, which your boss didn't bother to pay federal taxes on. In case you missed that class in law school, that's a crime. I know she hid them in the cleverly disguised sardine boxes, but we are a bit more sophisticated than she gave us credit for." Shelby leaned back in her chair and took a deep breath. She was tired, and the fact that this woman looked a lot like Cain was throwing her. Her own investigative skills and gaydar were pinging *family* in more ways than one.

"If you and the mental giants you're working for had bothered to open one of the crates, you would've found the little tax stamp you're talking about." Muriel snapped her fingers, and one of the lapdogs pulled a stack of papers from his leather-bound notebook and handed them to Lionel. "As for the sardine crates, I'll have to mention to Cain's Canadian distributor, Sardine's Liquor and Spirits, that you have a problem with their name. I doubt they'll change it since it's their family name. Who knows, maybe way back they were little fishers of little fish? You can take up the great question with Norris Sardine." The other younger attorneys behind her laughed, and Muriel joined in. "I know. I offered to change it to Morris Salmon, but he refused."

After Lionel read over the shipping invoices, which contained all the proper customs stamps, he ran to get a crowbar.

"This will only take a minute to clear up," said Shelby, reading the same papers. If they were legitimate, Cain had played them like blind sheep.

"Good, since you have about a minute to vacate my client's property. If not, I'll have the police come and remove you, along with every news crew we can get down here to film the government's harassment of a legitimate businesswoman. Would this be a good time to interject that said businesswoman was shot while she was receiving legal goods?"

"I don't know they're legal goods."

"Do you know Cain, Agent Daniels?"

"I've had the pleasure of making her acquaintance."

"Then you know every one of those crates holds bottle after bottle of federally and state-approved commodities. Leave before I have to put your name on the suit we're filing."

"But we've been watching Cain for months." The seriousness of the situation was dawning on Shelby. An FBI agent had shot and seriously wounded a citizen going about her business. The fact that he did it on orders from one of the city's crime bosses wouldn't help their case in the eyes of the public. As a group, they had been so busy watching Cain that it never occurred to them to watch their own.

"I'm sorry. Is this where I'm supposed to tell you that everything's going to be all right?"

Shelby looked up from the papers in her hand and winced when Lionel pried the first crate open. The nails giving from the wood sounded like fingernails running down a chalkboard. "Ma'am, I know you would like us to vacate the premises as soon as possible, but could you give me a few minutes?"

"Take all the time you need, Agent Daniels, as long as it doesn't take all morning. Could you also refrain from breaking anything else? Nothing upsets Cain as much as spilled booze." Muriel walked to her cousin's office and ordered the agents who had taken up residence to get out.

The young man who had written down the serial number of the broken crate was now busy writing up the fact that the desktop was full of mud. The agent sitting behind Cain's desk had thought nothing of putting his feet up when he took a short nap earlier that morning.

"Tell me there aren't any tax stamps on those bottles," Shelby said to Lionel, who was breaking open one of the boxes in the crate.

"This is the fourth one we've popped open, and I wish I could tell you no. She played us, Shelby, and like a bunch of fucking morons, we just trusted Kyle. Cain Casey's business is illegal liquor, but this one time she went more than aboveboard. Those papers that suit handed you have every *t* crossed and every *i* dotted. Hicks isn't going to like this. It's a complete media nightmare when you put Barney in the mix. We'll be lucky to convict Casey of an overdue parking ticket now."

"You've got to give her credit, though. God, we should've known when she just started talking in Wisconsin. Kyle's chased these people for years, and all of a sudden she starts giving details, dates, and times. Common sense should have told us all that it would be the one time she'd do it by the numbers."

Anthony and Joe joined them after they unlocked the back of one of the other trucks and opened some of the crates. All of them had the appropriate markings, meaning the agents shouldn't be there. In their game of cat and mouse with Cain, none of them had ever realized that they were the ones standing on the wrong side of the trap. They all knew if the winner had been conscious, she would have been laughing her ass off.

"Is everything in order?" Muriel asked, scaring them all because no one heard her walk up.

"We'll be on our way, and I can assure you, Ms. Casey, we'll conduct an inquiry into what exactly happened here last night. Here's my card." Shelby handed her own card over with a prayer that she wasn't about to be subjected to a complete dressing-down.

"My cousin told me to watch out for you, Agent Daniels. Her exact words were you were the smart one in the group." Muriel looked over at the three men backing Shelby up. "No offense, gentlemen."

"Thank you," said Shelby. "I was wondering about the last name and the family resemblance."

"My father thought some of us in the Casey clan should be on the up-and-up." When Shelby looked confused as to whom Muriel was talking about, she provided the complete family connection. "Jarvis, in case you're wondering. It was his idea for me to pursue a career as an officer of the court and all that jazz. If you all are finished with your less-than-successful fishing expedition, may I show you to the door? Oh, and if you left any of those nasty bugs behind, I'll send the extermination bill to you all personally. I'm already on retainer, so what's one more trip to court to make sure it comes out of your own salary."

The new guy with the muddy shoes stepped back into the office and returned about two minutes later. He nodded toward Muriel before climbing into the back of one of their cars.

When Muriel laughed softly, Shelby noticed how much she reminded her of Cain.

"I'm sure Agent Hicks from our office will contact you at your convenience, Ms. Casey," said Anthony, to break the silence.

"Tell Annabel I look forward to it, though she's another one who would benefit from a name change. Janet Bond, maybe. It sounds much more secret agent–like." She pointed to the door where some of Cain's men were already taking up their posts. "Gentlemen and Ms. Daniels, if you would please excuse me, I have work to do."

Seeing the personnel coming in, the four agents started walking toward the entrance. Whatever was up was big, since most of the men on Cain's payroll were arriving. One of them dragged a rolling bag behind him and stopped to talk to Muriel before he headed into the office. She nodded at what he whispered before she waved one last time to the curious onlookers.

Shelby turned to her coworkers and winked. The game was afoot again, and this time they would get it right.

❖

The doctor patted Emma's knee. "She's doing much better this morning, Ms. Casey. She had a good night and is responding well to the medications. The painkillers are one of the reasons she hasn't regained consciousness yet. Derby needs a few more days of rest to put her on the road to recovery." He answered the rest of her questions and then just sat with her.

Emma tried to process what the man who had put Cain back together had said. She took deep, calming breaths, trying to keep her tears and more-than-overwhelming emotions at bay. "Do you think she'll have a lot to overcome, once this is all over?" She knew that Cain would be devastated if she couldn't go back to the life she was used to.

"It'll take some time, but I think it's up to Cain to see how long that journey of recovery is going to be. I promise if she applies herself, she should be fine. Last night I wasn't this optimistic, but the woman lying in there has some amazing healing powers. Are you ready?"

Emma nodded and stood to follow him into the intensive care unit. The sight of Cain with all the tubes and equipment hooked to her made her slump against the doctor. Seeing Cain this vulnerable was threatening to make her breakfast reappear. When they had been together, Cain looked vibrant even in her sleep.

"She needs your strength now, Emma, not your hopelessness."

He left when she walked to the bed and put her head down on the uninjured side of Cain's chest. Dr. Elton had explained to her that he was a firm believer that his patients could hear their loved ones when they came to see them and talk to them in situations like this. He had assured her that when she got over the shock of what happened, her soothing voice would bring Cain back to those who loved her.

"Honey, I know I'm the last person you probably want to hear from right now, but I have you in the perfect spot to listen to me." She wiped her eyes and tried to sound teasing as she brushed back the black hair before running her fingers along Cain's jawline.

"This is my opportunity to work on that little part of your brain that's still crazy about me and is being beaten into submission by that tough macho part that likes to swagger most of the time. I'm here for you, my love, until forever." Her fingers stopped their caress and moved to Cain's lips, while she clasped the other hand lightly. "You are mine, but not for a short time. You pledged yourself to me forever, and that's what I want. Please give our family a chance. I want you to rest and get better. I've got some stuff to do, but I'll be back."

From her post at the door Merrick looked on as Emma leaned over the bed and kissed Cain on the lips. When they connected, Emma felt a flutter in Cain's fingers. "I love you."

The nurse behind the counter keeping watch on all the monitors glanced up and smiled. "Thank you for observing the time limit. Dr. Elton is hoping to move her into a regular room by the end of the week."

"Take good care of her."

Emma walked out with her two shadows, remembering to nod toward Lou and the other man who stood guard with him. It was time to see a man about her son.

CHAPTER THIRTY-ONE

When Emma arrived at the warehouse office, Muriel immediately stood, hugged her close, and didn't let go right away. "Emma, darling, you look fabulous. Cousin Cain won't be able to hold out too long when she wakes up. I spoke to the doctor, and he told me she's going to be fine." Muriel had put aside any anger she had left for Emma when Merrick explained the plan Cain's ex had come up with.

"Thanks, Muriel. She looks a lot better today, but I couldn't bring myself to tell her about Hayden. Have we heard anything?"

"There've been no calls, but that doesn't mean anything. It's not time to start worrying yet."

From behind Cain's desk, Emma snorted. "That's easy for you to say, Muriel. He isn't your son."

"Come on, I love the little guy. Of course I'm worried about him, but I realize what all this is about, and you're doing the right thing. You've changed, Emma, and that's good. I talked to Cain a lot when you left, and you know me. I had to drop my twenty-five dollars into the conversation."

"Isn't that supposed to be two cents?"

"Not with what I charge Cain. You probably wouldn't have left all those years ago if she'd made you more of a true partner. Once this is done, don't let her be the one to run away this time."

"I'm trying, Muriel. That's all I can do." Emma waited until the man sweeping the room was done before she moved on to more important topics.

When he finished the last section of the room he gave them a thumbs-up and spoke to Muriel. "The room's clean, Ms. Casey."

"Thanks, Frank. Why don't you clean the rest of the place? Those guys were in here for a while. God only knows what they left behind."

"Did the guys pick up my four packages?" Emma asked Merrick and Mook, not concerned Cain's attorney was still in the room.

Muriel Casey and her infamous cousin had a lot in common. Both had learned the ins and outs of the family business from their fathers, but Muriel hadn't lied to Shelby. Jarvis and Dalton had wanted her to pursue a law career because of the family business. Her sexual tastes were also similar to Cain's. Their parents hadn't been disappointed in their sexual preferences, but to have them be so open about their lifestyle made both Jarvis's and Dalton's dreams of grandchildren dim. Had Dalton only lived to see Hayden, he would have been delighted.

Muriel was two years younger than Cain, but unlike her cousin, she still wanted the pleasure of meeting a lot more women in the city, so settling down was out of the question. Even if she had considered it, watching Cain work through the pain of Emma leaving her put it right out of her mind.

Merrick leaned against the desk near Emma, like she did when Cain was in the chair. "Your packages are under some very watchful eyes at the club," she assured Emma. "Don't worry, I put our best guys on the job. With Cain out of commission, the feds are backing off. It's weird, really. Do they think business doesn't go on without her here?"

"Your boss just played them like a bunch of pimple-faced rookies, and they're reeling from what happened," Muriel interjected so they could move to the subject at hand. "The shipment sitting out there is legit."

"All of it?" asked Mook.

"Down to the no-name cigarettes in the last truck. My uncle Dalton always said be careful of jumping to a conclusion about anyone or anything. Even though someone's always done something a certain way, he may take another route every so often. Kyle learned that the hard way, and according to my connections at the federal building, he's in custody for shooting Cain."

Emma leaned forward in her chair and put her hands on the desk. "What are you talking about?"

"The story on the street is Kyle was working for Giovanni Bracato and shot Cain on his order. Mr. Bracato was using this as the culminating act to finish the turf war he's fought with Cain and the other families to take over all the neighborhoods and rackets in the city. With Cain still alive and Kyle in custody, it stands to reason he seized Hayden when he went out this morning unprotected.

"Nothing will happen to him, Emma. Not yet anyway. Big Gino needs him as an insurance policy for whatever talking Kyle's doing against him. My guess is he wants us to use our relationships and political connections to take care of that loose end." Muriel crossed her legs and tried to look relaxed before she asked a question. "But what happens if he doesn't take the bait you're going fishing with, Emma?"

"If something happens to Hayden, I'll trade Bracato's entire family, with his dead body at the top of the pile, for our son. I'll pull the trigger myself, if that's what's necessary for Mr. Bracato to see I'm serious. There's no way I go back to Cain and tell her I failed and let harm come to Hayden."

Everyone in the room nodded in agreement. If Giovanni put one bruise on Hayden, the streets would run red from the war that would erupt. Going against someone's child was just not done.

Merrick put her hand on Emma's back as a sign of encouragement and peered over her head at Muriel. "You want us to call you tonight?"

"I feel like a drink and some dancing, so you won't have far to look for me."

"Is that a smart thing for you, Muriel?" asked Emma. "You are, after all, an officer of the court."

"I'm also Cain's advisor on everything concerning the business. There's very little I don't know, Emma. I just don't share that knowledge with too many people. If that makes me a criminal as well, so be it, but this is my family too. To me that's all that's important."

"Good to know."

"Emma, we're ready when you are," Mook said when he got off his cell.

"Then let's go."

The car waiting outside had completely tinted windows in the back. Once Merrick had seated her new boss, and she and Mook climbed in, they all turned to the small brown-eyed passenger with his legs curled into his middle, crying.

"It's all right, honey," Emma cooed, as she took the crying child from one of Cain's men. The little boy looked up, and his crying slowed to just sniffles.

The driver glanced at Emma. "Christ. Glad you're here. The kid hasn't quit bawling since we snatched him in the park. Dumb nanny wasn't watching the stroller. Cain would've had her head for pulling a stunt like that."

Emma dried the baby's tears. "You sure are a cute one, aren't you? You don't have to be afraid. We're on our way to see your grandfather. No one is going to hurt you, little guy, so just relax." The little boy put his index finger in his mouth and leaned against her, closing his eyes as her soothing speech continued.

The car moved in the direction of Gino Bracato's warehouse. Muriel had called ahead and used her usual verbal persuasion to get them past the front door or, in this case, to the front door to pick up a lone Gino, shifting from one foot to the other as he watched for the car to arrive. He was obviously worried about the safety of the small passenger.

The FBI team assigned to Bracato, back on live surveillance, was surprised to see the man come out of his offices and get into the limo. The agents, shocked that none of Bracato's men got in after him and that the car pulled away quickly, called for backup to follow the mystery visitors and see what they were up to with Big Gino.

"Mr. Bracato, thank you for joining us on such short notice." Emma pulled the child resting against her shoulder tighter against her body and smiled. "I was enjoying the trip over here with your grandson."

"Listen to me, bitch. You hurt him, and I'll spend the rest of my days hunting you down."

"Merrick, if he curses in front of the baby again, please knock out some of those teeth. Good manners are so hard to instill in the young, Mr. Bracato. No sense in giving him a head start on how *not* to act."

After both Mook and Merrick eased their jackets open to show Bracato what would happen, he didn't move to get closer to her and the boy. Instead, he smiled and tried to turn on the charm, though Emma noticed a piece of spinach in his yellowed teeth.

"Maybe you should be the one who needs a lesson in good manners, Mrs. Casey. Stealing my grandson is just not done in this business. We are, after all, men of honor. Cain should have taught you that."

"Does that mean my son will be waiting for me at home when I get there?"

"What makes you think I have your son? He could've run off, for all I know, since he's the bastard son of that bitch Cain. Maybe he couldn't live with the shame of it all."

Emma closed her eyes and tilted her head upward to take a deep breath. After her short encounter with the idiot sitting across from her, she realized why Cain took so many cleansing breaths throughout the day. "Merrick, please tell the driver to stop the car."

"Yes, ma'am."

After another short tap to the window from Mook, Emma's order was obeyed.

"Get out."

"What about my—" Gino swallowed his smug smile when the man next to him pulled out his gun and just pointed it at the floor of the car. He didn't doubt that one word from Emma would change its position to the vicinity of his head.

"I had come today with every intention of giving you back your grandson as a token of my goodwill, but your behavior tells me that what Cain has said all along about you is true. Get out of the car, Mr. Bracato, and be careful how you treat my son. Take a walk back to your office and call your sons, all of them, and ask what move you should make next. Once they give you an answer, call me back and we'll talk again. Don't take too long, though. My patience is running thin, and I miss Hayden." Emma tightened her grip on the boy she held on her shoulder and motioned her head to the side to get the fat man moving.

Mook took the opportunity to press his gun at the base of Bracato's head. "I believe the lady asked you to leave."

"You're going to pay for this, starting with your kid, lady. My son Giovanni isn't quite as forgiving as his old man, and when he finds out you have his boy, he'll rip that little son of a bitch of yours to shreds."

"I'll look forward to your call, Mr. Bracato. Mook, I did promise our guest something if he cursed again, I believe."

Emma didn't even wince when she heard the blow to Bracato's head outside the car.

"You ucking astard, you knocked out my two ont eeth," the man yelled.

"It was a good way to get rid of the spinach, anyway," she said with a straight face. "Let's go home, guys, and introduce this little one to Carmen."

The kind old woman took charge of the baby from the minute they arrived. When Emma handed him over, he reached for her one last time, but went quietly with Carmen into the kitchen for a bottle.

After they disappeared, Emma asked Merrick to step into Cain's office. "I'm going to tell you something, and I want you to let me finish before you go off on me." She sat in one of the guest chairs, not feeling as comfortable in this office as the one in the warehouse.

"How can you be so sure that what you say is going to send me off the deep end?"

Merrick's arched dark brow reminded her so much of Cain she had to take a deep breath before she responded. "Because it's the same thing I shared with Hayden last night, and it sent him running into the waiting arms of Giovanni Bracato, so call it a hunch on my part."

Merrick pinched the bridge of her nose and nodded. "Okay, I wasn't going to ask, but since you brought it up, what was it?"

With no detail left out, she told the guard about Hannah, the secret she had kept for so long.

Merrick kept her word and didn't say anything until Emma finished. "Does Cain know?"

"It's why she threw up that day you went running with her. I made a mistake, Merrick, but I called my friends who are keeping Hannah, and they agreed to bring her to meet Cain and Hayden. I intend to stay in the city, even if Cain doesn't want us."

Merrick leaned forward and did something totally out of character. She put her hand on Emma's knee and looked up at her with a touch of sadness. "You don't know her at all, even after all this time, do you?"

"What do you mean?"

"Emma, she's never stopped wanting the things you took away. The closest I've seen a woman get to her since you left was, surprisingly, that FBI agent Shelby. You had a baby and kept it from her, though, and I'm not sure where she begins to forgive you for that. Turning you away, I'm fairly sure, isn't her style. Cain will always put her family first, but I don't know if she'll let you back in the way she did before. I have a feeling, though, little Hannah might just be your ticket."

"From your mouth to God's ear," Emma said softly, as she gazed out the windows behind Cain's desk. She and Cain had spent an afternoon in heated debate about the placement of the old family heirloom. She thought it left Cain vulnerable if someone wanted to take a shot at her, but living in fear wasn't Cain's style either.

"Come on, Emma. We have some idiots to move, and I have to figure out to where. Why don't you go up and take a nap? After this afternoon's meeting with Bracato, I'm thinking we should wait until at least tomorrow to make any moves."

Emma laughed, and some of Cain's expressions made sense to her now. "Make them sweat, right?"

"It's good to see you weren't just paying attention to her ass in those leather pants you liked so much. You're right. We make Bracato sweat and wait for him to panic." Merrick stopped at the door and turned around to look at her with a serious expression. "*You* aren't going to panic on me, are you, Emma?"

She shook her head and fought against her alarm. She had come too far to let nerves get in the way of getting her son back. "What about Hayden?"

"The boy got himself into this, so now he knows there's no quick fixes without Cain being here. He'll know to sit and wait, but he also knows we won't leave him behind."

"What would Cain do if she were here?"

The green eyes Cain had fallen in love with pinned Merrick with their open expression. It was easy now to see why Cain had such a hard time in the past telling this woman no. "Depends."

"On what?" asked Emma.

"If there's one scratch on her son. He comes back without a scratch on him, maybe Bracato gets lucky. That stupid fat ass hurts him, though, and she'll kill him even if she has to do it in the mayor's office in front of a million witnesses."

Emma steepled her fingers in front of her lips and thought about what Merrick had just said, knowing it was true. Finally she made her request. "Wherever you put them, Merrick, make sure it's private."

The answer gave Merrick another surprise for the day. In her wildest dreams she wouldn't have guessed Emma would last this long. "You got it, boss."

CHAPTER THIRTY-TWO

The beep of the machines next to the bed was lulling Shelby to sleep. She had been at Cain's side since she saw Emma leave earlier, wanting to sit with the mobster a while to convince herself that Cain would eventually recover. The guard Merrick had posted had searched Shelby before she entered, with her cooperation. She knew that if he was sure she wasn't carrying in anything she planned to leave behind, he was more likely to grant access.

She had been sitting for over three hours, trying to get some response out of the still woman on the bed. Cain looked different in this totally relaxed state, more like the son she had watched for so long when he was out with his mother. For the thousandth time she wished Cain had been an accountant so they could have something more between them.

"Come on, Cain. I know you're in there."

Muriel filled up the doorway, much as her cousin would have. "She'll come around, Agent Daniels. Don't worry. The doctor just told me they were cutting down on her pain medication and moving her soon. Is this some sort of new surveillance technique I'm not familiar with?" She indicated Cain's hand that Shelby was holding.

"I'm not here to make trouble for her, ma'am. Cain's my friend."

Muriel laughed, and the sound was so similar to Cain's, Shelby felt sad.

"But she's also been under your microscope for how long now?" Muriel lifted her big hands like a stop sign. "I'm just kidding with you, Agent Daniels. How's my cousin doing today?"

"All this quiet and stillness doesn't seem natural." Shelby touched Cain's cheek. "You're right, though. I did watch her for months, but it didn't prepare me for the day I met her."

"Well, ma'am, we Caseys like to leave an impression when we can. How about you wait for me down in the cafeteria, and I'll buy you a cup of coffee?"

"Please call me Shelby."

Muriel's phone started ringing, and she put one finger up. She listened and smiled at Shelby as whoever was on the other end finished talking. "Give me a minute, then bring her on up."

Muriel held her hand out. "Please pardon the interruption, Shelby, and I insist you call me Muriel. I hate to hurry you, but we have to be going."

"You're evicting me?"

"You're welcome to visit Cain whenever you wish, but Emma's on her way up and needs some time alone. I hope you understand."

Shelby kissed Cain's hand and accepted Muriel's escort downstairs. When the two passed a couple sitting in the waiting room holding a beautiful child, she stopped abruptly, stunned by the sight. The kid looked like a miniature version of Hayden. "Tell me she didn't do that to Cain?"

"Shelby, I'm going to ask you as a favor to forget you saw that little girl for now. I have no right to ask, but I don't want anyone to know just yet. My family's still reeling from what happened to Cain because of Kyle, and I want to make sure there's no one else on Bracato's payroll. I don't think even you know who to trust yet."

Running her hand through her hair to get it out of her eyes, Shelby nodded. Muriel was right. They couldn't know if Kyle had help. "If the secret comes out it won't be from me, Muriel. I promise."

They kept walking down the hall. "Does Cain know about her?"

"She knows about her."

"How could Emma do that to her?"

"How indeed?"

❖

The subject of their talk stood at the entrance to Cain's room. Emma had tried to follow Merrick's advice and take a nap, but sleep wasn't coming. With Hayden still missing, she sought comfort the only place she could find it. She inched toward the bed and sat on the edge. The tube coming out of Cain's mouth had left her lips chapped and dry, so she went for a wet towel.

"I wish you would wake up. There's so much wrong, Cain, and I'm not sure if I know how to fix it. At least not without messing anything else up. Please come back to me." She moistened Cain's lips with the cloth.

"Ms. Casey," said the large guard, who hadn't left the hospital since Cain had been admitted.

"Lou, right?"

"Yes, ma'am. I'm sorry to interrupt, but there's a couple waiting to see you. I wanted to give you a few minutes before I came in, though. I hope you don't mind."

"No problem." She nodded at the big guy before turning back to Cain. "Don't go anywhere, okay? I'll be right back."

Lou laughed as Emma headed out to the waiting room. "Don't worry, Mrs. Casey. I'll keep an eye on her and make sure she behaves until you get back."

"Thanks, Lou." The walk seemed longer as she left the intensive care unit and headed out to the waiting room. If it was reporters or more legal authorities, she was going to have a meltdown. Both groups had been tying up the phone lines at the house to the point that Carmen had taken the phones with listed numbers off the hook.

When she turned the corner, she felt as if someone had thrown her a life preserver before she drowned in a sea of turmoil. The small figure sitting on her friend Maddie's lap looked tense in the unfamiliar surroundings, but her face brightened overwhelmingly when Emma winked at her from the other side of the glass. For once the large number of men sitting in close proximity to her daughter didn't bother Emma. It was a comfort to see Jarvis taking such good care of Hannah.

"Mama!"

"Hey, how's Mama's big girl?" She knelt on the hard tile floor so she could accept Hannah's embrace.

The almost-four-year-old held on to her as if she was afraid Emma would disappear again. "We gots to ride a big plane here, Mama, and Aunt Maddie said I could meet Haygen and Mom too."

Hearing Hannah's excitement about the big day she had waited for made Emma cry. She felt like a failure for not giving the little girl the simplest of wishes before now.

Maddie put her hands on Emma's shoulders. "Emma, why'd we have to come here? Has something happened to Hayden? None of these guys would tell us anything."

"There'll be time later for me to explain, Maddie. Thank you and Jerry for coming and bringing Hannah, but I just can't talk about it yet." Emma stroked her daughter's hair, coming to a decision. "Do you mind waiting while I introduce Hannah to someone?"

"Go on, honey, and take your time. Jerry and I don't have any place to be."

Hannah glanced back and forth from her mother to Maddie, wearing a small frown. "I'm sorry, Mama."

"What for, my love?"

"I didn't mean to touch nothing."

Emma smiled and kissed Hannah's forehead. "Oh, baby girl, you aren't in trouble, I just wanted to talk to you before I took you to see someone. Do you remember me telling you about your mom Cain?"

The little head nodded.

"Well, she wants to meet you, but she got hurt and has a big boo-boo."

"We make it better, Mama?"

"We'll try, angel. Do you want to go and see your mom?"

When Emma walked back into the unit holding Hannah's hand, the nurses didn't dare tell her children weren't allowed. All of the men outside Cain's door stared at the little girl in the pink dress. Emma could imagine what they were thinking—that maybe it was a good thing the boss was out for the count at the moment.

She picked Hannah up as they entered the room and sat close to Cain's head. "Honey, I know you can hear me, so I want you to open your eyes and meet your daughter. Cain, she's waited so long for this. Please don't disappoint her."

Before Emma could stop her, Hannah reached out and put her hand over Cain's mouth. "Mom, it's me, Hannah. Mama said it was okay to come see you now."

The fog was thick where Cain was stuck, but she could hear voices. A panicked shock stalled her emotions because no matter how hard she tried, she couldn't open her eyes. Something had happened. She felt paralyzed. But no amount of concentration could make her remember. It was a soft slap to the mouth that made her eyes flutter.

"That's it, baby, come back to us. I need you," said Emma. It wasn't important that Hannah had crawled out of her lap and was pulling on Cain's top lip. She focused on the struggle Cain was going through to open her eyes. The hand she was holding came back to life, as did the monitor next to the bed as Cain's heartbeat increased.

Mother and daughter jumped a little when blue eyes opened without warning. Cain inhaled sharply, struggling to figure out what had a death-grip on her lip. The pain stopped her from moving around too much and from taking too deep a breath. Not having full control was making Cain panic.

"Don't try to move, baby. You've been hurt."

Really. I wouldn't have guessed that on my own. Cain blinked a few times and noticed Emma hadn't heard her comment. She could have sworn she had been actually talking. She managed to turn her head a little and found a beautiful sight—the little girl from the farm next to Ross's. This was her little girl, hers and Emma's.

"Hannah, this is your mom Cain, and she's been looking forward to meeting you. Only she might feel better if you stop pulling on her like that." Emma heard her own voice quiver and wished the introductions could have been like she had dreamed so many times, with Cain scooping the little girl into her arms and giving her a big kiss. The blue eyes looking up at her told her that was exactly what Cain would have done if she'd been able. "Baby, this is your daughter, Hannah Marie Casey."

"Love you." It came out in a whisper, but it was just as effective as if Cain had screamed it.

"Ma'am, could we get in there for a minute?" The nurse had an entourage with her, and someone was calling the doctor. Cain wasn't supposed to be awake with the massive amount of medication running through her.

When Emma grabbed Hannah and started to move out of the way, Cain's voice rose a little. "No."

"We'll be right over here, Cain. Don't worry. I'm not taking her anywhere." Emma stood back and watched as some of the medical team pulled the sheet back and checked Cain's injuries, while others attended to her vital signs.

When the head nurse took out a penlight and pointed it into Cain's eyes to check for pupil reaction, Cain rasped, "Take this out."

"Take what out, Ms. Casey?"

Uncoordinated, Cain was able finally to move her hand close to her mouth. "This, take it out." She put her fingers on the tube in her throat.

"I'm sorry, ma'am, but I'm not authorized to do so."

"Take it out, or I'll do it myself." The voice was low, but it made Emma laugh because it carried Cain's usual amount of venom.

"Ma'am, please calm down, or we'll be forced to sedate you."

"Go anywhere near her again with a needle, and you'll have to deal with me," Emma threatened from where she was standing. She had just gotten Cain back, and she wasn't going to let go so easily. "Is she all right for the moment?"

"Yes, but—" said the middle-aged woman.

"Then get out and we'll wait for the doctor."

"We just want to understand why this happened, Mrs. Casey. We're just trying to do our jobs. If you can't understand that, I'll have to remove you." The stout middle-aged nurse obviously wasn't used to being talked down to.

"You can try and remove her, lady, but make sure you bring enough people to take Freddie and me with her," said Lou, who stood just inside Cain's room.

Cain's surgeon had arrived at the counter surrounding the nurses' station and was glancing over the paper readouts from her monitors, and he chuckled as he listened to the fighting going on in the room.

Emma glanced toward the door as Dr. Elton opened it. With Cain's chart under his arm, he motioned all the healthcare workers out. "It's no wonder you're awake, with all the noise," he joked as he began his examination. He explained to Emma that Cain was a medical enigma to him. Her current condition was something he expected to see in a couple of weeks, if she survived at all, but her alert blue eyes and reflex response were almost normal.

"Take this out. Now." Cain's tone belonged to someone not used to being denied.

"Cain, I want you to understand something, so hear me out, okay?"

She swallowed rapidly and with difficulty because of the tube she was complaining about, but she nodded.

"Someone tried to kill you with a very large gun that shot even bigger bullets. I'm thrilled you're awake, but now I'm the boss, not you. The staff and I will try our best to make you comfortable, but you have a ways to go before we're done."

Cain motioned him closer and said, "I've got enough shit hooked up to me, and it's scaring my kid, so take it out. It's the first time she's seen me, and I don't want this to be what she remembers about the day."

"Mrs. Casey, could you and your daughter give us about twenty minutes? I promise it's just to clean Cain up and get her comfortable. If it's possible, we'll move her to a private room so you'll be more comfortable as well."

"No more drugs?" Emma asked with conviction.

"Unless she asks me, no more drugs."

As Emma and Hannah waited, the clock seemed mired in quicksand. Emma was about to go back into the room after forty minutes had passed, but then the doctor met her at the door.

"I don't understand how, but she'll be home in about a week."

She laughed at the thought of Cain flat on her back for a seven days. "If you can keep her that long. Cain isn't the best patient. Add to that her lack of patience, and a week might be tough."

"You don't understand. I thought she'd have to stay a month or two."

"No, Dr. Elton. You don't understand. Cain's an extraordinary person, used to doing extraordinary things. Right now she doesn't have time for this, so she'll will herself to mend."

"May your children take after her, then, Mrs. Casey. You go on in. She's asking for you." Dr. Elton patted her hand and left.

Go on in, she's asking for you. The doctor's comment echoed in Emma's head, making her dizzy. Memories of Cain dressing her down also echoed in her mind, but she had been lucky up to now. She had never been on the receiving end of the Casey temper at full throttle.

The time the staff had taken made a difference. Cain looked almost healthy with only the oxygen tube in her nose. The one she'd found offensive was gone, and Emma could only hope it was the staff who had removed it.

"I hurt too much to bite, so come here." Cain's voice was still raspy from the medical equipment, but it sounded glorious. The teasing comment was the first thing Cain had uttered to her that didn't carry with it a dose of anger.

"Cain, I'm so sorry for everything. I didn't come here to see you get hurt, but I'm grateful to you for saving my life."

She quit apologizing when, with a great deal of effort, Cain put up her hand and said, "She's a beautiful child, Emma."

"She's a Casey, Cain. What choice did she have but to be beautiful? I know it won't make things right between us, but I taught her to love you and Hayden." Emma sat on the chair next to the bed and rested her hands close to Cain's body. "She's talked about you for so long. I'm glad you found out."

Cain's side hurt like hell, and she wasn't up for a fight. "Your plan was to send me to jail so you could get Hayden back, so I'm sorry if I find your words more than a little hollow." The saddest thing for Cain out of everything that had happened was that she'd missed out on Emma's second pregnancy. She vividly recalled her first one.

Twelve Years Earlier in the Casey Bedroom in New Orleans

"Don't strain yourself today. I mean it." Cain was sitting on the bed putting on her socks as she lectured the woman lying behind her. Her seventh month of pregnancy was starting to wear Emma down and swell her up in unimaginable places.

"When are you coming home?"

The irritated tone directed at her didn't faze Cain. It was hormonal, and she figured the real Emma would return sometime after the birth. "Tonight early. I already talked to Vinny and told him I wasn't staying long, but the Gulf Coast property's being cleared today, and we're meeting with some of the county commissioners. If I could skip it I would, baby, but this is one meeting I can't miss."

Emma watched as Cain slipped on her belt, then her watch. The passion was gone. Now she knew what every pregnant woman meant— she really did feel like a beached whale and couldn't blame Cain for not finding her attractive.

"Maybe later you could go for a walk with Carmen? It's nice outside today."

"I'm not a pet, Cain, so stop being so condescending. Just go. I'm sure you're late by now."

If Emma expected the blue eyes to harden and her lover to give her the fight she was picking for, the exact opposite happened. Cain sat beside her and put her hands on Emma's cheeks. "I know you're tired, sweetling, and this big bruiser isn't helping any, but I love you. You rest, and I promise I'll be home early."

Emma nodded, then lowered her head so Cain wouldn't see the tears. It wasn't fair to keep taking out her bad moods on the person who loved her more than life. Cain pressed a soft kiss to her forehead. Then Emma felt the bed shift again and Cain was gone. Never had she wanted to beg her to stay more than in that one moment, but it was just a mood swing. Something so tragic would seem silly in an hour, so Emma kept quiet.

Trying to relax, she undressed and stepped into the shower. Reviewing her actions, she leaned her head against the shower wall and sobbed. She wanted to start the morning over so she could retract the harsh words, but now Cain was gone. "Emma, you idiot, it's not like she doesn't have her pick. Keep this up, and she'll go looking for someone who doesn't talk back so often." She laughed when no one disagreed with her. Talking to herself out loud was another side effect of pregnancy.

And then, suddenly, she wasn't alone. She cried harder when she heard the soft voice so close to her ear. "Ah, but she likes them feisty, lass. I want a partner, not a lapdog."

Cain's tall, nude body pressed against her back felt solid and wonderful, and Emma turned and pressed her cheek to Cain's shoulder.

"No tears now, sweetling. They'll ruin our morning." Cain ran her fingers through the wet blond hair. After seeing the sadness on Emma's face, she hadn't been able to get very far once she'd walked out of the bedroom.

"What are you doing here?" Emma turned her head up and kissed Cain's collarbone as she gazed up at her greatest wish.

"I live here, love. I'm the one you use as a foot warmer at night." Cain ran her fingers down Emma's neck, her lips following closely behind. She stopped just behind her ear and bit down gently, loving how it made Emma shiver.

"I know that, you sweet idiot. What I meant was, I thought you had a meeting?"

"I had a choice of bribing some old fat white guys into cutting us in on some gambling action, or bribing you into spending the day with me. It wasn't a close contest, so here I am. I want to spend hours showing you how much I love you and just how beautiful I think you are."

"Do you have any idea how much I love you?" Emma put her hand behind Cain's neck and pulled her down to claim a kiss. Any insecurities she had of Cain not finding her attractive disappeared when her partner's tongue pushed gently against hers and Cain's hands covered her backside, pulling her closer.

"How about we answer that question in the bedroom, Mrs. Casey?" asked Cain, when they pulled apart.

"That's me, and I always will be."

They had spent so many mornings like that, so many days when Emma had rushed down to Cain's office so she could feel Hayden moving around. Had Hannah been so active? Had the picture of Emma feeding her been as sweet and beautiful? Cain could never live those stories again, and her own Mrs. Casey had stolen them from her.

"I've learned something about myself in the last month, Cain. In the end I couldn't betray you just to regain my son. For the longest time I thought it was a fair trade. You got Hayden and I'd have Hannah, but it doesn't work. We have two children, and each of them needs us for different reasons. I'd love nothing more than for you to forgive me, but if that doesn't happen we need to learn to share them."

"If you were in my shoes, Emma, would you forgive?"

Emma admitted to herself that when she had come back and wanted to see Hayden, Cain had granted access. It wasn't Cain's fault that Emma had left and her son hated her for it, which was her burden to carry. So she answered truthfully. "No."

"Sweetling, that might be the first honest thing you've said to me in forever."

The endearment and the rest of what she had to confess started her tears. "There's more." Through the hiccups and sobs, she got out the rest. Hayden was gone, Cain was shot, and it was all her fault.

"Who has him?"

"Giovanni Bracato."

Cain forgot the pain for a moment and closed her hand into a fist. "That fat bastard's going to wish he'd stayed a gleam in his father's eye."

"I've already met with him." Emma leaned back in the chair and wiped her face. She didn't think Cain would coldcock her, but she wasn't taking any chances. The medication Cain was on could prove her wrong.

"You? I'm sure he found that highly amusing. What'd you do, ask him pretty please with sugar on top?"

Merrick's arrival was enough to defuse Cain's rampage and allay the nurses. "No, she had Mook knock out his front teeth and the rest of the boys kidnap all Bracato's kids, including his grandson, Little Gino."

Cain turned to Emma, who nodded in confirmation. "I wanted him ready to deal, and I thought his whole family would be worth Hayden."

"Listen to me carefully, the both of you. If you get him killed, start running before his body hits the floor. Run like the devil himself is chasing you, because you'll find you might prefer him to me." Cain glared at each of them in turn, and her voice was pure menace. "Nothing fancy whenever this goes down. You get my son and leave. Understand?"

"Yes," both Emma and Merrick answered.

"But, Cain—" Emma said.

"Get out."

Cain was done, but neither of her visitors moved. She leveled a murderous glare at both of them, and her voice dropped to its chilliest register.

"Get the fuck out."

CHAPTER THIRTY-THREE

Shelby stirred her coffee, hoping two pink packets of sweetener and three creamers would make it taste better. "Why is it you hardly ever blip on the radar Cain's constantly under, Muriel?"

"I'm around, Shelby, so you tell me."

"Cain's your only client?" Shelby watched as Muriel took a healthy swig from the Styrofoam cup and shivered. *This one must have the makeup of a killer too if she can drink this shit black.*

"Is this a coffee date or an interrogation? If your answer's 'date,' you must not do too much of it."

"This is not a date."

"So we'll go with the interrogation, then." Muriel had on her courtroom smile, which was making Shelby nervous.

"Can't a girl be just curious?"

"Most women are, Agent Daniels, but then again most of them don't have the ability to arrest you if their curiosity hits a nerve." With one more gulp, Muriel drained the cup. "What was the question again?"

"I forget."

"Somehow that seems highly unlikely to me." The smile got wider. "My cousin Derby is my only active client, yes, but I take care of the business as well as her. She's two years older than me, but I hear tell I'm better in bed."

"I doubt it." It slipped out before Shelby could censor it.

"See there, we've come to our first nerve, and unfortunately it's a strike against me. Derby has always had a little better luck with the pretty ones. Must be that gangster thing. Attorneys are more of an acquired taste."

Shelby laughed at Muriel's easy charm. "More like a pain in the ass. I spend my life trying to catch criminals, and people like you spend it trying to let them loose. And I thought I told you to call me Shelby."

"Since your next question was most probably if I've ever been involved in the family business, I thought I should address you accordingly. I wouldn't want it said in court I was disrespectful." Muriel pointed to Shelby's cup. "Another?"

"Just hanging around your family is death wish enough, thank you. Can I ask just one more question? I promise it has nothing to do with business."

"My phone number?"

Shelby shook her head and laughed again. "Maybe later, much later. What I want to know is Emma's story. I wasn't on Kyle's detail when Cain went up north, and she was history before I came to the city."

"I'm sure it's in Derby's file. Why not just read about it?"

"Because I want to hear it from you. Why'd she leave?"

There was no harm in telling the story, but Muriel was so good at her job because she was suspicious of everything. The world didn't revolve around money. It revolved around information. Something said innocently now could later be the final nail in the Casey family coffin, and she wasn't about to be the one to bury Cain.

"The truth is, this is Derby's story to tell, Shelby."

"This is off the record, Muriel. I came today because I owe Cain something. I'm sure I'll get my transfer now, and I didn't want to leave without knowing. Maybe there's something I can do to make her feel better. You know, pay her back in some way."

The confession sounded sincere enough to Muriel. "It doesn't change the fact that it's Cain you need to ask. Cain's not just my client, Shelby, she's my family. A cousin who's gone through more than her share of tragedy, all the while knowing she was being watched like a butterfly pinned to a board. The truth is, she trusts me more than most, and she hasn't told me everything about Emma."

"I can respect that."

"Thank you," said Muriel. She watched Emma rush by the cafeteria headed toward the front entrance, followed closely by Merrick. "Would you excuse me a moment? Better yet, why not go back up and visit Cain while I tend to something. I promise I won't be long."

"Trying to ditch me?"

"Of course not, Shelby. Call it comparison shopping. I'm sure you'll go for the younger model, given a chance."

"I'll wait for you upstairs. Don't stand me up."

"And let my cousin win out? Never."

Emma was racing down the sidewalk with a nervous Merrick chasing her down. Muriel took off in a slow jog, calling out to Merrick so she wouldn't be shot as she got closer.

"Emma, stop or I swear I'll put you over my knee when I catch up to you." She gripped Emma's elbow anything but gently when she did catch her and dragged her back into the hospital and to the most secluded place she could think of, the chapel. "Jesus Christ, did you learn nothing from what happened to Hayden?"

"She hates me, Muriel. I lost Hayden and kept Hannah from her, and now she hates me."

With two fingers under Emma's chin, Muriel forced her to look up. "I'd have guessed with all the time you spent up on that farm, you'd have spent some of it thinking."

"What do you mean?" Emma asked in a defeated tone.

"It's simple, Emma. You ran before, and what did it get you? Did you find happiness in anything but Hannah all those years you were gone?"

"No."

"Did you find the woman your mother wants you to be?" Muriel persisted.

"I can't be that person. Even if I could, she said I can't go back there."

"You don't have to go back, Emma, but you've got to stop running away. Derby Cain understands one thing, and that's strength. Show some and start running *toward* something, instead of away from her. If you don't, you're going to be lonely without her."

"She doesn't want me, Muriel. The sooner I come to grips with that, the sooner I can decide what I'm going to do with the rest of my life."

"One more talk with her is all I'm asking, only this time go in there and act like you belong at her side. You accepted the role Derby gave you as someone to be sheltered and taken care of, and look where it's gotten you. She won't give in unless you give her a reason to." Muriel stood and buttoned her jacket. Advice on legal matters was much easier to give.

"Why?"

"Why do I care?"

Emma nodded.

"Because she loves you more than she hates you. You fucked up, Emma, but so does everyone. Granted, yours was a fuckup of a magnitude you don't often see, but—"

"Okay, I get it. Any more trying to make me feel better and I may start crying again."

Laughter was coming out of the private room the ICU nurse directed Muriel and Emma to, enough laughter for Emma to shed her doubt and find her anger. She was used to women flirting with Cain, but Cain usually rebuffed them. This sounded like Cain was responding accordingly.

The biggest shock was that it was Agent Daniels she was playing with. "Agent Daniels, would you please excuse us," said Emma in way of a greeting.

"Sure, I was just waiting for my coffee date." The tension in the room was thick enough to make Shelby want to leave. The last thing she needed was for her superiors to read about her getting into a catfight over Cain Casey.

With a soft click of the door, Emma and Cain were alone again. Emma watched Cain take as deep a breath as she could, knowing it was the buildup to the storm.

"What in the hell was that?" Cain's question came out in a rush.

"Shut up."

"Excuse me?"

"I said shut up. It means be quiet and listen." She moved to the bed and fought the urge to poke Cain in the chest. "I'm not going anywhere, and I refuse to be left out of the loop anymore, so get used to it. Call it a hunch, but New Orleans has to be big enough for both of us, because I'm not going back."

She stopped to take a breath and went with poking the air in front of Cain's chest. "You're going to spend time getting to know your daughter, as I will our son. That means we'll be spending time together, sometimes even in the same room, maybe. I'm sorry for what I did, I truly am, but it's the last time I'm going to say that."

"Did you just tell me to shut up?"

Emma couldn't help it and hoped Cain had no head injury when she slapped the top of her head. "For God's sake, is that all you just heard?"

"No, I heard the rest. Don't worry. You hit me again, though, and injury or no, I'm putting you over my knee."

"Too late, your cousin's already threatened that." Her father's words about taking chances made her roll the dice. "Tell me you don't care anything about me, and I'll walk out now. We can arrange something through Muriel to see the children. You tell me, though, or I'm not leaving."

"Emma, you know I can't do that. You're the mother of my children, and I have to respect that."

"For once forget about your traditions and your honor. This is about you and me. Tell me you don't care."

Cain closed her eyes and tried to force herself to say the words "I don't care." It would be so easy to never again look at the greatest betrayal she'd ever experienced. "I can't. As much as I want to, I can't."

The joy in Emma's eyes came back when Cain spoke her heart.

"But that doesn't mean we can go back. I can't do that either."

"I don't want to go back, Cain. I want to move forward." Emma took another chance and held her hand out to Cain, not expecting too much. She blinked back tears when Cain took it. "If all else fails I'll spill a bunch of beer on you, since it worked so well for me in the past."

"I'm willing to be civil, Emma. Don't expect too much else. We had our chance, and we blew it."

"Is it Agent Daniels?"

"It could be anyone, but our time has passed." Emma began to pull away, and Cain squeezed her hand. "I can't, Emma. I barely survived the first time. I won't set myself up like that again, and I've got Hayden to think of."

"Fair enough. My fault, right?"

"Tell me more about Hannah?" A safe topic was what they needed to defuse the moment. Just because Cain had spent years cursing Emma's existence didn't mean she'd forgotten how soft her hands were, or how wonderful she smelled. Being this close was dangerous, but the part that did still care couldn't turn her away.

"How about I let Hannah tell you about Hannah? It's her favorite subject, after all. Unless you're tired." Emma moved her other hand to Cain's wound. It seemed like just a few hours earlier that she had looked so fragile.

"It hurts, but no more drugs. I'm alive and I can move all my parts, so the rest is just an inconvenience."

Forty minutes later Hannah had fallen asleep on Cain's bed after covering all the highlights of her life with great animation. From the moment the blue eyes turned her way, Cain lost her heart, and the past four years almost didn't matter.

"What happened with Hayden?" asked Cain in a whisper. The small little body pressed to hers felt like a dream.

"I told him about Hannah and he got upset."

She nodded slowly. "You told him I knew, didn't you?"

"Something else I have to apologize for. I said it without thinking, but I swear it wasn't to hurt you. He got angry and said something like he was being replaced and he wanted to be alone. I'm sorry, Cain. He must've run off after he dismissed all of us."

"Hayden knew better and he's smart, so he'll be fine as long as Bracato behaves."

"What does that mean exactly?" Emma kept her voice low, but Cain could hear the panic in it.

"He's dealing with a child who's a little advanced and who's a master wordsmith when he wants to be. Hayden starts taunting Big Gino, and I can't promise he won't come back without a bruise or two."

Green eyes opened in shock. "And you're okay with this?"

"That happens and I'll feed Bracato his kidneys with a spoon." The threat was real and delivered with the same calm tone. "Now, about tonight."

"I'm going, and you can't stop me."

"Just listen, okay? I want you, no matter what happens or how Hayden looks, to trade Bracato's for ours. I mean it, Emma. Nothing fancy. Don't let Merrick or anyone talk you into something stupid."

"This Bracato idiot gets away with all this? He took our son and had you shot."

"And he'll be dealt with in time. I don't want to wait, but he's left me in no shape to act now."

"But I can—" Emma started to give her pitch.

"You can milk cows, but this is out of your league. I'm not telling you that to insult you. It's to keep you whole. We are who we are, Emma, and what needs to happen to Giovanni isn't in you."

"What do you want me to do?"

❖

The room had only one small window, but it did have a good view of the sky. Not that the gray clouds were much to look at, thought Hayden, as he sat gazing out at the constant drizzle that had been falling almost as long as he'd been sitting in one of the hardwood chairs. What had started as a ride to clear his head had turned into a nightmare that he couldn't begin to imagine how to explain to Cain.

He had barely moved since the three men who had grabbed him turned the lock and left him alone. He had wanted to cry, but he couldn't give in to the weak part of his mind. So he did the only thing he could think to stem the tide of fear; he imagined how Cain would act in the same situation.

Behind him, someone put the key in the lock and opened the door with a loud squeak. Hayden squeezed the arms of the chair, but he didn't turn around.

Giovanni Bracato, a handkerchief in one hand to wipe away the drool from his numb mouth, sat down in the chair across from him. After his meeting with Emma, the big man had spent the afternoon in the dentist chair repairing the damage. When this situation was over, he and Emma would meet again.

"What you looking at, kid?" Almost every word out of Gino's mouth began with a distinct *s* sound.

Hayden couldn't help but laugh. "Mouth problems, Sylvester?"

"My name's Mr. Bracato, remember that. Who the fuck is Sylvester?"

"The idiot cat in the cartoons. You must not watch much TV, Sylvester. You want to let me out now? I've had a wonderful time here today, but I don't want to be late for dinner."

"Just like that bitch Cain, aren't you? She's not so big now, little man. All those wisecracks of hers aren't doing her any good since she's flat on her back. Cain found out what I've known all along. I'm better at the game and I won. Get yourself a watering can, kid, 'cause you ain't got nothing but a vegetable now."

"Oh yeah, then who's responsible for your dental work?"

"I owe the blond spawn who brought you into the world a return visit once I get my family back, so let's go." Gino got up so fast the chair slammed up against the wall, rattling the window.

"Where're you taking me?"

"I'm dropping you off where we found you. Don't think I'm doing this because I'm worried. I have all the time in the world to take care of your family. I promise I'm coming back to skin you alive, kid, only I want to do it in front of your innocent little mother. Sort of a payback for touching my grandson." He grabbed Hayden by the neck and led him out of the room to the garage of the building. Twenty minutes later he let him out a block from Cain's house.

"Put that bitch on the phone," Gino ordered when the number Emma had given him was answered.

"I see your trip to the dentist did nothing to improve your vocabulary. What can I do for you, Giovanni? I can call you Giovanni, can't I?" Emma hadn't been back in the house an hour when the cell phone ringing surprised her.

"Open the door and cut the crap. If my grandson isn't by the curb before the kid hits the door, I'll have him shot."

She dropped the phone and ran to the front door, calling for Merrick the whole way. Three houses down was the most beautiful sight she'd seen in forever. A healthy-looking Hayden was ambling back to the house, and if she wondered why he was moving so slowly, the gun pointed out the window of the large car behind him was her answer.

"He needs to see some kid before I can come in." Hayden's voice quivered, and he felt as if his knees would give out before he crossed the threshold, but he kept moving.

"Merrick, get Little Gino, and make it fast." Emma shouted the order to the running footsteps behind her since she refused to take her eyes off her son.

Carmen handed Gino to Emma and retreated into the house. In case of trouble, she wasn't going to be caught in the middle.

"Mook, give a heads-up to the guys along the fence. Anything happens and that car is a piece of history, got me?"

"Yes, ma'am."

Emma eased out of the house with the infant. "It's all right, Gino. It's your grandfather coming to pick you up. I'm going to leave you right here, and he's going to drive up." In a louder voice, she spoke to Hayden. "Go on and get in the house. It's going to be all right now, Hayden."

"But what about you?"

"I'll be fine. Just go so I'll know you'll be safe." She turned her back on the approaching car long enough to see Merrick pull Hayden into the house.

Giovanni had ordered the car stopped and had gotten out so as not to scare the boy in Emma's arms.

"I'm not real sure why you moved up the timeline for this, but thank you for returning my son."

"Don't thank me yet. Put him down, and my man will come and get him, so tell your dogs to keep their cool."

The boy was scooped up off the front lawn as soon as Emma put him down, but Giovanni wasn't in the mood for sentimental reunions and waved his man toward the open door. When he and the baby were safely back in the car, he turned his attention back to Emma. "Where are my sons?"

"Give me your word you'll leave my family in peace, and I'll make a phone call and have them released."

"And if I don't?"

"I'll let Cain decide what to do with them."

Giovanni swiped the white cloth in his hand across his mouth before he answered. If he despised Cain, this little woman was quickly gaining on her. "The bitch's in a coma." He saw Emma flinch.

"Then think of how long you'll have to wait."

Behind Emma, Merrick was warring between cheering the woman on or running out and slapping her. "Emma, what in the hell are you doing? We got the kid back. Let the rest go."

"I give you my word, I'll leave you all alone to lick your wounds. Just release my family and stay out of my business."

The car door slammed so hard Emma thought the window would shatter. With a squeal of wheels audible for blocks in the quiet neighborhood, the car took off toward the river.

The heavy oak door shut the world out when Emma closed it, and she had to take a minute to lean against it. Her heart felt like someone had shocked it, so she closed her eyes to get it to calm down. When she opened them again she saw something missing from her life for too long—her son, looking fragile and in need of his mother.

She moved slowly toward him, wrapped her arms around him, and waited. Hayden stiffened at first but finally gave in to the tears that had threatened all day. The staff disappeared into the house as mother and son sank to the floor. No matter the difference in their sizes, Emma never lost her grip and Hayden cried into her shoulder.

"I'm sorry," cried Hayden, saying it over and over.

"No, Hayden, you have nothing to be sorry about. I should've waited until both Cain and I could tell you about Hannah. But you have to know I love you both. I left here because I was a fool. Please don't make your sister pay for my mistakes."

"I'm sorry I ran away."

"Just promise me you'll think things through next time. I'm so glad you're home." Emma tried to push his hair out of his eyes. "I sure have missed you, and there's someone here dying to meet you. Think you're up for that?"

Hayden nodded and leaned more into his mother's body. "I thought about her when I was sitting in that room."

"What'd you think about?"

"What it would be like to have a little sister, nothing big. Does she look like you?"

"Honey, if you look at the million baby pictures we have of you, you've seen Hannah. Let's go in the den, and I'll run and get her."

With a strong hold, Hayden kept Emma from getting up. "He's coming back, he said."

"Who, Hayden?"

"Mr. Bracato. He said he wants to hurt all of us. He's the one who had Mom shot."

"He won't touch you again, I promise. I know what he did to Cain, but I'm going to do the one thing I should've done four years ago."

"What?"

"Trust her to fix it. She'll take care of us, and I have every faith she isn't going to fail. After all, these are her children we're talking about."

"But she's—" said Hayden.

"She's awake, son, and doing great."

Hayden pulled away a little and looked at Emma in shock. "She's awake?" His mother's nod made one thought pop into the boy's head. *Oh shit.*

CHAPTER THIRTY-FOUR

Hannah's here?" asked Hayden. He felt calm for the first time in days as Emma wiped away his tears. Finding he had a sister and sitting in the small room where Giovanni had locked him had left him in an uncomfortable limbo. In so many ways he had lost his place, or at least started to question his place, within his family. It was a new experience.

"I don't want to push you, but she's waited so long to see you. Hannah's never met you, true, but she talks about you and Cain all the time. Do you think you can forget you're mad at me for just a little while and give Hannah a chance?"

The look in Emma's eyes reminded Hayden of the loving mother he had lost. His last conversation with Cain came back to him. She had asked him to try to see Emma in a different light.

"You won't leave me again, will you?" His tears started again, and he felt desperate for something to hold on to other than Cain.

Emma placed both of her hands on his cheeks. "I made the worst mistake of my life when I walked out this door." She cocked her head toward the oak surface they were still leaning against. "It's something I can't ever take back, and it's something that will forever haunt me, but I'm here now. There will never be another day of your life that I won't be here. I love you, Hayden. You're my son and I love you."

"What about Mom?"

"I can't speak for Cain, but I can promise that we'll find a way to share in your and Hannah's life. Your sister needs to get to know you and Cain as much as I need to get to know you again. You're a wonderful boy, but I'd like to believe that I can offer things Cain can't."

He pulled away from her, but Emma moved with him. "Mom has given me everything."

"I'm not saying she didn't give you what you needed, but you need both of us. With Cain you'll find your strength, but I think with me you'll find—"

"My safe haven," he said.

"Yes." She pulled him forward, and for once he didn't hesitate. Hayden accepted the comfort Emma so freely offered. As she took in his warmth and presence, she sent her ex-partner a silent thank you. She owed the moment to Cain's generosity.

"Mama." Hannah's voice sounded small. She stood at the back of the foyer with her finger in her mouth, swaying like she was afraid of being sent away.

"Come here, sweetie." Emma kept one arm around Hayden but held a hand out to her daughter. "This is your brother Hayden."

"Really?" asked Hannah. Her mother's nodding head got her to break out into a run into Hayden's arms.

Emma bit back a sob when she saw Hayden's teary blue eyes as he held his sister tight. The size of his smile was one Emma saw only in her dreams.

"Hi, Hannah, how are you?"

For the rest of the afternoon the youngest Casey sat on Hayden's lap on the floor and rambled. She would reach out every so often to touch his face or his hair, as if to verify he was real. Hannah's experiences were limited to the farm and their neighbors, but Hayden listened to her stories with rapt attention.

In his heart, just like Cain, he knew he would spend a lifetime loving and protecting the little charmer sitting with him. It was exciting to have someone to look out for like Cain did for Marie. Hannah sounded like she had inherited the Casey smarts as well as their mischievous streak. But maybe giving Cain all the credit wasn't fair anymore. Both of the Casey children had become who they were because of Emma as well.

"You two want to go visit Cain at the hospital?" asked Emma.

"She's awake, you said?" Hayden's question sounded a little shaky.

"Mom has eyes like you, Haygen, and she let me sit on the bed with her," Hannah chimed in.

"She's awake, buddy, but I think she's still too weak to do any serious groundings," teased Emma, trying her best to ease any concerns he had. Cain was generous with her family, but what had happened with Bracato made it hard to gauge how she'd react.

"You must not know her well at all, then," he responded.

They piled into one car but were escorted to the hospital by two other vehicles full of Cain's men. Hayden's silence grew with each block they traveled, and he held Hannah's hand as she sat between him and Emma.

Merrick opened the door after studying the street and walked them into the lobby. As they rode up in the elevator, Emma made eye contact with the top Casey guard. Understanding, Merrick escorted the children to the waiting room so Emma could go in alone. The fact that neither of them had called to relay the news would not be lost on Cain.

She was sleeping when Emma entered, providing the perfect opportunity for her to study the face and body she missed so much. Growing up on a farm with no siblings hadn't prepared her for sharing space with another person, especially in her bed. But with Cain she had never had any awkwardness or adjustments. She had moved in shortly after they had consummated their relationship, walking on what felt like thin ice, trying to do nothing that would make Cain regret her decision to invite her.

Twelve Years Earlier in the Casey Home

The last of the moving men tipped his hat in her direction and started toward the front door of Emma's new residence. She didn't have much furniture or many knickknacks, given the frugal way she had existed in school, but Cain had hired a crew anyway, not wanting her to have to worry about anything.

Emma walked around the master suite studying the various pictures, smiling when she found more than one of the two of them. In the closet she ran her hand along the row of suits and shirts that hung neatly alongside her own things and wondered if she and Cain would have a long adjustment period.

Cain loved her—she was sure of it and had never doubted from the first time Cain had said it—but no woman had shared Cain's life this way either. When she stepped out of the closet, the object of her thoughts was sitting on the bed smiling at her. Across Cain's lap lay a bouquet of sunflowers, which seemed almost as out of place in the space as Emma felt.

"I remember you telling me when you lived with your folks you grew these outside your bedroom window so you could enjoy them in the summer. I also remember how happy you looked when you told me that story." Cain stood up and moved slowly to where Emma was standing. "These are for you, love." She handed the flowers over. "I didn't grow them, I'll admit, but I hope they make you just as happy."

"You make me happy," she said.

"I can only hope that's true too, because I don't ever want you to leave here, and I want you to feel like this is your home. If you don't, we'll look for another one."

Emma put her flowers down and moved into Cain's arms. "I don't ever want to leave, and I think the house is as perfect as you are. There's only one way to be sure, though."

"More flowers?" asked Cain teasingly.

Emma shook her head and looked up into the twinkling blue eyes. "More of you."

From that day on, a crystal vase full of sunflowers stood on the nightstand on her side of the bed. They always made Emma feel special because, unlike most of the things in Cain's life that she delegated to others, she always chose and bought the sunflowers herself. Over the years she became a fixture at least twice a week in the flower section at the French market.

"You look like you're carrying the weight of the world on your shoulders, sweetling."

The raspy voice made Emma realize that during her musings she had taken a seat on the bed to be close to Cain. "Sorry," she said as she started to move away.

"Don't go. I want to tell you something." Cain's movements were still a bit uncoordinated, but she managed to wrap her hand around Emma's wrist.

"I know I'm not your favorite person, but there's also a limit to how much I can take in a day, and it's been a hell of a day already." Emma was intent on getting up, sure that in Cain's weakened condition she could break the hold easily.

"Please stay. I don't want to pile it on, Emma. I want to apologize for my earlier outburst. Hayden's responsible for his actions, no matter what you told him. I shouldn't have jumped all over you like I did."

"Cain, I understand you were upset. You don't have to apologize." Emma relaxed and smiled because Cain hadn't moved her hand even though it was apparent that she wasn't going to get off the bed. "I should've waited until you were awake before I told Hayden about Hannah. It really isn't my intention to replace you or diminish your place in his life."

"Come on, Emma. You've got me on my back and apologizing to you. I say you should go with it and enjoy." Cain squeezed the delicate wrist under her fingers. "Now tell me what's got you looking even more depressed than when you left."

"Actually, I have good news for you."

"Tell me what's bothering you?"

"Why would you care?" The question wasn't sarcastic, and Emma didn't mean it to be.

"Does the why matter? Shouldn't the fact that I care enough to ask mean something?"

Emma dipped her head a little as if she expected a physical blow instead of an answer to her question. "I really don't want to play twenty questions with you, so could you just answer me?"

"I care because of who you are and what you mean to my life, Emma. I care because, despite our past and our future, you're the mother of my children. And because you are, I care about your happiness."

Green eyes that shimmered with tears peeked at Cain from behind a veil of pale blond hair. "Thank you. I'm sure admitting that was harder than taking a bullet for me."

Cain laughed, thinking Emma still knew her well. "So reward me for my show of compassion."

"I was thinking of sunflowers and better times. Silly, I know, but I was watching you sleep and it reminded me of those flowers. I grew them again when I left—well, for the first summer anyway. They made me cry so damn much I asked my father to rip them out." The tears she had tried to fight rolled down her cheeks. Emma had grown accustomed to them, but they did something to Cain.

"History can be a wicked mistress, can't she, lass?" Cain patted the hand resting on the bed and relaxed her face into a smile. "She can twist our most precious memories into our worst sources of pain."

"I gave up so much, and I won't ever get it back, will I?"

"You've gotten a little of Hayden back, haven't you?" Cain laughed at Emma's shocked expression. "Come now, sweetling. You and Merrick might've gotten caught up in the excitement, but someone in the house was bound to call me. How's he look?"

"Like you in all the pictures I've seen when you were his age. He was scared, but I think fear of facing you won out over anything Bracato could've done to him. Do you think just this once you could go easy on him?"

"Did he ask you to ask me that?"

Emma quickly covered Cain's hand with hers. "No. You know better. He would take a beating before he begged for leniency."

"Go get him, and don't worry about a beating. Even if I felt up to it, that's not my style."

The tease made Emma laugh, and the hand still under hers gave her a glimmer of hope for the future. "I'll go get him."

The guards around the waiting room were trying their best to keep their eyes on the hall and not on the little girl sitting on Hayden's lap giggling at the story he was telling her. Hannah had taken to her big brother in a way that surprised even the hardest of Cain's men. It was the first time Emma had seen their teeth, their smiles were so big.

"Hayden," Emma interrupted him.

"She's awake?"

Emma nodded. "It's all right. I talked to her, and I think she's too tired to be too mad."

"I wouldn't lay even money on that." Hayden left before his mother could complain about how a child his age shouldn't know about gambling and odds. The walk down the short hallway seemed to take an eternity. He knew in his heart that Cain wouldn't be mad. He didn't need confirmation from Emma about that. No, the woman lying in intensive care wouldn't be mad; she'd be disappointed, and to him that was worse. Anger would almost be easier to deal with.

They stared at each other in silence when Hayden reached the doorway of Cain's room. Cain visually scoured his body, making sure he was as fine as Mook had told her. "Come in and close the door." Her voice was rough from emotion.

"I'm sorry." Hayden stared at the now-closed door, his back to her.

"What are you sorry for?"

"For disappointing you."

"Hayden, come here, please." She held her hand up as high as she could manage, mentally cursing how weak she felt. "I'm not disappointed in you, son. Maybe I should be, but I'm so glad you're all right and whole that I don't care about the rest."

"But you wouldn't have made the same mistake."

"I'm not perfect, my boy, no matter what my mother thought."

The joke got him to sit on the bed.

"You made a mistake out of anger, which means you're a lot like me. You're still young, but with a few years under your belt you'll come to realize anger and love are the two strongest emotions and they'll make you do strange things."

"I just got mad you didn't tell me about Hannah."

Cain nodded, trying to find the right words to proceed. "Were you shocked to find out you had a sister?"

Hayden cocked his head to the side a little, much like Cain did when someone asked her something she considered idiotic. "That's not a serious question, is it?"

"Yes, it's a serious question. One I want an answer to."

"Of course I was shocked." Hayden threw his hands in the air as if to accentuate his point.

"Then imagine how I felt."

"But I thought—"

"You didn't have to think anything, son, because this was something I had to come to terms with on my own. But you can't think I knew all along and didn't tell you?"

Cain watched as anger replaced the confusion in Hayden's eyes. "She never told you?"

"My relationship with your mother is a little different from yours, so let's not confuse the issue here. What we're talking about is my relationship with you and the trust that entails. But just so you know, I'm not angry with your mom over what happened. True, she walked to the precipice of a major decision, but in the end someone pushed her off that cliff more than she chose to jump of her own free will. Punishment for those standing behind her will come in time."

"You don't blame her at all?"

Cain looked past Hayden to the door that had opened slightly. If her answer was totally honest, Emma would never have a chance in the boy's life; she knew him well enough to know. "No, I don't." The lie was a gift to the woman standing there listening.

"Is everything all right?" asked Emma.

Hayden turned and stared at her but stayed silent. He was young, but he wasn't a fool. Loyalty was as important to Cain as love. When his mother deserted them both, she had cut deep. Those types of wounds were hard to recover from, and he accepted Cain's fib for what it was— an invitation for him to know the woman who had left him behind, but hadn't forgotten him.

"We're fine, but we're not done," said Cain to Emma. The door clicked closed. "You're sure you're okay?"

"I'm fine, I promise. He just kept me locked in a room the whole time." His eyes never wavered from hers. "I think he weighed actually having me to what you'd do to him if he hurt me. You won out."

The laugh that rumbled up from Cain's chest was cut short by the stabbing pain of the gunshot wound. "If you've already figured everything out, then what do you think I should do to you for landing in Bracato's hands in the first place?"

"You should show some of that vast capacity for forgiveness you've shown Emma?" As extra incentive Hayden held up his crossed fingers and smiled.

"That's one route, but I hope you figured out what the lesson here was."

He opened his mouth to answer, but Cain lifted a couple of fingers in an effort to silence him.

"Anger, in and of itself, is a good thing, within reason, but it will be your greatest enemy if you don't learn to control it. You let your anger for me and your mother control your actions, and it made you an easy target." Cain was starting to get tired, and the pain in her chest was getting bad enough to make beads of sweat break out on her forehead, but this was important to her. "No matter what you do with your life, you'll be my son and I'll love you. You know that, right?"

"Yeah, I know and I'm sorry."

"Again, what are you sorry for?"

"For disappointing you."

Hayden looked at the person who was the one constant in his life. Cain had given him the one thing he treasured most—her attention. She talked to him as if what he thought and felt mattered to her, and always had, even when Emma was there.

How many afternoons could he remember running around the playground near their house and glancing toward the benches where the nannies would sit to oversee their charges. One minute he would notice only a sea of strange faces, and the next Cain would be there watching him.

She had taught him how to swing a bat, how to deal with bullies, and how important education was. Because she had taken the time and had taken such pleasure in teaching him, he had never hesitated about what he would do with his future. Some people said they loved their children; Cain had proved her love every day.

"Hayden, you found yourself in a dangerous situation and kept your head. That's not a disappointment to me. You're my kid and I love you, and when you leave my side and stand alone as your own man, you'll be better than most because you'll always think before you use your fists."

The soft hum of hospital equipment was the only sound in the room after Cain finished. She didn't have the heart to send Hayden away, but she was getting tired.

After considering what Cain had said, Hayden asked a very innocent question. In a way, though, it summed up everything they had been through. "Is that what you're afraid of for me?"

Emma peered through the window at Cain's face and noticed how the tight mask that concealed pain relaxed for a moment in a different sort of pain. She felt compelled to go in and see what they were discussing.

"What do you mean?" Cain asked.

"That I'll use my fists and lose the people I care about like you did? You hit Danny, and Emma left. Was that because you didn't control your temper?"

"No, Hayden," said Emma. "Cain didn't fly into a rage without thought. Cain thought with her heart. Someone had hurt me, and she reacted out of love." Emma gripped the rim of the door. More than once she had been in the position to listen in on a talk between Cain and Hayden, and again the tone and depth of Cain's lessons awed her. However, today Cain was trying to eliminate from Hayden's life the one thing that made her so unique. The uniqueness that had captured Emma's heart from the beginning and would make her son a special man to someone someday—Cain's passion.

"Emma, let's not fill his head with foolish notions." Cain's voice was barely a whisper.

"I'm not. I didn't mean to eavesdrop, but you're trying too hard to erase those things you see as lacking in yourself."

Hayden leaned back as Emma came closer and put her hand on Cain's face.

"I know you. What makes you so special is the fact that you're willing to fight for those you love." Cain's skin felt a little too warm, and Emma could only guess that the moisture was a result of the pain she saw in the blue eyes. "*I* was wrong, not you. I know what you want for Hayden, and I want the same things for him."

The sharp reply was poised on Cain's tongue, but she let it die away and gave in to the desire to close her eyes.

Emma had won another small victory. "Hayden, could you go out and keep an eye on your sister for me?" she asked.

A nurse met him at the door, pointing at the sign that read "Visiting Hours."

He put his hands up and shook his head. The moment had turned into something he figured both of them needed to get through without interruption.

The caress of a cool hand towel made Cain stir from the light sleep she had given in to, but she didn't open her eyes. As Emma ran a soft hand over Cain's head, Cain recalled the time they were together and she had gotten the flu. The tender touch then had made her feel so loved, magnifying now the loss of what Emma meant to her. When Emma had walked out, the memory of her skin pressed against her would wake Cain in the night. Intellectually, Cain realized there was a simple solution if all she needed was a warm body lying next to her, but it was Emma her heart still craved.

"You don't have to do that."

The voice stilled Emma's hand and tightened her nipples to the point where she felt as if she needed to cover her chest to hide the effect from Cain. Her soft timbre reminded her of her nights in Cain's bed.

"I'm taking advantage of your weakened condition, so be quiet."

"You know something, shorty?"

"The pain must be getting bad. Either that or you're delusional if you think you're going to get away with calling me that," Emma teased back.

"I'm beginning to think you're enjoying having me here with no choice but to succumb to your wiles."

Emma placed the nurse's call button closer to her hand and stopped what she was doing. "I'd trade places with you in a heartbeat, I already told you that, and if you want I can get someone else to do this. This isn't about pushing you."

"I didn't say I wanted you to stop."

The blue eyes opened and pinned Emma with a look she hadn't seen in forever. Cain almost looked like she cared.

"How about you and me make a deal until all this is over and we settle back into some semblance of a normal life?"

"What did you have in mind, Cain?"

"Well, we share a name and all these kids running around, so what do you say to being friends? That's one thing we haven't tried in a while."

"I'd love that. You'll see with time that I mean what I've said to you. I'm here, and I'm not going anywhere ever again."

Cain gave in to her fatigue and closed her eyes. "One day at a time, sweetling. Let's not get ahead of ourselves." The feel of the towel disappeared, but not the fingers running through her hair. Their presence put her to sleep.

❖

Merrick was sitting behind Cain's desk at home getting some business done when the phone rang. They had gotten back from the hospital after the nursing staff wouldn't be put off anymore and evicted Emma from her spot on the bed. After a late lunch the Caseys had retired upstairs for naps.

"Runyon," she barked into the phone.

"Merrick, this is Blue over at the club." The man sounded winded and rushed.

"What's going on?" She reclined in the comfortable chair and glanced out the window. Six guards perched on the fence line not far from where she was sitting.

"Some fucker just blew the shit out of the place."

Giovanni's eldest son looked on from a few blocks away, the detonator still in his hand. They would take out every one of Cain's holdings, showing her she had no safe place to hide, and they wouldn't stop until all of the Caseys were dead. The blond bitch who had the audacity to touch his son would pay the ultimate humiliation before he personally slit her throat. He smirked as he thought about making Cain watch as he fucked her precious little wife before he took her out.

"Tick tock, Casey. Your time's running out, and I'm holding the stopwatch."

About the Author

Originally from Cuba, Ali now lives in New Orleans with her partner. As a writer, she couldn't ask for a better, more beautiful place, full of real-life characters to fuel the imagination. When she isn't writing or working in the yard, Ali makes a living in the nonprofit sector.

Look for information about her books at www.boldstrokesbooks. com.

Books Available From Bold Strokes Books

Sweet Creek by Lee Lynch. A celebration of the enduring nature of love, friendship, and community in the quirky, heart-warming lesbian community of Waterfall Falls. (1-933110-29-5)

The Devil Inside by Ali Vali. Derby Cain Casey, head of a New Orleans crime organization, runs the family business with guts and grit, and no one crosses her. No one, that is, until Emma Verde claims her heart and turns her world upside down. (1-933110-30-9)

Grave Silence by Rose Beecham. Detective Jude Devine's investigation of a series of ritual murders is complicated by her torrid affair with the golden girl of Southwestern forensic pathology, Dr. Mercy Westmoreland. (1-933110-25-2)

Honor Reclaimed by Radclyffe. In the aftermath of 9/11, Secret Service Agent Cameron Roberts and Blair Powell close ranks with a trusted few to find the would-be assassins who nearly claimed Blair's life. (1-933110-18-X)

Honor Bound by Radclyffe. Secret Service Agent Cameron Roberts and Blair Powell face political intrigue, a clandestine threat to Blair's safety, and the seemingly irreconcilable personal differences that force them ever further apart. (1-933110-20-1)

Protector of the Realm: Supreme Constellations Book One by Gun Brooke. A space adventure filled with suspense and a daring intergalactic romance featuring Commodore Rae Jacelon and a stunning, but decidedly lethal Kellen O'Dal. (1-933110-26-0)

Innocent Hearts by Radclyffe. In a wild and unforgiving land, two women learn about love, passion, and the wonders of the heart. (1-933110-21-X)

The Temple at Landfall by Jane Fletcher. An imprinter, one of Celaeno's most revered servants of the Goddess, is also a prisoner to the faith—until a Ranger frees her by claiming her heart. (1-933110-27-9)

Force of Nature by Kim Baldwin. From tornados to forest fires, the forces of nature conspire to bring Gable McCoy and Erin Richards close to danger, and closer to each other. (1-933110-23-6)

In Too Deep by Ronica Black. Undercover homicide cop Erin McKenzie tracks a femme fatale who just might be a real killer…with love and danger hot on her heels. (1-933110-17-1)

Stolen Moments: Erotic Interludes 2 by Stacia Seaman and Radclyffe, eds. Love on the run, in the office, in the shadows…Fast, furious, and almost too hot to handle. (1-933110-16-3)

Course of Action by Gun Brooke. Actress Carolyn Black desperately wants the starring role in an upcoming film produced by Annelie Peterson. Just how far will she go for the dream part of a lifetime? (1-933110-22-8)

Rangers at Roadsend by Jane Fletcher. Sergeant Chip Coppelli has learned to spot trouble coming, and that is exactly what she sees in her new recruit, Katryn Nagata. The Celaeno series. (1-933110-28-7)

Justice Served by Radclyffe. Lieutenant Rebecca Frye and her lover, Dr. Catherine Rawlings, embark on a deadly game of hide-and-seek with an underworld kingpin who traffics in human souls. (1-933110-15-5)

Distant Shores, Silent Thunder by Radclyffe. Dr. Tory King—along with the women who love her—is forced to examine the boundaries of love, friendship, and the ties that transcend time. (1-933110-08-2)

Hunter's Pursuit by Kim Baldwin. A raging blizzard, a mountain hideaway, and a killer-for-hire set a scene for disaster—or desire—when Katarzyna Demetrious rescues a beautiful stranger. (1-933110-09-0)

The Walls of Westernfort by Jane Fletcher. All Temple Guard Natasha Ionadis wants is to serve the Goddess—until she falls in love with one of the rebels she is sworn to destroy. The Celaeno series. (1-933110-24-4)

Change Of Pace: Erotic Interludes by Radclyffe. Twenty-five hot-wired encounters guaranteed to spark more than just your imagination.

Erotica as you've always dreamed of it. (1-933110-07-4)

Honor Guards by Radclyffe. In a wild flight for their lives, the president's daughter and those who are sworn to protect her wage a desperate struggle for survival. (1-933110-01-5)

Fated Love by Radclyffe. Amidst the chaos and drama of a busy emergency room, two women must contend not only with the fragile nature of life, but also with the irresistible forces of fate. (1-933110-05-8)

Justice in the Shadows by Radclyffe. In a shadow world of secrets and lies, Detective Sergeant Rebecca Frye and her lover, Dr. Catherine Rawlings, join forces in the elusive search for justice. (1-933110-03-1)

shadowland by Radclyffe. In a world on the far edge of desire, two women are drawn together by power, passion, and dark pleasures. An erotic romance. (1-933110-11-2)

Love's Masquerade by Radclyffe. Plunged into the indistinguishable realms of fiction, fantasy, and hidden desires, Auden Frost is forced to question all she believes about the nature of love. (1-933110-14-7)

Love & Honor by Radclyffe. The president's daughter and her lover are faced with difficult choices as they battle a tangled web of Washington intrigue for...love and honor. (1-933110-10-4)

Beyond the Breakwater by Radclyffe. One Provincetown summer three women learn the true meaning of love, friendship, and family. (1-933110-06-6)

Tomorrow's Promise by Radclyffe. One timeless summer, two very different women discover the power of passion to heal and the promise of hope that only love can bestow. (1-933110-12-0)

Love's Tender Warriors by Radclyffe. Two women who have accepted loneliness as a way of life learn that love is worth fighting for and a battle they cannot afford to lose. (1-933110-02-3)

Love's Melody Lost by Radclyffe. A secretive artist with a haunted past and a young woman escaping a life that has proved to be a lie find their destinies entwined. (1-933110-00-7)

Safe Harbor by Radclyffe. A mysterious newcomer, a reclusive doctor, and a troubled gay teenager learn about love, friendship, and trust during one tumultuous summer in Provincetown. (1-933110-13-9)

Above All, Honor by Radclyffe. Secret Service Agent Cameron Roberts fights her desire for the one woman she can't have—Blair Powell, the daughter of the president of the United States. (1-933110-04-X)